D1329311

UNDER VIOLENT SKIES

An absolutely gripping crime thriller

JUDI DAYKIN

JOFFE
BOOKS

First published 2020
Joffe Books, London
www.joffebooks.com

**Please join our mailing list for free kindle
crime thriller, detective, mystery, and romance
books and new releases.**

We love to hear from our readers! Please email any
feedback you have to: feedback@joffebooks.com

ISBN 978-1-78931-535-6

AUTHOR'S NOTE

It has been my great delight to call Norfolk my home for the last forty years. As with all regions, we have our own way of doing and saying things here. If you would like to pronounce some of the real place names in this book like a local, the following may help:

Happisburgh = Haze-bruh

Wymondham = Wind-am

Sea Palling = Sea Paw-ling

Norwich hides its 'w', and North Walsham is just North Walsham, though it often rocks!

These violent delights have violent ends,
And in their triumph die, like fire and powder . . .

William Shakespeare, *Romeo and Juliet*

PROLOGUE

Clouds blotted out the moon. The night was much darker than Adam had anticipated, and he couldn't use a torch as he didn't want to alert the men to his presence. In the distance, an unearthly orange glow suffused the sky beneath the clouds. Everyone around here knew that glow. It came from Bacton gas terminal, where the lights blazed all night, every night, ever on the alert in case of terrorist attack. He struggled through a gap in the hedge and clambered down into the drainage ditch at the road end of the field.

He was already short of breath. 'Not built for this stuff anymore,' he muttered. Not now that retirement and a fondness for real ale had given him a proper belly.

There were several inches of rust-coloured water at the bottom of the ditch. Under that was a layer of sticky mud. Thank God it had been dry recently, or he would have sunk a lot deeper. In spite of the warm night air, the feel of the cold water splashing his trousers made him shudder.

These ditches cut through many of the farmers' fields. Adam had checked two days ago that this one made its way to the barns that were his target. Somewhere to his right, he could hear the hiss and beat of an irrigator moving back and forth. Salad crops, potatoes, carrots, they'd all be needing a bit of help in this dry spell.

Farming! Who'd have guessed it? He shook his head, then cursed as he stumbled and made a grab for the bank, slicing his hand on the wild grass that covered it. Swearing, he rubbed the bleeding hand on the leg of his jeans. At least here the hedge stood high above the ditch, so he could move upright. Brambles reached out thorny fingers to snatch at the brand-new camera, which was swinging around on its strap and bouncing off his beer gut. Near to the barns there were no hedges.

On his reconnaissance trip, he had carefully chosen a piece of overgrown scrubland behind a high hedge to leave his car. It should be invisible to passers-by, and only the occasional local would use a minor road like that. Last night he had parked there and waited in vain, only leaving when the July dawn began to cancel out the Bacton glow. Tonight, he'd returned to watch again. Just after midnight, a solitary vehicle made its way down the road, pausing briefly to drop off three men at the rutted, bumpy cart track which led directly to the weather-worn barns clad in corrugated iron. One of the men was carrying a large toolbox.

Adam changed his shoes for wellingtons, hung the camera around his neck and locked the car. Never quite confident that he had mastered the thing, he left his mobile behind in case it should ring. Not fancying his chances against men like these, he couldn't approach from the track. Besides, his intention wasn't to tackle them but to collect hard evidence.

He grinned at the prospect. 'I'll show them I haven't lost my touch.'

Twenty yards from his target, the hedge ran out. He edged along with his shoulders bent, the camera swinging wildly. He steadied it with a muddy hand and peered over the edge of the bank.

There were two barns, one larger than the other, sitting at right angles around a concrete yard. Like many farmers in the area, Jack Ellis kept various pieces of agricultural machinery remote from his house but near the fields. The doors to the smaller barn stood open. Inside, Adam could see the flicker of torches darting like fireflies about the walls and ceiling. He wriggled his bulk onto the bank to steady himself and the camera. These thefts were happening all over the region these days, but no one seemed willing or able to find enough evidence to stop it. Well he, Adam Crane, was going to provide all the photographic evidence needed to complete the dossier he had already drawn up. He had a damn good idea which locals were involved.

There was a grinding noise from inside the barn, followed by a clang as something fell to the ground. One of the men was speaking. Adam couldn't make out the exact words but by the tone of his voice, he was trying to hurry the other two. Someone opened the bonnet of a car. Now all the torches were pointed to the same place, the shadowy figures peering into an engine.

Taking the lens cap off and placing the camera carefully on the edge of the bank, Adam zoomed in like a paparazzo spotting a film star. He pressed the shutter.

Shit, shit, shit.

The camera fired off a series of rapid shots, the flash lighting the darkness like a strobe. Urgent voices from the barn made it clear that they'd seen it. Adam shot down the bank, then struggled along the ditch, trying hard not to make any noise, until he reached the cover of the hedge. He slumped against the bank. 'You fucking idiot,' he hissed to himself.

His heart was pounding, his chest heaving with fear and unaccustomed exercise. Forcing himself to peer through the tangle of vegetation at the base of the hedge, he could see the beams of two torches heading out of the barns, shadowy figures behind them. Their movement triggered the outdoor lights fastened above the doors, which blazed across the yard and into the field beyond. The two men were backlit so that he couldn't make out their features.

One of them began to move towards him along the bank above the ditch. The other moved in the opposite direction along the cart track. The light from the yard cast an inky shadow from the hedge into the ditch. At least he'd had enough sense to wear black clothes. Knowing that any movement would attract their attention, he fought the impulse to get up and make a run for it. He braced himself, and dropped to one knee. The evil-smelling water soaked his trousers and ran like ice into his boots. He waited, shivering. The man came to a stop at the hedge and shone his torch around. Adam tried to hold his breath. The yard lights timed out, then cut in again. His pursuer walked back along the top of the ditch.

He'd got away with it. *Fuck, that was close.* Adam took a deep breath.

The man dislodged something lying in the grass and bent to pick it up. Holding it up to examine it in the light from his torch, he whistled and beckoned to the other man on the cart track. They inspected the item.

'Camera lens cap. Someone's spying on us. Can't have gone far.'

The second man swung his torch around, searching the ditch and field beyond. The splintered beam passed through the hedge, inches above Adam's head. They moved along the ditch, one in each direction, their powerful torches swinging in arcs, like prison searchlights.

Fear galvanised Adam. He shot upright and began to race along the ditch like a startled animal, spattering water wildly, not caring how much racket he was making. With a yell, one of the men jumped into the ditch and started to chase after him. Adam lumbered along, sheer panic flooding him with adrenalin. In all his sixty-five years he had never been more afraid than he was now, not even on riot duty. He could hear his pursuer gaining on him until there was a sharp cry, followed by a sudden splash. Adam hoped the man had been caught in the same brambles he was fighting. It had given him a slim chance.

An engine turned over and, headlights on full, a Land Rover Defender careered out of the barn at speed. Someone had managed to get the vehicle started.

'Come back,' Adam heard the man on the bank shout to his pursuer. 'Faster in the Landie.'

They'd be armed, these types always were. He'd be safer in the middle of the fields, harder to find. Adam struggled on. His chest felt as though it was bound with a steel band. He drew short, rasping breaths and his vision clouded with red flashes. The mud in the bottom of the ditch was sucking at his boots and his thighs burned with the effort of pulling them out. One wellington became embedded in the slime. Not daring to stop and retrieve it, he stumbled on. The rubbish in the bottom of the ditch sliced into the sole of his foot, the overgrown grasses lacerated his arms and face. Brambles grabbed at his clothes like demon fingers trying to hold him back. Panting in terror, blinded with effort, Adam lurched into a blank wall. It was a dead end. He must have taken a wrong turn into one of the connecting ditches. He slid down the bank in despair. Everything hurt.

Above the noise of his gasps, Adam could hear the Land Rover. The arguing men were still scanning the field with their torches. The headlights began to bounce out of the yard and along the track towards the main road. His wrong turn had brought him close to the track. Too close. There were no hedges here to protect him.

He crawled frantically away from the track on his hands and knees, and burrowed beneath a thick clump of undergrowth at the bottom of the ditch. He lay on his side in the stinking red mud, stretching his neck to keep his face out of the rusty water, willing his breathing to slow. The vehicle approached along the track, stopping every few yards, the men climbing out to search the fields and ditches. But in spite of their thoroughness, by some miracle, they drove on by. When they moved past, he almost pissed himself. Not that anyone would have noticed — he was completely soaked.

The men reached the road and stopped. After a short, furious argument, they gave up. The vehicle doors slammed and Adam heard it drive off along the narrow lane towards Happisburgh.

He lay in the vile water for a long time, shaking with cold and shock. Slowly, he edged out from underneath the scrub. Peering cautiously over the top of the bank, he made sure that there was no one around, no silent guard left to wait for him. Exhausted, he stumbled up onto the track. His body was covered with scratches, cuts and bruises, his clothes soaked and ripped. No point in trying to hide now. He began to limp along the track to the lane and his car. The new camera swung from its strap, smashed and dripping blood-red water. There would be little chance of salvaging any pictures.

'I'll pay for this tomorrow,' Adam grumbled, hobbling along. 'Come to that, I'm bloody paying for it now.'

The road under his bootless foot was rough, and he winced with every step. Nearing the gap in the hedge where he had hidden his car, he fumbled with bloodied and unco-operative fingers for his car keys.

Then, without warning, headlights blinded him.

CHAPTER 1

It felt like such a release, being able to close the door to her very own flat for the first time in her life. At last, she was shutting out the previous few weeks, and the bitter argument that had grown between herself and her mother ever since she'd announced her intention to leave home. Only London prices had kept her there until she was thirty-five years old.

Downstairs, the front door slammed. Sara went out onto the small decked balcony and looked down. In the street, three storeys below, a young man turned to look up at her and waved.

They'd met at lunchtime while Sara and Javed, her step-father, were struggling to carry a huge box upstairs. Her new neighbour, Chris, who told them he had come home for a break, helped them carry her possessions up. Once the last box was upstairs, Chris had taken them across the road for lunch in the independent coffee shop, of which he was the proud owner. This evening he had knocked on the door and offered to fetch a pizza. He seemed a nice guy, if a bit over keen. She'd accepted his offer.

Watching him now, Sara thought him rather handsome, with his neatly trimmed beard and curly brown hair cropped close around his ears. She was taller than him, but then she was taller than most people. For a moment, she relaxed and allowed herself to admire the view across the rooftops of central Norwich. To her left, the cathedral spire rose above the city, as it must have done for centuries and, as if by magic, a castle floated above the houses. The city had an aura of gentility. Down in the narrow street, there were several restaurants, Chris's café, a variety of fashionable shops and plenty of people.

The warm August air rose gently up, bringing the scent of Norwich with it. Garlic from the restaurant kitchens, fresh ground coffee from the café, an overlay of recently cut grass from the nearby park. The whole place felt quaint in comparison to Tower Hamlets and the family home she had shared with Tegan, her mother.

There the houses crowded up to one another, cars occupied every available parking space, and the unceasing rumble of traffic filled the background. On some days, especially hot ones like today, the London aroma combined the stench of overflowing rubbish bins with traffic pollution, or the alley next to her Mum's ex-council maisonette that was used as a temporary urinal. On other days, a fresh breeze would blow up from the Thames dockside just a few streets away, filling the air with cleansing river ozone.

There was still plenty of work to be done. Turning back into the living room, Sara sighed at the packing debris which littered every surface. The bedroom was in better shape. Her new bed, a hopeful double, was made. The contents of her suitcase were spewing out onto the floor. Pulling out the rest of the clothes, Sara unearthed her treasure. With care, she carried the tin box into the living room. She swept aside the cardboard and plastic, placed the tin in the middle of the new coffee table and made a space on the sofa to sit down.

Originally a deep royal blue, now the tin's colour was fading. Oriental lettering decorated the sides. Etched on the lid and embossed in gold was a depiction of two long-legged birds performing a mating dance. Perhaps it had once held biscuits, or expensive chocolates, or a precious gift of some sort. Now, it contained a handful of letters and a few old photographs, dating back to the 1980s. They were the key to a question which her mother refused to answer. Who was Sara's father?

She had found it by accident. Digging out some old clothes for Tegan to wear to an eighties disco at the February social, Sara had discovered the long-forgotten tin stuffed behind a pile of old handbags and shoes in the spare bedroom wardrobe. Simple curiosity had made her lever open the lid. The contents had exploded her life.

For weeks, Sara had read and reread the letters until she knew them by heart. She had studied the pictures until she thought her eyes might burn them to dust. They jumped into her thoughts, unbidden, while she was at work. The grainy image of the man she now presumed to be her father troubled her dreams. Unable to talk to her mother about it for fear of upsetting her, Sara had finally accepted that she would have to find another way to solve the mystery. She wanted to track down her dad before her obsession damaged the rest of her life, even if he didn't want to meet her.

Dearest Tegan,

The days are long without you. It's rather boring up here, hardly any excitement. A small jeweller's shop in a city centre back lane was robbed yesterday, apparently by two black guys, supposedly Jamaicans, with London accents. Everybody turned and looked at me as if I should know who it was, just because I used to be in the Met.

It's very middle-class too, though there are some rough estates. But it's nothing like Brixton! They don't have the same community spirit either. You helped me see that side of life where I hadn't before. I miss our barbecues and your mum's jerk pork. Who'd have thought it?

I'll call you on Wednesday, but it will be after 10 p.m., as I am on the late shift.

All my love.

A

So here she was in Norwich, because the letters had originally been posted from here. She patted the blue tin as if to assure herself it was real, then placed it out of sight behind the television. After all, moving to Norfolk and following in her missing father's footsteps might be little more than a romantic notion. All Sara knew was that her instinct told her she could do more here, and a good copper always listens to their instinct.

The downstairs door slammed shut again. Footsteps climbed the stairs and there was a knock at the door.

'Pizza delivery,' called Chris's friendly voice. She opened the door and let him in.

CHAPTER 2

Agnes didn't get many visitors, especially at eight o'clock on a Sunday night. She had just settled down with a cuppa and a packet of biscuits to watch TV when the doorbell rang. With a sigh of exasperation, she levered herself out of the sagging armchair and walked stiffly to the front door. She didn't take the chain off, even though it wouldn't be much of a barrier to a determined assailant. Most of the other houses in these remote lanes were second homes these days. Her nearest neighbour was over a mile away.

'Evening, Agnes. Hope I'm not disturbing you.'

'What do you want, Des? I'm just about to watch a programme.'

'Oh, sorry.' Des Dixon didn't look sorry. 'Can I come in?'

She'd known Dixon for years, and he was unlikely to give in easily if she refused. Better to find out what he wanted this time.

'I suppose so.' Agnes closed the rarely used front door, undid the chain and then reopened it. With arrogant familiarity her visitor strode across the hallway to the living room. By the time Agnes had shut the door and followed him in, he was already seated on the sofa, lounging back against the cushions as if he'd lived there all his life. She sat back down in her armchair.

'Cup of tea, then?' Agnes reached to turn down the volume on the television.

'No tea. I just wondered if you had thought about my offer on the house.'

'I didn't need to think about it. I told you, I'm not interested.'

'Would it help if I found some more money? Made a higher offer?'

'No.'

'I've been doing a bit of research. I could raise my offer to £350,000. Just for the house and garden.'

He'd made his last offer a few weeks ago when they'd bumped into each other at the Norfolk Show. Agnes suspected that the meeting was planned, and not accidental as Dixon had made out. She could have looked prices up on the internet but she'd not bothered. These days Agnes rarely went off the farm except to do her shopping in North Walsham or Wroxham, where estate agents' offices peppered the high street. She hadn't looked at them either. She was quite sure, however, that a five-bedroomed, detached farmhouse with a two-acre garden, a barn and outbuildings, would be worth more than £350,000 even though the place had become somewhat dilapidated since her husband had died.

'Can we talk about the land or barns?'

'No, Des, we can't. What makes you think I've changed my mind?'

'Nothing. I was just passing, thought I'd ask.' This was so unlikely that Agnes couldn't hide her surprise. Dixon never did anything without a purpose. He smiled, which made him look even more like the shark that Agnes knew him to be. 'I have a bit of cash in the bank. It could be yours.'

One thing a farmer always knew was the value of their land. It was the only thing Agnes had checked on the computer. She had 700 acres, about half of which were arable fields, the rest grazing marshes. It was easy enough to work it out. The empty Victorian barns, half a mile along the lane, were a developer's delight. They'd be second homes in a flash if she let them go. Dixon had been trying to get his hands on all of it for years, circling her old age like a vulture. And there was still Mark, her son, to consider. How typical of Dixon to think of £350,000 as 'a bit of cash.'

'I've told you, none of it's for sale.'

'You could buy yourself a lovely bungalow nearby. No renovations to do, no stairs to climb. You can still farm without being on the land.'

'Christ, Des, I'm only seventy. I'm not ready to curl up my toes yet.'

Dixon shifted forward on the sofa, bringing his face far too close to hers. She could smell his breath. He'd been drinking.

'Such a big place and all on your own. You can't manage it for ever, you know. You'll need help.'

'Des Dixon.' She pulled back. 'How dare you sit there on my sofa, in my home and talk to me like that. Besides, I have Frank to help me. Mark will come home to the farm when he's ready.'

'Yes, in time, perhaps.' Dixon smiled, sat upright again. 'And I suppose you and Frank have managed so far.'

Agnes wasn't sure if this was a compliment or a threat. She needed to be careful. For many years now, Dixon had been systematically buying up all the small farms in the district. Agnes's farm sat between this growing agri-business empire on one side and Jack Ellis's place on the other. Agnes and Jack's were the only two adjoining farms Dixon hadn't managed to get his hands on.

'Perhaps I'll make a few enquiries,' she conceded, 'but I'm in no hurry. Please stop pestering me about it.'

'All right. Promise you'll give me first refusal?'

'Maybe.'

Dixon relaxed, leaning back against the cushions. An uneasy silence descended.

He'd been quite handsome when he was young, Agnes remembered, watching him from the corner of her eye. He was a tall, well-built man. His hair was beginning to go grey around the temples, and like many people in their fifties, he was gaining weight. Dixon had a poor reputation among the local farming community. He was ambitious, and showed a ruthless streak when cutting deals or dealing with staff. His short temper hadn't improved since his wife had left him three years ago. Rumour had it that he could be free with his fists.

For a moment Agnes wondered if he would ever threaten her physically. Surely her years protected her somewhat? She might be small, her hair might be grey, but she was not yet either frail or lacking in spirit. Would Dixon like to be accused of hitting an old lady? Once the thought had entered her head, she couldn't dismiss it. Who would know he had even been here? She'd had no CCTV camera in the yard since her old one had given up the ghost months ago. Frank had kept going on about getting it fixed. She picked up her mobile from the little table next to her chair, where her cup of tea was growing cold. Glancing at Dixon, who appeared occupied with the television, she typed a quick text to Frank.

Call me.

Two years ago, Frank had been working for Dixon until the mild-mannered younger man had been shouted at once too often and swung a punch at the farmer. Dixon's aim was more accurate, and Frank had been sacked on the spot. So now he worked for her. Agnes knew she was lucky to have him, and had come to rely on Frank. He was a natural farmer with a genuine feel for the land they worked together.

'How are you getting on with the boys in the barn?' Dixon asked.

'Fine. They don't bother me. Stay late, don't they?'

'Well they work all day for me, then do the car repairs in the evening. It was good of you to loan it to them.'

'It's been empty a while.'

Agnes knew that agreeing to this hadn't been her best decision. Dixon had caught her moments after her son Mark's last brief visit in April. Mark had left hurriedly after breakfast, in spite of his promises to stay the weekend, and she'd been feeling hurt and confused. Distracted as she was by her son's behaviour, Dixon had managed to bully her into allowing some of his seasonal employees to use one of her empty barns to do up old cars.

'When your lettuce is ready on Long Acre, I'll send them over with the packing rig. The men will do that field of yours in half a day.'

'Thank you.' Agnes knew it would be a good saving for her.

'Little Gems, isn't it? Who's it for by the way?'

'Kay's.'

'Got the packing trays?'

'Not yet.'

'I'll sort that for you. Don't worry.'

Another favour gave Dixon yet more leverage. Agnes's mobile suddenly rang. With relief, she picked it up and brandished it. 'I'll just answer this.'

'Sure. Look, I'll leave you to your programme. Don't worry about seeing me out.'

Nodding, Agnes stood up and accepted the call.

'Are you all right?' Frank asked.

'I am now.' She went to the living room door and waved goodbye to Dixon as he let himself out.

'What's up? Shall I come round?'

Agnes explained, watching Dixon until he closed the door, and followed him to put the chain back on. She went to the kitchen, holding the mobile firmly to her ear. Then, making herself obvious in the window, where she could see into the yard, Agnes waited.

'He's going now,' she told Frank, watching Dixon climb into his brand-new Range Rover. Shiny, black and expensive, it had those windows that you couldn't see through, which always made Agnes feel the driver had something to hide.

15

They'd been on the dealer's stand at the Norfolk Show, starting at £100,000. Her home was only worth three and a half of these monsters, according to her skinflint neighbour. Her old Defender looked shabby beside it.

'CCTV needs mending.' Frank was never one to waste words. 'Shouldn't be on your own up there.'

'Let's talk about it tomorrow.'

'Are you sure you'll be ok?'

'Yes, I'm sure. Thank you so much for calling. It just showed Dixon that I wasn't on my own.'

The Range Rover shot out of the yard, gravel spattering from beneath its tyres. Agnes refilled the kettle and slammed it back on its base. Her hands were shaking. An encounter with Des Dixon always left her feeling like this. And then there was Mark. She needed to talk to her son — she didn't know where she stood with him. She ought to try ringing him again, though these days he never answered.

But not tonight. Tonight, Agnes intended to rewind the TV satellite box and watch her favourite show. She made a fresh cup of tea, then settled back into her ancient armchair to try and recoup something of her evening.

CHAPTER 3

It was threatening rain. Sara's mood matched the grey and heavy sky outside. A cup of cold coffee stood on the window ledge of her bedroom. Nerves had stolen her appetite. Deciding it was best to look smart, rather than dress in more practical clothes, she pulled on her favourite navy blue trouser suit and matching pair of leather court shoes. The suit had been a bargain in the sale at L.K.Bennett, and it made her feel that she looked efficient, a necessary confidence boost this morning. The day would undoubtedly be about meeting the team, and she wanted to make a good impression on her first morning. So much depended on how the next few days went.

Fear of being late made her leave too early. The city centre traffic was already building up as she drove out from the tiny car park at the rear of the flats. Chris had warned her that the medieval city layout equalled awful rush-hour traffic. The police HQ wasn't in Norwich but in a small town called Wymondham, about fifteen minutes south of the city. There was plenty of parking, and her jaunty red Fiat 500 stood out among the dark-coloured vehicles which filled most of the other spaces. Sara took a deep breath, and went into reception.

'You must be the new DS,' said the duty sergeant with a broad smile. 'Welcome to Norfolk. I'm Trevor Jones. You can always find me here. At least, that's what the wife says. Have a seat while I track down DI Edwards.'

Jones called up, and in the same genial tone offered her a coffee. She declined. They kept her waiting for twenty minutes, and then as if to compensate, her new boss came down in person to meet her. DI Edwards looked just as she remembered from her interview — in his late forties, slim, muscular and tall, his dark hair peppered with silver. His greeting wasn't as warm as her hypersensitive state would have preferred. His handshake was brief, his smile lukewarm.

The Serious Crimes Unit office was at the end of a corridor on the second floor, opposite the toilets. It looked as if it had been placed here on purpose, as far away from the other departments as possible. Edwards held the door open. The rest of the team, such as it was, waited at their desks. The atmosphere was subdued. A room with glass walls and door occupied one corner. Standing inside and gazing out of the window was another figure Sara remembered from her interview. Assistant Chief Constable Miller, in his full glory and uniform. He swung around when the door opened, striding towards her across the office as straight as an arrow, his hand outstretched.

'Welcome to Norfolk Police, DS Hirst,' he said. 'I hope you'll enjoy it here.' He pumped Sara's hand vigorously.

'Thank you, sir.' Sara hadn't been expecting him to be there. She glanced at the other team members. There were only two of them.

'Let me introduce your new team,' said Miller. He gestured to a middle-aged, slightly tubby man. 'DC Mike Bowen, Norfolk born and bred. He can help you with local knowledge.'

DC Bowen made no effort to leave his seat or speak, and his eyes seemed to challenge her for some reason. The ACC ignored Bowen's rudeness and moved on to the other team member, an athletic-looking woman in jeans and a smart summer jumper. Her bright blonde hair was swept back into a ponytail and her mouth was open.

'DC Ellie James,' Miller continued, oblivious to the look on the other woman's face. Sara sensed an uncomfortable atmosphere in the office, which Miller was either impervious to or was actively ignoring. 'Soon to be DS, isn't that right, Ellie? Just passed her sergeants' exams.'

Behind her, DI Edwards cleared his throat but ACC Miller ploughed on.

'SCU needs officers like you, DS Hirst. You might not find it as exciting as the Met, but you will certainly improve our scenery.'

Sara heard DI Edwards pull in a breath, as Miller continued in what he probably hoped was an avuncular tone. 'Now, if you have any problems, come to me. My door is always open.'

Then he left, breezing down the corridor like a small hurricane, ignorant of the damage left behind. With a strangled sob, DC James pushed past Sara and rushed across the corridor to the ladies' toilet. Had her new big boss really just told her she would 'improve the scenery?' Sara struggled with the thought. Her looks had nothing to do with her capabilities. And why was the blonde woman so upset?

'Where shall I sit?' she asked. The office had several empty desks.

'Take your pick,' Edwards said. 'We're a bit short-staffed, so it's up to you. Ellie uses that one, Mike is over there. The one by the window might be nice. The computer people will be down in a bit to sort you out.'

Her new boss was gabbling like a teenager caught looking at porn magazines in the corner shop, and Sara wondered why he seemed so embarrassed. He retreated into his corner office, sat down and began to leaf through some files, leaving her abandoned in the middle of the room. DC Bowen had turned his back and was concentrating on his computer screen. She chose the desk by the window and dumped her bag on it.

'Is there anything I can do?' she asked.

'Yeah, put the coffee on,' said Bowen.

'Okay.' Sara wasn't sure if this was a joke but smiled anyway. 'Where do I fill it?'

'Ellie usually gets the water in the ladies.'

Sara took the empty glass jug and went into the toilet. The young DC was splashing water on her face.

'Do you really fill this in here?' Sara asked. The other woman nodded. Taking a moment to fill the jug with cold water, she waited for DC James to regain her composure. 'Are you okay? Why are you upset?'

'It's not your fault,' the DC muttered. 'It's just that I thought — we both thought — that I would get the promotion.'

Sara paused to assess this statement and could only come to one conclusion. 'You mean my job?'

'Yes. I took my exam just before the interviews.'

'And they interviewed you?'

'Yes. Mike and I sort of assumed that I would get the post, as I'm already part of the team. Especially as everything has been up in the air since the reorganisation.'

'They offered me the job weeks ago. Didn't they tell you?' Sara said.

'No. I assumed no news must be good news. When the ACC came down, I thought they were going to tell me I'd got it. Instead, I found out about you.'

'While I was waiting downstairs?' Sara was horrified. 'I can understand why you're upset.'

'There aren't many jobs available around here,' DC James said. 'It could be ages before another one comes along.'

'And DC Bowen wanted you to have the job? He didn't want it for himself?'

'That's what he told me. He's never taken the exams, doesn't seem to want to.' James looked directly at Sara. 'We ought to get the coffee on. They'll be waiting for it.'

'Do you always make the coffee?' asked Sara.

'Usually. Look, none of this is your fault. You can call me Ellie if you like.'

'Thank you.'

The pair headed back into the office. Ellie took the jug and started up the coffee machine. Sara walked over to where Bowen sat at his desk. He looked up and scowled, and their eyes locked. He looked away first, his chair clattering on its castors as he stood up.

'What are you working on?' she asked.

'Theft.'

'Just the one?'

'No, lots of them.'

Bowen looked at her defiantly. He wasn't going to accept her without making her work hard for it. Sara set her jaw to stop her face betraying any emotion and took the risk.

'Ellie here tells me that neither of you knew that I'd been given the job,' she said.

'Maybe. Maybe not.' He paused. 'She's a good copper, deserves her promotion.'

'I'm sure she does. How do you know I don't deserve the same?'

'I don't, but she's one of us.' Bowen grabbed some pens from his desk and moved to a table with a large map on it.

Sara went to the DI's door and knocked, even though it was open. 'Can I have a word, sir?'

'Of course, come in. What is it?'

'Just want to get my bearings, sir.' She closed the door and sat down. Her human resources file was open on his desk. 'It appears my presence is a bit of a surprise to the rest of the team.'

'Ah, yes.' He had the grace to look embarrassed. 'To be fair to them, I hadn't confirmed it until today, though they knew we had interviewed several people.'

'Including internal candidates?'

'DC James was the only internal candidate. She and Mike assumed things that I wasn't able to confirm or deny until ACC Miller had approved your appointment. They'll get over it.'

'I hope so, sir.'

'I've worked with them both for years. We're a good team. But Ellie could be promoted to any department, as you know.'

So, loyalty had robbed him of the words to disappoint a hard-working team member. Sara wasn't sure what to make of that. Did it make him weak, or caring? Or had he been shirking his responsibilities, so that Ellie had gone on assuming the job was going to be hers even as Sara had been working out her transfer notice in London. She had to give them all the benefit of the doubt.

'Ellie mentioned something about a reorganisation,' she said.

'Yes, about six months ago. I did mention it during the interview.'

Perhaps one of them had talked about it. Sara had been far too nervous at the time to remember the finer details.

'We used to be one large team. We dealt with everything from murder to gang crime. Recently we've seen a huge rise in drug-related issues, so the Chief Constable decided to split the teams. We now have a dedicated vice squad, a separate drugs team, and SCU mop up anything that the others don't think is in their patch. Norfolk isn't that violent a place.'

'Half your team went elsewhere?'

'More than half. Then one of my long-serving team members retired, our civilian admin got a job in the city, and here we are.'

'All in six months? That is quite an upheaval, sir.'

'That's one way of putting it,' he said.

'I think there'll be fresh coffee soon. Perhaps you'd like one?'

'Yes, in a minute.' He fiddled with his pen. 'Look, it's not personal.'

So they all keep saying. Sara watched the DI without replying.

The DI ploughed on. 'It's just that I thought it might be easier for a local candidate. People here can seem a bit stand-offish, especially with anyone they consider to be an outsider. It helps if you know about the local mindset, the farming community, the city, the university.'

He had wanted Ellie. Presumably, given his greeting, she had been the ACC's choice. Sara's heart sank. It was going to make things much more difficult if her boss was testing her as well as the team.

'I see. I'm sure I will do my best, sir.'

'So am I.' Edwards was gabbling again. 'You come highly recommended. I'm a Newcastle lad myself. It's taken me years to be accepted. I'm still not considered a local, though I've lived here for twenty years. You may well encounter prejudice or find it hard to gain people's confidence, especially in the countryside.'

Sara nodded. 'Everyone takes time to settle into a new post. Coffee, sir?'

He sighed. 'Yes, please.'

The coffee machine was glugging away in its corner. A selection of not very clean-looking mugs sat on a tray next to it, with a bag of sugar that was going crusty. At least the milk looked fresh. Sara selected four of the least grubby mugs and took them to the desk where the rest of the team had gathered.

'Mike, why don't you fill us in on our latest case?' said Edwards, as Sara plonked the cups down. Bowen looked up from the county map, which he had been colouring in with felt pens of different acid hues.

'It's not very exciting. Just a few random bits of agricultural theft.'

'Agricultural theft? You mean they steal farms?' Sara smiled. It wasn't much of a joke but Bowen laughed. It wasn't a kindly or conciliatory laugh.

'This is the countryside. Oh, there's Norwich of course. Usually, the most interesting thing about the city is the fighting on Prince of Wales Road on a Saturday night. Nightclub land. Most of what we do is about farmers or domestics or burglaries. If you wanted excitement, you should have stayed with the Met.'

'The thefts, Mike,' Edwards snapped. Bowen scowled.

'It sounds very restful.' Sara tried the friendly approach again. 'The Serious Crimes Unit with no serious crimes to solve.'

'We deal with the worst that Norfolk criminals can throw at us.' Ellie brought over the milk and the near-solid bag of sugar. 'To be blunt, it's not normally that serious. Not now that drugs are a separate team.'

'We get imported crime too,' Bowen added, snatching up his felt pens as if someone might steal them away from him.

'Imported crime?'

'Londoners mostly, who think we're a soft target. Bunch of them came up here to do a bank robbery a while back, got stopped by the firearms unit less than a mile from the scene.'

'Yes, well, that was luck really,' said Ellie with a smile. 'The bank was up in Hellesdon, and the team were on a training exercise at Norwich Airport, five minutes away. How do you take yours?'

'If I can't get a cappuccino, then milk no sugar.' She indicated the map. 'So, what's all this?'

'We've had several farm thefts reported.' Ellie pulled it round to show Sara and indicated a stack of buff folders. 'We were just plotting them on the map to see if there was a pattern.'

Edwards loaded his coffee with milk and took it back to his office without adding to the conversation. Ellie talked Sara through the colour coding they'd devised. Bowen watched them with his arms folded, making no attempt to explain, in spite of the DI's request that he do so. Sara's only knowledge of the geography of the area came from the internet. It was difficult for her to follow the stream of information, and she was grateful when someone new arrived in the room. The young man explained that he was from IT, come to set up her passwords.

'While Matt's doing that, shall I show you round?' asked Ellie.

Sara smiled. 'That would be great. Especially the most important places, like the canteen.'

The building had three floors, curved around the sides of a central glass atrium. There were the usual cells and interview suites on one floor, team offices and admin areas like accounts on the others. The canteen was busy, the food smelled nice, and Sara's stomach began to grumble. Her appetite must be returning. Not all the departments were based there, Ellie explained. Some worked out of different office buildings. It didn't take long to get back to their room, and they must have done so more quickly than expected. Bowen was standing in the DI's office holding a file, his back to the main room. Edwards sat behind the desk.

'Miller says we're getting lax, need a stir up,' Edwards was saying. 'You have to get on board with this.'

'Nothing wrong with us.' Bowen flicked angrily through the pages, then held it up with a photo uppermost. 'It doesn't do her justice, does it?'

'No.'

'She's going to stand out plenty, though, pretty as she is. The only black officer in the whole damn force.'

'For fuck's sake, Mike.' Edwards grabbed the file. 'You're such a bloody dinosaur. Be careful what you say or you'll get a complaint made against you. Wise up.'

IT Matt looked up as the two women came in, then glanced across at the men. There was a moment's frozen silence. Whatever friendships existed in the team, Bowen had no right to be looking at her HR file. Whatever else was going on, Sara knew she had to deal with this. She walked to the office, took the file from Edwards's hand and looked at the photo.

'Not a great likeness, is it?' she said. 'My grandparents came over on the Windrush. My mother was born here and is as British as you, though she still considers herself partly Jamaican. My father was an East End boy, white as a snow-flake. So yes, a British-born officer of colour. Still a Londoner by rights, though. Am I really the only one?'

'Not entirely,' Edwards replied. Sara handed the file to him. Bowen shuffled back a couple of steps and turned away so she couldn't see his face. The phone on the DI's desk began to ring.

She returned to her desk and thumped down in the chair next to IT Matt. *What a great start — sexism and racism in under an hour. Now my new boss will have me down as difficult, though he created the issue in the first place.* As she made a note of her new passwords, she could see that Edwards was scribbling away furiously.

'If you have any queries, this is my extension.' IT Matt wrote a number on a scrap of paper. 'I'm on call during the day all this week.'

'Well, life just got a whole lot more interesting,' said Edwards. He marched out of his office, holding up his notepad.

'Why?' asked Ellie. 'What have we got?'

'A body. In a ditch.'

'Murder?' Bowen looked almost gleeful. 'We haven't had one of those in ages.'

'How long?' asked Sara.

'About a year now. Like you said, a Serious Crimes Unit with no serious crimes,' said Ellie. 'The last one was domestic violence anyway. She confessed after a few days.'

'Yeah, lezzy couple out at Aylsham. Jealousy. Took a shotgun to her partner,' Bowen said.

'DI Edwards may have a point.' Sara got to her feet, pulling herself up to her full height. 'You seem to need a more progressive vocabulary, DC Bowen. Though the Met have a word for people like you.'

She let the silence hang just long enough to be uncomfortable, then said, '"Unreconstructed."'

Edwards choked back a laugh. Bowen looked confused. Ellie let out the breath she was holding.

'Although "dinosaur" covers it just as well.'

Bowen grinned at Sara. 'Fair enough. Just go easy on me.'

'So, is it a murder?' Ellie sounded excited at the prospect.

'Too early to be certain. Uniform have just called it in. Some farmworker trimming hedges found the body. They reckon it may have been there a few days, given the state it's in.'

'Well, it's got to be better than all these damn thefts. Are the SOCOs on their way?' Bowen was already pulling on his jacket.

'Yes, they are, and so are we. Grab your stuff. We're off to East Ingham. It looks like we might be busy.'

CHAPTER 4

What a fool she had been. She was trapped. Or as good as. The door might be unlocked, but where could she go? Lenka had no one to talk to. Who would believe her? She had no papers, no passport. No one knew she was here.

This morning the sky had turned steel grey. A steady light rain was falling. Kirill drove the minibus down the cart track towards the road. It was time for the next set of chores. She began with the breakfast dishes stacked on the small work surface. Feeding eight men and two women twice a day from a caravan kitchen was a challenge for anyone who wasn't trained to do it, but she managed, and at least it relieved her of the other duty. That fell to Mouse. She ran a bowl of warm soapy water, while behind her, Pavel was pulling on his coat. There was a clink from his pocket, the sound of metal against a mobile phone case. Lenka knew that it was a gun. He grunted a goodbye and stepped down from the caravan into the warm August rain.

Lenka wasn't sure about Pavel, though he never said or did anything to her. He looked to be the oldest of the group, was wiry but strong and had little to say for himself. He didn't go out with the other crop pickers. Instead, most mornings, he left after the minibus to take a path across the fields and over a small hill that blocked Lenka's view. Sometimes he stayed out all day. Other days he returned in the middle of the afternoon, covered in dirt and grease, to take a shower and a nap, then, after their communal evening meal, he'd go out again with Kirill and the farmer.

Standing at the sink, she watched him walk across the fields behind their temporary home, two elderly static caravans embedded in rough scrub in the middle of farmland. The only drivable access was down a bumpy dirt track that wound across the fields from the farmhouse near the road. Her days were all the same. She had an early start to make breakfast and prepare packed lunches for the men before they left for work. After that, she would wake Mouse up, make the beds, do whatever cleaning or washing was necessary. Later she would prepare the evening meal for them all, cleaning up afterwards. Most days she could sneak some time to watch TV, which was helping with her English. It wasn't much of a life but it was better than when she had first arrived in London, and they dumped her in a brothel. It turned out that she was better at cooking than casual sex, which is why she had ended up here.

She stacked the pots on the drainer. There was Matus too. He was the youngest of the men, handsome in his way, with a shy smile. They were of similar age, and Lenka often wondered how he had ended up working with the gang, who were mostly middle-aged, weather-beaten and tough. Best of all, Matus was Serbian like she was, so they could sometimes talk, though it might be dangerous if Kirill noticed. She was a servant, useful so long as she did her job and kept her mouth shut. Pavel was a Serb too.

'I've brought you something,' Matus said one evening after he had been to the supermarket. Lenka wasn't allowed to leave the caravans, so once or twice a week, Matus would go out and bring whatever was on her shopping list. Shyly he had pulled a crumpled women's magazine from the inside pocket of his jacket. It was folded and torn, but it was hers, a present. She had started to cry.

'Thank you,' she whispered, holding the magazine tight in her slim, bony hands.

'Hey, no need for tears.' Matus put one hand gently on top of hers.

Lenka hid it temporarily in the cupboard while she unpacked the shopping, and then stuffed it into the pocket of her chunky cardigan to sneak it to her room when she finished a few minutes later. She used it to try to learn to read English. That was the first time Matus had been kind to her. Other gestures followed. Fleeting smiles, his hand brushing hers when he brought things to the kitchen, more little gifts like magazines or bars of chocolate. She sometimes wondered if the rest of the gang would care if Matus came to her room at night. She knew why he didn't. Where he went, others might follow, and Kirill had forbidden anyone to touch her.

Lenka finished the washing up and put on a fresh pot of coffee for herself. No one would count the scoops from the bag. Then she took a key from the hook by the door and ran quickly through the rain around to the door of the second van, without bothering to put on a coat.

'Mouse,' Lenka called as she unlocked the bedroom door. 'Mouse. Come on, breakfast.'

A small, fragile-looking woman was sitting hunched on the edge of the bed, staring out at the rain through the grimy, distorted plastic of the bedroom window. Her long hair hung limply down her back, and Lenka could see a fresh bruise turning the flesh around her eye purple.

'Stupid. I keep telling you, don't fight. Some men like it more that way.'

'I escape. Soon I go.' It was Mouse's perpetual complaint. 'Bastard Bohdan.'

'Come with me. Fresh coffee. TV's on.'

Gently, Lenka pulled Mouse up from the bed, handed her the long tatty jumper she used to cover herself with, waited while she used the bathroom. Her real name was Anya. She had acquired her nickname because she was so tiny, but Tiger would have been better, or Wildcat. When she'd first arrived at the caravans, she'd fought and spat — at life, the men, the sex, her captivity, had attempted to escape. They'd soon caught her, and locked her in. Lenka looked on in horror as Mouse's bruises grew and her treatment got rougher. After three months of this, Mouse's fight had altogether vanished, leaving her shrunken and depressed.

Not all the gang visited Mouse. The days were long and physically hard — often the men were too tired for sex. Pavel rarely acknowledged her existence. Kirill kept himself apart from anything that wasn't business.

They made their way past the improvised firepit and through the collection of old tables and chairs that the gang had gathered between the caravans. Sitting around the pit on fine evenings, the men would smoke and drink, play cards and talk in broken English, the only language they had in common. Some of them were Serbian, others from Ukraine. Lenka had no idea why they were such a disparate group, but they all seemed to have known either Kirill or Pavel before they arrived here.

Lenka was hurrying. Mouse wasn't. Her head was turning this way, then that, eyes scanning the area.

'Do not think about it,' said Lenka, grabbing Mouse's arm. 'You're not even dressed properly.'

'I escape. I run. Let me.' Desperately, the tiny woman tried to peel Lenka's fingers off her arm one by one. Unable to release the grip, Mouse pulled jerkily away, trying to wrench herself free. Her feet slipped on the freshly damp grass, making her land heavily on one knee, where she knelt with her head bowed, rain soaking her.

'If I let you go, they will kill me. Now, come,' Lenka pleaded. 'Coffee, toast, TV.'

'Please, help me.'

'I can't.' She pulled Mouse to her feet, rough in her frustration. Lenka wasn't supposed to let Mouse out of the other caravan, though she often did when the men were all out working. Now the small woman was trying to run away, which Lenka felt was a poor return for her kindness and rule-breaking. Mouse's knee was muddy. There was fresh blood. A new wound to add to her black eye. 'I fix that. Come with me. Please.'

Being Mouse's jailer wasn't something Lenka enjoyed having to do. They were both trapped in different ways. Lenka's fear of Pavel's gun was genuine, and she didn't doubt he would use it if he felt the need. She was far more terrified of Kirill. His manic rages were barely controlled and he would snap into violence without warning or remorse. One evening, one of the gang had teased Kirill as they stood smoking around the firepit. Bohdan was a big man with a tough attitude. Kirill was shorter but equally well-muscled. With a scream of rage, Kirill had floored Bohdan with a single punch, then knelt on his chest, hands squeezing the larger man's throat so hard that his breathing almost stopped, while Kirill whispered threats in his ear. Bohdan had let him do it, though Lenka suspected he would find a way to get revenge for it before the end of the season. Since then, the gang had tended to avoid upsetting Kirill.

Lenka knew that the picking season would be ending in a few weeks, then she could take action. For now, she was working on her English and waiting. She could also lock her bedroom door from the inside, which helped her sleep at night. Lenka was afraid that if she shared her plans with Mouse, the other woman might use the information in the hope of improving her situation. The more they beat Mouse, the less Lenka could trust her, no matter how sorry for her she felt. Besides, it was too soon. She still needed to form her plans.

Out of the rain, Lenka sat Mouse on one of the bench seats by the kitchen table to clean up her knee. She covered the wound with sticking plaster. The younger woman sat staring into space, shaking, though it wasn't cold.

'Stay there,' Lenka instructed. Swiftly fetching a blanket from her room, she wrapped it over Mouse's legs. 'If I make something, you will eat it?'

Mouse nodded, then asked, 'How will they kill you?'

'Pavel has a gun.'

'I don't know this. Pavel, he doesn't come near me.'

'Or Matus?'

'No. Not Matus.' Lenka brought a towel to dry Mouse's hair. 'They will kill me too.' Tears began to drip down Mouse's face, oozing from the tip of her nose where they mixed with stringy mucus. 'They will beat me until I die. Or they will fuck me until I am dead. Then Bohdan will fuck me until I rot.'

'You are just tired and hungry. I told you, don't fight them.' Lenka pushed tissues into the battered hand, then busied herself in the kitchen. Mouse pulled the blanket higher. Turning to watch the TV, she rubbed at her dripping hair.

They were settling down to toast and coffee when, unexpectedly, Kirill returned. He normally stayed out all day with the gang. Now the minibus skidded to a halt outside on the greasy grass. Lenka half rose from her seat and looked out in panic. Mouse huddled deeper into her jumper, stuffed the toast into her mouth, then slid under the table to hide. Kirill swung out of the driver's seat, slamming the door hard.

He didn't come into the caravan. Instead, pulling out his mobile phone, he punched at the screen angrily. As Lenka watched, their farmer landlord drove up after him, also in a hurry. He climbed out, leaving his engine running. The two began to talk excitedly together. Lenka couldn't hear much of what they were saying and could only understand a fraction of what she could hear. Something had gone very wrong. Seized with fear, she had a vision of Matus lying in a field somewhere, injured or even dead. Unaccustomed courage flooded her, she wrenched open the caravan door and ran towards the two men.

'What are doing, stupid bitch?' Kirill shouted when he saw her.

'Matus. Is Matus hurt?'

'Get back in the caravan.' The farmer turned towards her, his face dark with anger. 'Wait. Has Pavel gone already?'

Lenka nodded.

'Fuck off inside,' barked Kirill, raising his hand to slap her. Lenka obeyed, she didn't want a black eye like Mouse. The two men climbed into the farmer's vehicle. He turned it in a couple of violent manoeuvres and, gunning the engine, they bounced down the track back towards the road. Under the table, Mouse moaned with fear. Lenka watched them until they got to the end of the track and pulled out onto the road. Then she leaned down and patted Mouse.

'They have gone.'

Whatever was going on, Lenka had never seen Kirill look so rattled.

CHAPTER 5

The DI sent Ellie and Mike off in one car and took Sara in his own. Protocol usually dictated that the junior officer drove, but Edwards strode round to the driver's side without so much as a glance at her. She didn't know what to make of their sudden enthusiasm at the idea that there might be a murder to investigate. They looked almost joyful. Surely it couldn't be that dull here? They sped around the bypass, shooting off on a roundabout marked *Norfolk Broads*. A few minutes later he barged through a small town on a river, with boats moored on a quayside.

'This is Wroxham.' Edwards turned on his siren to scatter tourists and locals. '"Gateway to The Broads." Full of tourists at this time of year.'

It was starting to drizzle. The windscreen wipers squeaked intermittently. Sara could feel the wheels sliding on the greasy road. Beyond Wroxham, they turned off the main road into a tangle of minor lanes so narrow that there were regular passing places. She'd never been on a road like this in her life. You couldn't tell what might be coming towards you, or what lay beyond the hedges which crowded in on the car. True, London roads were often hemmed in with parked cars, or frantically busy with traffic, but a bit of siren and lights routine usually got them through. Here it wouldn't help in the slightest, and the greenery looked impenetrable. Bursting out of a group of trees, Sara caught sight of the countryside. If it wasn't quite as flat as her internet searches had led her to believe, the wide expanse of fields and big skies were exactly how she had envisaged it. After a couple of false turnings, which made Edwards furiously reverse the car, they rounded a bend and found the lane he wanted. Bowen and Ellie were already there.

'Take the scenic route, boss?' Bowen was grinning.

A patrol car blocked the road at the far end of the lane, where Ellie stood talking to one of the officers. Bowen had swung their car round to block the road coming the other way. Edwards abandoned his car behind Bowen's and strode off, leaving Sara to keep up as best she could. Hampered by her neat shoes, she almost had to jog.

'Body's in the ditch up there,' she heard Bowen say. 'This chap found it when he was working.'

Bowen pointed to where another uniformed officer was talking to a man dressed like the archetypal farmer in a checked shirt, sleeveless jacket, jeans and work boots. He stood looking round in a bewildered way. His face beneath the thatch of brown hair was lined where the outside work had aged him prematurely, burnishing his skin with a tan and the burn spots that Sara normally associated with older people. He might be thirty-five or forty. They were standing on a raised verge. A deep drainage ditch, overgrown with tall grass and brambles, ran in front of the untidy hedge on one side of the narrow lane. In the field beyond, Sara could see a tractor with a piece of long-armed machinery attached to it. Edwards climbed the small bank and Sara followed.

'Morning, sir,' the uniform said. 'This is Frank Walsh. He discovered the body.'

'Mr Walsh.' The DI acknowledged the man. 'We'll need a statement, of course, but perhaps you could fill us in briefly.'

'I just thought I'd do a bit of hedging,' the man began. 'I don't get much chance, so while we were waiting for the salad stuff to—'

'Briefly, Mr Walsh.'

'Well, I thought it was wrong.'

'What was?'

'The awful smell. So I had a look, and there he were.' The man turned his gaze back up the road.

'If you can give your details to my DS here, we'll call on you later for the details.'

The DI walked off up the lane towards Ellie. Bowen looked at Sara with a small triumphant smile, then tagged along. It was a DC's job to do this, not the DS. Sara pulled out her notebook and took Walsh's address. The rain was persistent now — she was going to get soaked.

'Are you all right, sir?' she asked.

'I suppose so. Weren't expectin' it.'

'No, not something people normally come across.'

'Oh, I see dead things all the time,' said Walsh. He was twisting his work-calloused fingers, which Sara could see were shaking. 'I empty the vermin traps at the farm. Then there's the roadkill. You know, hedgehogs, sometimes deer, even badgers. But I hint seen roadkill like that before.'

He stared after Edwards, who was looking down into the ditch with Bowen by his side. It took a moment for Sara to adjust to his local accent.

'Is there someone who could sit with you for a while?' she asked. 'Or somewhere you could go? Get a cuppa, perhaps?'

'I should tell Agnes.'

'Agnes?'

'My boss. Owns the farm.' He waved at the field behind the hedge, where the tractor stood abandoned.

'She'll need to know. We'll have to cut the lane off for investigations.'

Walsh pulled a battered-looking mobile from his work waistcoat and squinted through the rain at the screen. After wiping it with his sleeve, he selected a number.

Sara turned away to give him some privacy, checked her own phone and saw that she had no signal at all. Edwards stood with his back towards her, talking to Ellie. To her horror she saw Bowen start to step down into the ditch, one gloved hand on the verge edge, the other reaching out to retrieve something. He would contaminate the evidence. Her new shoes tapped a tattoo on the tarmac as she moved rapidly to stop him.

'I don't think you should be doing that,' Sara said. Bowen quickly pulled himself back up the ditch onto the verge.

'Can't reach it anyway.'

'We should wait for the SOCOs.'

'Yes, of course. I just wanted to see what that was in his pocket. Look, there.'

Sara looked down. What she saw made her want to vomit. During her years of service, she had seen her fair share of bodies. People mangled in car crashes, suicides with their bulging eyes. Once, an elderly man who had died alone. Unmissed for days, his body reduced to a feast for maggots, it had been the storm of flies buzzing at the windows that had finally alerted a neighbour. They had swarmed past Sara as she and a fellow officer had broken in the door. But this was quite a new experience.

The body was probably an older male. It lay on its back in the ditch, red-orange mud holding it down like glue, an orange tidemark on the arms and body. It too was stirring with maggots and flies, but they hadn't done the worst damage. The flesh on the face and neck was torn away. Fingers on both hands and part of one foot were missing. Both eyeballs were gone, the tongue pulled out of the jaw and gouged to ribbons. Walsh was right. The smell was rank.

'Dear God, who would do such a thing?' She was trying to keep the bile down herself.

'Well, I doubt he went in there looking like that.' Bowen smirked. 'Once he started to stink, that would have attracted the animals and birds. If you came from the country, you'd know about that.'

'We have no idea what happened yet.'

'Yeah? Well, I'd lay twenty quid most of that damage was inflicted post-mortem. Fancy a bet?'

Sara didn't. She'd seen the damage rats could do to bodies in London. Who knew what the local wildlife might be capable of?

'If there is something in his pocket, it would be the quickest way to identify him,' insisted Bowen. He moved to stand close beside Sara. She knew he was deliberately invading her personal space, capitalising on her show of discomfort, testing her. If she moved away, it would be a capitulation. 'Look, something's poking out. We could reach it.'

Suddenly Sara felt a hand in the small of her back. None too gently it pushed her. She slipped down the wet grass on the side of the bank. Too late, she realised the smart court shoes gave no purchase. As she shifted her weight sideways to save herself, her right foot landed in the red glue in the bottom, missing the body by millimetres. It shifted in the slime, releasing a gust of stinking decay which made her heave uncontrollably.

With half-screwed up eyes, trying to close her nostrils, she scrabbled at the grass on the side of the bank to stop herself going any further. A hand reached down and grabbed her arm. It was the DI.

'Up you come,' Edwards said, pulling her back out of the ditch. He's stronger than he looks, Sara thought as she took a couple of steps away and vomited on the verge. She could hear Bowen laughing.

'What the hell do you think you were doing?'

Now she had a choice. If she accused Bowen of pushing her, she would never be forgiven, would never fit in. It was her first day, she couldn't afford to get this wrong. The smell of the body, combined with the stink of vomit, caught in the back of her throat. She pulled a tissue from her jacket pocket to wipe the spit from her chin. It hadn't taken long for the DC to find a good moment to haze her. No doubt it was retaliation for stealing the job from his friend and then calling him a dinosaur. Bowen stood, arms folded, waiting to see what Sara would do, his head cocked on one side like an inquisitive dog.

'Sorry, sir.' She looked down at her dirty feet. 'Think my shoes aren't up to the job. Must have slipped.'

She saw Edwards look at Bowen, then at Ellie, who had moved closer. 'Let's leave it at that then.' Edwards didn't sound convinced. 'Sort out some better footwear.'

They heard vehicles approaching from the north end of the lane and the SOCOs began to arrive. A black Mercedes was following the white CSI vans. Edwards moved off to greet them, much to Sara's relief. When she looked back at him, Bowen was silently applauding.

'Here.' Ellie offered her a bottle of water. Sara grabbed it and rinsed out her mouth. Her shoe and trouser leg were caked in the red mud from the ditch. So much for making a good impression on her first day.

'That was a bit much,' said Ellie in a low voice. She led her away. 'Come on. I've got some wipes in my bag. I always carry a packet.'

Sara had managed to make herself a bit more presentable by the time the SOCOs began pulling on their white suits and setting up their tent. Edwards motioned to the others to join him.

'We'd best let them get on. What's happening with the farmer?'

'He phoned his boss, I think,' said Sara. 'Someone called Agnes.'

'I'd like you to get his full statement. Find out what's going on so we can organise cars.'

Sara walked along the lane to where the farmer waited, the wet shoe rubbing against her heel.

'Did you get hold of your boss, Mr Walsh?'

He nodded. 'Yes, she's coming over. It's only a couple of miles, won't be long. You can call me Frank.'

'Perhaps we can get your statement when you've had a cuppa?'

'Yes, of course. Don't know what I can say that will help. I just found him, is all. You all right?'

Sara smiled and shrugged. The rain was easing off now, the clouds breaking up. There was the sound of a vehicle approaching at speed. Frank's brow wrinkled in surprise.

'That's not Agnes,' he said.

The black Range Rover came round the bend so rapidly that the driver had to do an emergency stop. Tyres squealing, the vehicle swung to the left, narrowly avoiding ramming Edwards's car. Spattering dust and gravel under its locking wheels, the huge vehicle shot up the bank, its brakes screaming, as Frank and Sara scrambled out of its way. It rose from the road, front wheels inches away from where they had been standing, back wheels on the tarmac, grinding to a noisy halt, its engine hissing like some fantastic beast. Everyone turned at the noise. The windows were tinted, making it impossible to see inside. The passenger window began to wind down, and Sara glimpsed two men.

'Idiot!' The driver swore and wound the window back up. The vehicle revved noisily but didn't move as, Sara assumed, the two men inside checked out the scene down the road. Heart thumping from the close call, she strode angrily along the bank towards it. In response, the driver turned the vehicle and shot back the way it had come. Sara grabbed her notebook and started to scribble down the licence plate.

'Don't worry about it,' said Frank. 'I know who that was.'

Then he burst into tears.

CHAPTER 6

Agnes grasped the photo of Mark as though it might give her an answer that she couldn't get from him in real life. She was at her study desk, in theory sending out her grazing invoices but dreaming of a visit from her distant son. Cambridge wasn't that far away — the distance was emotional, not practical. Her mobile rang.

'Mark?' she asked.

'Agnes, we've got a problem,' said Frank.

Of course. How could she have imagined that Mark would call her?

'Is it the tractor or the hedger?' It wasn't unusual for the farm machinery to break down. Replacing things was another thing she didn't get around to anymore. Frank managed by cobbling repairs or buying the occasional part.

'Neither.'

'Are you all right? You haven't had an accident, have you?'

'No, no, I'm fine.' Frank still seemed hesitant. 'It's just . . .'

'Whatever is the matter?'

'Police are here. I found something. In the ditch.'

'You found . . . something?'

'Well, more like some*one*.'

Agnes slumped against the back of her chair. 'Jesus, Frank. What's going on?'

'Police say you ought to come over. Lane'll be shut, though.'

'OK, I'll be there in a few minutes.'

Agnes closed the call with a shaking hand. Memories overwhelmed her. For a moment, she couldn't stand up. A late autumn afternoon, unanswered mobile calls, growing panic, dashing through the darkening lanes in her rattling vehicle. The tractor stalled at the end of the field, its nose in the hedge, the plough still in the ground. Her husband slumped over the steering wheel, already gone.

Trying to calm her heart rate, she grabbed her keys, locked the back door and made for the field where she knew Frank had intended to do some hedging this morning. Found someone? What on earth did he mean by that? Mercifully, she was some yards from the turning when she saw Des Dixon's monstrous black Range Rover hurtle out of the lane without pausing.

'That man gets everywhere,' she grumbled. At least she wouldn't have to acknowledge him, he was heading in the other direction at considerable speed.

She stopped at a cordon of blue and white tape. Frank was standing on the bank of the ditch talking to a woman, who was handing him a tissue. A white tent had been placed over the ditch further up the lane, where several people were milling around in protective suits. There was an air of unreality about it all. You rarely saw this many police here, not even if you'd had a break-in.

'My boss,' Frank explained to the officer.

She nodded at the woman. 'Agnes Richardson,' she said. 'Frank, what on earth is going on?'

'I'm DS Hirst.' The woman held out her hand, which Agnes shook briefly before laying a consoling hand on Frank's trembling arm. 'I think Frank has had a nasty shock. Perhaps we could get him away from here for a while?'

'Body in the ditch,' Frank murmured. 'I could smell it. Thought it were a deer.'

'But it's not?'

'I'm afraid not, Mrs Richardson. It's a person.'

'Then that bloody Dixon,' — Frank's gaze shot back down the lane — 'nearly ran us down. Driving like a loony, just like always.'

'I'll take Frank back to mine,' Agnes said. 'It's nearest, and his car's there.'

'We'll need a statement.' DS Hirst looked up the road at the gaggle of people.

'Tea.'

'Sorry?'

'Tea's good for shock.' Agnes started to lead Frank away. 'You know how to find me?'

'Yes.' The detective sergeant didn't sound sure. 'I have your address and Frank's home address.'

'We'll wait at the farm for you. Dare say you could do with a cuppa yourself. You look a bit damp.'

Agnes drove a silent Frank back to the farmhouse. She was desperate to know what was going on but didn't press him. They settled in the kitchen, quietly drinking mugs of strong tea until he had shaken off the worst of it.

'I'm sorry.'

'What on earth for?' Agnes opened a new packet of biscuits and placed them on the table between them.

'It'll be a lot of trouble.' Frank helped himself to one. 'Police everywhere, and they'll be pestering us.'

'Can't be helped. I wonder who the poor soul is?'

'Foul,' said Frank. He dunked his biscuit, pushing the soggy digestive into his mouth. Agnes munched along with him, nodding and waiting. Frank remained silent.

The rain had cleared, and the clouds had broken by the time another car pulled into the yard. The woman who had called herself DS Hirst climbed out, along with a man. Police officers always came in pairs. They also liked tea.

'This is DC Bowen, and I'm DS Hirst,' the woman said.

'Tea's on, have a seat and help yourself to biscuits.'

Agnes was surprised to see the DC grab the packet and lever out a biscuit. He took a bite before remembering his manners and offering the packet to his partner. The woman shook her head, though she looked hungry. Agnes put down a cup of tea next to her, which was accepted gratefully.

'So, Frank, tell me what happened,' said DS Hirst. 'Take your time.'

'Thought I'd do a bit of hedging,' Frank said, looking between the two officers. 'Seeing as how we're waiting.'

'Waiting?' DS Hirst asked. 'Assume I know nothing about farming.'

The DC snorted into his tea. They all looked at him, Hirst with a barely concealed frown.

'You could wait in the car, DC Bowen,' she said, and Agnes silently awarded her a brownie point. He mumbled a half-hearted apology and stuffed another biscuit into his mouth. Frank explained how a day or two's hiatus in the summer was rare, there was so much harvesting to be done. This year had been dry, so the crops were out of sync, leaving him with the chance to do some tidying up.

'Usually leave it until the autumn, but it seemed a shame to waste the day.'

'You took the tractor over to the field first thing?' the DS asked.

'Yes, about eight. I'd been goin' a while, then I needed . . .' Frank began to blush, the colour rose swiftly to the roots of his short, brown hair.

'Yes?'

'I think Frank means he needed to answer a call of nature,' Agnes explained. 'Most of the workers go in the hedge if they get caught short.'

Frank nodded. 'Then that awful smell. I knew it was death. Sometimes the deer come down to eat the salad crops and get hit by cars. Their bodies stink, especially in hot weather. So, I climbed over the gate and walked down to see. Buzzing with flies, it was, when I pulled away the grass

— them clothes, that face. Made me sick.' Frank glanced at the DS.

'Me too,' the woman admitted. She was ignoring her partner's smug face. Agnes allocated her another brownie point.

'I saw. What you go down there for?' Frank's question caught out both the officers.

Hirst looked at Bowen, who didn't meet her gaze, then said, 'I slipped. Do go on.'

'I called Wroxham.'

'Wroxham is the nearest rural police station,' the DC muttered to Hirst.

'And they came out?' Hirst asked.

'Yes, straight away. Made them go green an' all. Then they called someone else, then you all turned up and the others with the tent and stuff and then bloody Dixon. Damn 'im. Cud've killed us both.'

Agnes wondered which had upset Frank more, finding the body or the near miss with Dixon. It made her feel angry on Frank's behalf.

'This was the man in the black Range Rover?' Hirst asked.

'Don't know what he was doing there. No need to be.' Frank was getting angrier. 'Interfering, that's what he'll be doin'.'

'I should explain that Des Dixon isn't much liked around here,' Agnes said. 'Frank used to work for him until Dixon sacked him. When I found out, I asked Frank to come and work for me. Best thing I ever did.'

'Me and the missus is still grateful. Don't know what we would have done. Could have lost our home and everything.'

'So how long have you been here, Frank?' Hirst asked.

'Couple of years.'

'Since my husband died,' Agnes added. 'I couldn't manage the farm alone. Now Frank does the hard work and I do the paperwork. Suits us both.'

The two officers got to their feet, and made arrangements for Frank to complete a formal statement at Wroxham the following day. Agnes watched them drive away. The man was at the wheel, while the woman made notes in her book. DS Hirst had asked for Dixon's address, which Agnes hoped meant that he would also be receiving a visit. It would serve him right.

'Is the tractor locked up, Frank?'

'Yes, I did it while I was waitin' on the police.'

'You get off home, then.'

'I should have a look at your CCTV.'

'Tomorrow will do,' she said. 'Spend some time with your family. You've had a nasty morning.'

Frank still took time to lock up the barns before Agnes could pack him off to his wife and young son. The anger that had been simmering inside her since Des Dixon's visit the previous night now pushed her into action. If Mark wasn't going to come home to help her, she'd have to do it herself. She'd had enough of Des Dixon's obnoxious ways and didn't owe him any more favours. She was going to go to the barns and tell her visitors that they had to clear out.

CHAPTER 7

Bowen drove back to the lane in silence. Sara didn't feel like talking either. In spite of Ellie's wipes and Sara's best efforts to get clean, the car had a faint odour of vomit. The DI was standing by the tent over the ditch, talking to an older man in a white coverall.

'This isn't blood.' The man pointed to the legs of his protective suit which were soaked in red mud. 'In case you were wondering.'

'I wasn't,' said the DI.

'Much of his face, several fingers and toes are missing — animals and birds I would surmise. So full identification may be down to DNA. Given the state of decay, I'd say he's been there several days. I can be more accurate once we get him on the slab. But it's not recent, and his leg seems to be broken. We should be able to move him soon, and I'll get the post-mortem finished by tomorrow morning.'

'No other way to identify him?' the DI asked.

'There are some items in his jacket. I'll get SOCOs to bag them up first and let you know when you can have them. Shouldn't take long. I can tell you that he's a Caucasian male, early sixties, overweight. Seems to be wearing rather too many clothes given the hot weather we've been having recently.'

'Anything particular about them?'

'They are all black if that helps. Oh, and I'll need to take a DNA sample from your new lady for elimination purposes.' The man nodded at Sara, who felt herself blush. 'Just in case she's contaminated the scene throwing up like that. Your first body?'

'No, sir.'

The DI turned to the team. 'Did you get the statement?' Sara nodded.

'Good. Let's get back to the office. Ellie, you can take Sara. Mike, you're with me.'

Edwards allowed Bowen to drive, Sara noticed with annoyance, as they headed back to the cars, though she was grateful that Ellie went around to the driver's side of the other car and climbed in. It had been a long morning, and she was starting to feel rather shaky. Her stomach growled. She needed to eat something and keep it down — no point in getting a reputation for being soft.

'Who was that?' she asked.

'Dr Stephen Taylor, our main pathologist. He's a nice guy, though he's due to retire soon. We'll miss him.' Ellie turned back through the tangle of lanes towards the main road. 'Are you okay?'

'I'm fine.' Sara looked away from Ellie and shrugged. 'It was just first day nerves, I guess. How about you?'

'It's not been easy for any of us. We didn't come in expecting to meet you, any more than you expected to get that bullshit from Bowen.'

'Could you see?'

Ellie didn't reply immediately, then said carefully, 'Mike's a long-serving officer who found his niche in SCU and hasn't gone for further promotion. He's settled, I suppose.'

'Or set in his ways?' Sara suggested. 'He certainly has a way of talking that I haven't come across in a while.'

'Old-fashioned, you mean? The boss does have to defend him now and then. Don't mistake that for incompetence.

He's a good detective, has a sharp mind. That's no excuse, though, for doing that to you. I suspect he'll be getting a bollocking on the way back to the office.'

'Just a bit of hazing, bound to happen,' said Sara. She looked down at her leather court shoes. 'Think my shoes are dead, though.'

Ellie smiled. 'Walking boots. That's what we all wear, unless you're going off to interview someone posh. We have lots of posh people in this county. I keep a pair of pop socks and smart shoes in my desk drawer.'

'What about you? You've passed your exams. You must have ambitions. I'm sorry if I upset your plans.'

'You weren't to know. They'll find me something soon.' Ellie sounded as if she didn't quite believe what she was saying.

'Well, at least there'll be something to investigate with this poor man. We can work on this one together. I'd appreciate your help in getting to know the area, the other teams. Can you tell me where I can buy walking boots?'

Ellie nodded. 'Is that your stomach?' she asked.

Sara rubbed her belly and laughed. 'Couldn't eat this morning.'

For the rest of the journey, Ellie tried to explain the geography of the area. The Norfolk Broads to the north and east of Norwich, the crumbling North Norfolk coastline, the ageing seaside resorts and the city of Norwich like a hub of a cycle wheel with the roads leading into it like spokes. If you got as far as King's Lynn, you were in the Fens and heading towards Lincolnshire.

'You find water everywhere, rivers or sea. It's still pretty rural, and most people work in either agriculture or tourism,' Ellie finished. They pulled back into the HQ car park. The boss had beaten them back to the office.

'Can you do an initial missing person scan?' Edwards asked as they came in. Bowen had managed to put a pot of coffee on, Sara noticed. 'Say in the last three weeks or so. Though I don't hold out much hope.'

'Sure. Could he be a tourist?' Ellie asked.

'I suppose so. Do a general sweep, see if anything comes up.'

'I'll start now.' Sara logged into her computer, grateful that it responded to her new passwords. She hoped no one could see her as she eased her soggy shoes off under the desk.

'Special job for you, Mike,' the DI said. 'I think you owe us all a sandwich. Get down to the canteen and sort it out.'

Sara and Ellie shared a glance as Bowen went out of the door. Presumably, the bollocking had taken place.

'You do eat bacon butties, don't you?' Edwards asked her.

'Yes, sir. Not a veggie.'

Ellie got down to work, pulling up maps and satellite pictures of the site, printing them out and pinning them to the incident board. Sara trawled the database without success. Eventually, Bowen returned with a pile of foil-wrapped bacon rolls. He dumped them on the spare table with sachets of ketchup and brown sauce, helping himself before he went back to his desk.

'No patients wandering, no husbands walking out — well, at least not of the right age — no tourists lost their way. Nothing.' Sara sighed. 'I suppose he could be from elsewhere in the country. I'll give that a go.'

Gratefully, she selected a roll, opened the foil and squeezed ketchup onto the bacon. The smell was divine. She took a large bite, squishing tomato sauce out of the sides. 'Nice one, Bowen,' she said. He nodded. As the other two loaded up their rolls, Sara outlined the basics of their interview with Frank.

'So, they think this neighbour was the driver. Did you take his plate number?'

'Yes, sir.' Sara held up her notebook. It was new. The number plate was her first entry, which felt both odd and full of promise at the same time.

'Mike, check that out.'

Sara's bacon roll had vanished in a few bites, and her shaky feeling began to subside. All she had to do now was keep the damn thing down. She studied the maps that Ellie had pinned up, trying to get her bearings.

'Technically, Mrs Richardson's farm is in a village called East Ingham.' Ellie's fingers circled on the high detail map, then moved on to one with a wider view. 'It's a hamlet, just a few houses and farms. This is the nearest village of any size.' Her finger landed on a village called Happisburgh strung out along a minor road. 'It's pronounced Haze-bruh. Did you spot the red and white striped lighthouse?'

Sara nodded. It was hard to miss the thing even in the grey misty rain of the morning.

'That's the place. You see it on all the postcards.'

'Got him, boss. Desmond Arthur Dixon.' Bowen read out the search result. 'They called him Des, so that makes sense. Ridlington Manor Farm. He wasn't far off his patch.'

'There was no love lost there,' said Sara. 'And his driving leaves a lot to be desired. I thought there were two men in the vehicle. Could you see?'

'Nah, you were closest. It's only been registered for three months.' He opened another screen and whistled. 'Didn't think farming was that lucrative, the way they're always moaning. This one's top of the range, about a hundred grand.'

Ellie returned to her desk and searched on her computer. Edwards and Sara located Dixon's farm on the big map, and she stuck coloured pins in the two farms to identify them.

'He's Mrs Richardson's neighbour,' Edwards said. 'Only a few miles as the crow flies, but further round the lanes.'

'Look at this. I googled him.' Ellie brought up an old newspaper article. 'Won some farming industry award. This isn't so nice though. Looks like Mr Dixon has a bit of a profile. Might be known to us. Something to do with a fight at the local pub a few months back.' Ellie opened another tab. 'Acrimonious divorce, wife claims violence.'

'Did we ever go out to that?' asked Edwards. 'Have a look, Mike.'

'On it,' replied Bowen.

'What has our friend been up to?' The DI moved over to the DC's desk. 'This old boy says he got harassed.'

'Mr Dixon is all over this like a bad rash.' Bowen was grinning. 'I'll print the reports out. Complaints from the wife. Ex-wife. Complaints from neighbour Jack Ellis. Arrested after a punch-up in the Hall House pub, got off with a caution.'

The office's large printer began rattling as reports and news articles streamed out. For balance, Ellie also printed the one about the award, along with a photo of Des Dixon from a farming magazine. Edwards surveyed the information.

'I think a visit is in order, don't you? Nobody nearly runs down half my team and gets away without one. Sara, you're with me — time for another drive. Mike, Ellie, keep digging. Find out how big his farm is and where all the land is. Anything else you can think of. I don't like the sound of our Mr Dixon.'

Sara pulled on her soaking shoes, wincing at the slimy feel of them, and grabbed her stuff. The DI took the photo from the magazine, folded it up and put it in his pocket. When they reached Wroxham again, the traffic had snarled up. Edwards crawled along in the queue of cars.

'No point in rushing,' he said. 'There's just the one little bridge, and we have to cross the river somehow. People tend to forget we have to worry about crossing over all this water. The only other bridges are fifteen miles that way or ten miles the other way.'

'It can be a problem in London, too. People forget because it's not an issue on the Tube.'

'And it's high season.' Edwards's mobile rang. He grimaced. 'Yes, Mike?'

'Thought I ought to ring you straight away. Stephen Taylor's just called. They got the body back and checked out that jacket.'

'And?'

'We got lucky. The things in the jacket pocket were mostly camera stuff. Underneath all that was a credit card with a petrol receipt. You're not going to like this.'

'Get on with it, Mike. Who is it?'

'It's one of ours.'

'What? Who?' The car jerked to a halt.

'It's Adam Crane. The dead guy is retired Detective Sergeant Adam Crane.'

CHAPTER 8

The grey clouds had broken and it was sunny again. The anger that had driven Agnes out of the farmhouse hadn't had time to soften in the half-mile drive to her barns. She turned smartly into the yard, braking the old Defender hard on the overgrown and patchy gravel. Years ago, they had kept a few animals here. Sometimes sheep, more often cattle. Her husband would buy a few at the market in Norwich and bring them back here to fatten before returning them to the abattoir. It hadn't earned them much money but he'd enjoyed having the animals to take care of. As the couple grew older, it became too much of an effort, and they'd stopped doing it, instead renting out the fields and marshes to other farmers who'd used them to fatten stock of their own.

The barns had fallen into disuse since then and were in poor repair. Two large double-height barns with twin doors, half a dozen stables and a couple of open-fronted cow byres formed an oblong around the central yard. They were old, constructed in red brick and flint, once common in the buildings here and now so beloved of the barn converters. There had been several offers for them in the last couple of years, all of which she had refused. Most of the buildings were full of broken farm junk, not to mention old household items that

Tom had never felt able to throw away. One of these days she was going to have to get around to sorting it all out, she supposed. Dixon's crop pickers had been the first people to use the barns in years. Well, she'd had enough. The man was a bully.

Agnes had assumed that the men would be out picking and the place would be empty. She had brought the keys to the barn, wanting to check it out before calling on Dixon to deliver her ultimatum. But the doors were open. Inside, a radio was loudly playing Radio Five Live. It must have masked the sound of her arrival, and for a moment, she was able to look around the barn. Sunshine flooded through the open doors behind her and drifted down from regularly placed slits high up in the walls, the old-fashioned method of ventilating the space. Dust danced in lazy motes in the shafts of light. She could smell engine oil and diesel fumes.

A new-looking Defender stood in the middle of the floor, its engine hoisted up by chains on a lift that looked like a large, red spider clawing at a trapped fly. An old bench stood against one wall, covered with tools. There was a quad bike parked against the back wall, a trailer still hitched on. Rough wooden packing crates of various sizes stood around the edge of the barn, some sealed and marked up with stencilled addresses, others empty, waiting to be dealt with. In one corner, the men had set up a sort of rest area, with tea-making paraphernalia and some bits of broken furniture. Agnes recognised the sagging sofa and armchairs. It was her old suite which they'd dumped in one of the stables years ago intending to take it to the tip at some point. The men must have found it and dragged it over here, though they would have needed to break off the lock to have done so. The idea offended her.

Bent over a large packing crate behind the vehicle was a middle-aged man. Dressed in dirty jeans and an oil-stained T-shirt, he had short, dark hair and looked as if he needed a shave.

When she called, 'Hello,' the man jumped in an almost comic fashion, dropping what he was holding into the crate. He scurried over to turn the radio off.

'I'm Mrs Richardson.' She tried to keep her voice neutral. 'I own these barns. Are you staying at Mr Dixon's farm?'

The man looked at her blankly, raising his hands and shrugging. His eyes darted from her to the rest area and back again as if he were unsure what to do.

'You're working on this one?' She pointed at the Defender. The man strode forward to intercept her as she moved towards it. 'It's newer than mine.'

Again, the man shrugged, gesturing aggressively with his hands, standing between Agnes and the vehicle to prevent her from getting any closer to it.

'I thought you were doing up old cars?'

As she tried to look past him, the man swerved from side to side, managing to block her view each time, until she stepped smartly around him and the vehicle, moving towards the quad bike at the far end of the barn. He followed her, jabbering something she couldn't understand, and grabbed her by the arm. She swung round to face him, looking pointedly at his dirty, oil-stained hand. He removed it, holding both hands up in a pacifying gesture.

'Don't you speak English?'

'No. No. No English.' The man shook his head, apparently relieved to have understood something.

'I see. Well, these are my barns. I'll go where I like.'

Agnes went over to the quad bike. The keys were still in the ignition. She felt that she ought to recognise it, but if she were honest, it could be one of many. All the farmers and smallholders had these things, the trailers were common too. The man was still hovering closely behind her. If he couldn't understand her, there didn't seem any point in continuing. Agnes turned to leave. 'You tell Mr Dixon I want you out of here. You can't use these barns anymore. I'm giving you notice to quit.'

'No speak English,' the man called after her.

Agnes turned her vehicle down the lane towards Happisburgh with a shudder. The bizarre encounter had made her feel uncomfortable. She could still feel the grip of his hand on her arm and there were greasy marks on her skin where his fingers had grabbed at her. The sight of them revolted her. She had no issue with the fact that the man couldn't speak English. These crop picking gangs did the work that local people often preferred not to and were valuable to the farming community. But if he didn't speak any English, why was he listening to a radio station that was mostly sports talk? Why not music? Dixon had said the men were doing up old cars, but that Defender was no more than a few years old and valuable on the second-hand market. What about the quad bike and trailer? It didn't take a genius to suspect they might have been stolen. Dixon was capable of anything if there was money to be made.

Turning through Happisburgh, she drove to the coast road, turning left and left again in a big square that brought her to Dixon's farmhouse. The farms backed on to each other, the two houses only separated by a handful of fields, but there was no drivable path between the two. She rang the front doorbell, then knocked hard at the back door, but the house was empty. The farm buildings on the other side of the yard were also locked up. Perhaps it was a good thing, she thought, belatedly remembering Frank's words about being careful when she was on her own. No one could see her from the road if anything happened, if Dixon decided that her age didn't protect her. The thought made her uneasy, and she drove home by the shortest route.

Back inside, Agnes couldn't settle. The farmhouse felt particularly lonely and quiet after such an odd day with its unexpected visitors. She scrubbed at the marks on her arm with a grease cleaner until they came off, leaving the skin red. Her natural reaction, to make tea, didn't help. The drink grew cold on the kitchen table. Her appetite had vanished too, and the biscuit packet stood on the table untouched. She tried to call her son again. There was no reply at his home number, and his mobile went straight to voicemail, as usual. She wished that she'd allowed Frank to mend the CCTV.

Agnes was not an anxious person by nature, but now she did something she would never normally consider necessary in the middle of the day. She deadlocked the front door and secured the chain in place, then she locked the back door and drew the curtains. For the first time since her husband's death, Agnes felt herself to be old and vulnerable.

CHAPTER 9

It had been a quiet afternoon in the caravan. Mouse had fallen into an uneasy sleep on the seat behind the table, so Lenka had covered her with the blanket and left her to it. As the TV had run through its afternoon schedule, Lenka had concentrated on practising her English. She especially liked the one about doctors after the early afternoon local news. Mouse had slept through it all, not waking until Lenka shook her at 3 p.m.

'Have a shower, wash your hair. It will make you feel better,' Lenka said, trying to soothe the frightened woman. Kirill's sudden return that morning had terrified Mouse, who kept staring out of the window with a haunted look. But she did as Lenka suggested. Once Mouse had finished her shower, Lenka took her back to her room. As she made to leave, Mouse grabbed Lenka's hand and held it to her cheek.

'Thank you,' Mouse whispered. 'No one else helps me.'

'I'm sorry,' Lenka replied. She pulled her hand away. 'I do what I can.'

Soon, Lenka promised herself as she locked the bedroom door and wiped away a tear. *I'll be able to go soon, and I'm going to take her with me.*

The farmer, Dixon, dropped Kirill to pick up the minibus just after Mouse had returned to her room, but neither came into the caravan. Instead, both vehicles left by the track, Dixon back to his house and Kirill driving off to collect the gang from their picking job.

Lenka began to prepare the evening meal, choosing her ingredients and settling in to chop vegetables. The TV had reached some programme about selling antiques when she was surprised to see Pavel walking back across the fields. Lenka rarely saw Pavel do anything quickly. He wrenched open the door, radiating anger. She kept her back to him, peeling potatoes in the sink, her shoulders hunched defensively.

'What's going on at the house?' he demanded.

Lenka shrugged. The kitchen window faced the other van, not down the track to the farmhouse. Pavel put a hand on her arm and spun her round. She was lucky not to peel her hand instead of the potato she was holding. He pointed out the opposite window.

'Who does that car belong to?'

Lenka looked at the farmhouse. In the yard next to the farmer's monstrous four-by-four was a sleek, dark-coloured saloon. There were three figures.

'You go find out.'

'Me?' Lenka was horrified.

'I had one visitor earlier today. Now he has two. Something's up. Go. Listen.'

'Kirill will beat me if they catch me.'

'Then make sure they don't.' Pavel grabbed the peeler from her hand, pulled her out through the caravan door and shoved her down the path towards the house. The cart track from the vans to the backyard of the farmhouse was dotted with occasional trees and tangled briar patches. When Lenka looked back at Pavel, he shooed her like she was a stray animal. Lenka didn't dare test his temper any more than Kirill's.

Staying low, Lenka scurried along the scrubby undergrowth, pausing behind one tree to check she hadn't been seen before moving onto the next. The cover ran out about twenty metres from the yard, where a low wall separated Dixon's well-kept garden from the field. It was as close as she could get. The farmer was talking heatedly to the two people. The first was a middle-aged white man, the other a black woman.

Lenka was surprised. In Serbia, she had seen few black people, just a handful of locally born Muslims who lived on the outskirts of her village. It wasn't even the sort of place that refugees had turned to during the recent crisis. The authorities had made it clear that they weren't welcome. Serbia was no more than a staging post on their journey to Western Europe.

Furthermore, although the two men were doing all the talking, the woman showed no signs of being subservient and was writing things Dixon said down in a notebook. The only female officials Lenka ever saw belonged to places like orphanages or hospitals and were rarely in charge of things. All this was beyond her experience.

The farmer became angrier as the conversation went on, his voice rising, his hands waving. The little she could catch was a good test for her English, Lenka thought, her heart hammering as she peered over the low wall.

'That was all dealt with,' Dixon was saying. 'I apologised to the landlord, and he accepted it. Why are you raking all this up now?'

The man replied in an even tone, which meant Lenka couldn't hear the reply.

'I can drive where I like. It's a free country. At least it was last time I looked.'

The man interrupted.

'Yes, well, maybe I was driving a bit fast. But that lane's a short cut. I use it all the time.'

Now the woman asked something. Dixon looked at her in surprise.

'I don't have to answer that,' he snapped.

'Just answer the question, Mr Dixon,' said the man. 'Who was in the car with you?'

'I've had enough of this.' Dixon folded his arms as if to keep his hands from lashing out. 'You can leave now. I don't even know why you're here, bothering me like this. It's police harassment, that's what this is.'

Police? Were these visitors police officers? Neither Pavel nor Kirill were going to like that. As Lenka watched, the woman scanned the fields towards the caravans. For less than a second, Lenka thought their eyes met. Ducking her head down, Lenka realised that she could do it now. Run up to the visitors, ask for asylum, for help, but her limbs froze. What about Matus? What about Mouse? Would these strangers believe her or Dixon? He was bound to have ready answers to anything she tried to stutter in her broken English. As she frantically tried to decide what to do, she heard the man say goodbye to Dixon. The moment of opportunity had passed. Her courage had failed. The two visitors were returning to their car and Lenka felt exposed. Staying low behind the scrub and briars, she crept back to the caravans. Pavel was inside the kitchen watching for her out of the window, still clutching the potato peeler.

'Police,' she said. She pulled the door closed behind her, breathing heavily. 'They are the police.'

Pavel gasped. The peeler clattered on the worktop. His hand strayed to his jacket pocket, where Lenka knew his gun would be. As they watched the dark saloon drive out of the yard, the minibus turned in. Lenka grabbed the peeler in a panic. They were earlier than she'd expected, and Kirill didn't like to be kept waiting for his meal. She had the vegetable pans on, as well as onions and mince frying in the big skillet just as the minibus pulled up. The picking gang filed off the bus. All six of them walked wearily to their various bedrooms where, earlier in the day, Lenka had left fresh towels for them. A warm shower would be welcome after the wet morning, and it would give her time to get the meal ready. Pavel climbed into the bus before Kirill could get out. Lenka didn't doubt that their short but heated exchange was about the visitors. Kirill came into the van.

'Food. When?' Kirill demanded.

'Twenty minutes.' Lenka flinched, expecting him to be angry. Instead, he grunted and climbing back into the minibus, drove back down the track to the farmhouse. Pavel watched him, then went for his shower.

By the time they had all cleaned up, Lenka had the meal dished up, cake sliced for pudding and a big pot of tea ready to pour. Kirill hadn't returned, so she left him a serving along with the two helpings she always kept back for herself and Mouse. The women would eat together in Mouse's room after the men had finished. The pickers ate wolfishly, with little conversation and without manners. The work they did was physically hard, calories were all they wanted. The evening was turning pleasant after the rain, so it wasn't long before the men had the fire going in the pit, and had settled down to drink tea or beer and play cards as usual. Even Pavel went with them for a smoke. Lenka stacked the dirty pots, while Matus helped clear the tables.

'Good day?' he asked when they were all outside.

'Strange. Kirill went off in a hurry this morning. Pavel says he had a visitor at the barn. Then the police turned up at the farm.'

'Police? How do you know?'

Lenka told him of her little spying escapade. Matus listened open-mouthed.

'He's no right to make you do that.'

'It's OK. No one saw.'

'He put you in danger.'

'He trusted me too.' She didn't want to cause any trouble. 'I'm taking the food round to Mouse.'

Matus picked the key off its hook. 'I'll help you.'

Most of the men took no notice when they passed with the two trays. Only Bohdan watched them, his face twisted with a sneering grin. It didn't take long to finish the food. Mouse stuffed the plate with the cake under the bed 'For later.'

As they left Mouse's room, the door key was hung on a hook outside the door. It signalled that she was available. The last man would hang it back up in the kitchen when he had finished. Tonight, the men seemed content to relax around the firepit. They were still there when Lenka had finished the cleaning. She made another pot of tea and took it out to them on a tray. Bohdan, who had been watching and waiting, levered himself up from his derelict garden chair, looked at Lenka, then without a word, went round to visit Mouse. She handed round the cups of tea, made as each man preferred it, leaving her own until last. As she picked it up, she heard a crash and Mouse crying out in pain. The others heard it too. Pavel tensed, his face full of disapproval. But no one went to help the girl.

'Bastard,' they heard Mouse say, then the sound of a slap. At that moment, Lenka hated Bohdan more than ever. He was by far the largest of the gang, his physique reminding Lenka of a heavyweight boxer or a wrestler. A broken nose and several tattoos suggested he had survived more than one fight or prison stay. The other men deliberately ignored the noises, though none of them laughed. Matus hunched down in his chair as if he were trying to hide from the consequences of his passivity.

Lenka took her mug of tea around to the other side of the caravan. Matus followed her a few minutes later. The light was beginning to fade as they sat against the side of the van, below the level of the windows, hoping to escape notice.

'You could help her,' she said.

'How? Bohdan is much bigger than me, and the others wouldn't help.'

Lenka knew this was true, but she still wished Matus could find the courage she lacked. 'It's not right.'

'I know.' Matus put his arm around Lenka's shoulders. 'But I'd do anything to protect you.'

She nodded. They gazed across the field to the farmhouse and yard. The minibus was still there, Kirill presumably inside the house. There was also a large, beat-up white van, which often turned up later in the day after the other farm workers had gone. Matus's arm was still lying on Lenka's shoulders when Pavel strolled around the end of the van. He drew on his cigarette, sizing up both situations.

Matus left his arm where it was. Pavel made no comment, giving a vague wave of his hand.

'Kirill still hasn't eaten,' said Lenka. 'He'll be angry.'

Pavel nodded.

'You had a visitor as well?' Matus asked him.

'Old lady from the next farm. I pretended I didn't speak any English. She was very angry, looking for Dixon over there.' They watched the farmyard for a while longer. Pavel stubbed out his smoke and drained his tea. 'Going to get an early night. Don't let the others catch you.'

Matus and Lenka sat there for almost an hour before Kirill finally brought the minibus back to the vans. Lenka went to warm up his meal, but he never ate it.

CHAPTER 10

It was well after seven. The stairs to Sara's flat felt steep, and she was grateful there was no one to see her come in. Her first day had been exhausting in so many ways. When she kicked her shoes off in the kitchen, she noticed they had a strange orange tinge. No doubt something to do with the weird colour of the water and mud in the ditch. Well, she wasn't going to show her ignorance and ask. She dragged off her suit and shoved the trousers into the washing machine, then scrubbed the inside of her shoes under the tap, wondering if they would ever dry.

A hot shower washed away the mud and smell of vomit, and she scrubbed extra hard at her teeth to remove the taste of bile and coffee. But nothing could clean away her disappointment. How could she have allowed herself to be drawn into a situation with a junior officer who clearly had something of a reputation?

Her new boss had let her down as well. She felt bewildered and angry with DI Edwards's actions. It simply wasn't fair that he had landed her in this situation with the rest of the team, no matter what his motivation. But then, as her mum would have said, no one ever said life was going to be fair. You had to deal with the situation as it was, not how you would have liked it to be. As she towelled herself dry, she felt a pang of loneliness. In the past, she'd have talked through a bad day with her mum. Now she couldn't. The argument they'd had when Sara had announced her move played out in her mind again as she rubbed her hair.

'I don't see why you have to go there. What's wrong with what you're doing here?' Mum had demanded.

'I want a place of my own.'

'You could get a place here. Why go there?'

'I can't afford anything here, you know that. Besides, it's a good promotion. I'll be in a smaller team. I can make a bigger impact. Do more good.'

'But why that dump of a place? You're throwing away all our efforts.' Sweat had broken out on her mother's face, and tears had welled up in her eyes.

'It's what I want, Mum.'

'Then why not another big city? Better opportunities? I can't bear it. After all we did to get you through university. All those endless shifts your granddad worked. All that hair I washed and cut and pampered, just so you didn't have to. Now you're throwing it all away.'

Her mother's partner, Javed, had been sitting beside her on the sofa. He was a kind man and Sara liked him. He'd tried to pull Tegan into a hug. 'Come on, baby, calm down.'

'Like I ever had any choice. I did what I had to do.' Tegan had struggled out of Javed's embrace. 'You don't understand, girl. I wanted you to be free, to do better than me.'

'I am free, Mum, and this is my choice.'

'You think you've had it bad here, been passed over for the better jobs 'cos of your heritage? You wait till you get up there. No one else will be the same colour as you.'

'My heritage?' Sara had echoed. She'd never known her mother to talk like this. 'I don't know what my heritage is. You won't tell me.'

'You have me. You have Granddad. What more do you want?'

'Let's leave Granddad out of this.' Sara's anger had begun to match her mother's.

'Why? Just because he's in a home now? You think it don't matter anymore what he does for you? Just because he doesn't always recognise you when you bother to visit?'

'He doesn't recognise either of us.'

'He looked after us both plenty good enough. You ungrateful, don't-care-girl. You talk big, doing your famous job. No time for your family. If you do this, I will never speak to you again.'

'That's unfair, Mum.'

Javed had intervened in that calm voice of his. 'I think we should all take a break now.'

In the weeks that followed, they'd tiptoed around each other, nursing their anger along with their secrets, Javed trying to act as mediator. Once the lease on the flat in Norwich was signed and the move inevitable, her mother had lapsed into complete silence, refusing to help at all. Exasperated, Javed had defied Tegan for once and hired a van to help Sara move, before it all became too unbearable.

Her mother had been right, Sara realised, pulling on a tracksuit. She slammed an unappetising ready meal in the microwave. It had turned out that she was the only one of Jamaican descent in the Norfolk constabulary. There was one Chinese officer, a local lad whose family ran a restaurant, and one Indian officer who'd moved from somewhere in Yorkshire. They were the only other representatives of 'multicultural' Britain, Ellie had told her. It was such a cliché that it made Sara's blood boil.

The only good thing about the day was that her internet service was finally connected. Sara routed her laptop through the TV as she picked at the tasteless food. A quick search told her that the red colour in the water and mud deposits were due to iron oxide. It was a common feature of that area of farmland and worse after a long period of drought. The body had had an orange tidemark around the upper clothing.

She heard the door to Chris's flat banging open and shut, his feet going up and down the stairs several times but without coming up any further. Sara felt guilty to be grateful. Once the food was gone, she sat on the little balcony, sipping camomile tea, as recommended by her mother for calming the nerves. In the street below she could hear voices from the nearby pub as people came outside into the warm summer evening for a smoke. After a while, from inside the pub, she heard the sound of a guitar and a singer. Other voices joined in with the chorus. Sara didn't know the song, though it sounded pleasant enough.

Her equilibrium began to return. She retrieved the oriental biscuit tin from behind the television, placed it on the little wooden table next to her mug and opened it. The letters were all there in chronological order, beginning in April and ceasing in November. She smiled grimly. Some things hadn't improved much in Norfolk.

Dearest Tegan,

I am speechless, angry beyond belief. Did you see it in the papers? It made the Daily Mail. You remember I told you about that jeweller's shop? Well, they decided that seeing as I couldn't tell them who the thieves were, they would hold a reconstruction. But there are no Jamaicans in the force here. No Indians, Chinese, or anyone who is not white, in fact. Not so many women, come to that.

So they bought a couple of afro wigs, blacked up two bobbies and took pictures of them joking outside the shop. As if that made it all right. They were laughing about it. While your brother and his friends get endlessly arrested on 'sus' just for looking at someone wrong. It made me so angry, but I daren't do anything about it. It's like this place is in some kind of time bubble, like it's still the 1950s. You can still buy golliwogs in the toy shops.

I'll call you on Wednesday.

All my love.

Sara read the second letter, even though she had memorised them all.

Dearest Tegan,

I'm sorry, I think I might have made a terrible mistake in coming here. It's quiet enough at work, and the housing is cheap. The extra money will go much further. But I don't see any Black faces at all, it would be so difficult for you. After you have suffered so much, I don't want you to feel like that all over again. Perhaps I should have tried for a bigger city, but it's too late now.

Worse for me is that the police here don't seem to have learned anything from the riots. At least they don't use 'sus' like we used to. Mostly because there aren't any Black people to stop or search.

I have a weekend off coming up, so providing no one gets murdered, I will be able to come home to see you both. I miss you so much.

All my love.

She folded the letters and put them back into their envelopes, removing a faded photograph of her mum looking happy and proud, holding up a tiny baby, which Sara presumed to be herself. Standing beside her, a tall, handsome white man with a big grin on his face. He looked just as proud and happy as her mum.

A round of applause floated down the street from the pub. Sara repacked the tin, hiding it behind the television again. She needed to focus on her job for now and not be distracted by the past. She wasn't going to be able to change anything if she got a reputation for being difficult or losing her temper. Some rest was in order, and tomorrow she would try to do better.

CHAPTER 11

Kirill climbed out of the minibus and slammed the door, an angry scowl creasing his features.

'Pavel,' he shouted. 'Bohdan, get out here.'

Pavel emerged from his room. Most of the gang, including Matus, were sitting around the makeshift firepit, smoking or pulling tiredly at tins of beer.

'Where is Bohdan?' Kirill demanded of everyone. They looked at each other. 'With woman?'

No one spoke. Kirill stomped into the second caravan and flung open Mouse's door, making her scream. She was alone. He slammed the door shut, pausing just long enough to lock it. He strode back to the firepit. Kirill was losing control.

'He went out,' one of the men said. He flinched as Kirill approached.

'You do not go out without my permission,' Kirill raged. 'Where's he gone?'

'Maybe he went to the pub?' said another, although they all knew that Kirill had forbidden them to do this.

'Bastard. How dare he disobey me?' he screamed. He stormed into the caravan as Lenka was placing his dinner plate on the table. Kirill was behind her in two strides, grabbing her arms, forcing her round to look at him. He leaned heavily against her, and she could feel the edge of the table biting into the back of her legs. 'You're always here. Where did he go?'

Terrified, Lenka shook her head. Kirill raised his arm to hit her, but a hand grabbed it.

'She was in her bedroom,' Pavel said. He pulled Kirill away from Lenka. 'Me too. We've not seen anything.'

Lenka scrambled onto the bench by the table, pulling herself into a defensive ball. Kirill screamed in rage, a noise void of meaning but so loud it made her ears vibrate. He pushed Pavel hard in the chest. The older man staggered backwards, where Matus just caught him as he came into the caravan. Turning back to the table, Kirill grabbed the plate of food and hurled it at Lenka. As the plate scythed towards her, she raised her arms across her face in defence. The plate hit the wall beside her, shattering into half a dozen sharp pieces, raining down hot food and ceramic shards, which lacerated her raised arms.

'Enough!' Pavel shouted. 'Leave her alone.'

To Lenka's amazement, Kirill swung round, pushed past both Pavel and Matus and stamped outside. In spite of her fear and her bleeding arms, she unknotted herself to look through the window.

The men scattered as Kirill rampaged around their makeshift rest area, raising chairs over his head to smash them on the ground and kicking over the firepit. The logs rolled out onto the bleached grass, starting little fires. Pavel and Matus dived out of the caravan and began to stamp on them as they bloomed. One of the other men dashed into the kitchen to fill the washing-up bowl with water and rushed back outside to douse the embers from the rocking firepit. Kirill pushed over the drinks table and threw the bottles around, completely out of control.

'Stop it!' Pavel shouted over the chaos. 'Stop it now!'

Everyone else shrank back as Pavel tackled Kirill, grabbing him around the waist and trying to throw him to the ground. He couldn't manage it, Kirill was by far the stronger of the two. But his rush had thrown Kirill sufficiently off balance to send him stumbling back. The pair staggered across the grass, locked in a weird embrace.

'Help me,' Pavel shouted, as Kirill struggled out of his grasp. Matus and two others ran at Kirill, pushing him further away from the debris until he tripped on the rough grass and collapsed onto the ground.

He lay face down on the grass, panting, surrounded by broken plastic chairs, bottles, tins, logs, the steaming firepit on its side with a large dent in it. Pavel moved towards him, his hand reaching for his jacket pocket. Kirill turned his head to watch him approach. His eyes widened.

Lenka's breath stopped in her throat. She watched in horror as Pavel leaned on Kirill's back with one knee. He pulled the gun from his jacket and held it against the back of Kirill's head. Then he leaned forward and spoke into Kirill's ear. She couldn't hear what was said. As soon as Pavel released him, Kirill climbed into the minibus and drove off. Pavel tucked the gun back into his inside pocket. The weapon was no longer a secret that only Lenka knew — if it had ever been a secret at all.

Her shaking gradually subsiding, Lenka fetched the waste bin to clear up the broken plates and scattered food. They kept a first aid kit in the kitchen, ready for the cuts and sores that the men frequently acquired while they were working. She washed her arm under the tap, then spread a little antiseptic cream on the cuts and stuck plasters over them. It almost looked like she had tried to slash her wrists — not that this was an option she had ever considered.

The men picked up the worst of the mess outside and headed to their beds. When she had finished cleaning, Lenka turned off the TV and went to her room. She lay awake, hiding under her bedclothes like a child, the door locked, until she heard Bohdan return in the middle of the night. The minibus arrived back at the same time — Kirill must have been watching for him. On the other side of her window,

Lenka saw the flare of Bohdan's lighter as he lit a cigarette. Kirill slammed the minibus door and marched up to Bohdan.

'Where did you go?'

'For a walk,' was Bohdan's unlikely reply. 'Needed time to think.'

'What about?'

'Home. Going home.'

'We'll go when I say so.'

'Sure, but the season is nearly over.' Bohdan took another drag on his cigarette, then scrubbed it out with his foot. 'I need my share soon. You better have it ready.'

Kirill didn't reply. Lenka heard a thump as Bohdan pushed Kirill aside, then footsteps in the dry grass as he crossed to the other caravan. There was a silence. Kirill climbed into the caravan and went to his room, which was next to hers. She heard him throw himself on his bed. It was nearly dawn — Lenka could see the light beginning to change through the curtains. She would have to be up at six to get breakfast ready before the gang headed out to wherever today's picking job would be.

If the men were going home soon, it was time to stop dreaming and start planning.

CHAPTER 12

Sara chose what she thought to be more suitable clothing the next morning. Smart jeans and a simple blouse, trainers that would at least enable her to keep her footing until she could find time to buy some walking boots. Being practical was more important than looking smart enough for a court visit, and she felt more comfortable this way.

The call was for eight. Sara was there early, as were the rest of the team. Edwards was in his office. He glanced up as she came in and nodded. Bowen followed her with hot bacon rolls from the canteen. Ellie was leafing through a thick file from personnel. Sara sorted out the coffee machine. They settled around one of the spare desks.

'Adam Crane,' the DI said. He opened the file Ellie had handed him. 'Retired about ten years ago. Detective Sergeant, CID, I worked alongside him for several years. He was a good man. Do you remember him, Mike?'

'A bit. I wasn't in this team back then.'

'He had a minor heart attack, enough to put him on light duties. I think he'd had enough by that point and took early retirement at fifty-four. That would make him about sixty-three, sixty-four by now.' Edwards checked the file. 'Here we are. Sixty-four. Birthday was in April.'

'So, what the hell was he doing in a ditch up near East Ingham?' asked Ellie.

'He lived near there. Five Lighthouse Lane, Happisburgh. At least, he did when he retired. Ellie, check that out, will you? Wonder what he did after he left.'

He pulled the ID photo of the dead man from the file and stuck it on the board. It wasn't a flattering image — hair greying and face fattening. It must have been taken not long before his illness. Something about that face was making Sara uneasy.

'What did he do before he joined Norfolk police?' she asked. 'Perhaps he went back to that? Or did he join from school?'

'He wasn't a local lad.' Edwards checked the file again. 'He joined from school at eighteen, but in London. Came here in 1983, moved up from the Met to take a promotion here when he couldn't get one down there.'

The DI's voice trailed off. Sara could feel them all pause to look at her. Just like she had, she could feel them all thinking. Just like her father before her. She looked more closely at the older man in the photo, and the image made the back of her neck tingle. Surely it couldn't be that simple? No, her father could easily have moved to another force or got a different job. What she needed to do was to check the personnel file that DI Edwards was still holding.

'I do remember him now,' Bowen said, making Sara jump, then smile inwardly. You could put one of those little cartoon light bulbs over his head when Bowen had a genuine idea. 'He used to moan about how boring it all was, nothing like the excitement in London. I wouldn't be surprised if he'd gone back.'

'Well, he doesn't appear to have,' Ellie said. She pointed to her computer. 'At least, he's still on the electoral roll for that address in April this year.'

'Any other family?' Edwards asked.

'Nope. At least, nobody else mentioned on the electoral roll.'

'OK, so we'll need a search warrant, then, if there's no one else to give us permission. Mike, you get on to that. Ellie, let's see if you can find any trace of what Adam got up to after he retired, or any evidence of family. Sara, get onto SOCO and see how they are doing up at the scene. Then chase Stephen Taylor. I'm going to talk with Miller.'

He took the personnel file with him. It was every copper's nightmare, to find a dead colleague, active or retired. No doubt there would be plenty of pressure to sort this one out.

Sara checked the address. Her online search showed a small row of cottages. Crane's home was at one end and looked distinctly dilapidated compared to the others. A battered Freelander stood on a patch of gravel at the front where the other cottages had small, pretty gardens. She wondered if he had fixed the place up more recently. Most of these rural street views had been done several years before and were never updated.

By mid-morning, Ellie had pinned up what little information she could find on the retired Adam Crane. Bowen completed the paperwork for the search warrant, and the pair of them went into the magistrates' court in Norwich to find a judge prepared to sign it. Sara finally managed to get Dr Taylor to answer his phone.

'I've been working on him all morning.' Taylor sounded put out that they were chasing him already. 'He's getting priority treatment. I'm prepared to say more now if you want to come over with the DI.'

The pathologist worked at the Norfolk and Norwich University Hospital, which entailed another trip to the outskirts of the city. Sara was beginning to believe that there was nothing at all near the police HQ at Wymondham. They seemed to be forever travelling from one place to another.

The corpse of Adam Crane lay on the examination table, a sheet drawn discreetly up to his chest. The face had been repaired a little, though there was a limit to how much Taylor could do after the animal damage. The chest and neck had stitchwork in them. Even at this distance, Sara could see that he would be hard to identify visually.

Various items lay in bags on a high bench at the far end of the room, where the pathologist was perched on a stool writing on his computer.

'DI Edwards, DS Hirst.' Taylor nodded to the pair of them. 'Sick bucket's over there if you need it.'

'Thank you, sir.' Sara winced at the implication. 'I think I'll be fine this time.'

Taylor swung round on his stool to face them. He wore a dapper suit under his lab kit, complete with waistcoat and bow tie. The summer weather outside had little to do with the colder temperature of the mortuary.

'So, Stephen, what are you prepared to tell us?' Edwards began.

'Been dead about a week. That credit card was used to buy diesel in Norwich on the twenty-seventh of July.'

Taylor held up the evidence bag with the card and receipt in it. The paper had red stains on it, but the print was still readable.

'Used the same day he died?' Edwards asked.

'Well, that's difficult to prove at the moment. Bank statements would be helpful, no doubt.'

Edwards turned to her. 'DS Hirst?'

'Request put in this morning, sir. Mobile phone records as well.'

'I've sent away body tissue samples for full analysis. Given the state of the decomposition and level of maggot infestation, I'm fairly happy with on or just after the twenty-seventh.'

'Are we sure it's his card?' the DI asked.

'Well, of course, it could be someone else's card. I've put out a search for dental records to confirm his identity and requested a DNA test just in case he's on our records. But it's a reasonable assumption at the moment.'

Police officers were not obliged to give samples for DNA profiling unless they were needed for some reason. Having retired ten years ago, Adam Crane may well not be on the database. Sara knew what was coming next.

'On the other hand,' — Taylor looked at her — 'I will need to do one for you. Sorry. You can always get it removed once the case is over if you wish to.' Taylor pointed to another evidence bag, containing camera filters, lens caps and a cloth to clean the lenses. 'The card was at the bottom of his pocket, trapped under this lot.'

'All camera equipment?' Sara asked.

'Yup.' Taylor nodded. 'No sign of a camera on or near the body.'

'What about car keys?' she persisted. 'Did he walk there?'

'She's good, isn't she?' Taylor glanced at Edwards. 'No car keys either, which is rather odd. It's quite remote. Notice anything else missing that you'd expect?'

Sara checked the bags along the bench, and then said, 'No mobile phone?'

'Interesting, isn't it? Everyone has one these days. He wasn't fully dressed either.'

'With all these clothes?' Sara moved along the bench, looking at the evidence bags with Crane's various layers of clothing in them. Edwards stood watching. He was testing her. Sara knew she was equal to this challenge.

'Clothes, yes,' Taylor said. 'But he only has one boot. A Hunter wellie, to be precise. I wonder what happened to the other one? Furthermore, those clothes have substantial rips in them.'

'How? When he fell into the ditch?' Sara asked.

Taylor nodded. 'Possibly. There's a lot of damage for a single fall. It looks more like he got trapped in a hedge and had to struggle to get out.'

When Sara hesitated, the DI steered them back to the main issue. 'So? Cause of death?'

'That's where it gets really interesting.'

The pathologist was warming to his theme now. He slipped off his stool and led them to the body on the table. Viewing cadavers was part of their job, though Sara doubted if she would ever get as used to it as someone like Dr Taylor. She steeled herself to take a proper look, willing her stomach to behave itself. Taylor pulled up the sheet to expose the feet and legs.

'There are cuts and bruises underneath one foot. In spite of the animal damage, I suspect he walked some way without the missing wellie. That leg is broken.' He pointed to the right leg. 'The other had also been damaged, but not broken through.'

Sara frowned. It seemed that the victim had somehow lost weight. The pathologist glanced at her. 'Problem?'

'It's just that he seemed bigger yesterday. Fatter, somehow.'

'He still has a paunch, for sure.' Taylor looked at her as if trying to gauge her reaction. 'Want the full gory details?'

Sara nodded. This test she was volunteering for, to prove she wasn't squeamish.

'OK. He's been on his back in the ditch for several days. It's been hot, so in spite of the clothing, the body has begun to decompose and is maggot-ridden. Have a look.' Taylor pressed the surface of the thigh so Sara could see the maggots underneath. They lay like small drug capsules in groups under the flaccid skin. 'Blowflies, I expect. I've sent some away for testing to be sure.'

He looked at her as if to check whether he should go on. Sara nodded again.

'They would be best able to access his upper body, his stomach, upper thighs. The animals would help by exposing the flesh when they ate the extremities. As the maggots feed, they not only reduce the flesh but they produce faeces. In fairly short order, that produces gas, which distends areas like the stomach and scrotum. The level of activity and decay is one way I can be fairly sure he's been there about a week. I let the gas out when I got him back yesterday.'

As he put the sheet back down, the pathologist looked at Sara again. She returned his gaze. The maggots hadn't worried her, nor the level of decay and injury. If anything, seeing

Crane laid out on the mortuary table made it less personal and more academic. Whatever might be in that personnel file, he was a victim, and the team would try to find out why. With quiet pride, Sara felt her professionalism returning. Taylor moved up to the head.

'Look here.' He pointed to one side of the skull, where Crane's hair had recently been cut away. 'There's a fracture to his skull.'

'Beaten up, then?' Edwards asked. He bent down to look more closely.

'I'd normally associate these kinds of injuries with a car accident, or more likely, being knocked down by a vehicle. If he was hit at sufficient speed, it could break his leg, send him up in the air, and his skull could have fractured either by impacting on the car or the road.'

'Hit and run?' Edwards looked up.

'You'd think so, wouldn't you? I checked his trousers. There's no immediate signs of car paint.' Taylor paused. He smiled with apparent satisfaction. 'No, this is definitely murder.'

'How can you be sure?' Edwards asked.

'He's been strangled. His hyoid bone is broken.'

CHAPTER 13

To Agnes's surprise, Frank turned up for work at his normal time on Tuesday morning. He let himself in the kitchen door to discuss his daily tasks, as if nothing unusual had happened the previous day.

'How are you?' she asked. She poured him a mug of tea and spooned in the three large sugars he preferred.

'I'm ok.' He sat at the table. 'What about you?'

'Not bad, I suppose. Still a bit shocked, if I'm honest.'

'Did you speak to Mark last night?'

'Left a message,' she replied, thinking, *Yes, three times.*

'Police are still in the lane. I checked as I come round.' Frank slurped his tea. 'What would you like me to do today? Shall I go get the tractor back? I can bring it across the fields without doin' too much damage.'

'I think that's best. Check out the salad in Long Acre too, let me know how soon you think it can be picked.'

'That won't take long. I could take a look at the CCTV camera. Or cut your grass?'

'Cut the grass, please,' Agnes rather liked the idea of having Frank around the yard today. 'Actually, do the CCTV if you have time.'

'I ought to go to Wroxham too, make that statement the police want. You could get a bit of shopping while I'm with them. I'll check that camera, anyhow. See if it needs any parts.'

Before long, the tractor rumbled back into the barn behind the house. Agnes settled in her study to finish the grazing invoices that had been interrupted by all the commotion of yesterday. The sound of Frank riding the mower around the lawn reminded her that her son loved that little job when he bothered to visit. She tried Mark's mobile again. It was still going to voicemail.

She had sent the invoice emails by the time Frank returned to the kitchen, his early jobs completed. He had the CCTV camera in his hand. 'There's a place in Wroxham. Perhaps they could have a look.'

They took Agnes's old Defender and wound through the lanes, round a small unnamed Broad and through a straggly local village, until they eventually turned into the main road. Agnes was concentrating on the traffic, Frank looking out the passenger window.

'There they be,' he said, almost to himself. Agnes glanced past him to the fields beyond. She could see the picking gang that lived on Dixon's farm, moving behind a tractor with a salad conveyor attached to the back. With the deftness of much practice, they were stooping to cut broad leaf whole lettuces, then placing them into the plastic cups on the conveyor. It was back-breaking work.

'How is our salad coming on?' she asked.

'Three or four more days would do it just right,' was Frank's opinion, which Agnes trusted implicitly. 'Next Monday, even.'

'I'll speak to Des, then. He promised those boys would come over to do it for us.'

'Why not Kays?' Frank turned to look at her in some surprise.

'Kays will get the crop. It's a favour. I won't have to pay the pickers, and we need every penny we can save.'

'Think I need to find a cable for that camera.' Wearing a frown, Frank returned to looking out of the window.

They left the Defender in the Roy's store car park, Frank heading off to the police station, while Agnes did her supermarket shopping. The stock in one aisle consisted of tins and packets marked up in Eastern European languages. There were sufficient temporary workers from what Agnes still thought of as the Eastern Bloc to make it worth the shop's while to cater for them. After the visit to the barns, she knew that the men Dixon housed were part of this seasonal influx.

The memory of the man with his greasy hand on her arm made her shudder. She hadn't slept very well, and now her resolve to get them out the barn was diminished by tiredness. Pausing in the middle of the aisle, she surveyed the unfamiliar food. It wasn't the workers that worried her — they were there to earn a living. Their accommodation was often poor, and a few comforts like familiar treats weren't something she begrudged them. No, it was the idea of confronting Dixon that frightened her.

Agnes packed her shopping into the back of her vehicle, then treated herself to an expensive coffee in the new café by the riverside while she waited for Frank to finish. She watched the holidaymakers with amusement. The larger Broads cruisers were queuing up on either side of the tiny bridge to wait for the pilot to drive them underneath. Smaller day boats puttered around the water, families in life jackets and dads at the helm. With a grand toot, the riverboat pulled out of the boatyard for a sightseeing trip, the top deck jammed with people eagerly pointing at everything in sight. It was pleasant to sit here in the sunshine, flicking through a magazine. Her fears of the previous evening eased in the sunshine and warmth, and she came to a decision. She wasn't going to allow Dixon to intimidate her.

'We're going to take a detour on the way home,' she told Frank when he joined her. 'I want you to come with me to visit Des Dixon.'

'He been pestering you again?'

'I just want to arrange for the salad picking,' she said. She also wanted to see if she could spot where the crop pickers were living. If Frank was with her, Agnes felt she might have the courage to tell Dixon to his face that she wanted those men out of her barn.

You had to know these lanes well, or it was easy to get lost. Many of them followed old field boundaries, skirting in and out of tiny hamlets, crossing rivers and dykes. You could easily tell when you came to Dixon's land. He had ripped out most of the hedges, combining small fields into larger ones that were easier to work but were the bane of the environmentalists. Agnes disliked the practice as much as the eco-warriors did.

She realised Dixon wasn't in as soon as they pulled up in the yard. His shiny black monster of a vehicle was missing. There was no sign of life in the house. Agnes knocked on the door just in case. When there was no reply, she felt free to wander around the yard, checking out the barn door. It was locked.

'What are you looking for?' Frank asked.

'I just wondered where these men of his lived.'

'In the caravans.'

'What caravans?'

Frank took her to the bottom of Dixon's garden and pointed down a cart track. Beyond the trees and scrub, Agnes could see two large static caravans.

'Been there all summer. I sometimes sees them from our fields. There's a footpath, it leads to East Meadow.'

Between the two caravans, washing was drying on lines, flapping sedately. As they stood looking, a figure came out and began to take down the clothes. Agnes was shocked to realise that it looked like a woman. She started to walk down the track to get nearer.

'Who's that?' Agnes asked Frank when he caught up with her. The figure, with its back to them, was putting the clothes into a basket. Agnes kept going, towards the figure walking away between the two caravans with her load. By the time the two of them got to the open door of the van, the young woman had sorted the clothes into several piles on the kitchen table.

'What do you want?' The girl turned to face them, folding a shirt. She didn't seem surprised. Agnes realised that she must have been watching them through the window.

'Afternoon. I was looking for Mr Dixon.'

'Not here. No one but me.'

The muffled sound of a voice from the other caravan gave the lie to that. Agnes glanced around.

'Just TV,' the girl said. Her attention was focused on Frank. 'You should go.'

Agnes held out her hand and introduced herself. 'I'm your neighbour, on that farm over there. I didn't know there were any women here.'

'Just me, I am the housekeeper.' She didn't take the proffered hand.

'Frank, can you nip back and fetch the Landie?' Agnes asked. 'I'm not sure I can walk back again.'

Frank nodded and took the keys Agnes was holding out to him. It was nonsense, of course, they both knew it. But the girl didn't, and his presence was intimidating her. He would only be a few minutes.

'Must be lonely here for you, all on your own,' Agnes began.

'Much to do. I am busy.'

'Your English is very good. Did you teach yourself?'

'From TV. It's good?' The girl smiled.

'Excellent. What did you say your name was?'

'Lenka.' The young woman bit her lip.

'I tried to speak to one of the men yesterday, up at my barn. He couldn't speak any English. Not like you.'

Lenka became restless at the mention of the barn. She glanced at the path across the field, then looked up the cart track at Frank as he walked back to the yard.

'No one here,' she insisted.

'You can walk to my barns from here.' Agnes smiled. 'My house is only half a mile or so down the lane after that. If you ever get lonely, you could pop round for a cup of tea.'

'I must not leave here, not allowed,' she said.

There was a bang from the other caravan. A voice called out, making them both jump. Agnes couldn't make out the words, but it sounded female. She could see Lenka begin to panic.

'You must go. I'll get in trouble if they see me talking to you.'

'Why?'

'Please go.'

Lenka pushed her way past Agnes through the doorway, stepping down onto the grass. She turned and grabbed Agnes by the hand to lead her back to the track. There were raw cut marks on the girl's arms, sticking plasters doing a bad job of covering them up. Agnes allowed the girl to tow her away from the vans.

'I'm going,' she promised. She pointed at the marks. 'Had an accident?'

'I broke a plate. Stupid.' Lenka was trembling. The sound of Frank starting the Defender made her look up the track in horror. 'Please leave. The men will be back soon for their food.'

'Why are you so afraid, Lenka?'

'Not afraid. I have work to do.'

The other voice was shouting something from the far caravan. Someone was hammering on a wall or door.

'Who's that?'

'No one. Only me here. Please go.' Lenka was begging now.

Agnes had no idea what was going on and felt out of her depth. The young woman, Lenka, looked distressed, almost terrified. Normally Agnes never interfered in other people's affairs, it just wasn't her way, but this smelled as bad as a rat's corpse rotting under floorboards.

'Where are you from?'

'London.'

'How long have you been here?'

'Since a few weeks. Just a summer job.'

Frank brought the Defender up to the vans and turned it round ready to leave.

'You must go.' Lenka urged her towards it, spun around and hurried away.

'Just walk past the barns onto the lane and turn right,' Agnes called after Lenka, though she couldn't be sure if the young woman was listening. 'Mine's the next house down. A fit youngster like you can do it in twenty minutes.'

None of this made any sense to Agnes. If the girl was a housekeeper, doing a summer job, why was she so afraid? She didn't think any of the other picking gangs she knew of had housekeepers. Why wasn't she allowed to leave the caravans? Who or what was stopping her?

Agnes climbed into the vehicle. Frank drove them back to the road in silence.

'I don't like this, Frank. What the hell is Dixon up to?'

CHAPTER 14

So, it was murder. Sara knew that the hyoid bone was rarely, if ever, broken other than during strangulation. They headed back out to the coast. Edwards phoned the news to Bowen and Ellie at the magistrates' court, and the search warrant was immediately signed off.

'Some of the SOCO team are still searching the lane,' Edwards said. They turned off the main road. 'Given the age of the body, I don't see the advantage in rushing the full team out to the cottage this afternoon.'

Sara's impatience to reach Happisburgh made her squirm in her seat. If she couldn't get at Crane's personnel file, there might be a clue to the man's background in his cottage.

'They can start a preliminary sweep this afternoon. Then relocate from the lane in the morning.'

'Yes, sir.'

'Ellie and Mike will meet us out there, and we can get a quick feel for the place.'

The row of cottages was on the outskirts of the village. They looked different from the online image. Only one cottage retained its full garden, the rest had been gravelled over in varying degrees to create parking spaces. The other four all showed signs of occupancy and care — flowers in pots, freshly painted front doors, clean cars. Number five was dilapidated. The brickwork was rendered in plaster and painted in cream. The paint was flaking and bits of the plaster had fallen off, making it look like diseased skin. There was no vehicle in the space that been had created for it.

Three CSI vans stood waiting in the lane. Bowen was outside Crane's cottage, the warrant in his hand. Ellie stood by the open boot of the car, door enforcer ram propped up and ready for use. Sara wondered at the way Bowen must drive. Somehow, he always seemed to arrive ahead of them. Their presence had brought the neighbour from number one out to see what was going on.

'Everything all right?' asked the woman.

'With me,' Edwards muttered, and they went to speak to her. He introduced himself and Sara.

'I'm Gilly Barker,' the woman said. She was wearing a long apron over a floral dress. Her hands were covered in flour. She wiped them before shaking his hand.

'Sorry about that. I was baking a few bits for when my grandkids come round tomorrow. They like Granny's home-made cakes. Can I help you at all?'

'Do you know the man who lives in the end house?'

'Sure. Adam and I have become good friends since he retired. We're both on our own now.'

'Have you seen him recently?'

'Now you mention it, no, I haven't.' She frowned. 'Not for a couple of weeks probably. I've been busy babysitting, with it being the school holidays, so I suppose I hadn't noticed. Is something wrong?'

'We think there may be a problem,' said Edwards. 'We're going to have a look around his cottage, to see if we can find anything that might help us. We have the proper paperwork.'

'Do you want the key, then?'

'You have a key for number five?' asked Sara.

'I keep a spare for him in case he locks himself out. Would you like it?'

She addressed this to Edwards, who nodded. 'It would save us having to damage the door.' Mrs Barker brought the key from her cottage and handed it over. 'Could you give my officer here some background about Mr Crane? As you were friends?'

'Of course. Do come in, my dear. Do you like cake?'

Reluctantly, Sara followed the woman inside, while the DI took the key to the search team. She would much rather have been there for that first moment in Crane's cottage. The thought of what she might miss made her twitch and she felt excluded from the team. None of which was the neighbour's fault, she reminded herself.

The cottage was narrow. The front door opened straight into the living room, where a comfy armchair and sofa faced an open fireplace. A television stood on a shelf in the alcove to one side of the chimney, surrounded by knick-knacks. The room was immaculately tidy. Two doors stood at right angles at the back of the room. One led into the kitchen. The other, Sara assumed, must lead to the stairs that were hidden behind the wooden wall.

Mrs Barker's kitchen was warm and friendly. It ran the width of the cottage. The sink under the window looked out onto a well-maintained garden. The sunshine lit up rows of tall flowers against the wall of the small extension at the rear of the cottage. Flowery tea towels hung in front of an Aga, sponges and scones were cooling on wire racks issuing the tempting aroma of calories. Beach towels, children's swimming costumes and a blanket hung over an airing rack suspended from the ceiling.

'Victoria sponge or scone?' asked Mrs Barker. She was making mugs of tea that belied the hot afternoon outside. Sara chose the sponge. A plate with a large slice of cake, a fork and hand-embroidered napkin arrived. The older woman seemed to need a few minutes busying herself about the kitchen before also sitting down with her plate and drink.

'So, tell me about Mr Crane,' Sara said. She took a bite of the cake, which tasted as delicious as the aroma had promised.

Not much of a cook herself, Sara appreciated homemade food and the comfort it always seemed to offer her.

'Let's see.' Mrs Barker popped a lump of sponge into her mouth as if to delay a reply. 'We've been neighbours for years. He must have moved out here in the late nineties. We didn't see much of him then because he was still working.'

'You became friends later?'

'After my husband died.'

The world is full of widows, Sara thought. Crane must be a rarity.

'Was Mr Crane a widower, then?'

'No, I don't think he was ever married. He never mentioned a wife to me. Talked about a girlfriend sometimes. I think that was before he came here.'

'Before he moved to the village?'

'I'm not sure, it may even have been before he moved up from London.'

'You knew about that?'

'A little. Sometimes, when he'd been drinking, he would talk about his time there.'

'Did he regret coming here?' Sara asked. Crane had once taken the same journey she was beginning, and it suddenly felt important for her to know if he had come to enjoy living here. It must have been as alien to him then as it was to Sara now. She realised how odd the question must have sounded. Mrs Barker didn't appear worried by it.

'I don't think so.' She smiled. 'I think he enjoyed his work until he was taken ill. He had a heart attack, you know.'

Sara nodded. 'Was he living here when that happened?'

'Yes.' Mrs Barker's face clouded. 'It was my Ian that found him. Adam must have been coming home from work or something because he was lying on the ground outside his front door. Luckily, Ian spotted him as he drove past. We got to know him better after that, then Ian died a couple of years later.'

'I'm so sorry to hear that.' Sara tried to make the words sound less trite than they were. She put her fork down, feeling it was inappropriate to be shovelling cake when her host was reliving painful memories. 'Are you all right to carry on?'

Mrs Barker nodded. 'It all happened years ago.'

'Then Mr Crane left the police?'

'He seemed to enjoy his retirement, at least at first. Did a bit of freelance stuff, wrote the odd security report for a firm in Norwich. Went to the pub quite often, volunteered at the lighthouse in the summer. Used to come round regular for tea and cake, do the odd job for me. It's company, isn't it?'

There was a polite knock. Through the open front door, Sara could see the DI on the step.

'Mrs Barker? It's DI Edwards. May I come in?'

'Of course. Do join us. Tea?'

Sara stood up as he came in, guiltily wiping at the cake crumbs around her mouth. Mrs Barker smiled at him, then began to busy herself with making tea again. 'Would you like some cake, too? Do sit down.'

'Mrs Barker's been telling me about Mr Crane's retirement,' said Sara. Edwards sat at the table, and Mrs Barker placed a slice of cake in front of him.

Edwards lifted his fork and scooped up some cake. 'Don't let me interrupt you,' he said.

'We didn't live in each other's pockets, mind you.' Mrs Barker rejoined them at the table. 'He started to change a couple of years ago.'

'Change? In what way?' Edwards asked.

'When that man moved into the village.' Mrs Barker began to frown. 'You can't stop someone buying a house, of course. But he wasn't popular here.'

'Which man?'

'Surely you must know him? I thought you kept tabs on that sort. He was always causing trouble, shouting his mouth off.'

'Who are we talking about?'

'Ray Fraser. Anyway, it upset Adam a lot. He didn't like him at all.'

'I'm not familiar with Ray Fraser,' said Sara. 'Why was he unpopular?'

'We were always a quiet place.' Mrs Baker seemed to be choosing her words carefully. 'Everyone has a right to their own opinions, of course. Brexit caused a bit of falling out, but people put it to one side. You have to get on with life, don't you?'

'Not Fraser?'

'I'm not into politics myself,' Mrs Barker continued. She glanced at Sara. 'I find all that hatred so unnecessary. Fraser was extreme, always going on about immigrants stealing jobs and how it wasn't like the old days. That foreigners should be sent home, that England should be for the English.'

Sara could feel Edwards watching her. Presumably, this was the sort of thing he had meant yesterday morning, and he was waiting for her reaction. She smiled at Mrs Barker. 'I'm a Londoner.'

'See what I mean?' Mrs Barker asked. 'I never judge a book by its cover. Besides, we have lots of foreign workers around here, and they don't cause any trouble. I don't want my grandkids picking crops for a living, so what's the problem if they want to come here and do it? Fraser loved stirring things up.'

'Was Mr Crane especially vocal against him in some way?' Sara asked.

'Oh, yes. They had a fight in the pub a couple of months ago.'

'Fight? You mean argument?'

'No. Adam punched him, knocked him out too. Left him on the pub floor, unconscious.'

CHAPTER 15

Her legs couldn't hold her up. Lenka knew her life wouldn't be worth living if any of the gang had seen her talking with the woman. As the Land Rover bumped its way back down the cart track, she leaned against the outside wall of the caravan and slid slowly down to the grass. Every part of her was trembling. Mouse was still shouting and banging on her door. It was more than Lenka could cope with.

'Shut up!' she screamed at the other girl. 'For God's sake, shut up.'

The banging ceased, and sobbing replaced it. Both of them were sobbing.

Lenka wasn't sure how long she sat there, tears slowly subsiding, before the afternoon news came on the TV. It was her signal to start the men's evening meal. She struggled to her feet like a newly born animal, legs splayed out, hands reaching for the door frame to help her up. Work was the answer. It kept the thoughts at bay, the fear in check. She washed her face, then, heaping potatoes into the sink, she began to peel mechanically. She was frying burgers when Pavel walked back across the fields.

'Why is Mouse crying?' he asked as he came in.

'Don't know,' Lenka lied. Keeping her eyes on the food, she panicked and blurted out the first excuse that came into her head. 'She's lonely, fed up, maybe.'

'You too?'

Lenka turned her head to look at Pavel. He was watching her.

'Well?'

'I guess.'

'You like Matus?'

'Why do you ask?'

'I think he likes you.' Pavel smiled at her. Actually smiled at her. 'The others, they leave you alone still?'

'Yes. No problem.'

'Don't let them get jealous.'

'I know. Mouse . . .' Lenka's voice trailed off, unable to come up with words she dared to use. Pavel lost his smile.

'She's a whore,' he muttered. 'Even before she came here. Still one now.' Then he went to his room.

When they returned that evening, the gang seemed subdued. The meal was quickly eaten, the dented firepit lit, beers taken from the fridge. There was no enthusiasm in any of it. Kirill took the minibus back to Dixon's farmhouse before most of them had finished. Lenka cleared up, then took the food tray to the other caravan.

Mouse lay on her bed, curled in a foetal position. Her face was blotchy with crying, silvery trails smeared across her pillow. Lenka brought a toilet roll and flannel from the bathroom and encouraged her to clean herself up. Mouse sat up and obeyed. When Lenka placed the food tray on the bed beside her, she didn't eat.

'Can I ask you?' Mouse spoke as Lenka reached for the untouched tray. Her voice was so low that Lenka had to lean in to hear the words. 'Before the men came back. Who was that?'

'Nosey neighbour.' Lenka felt the need to be cautious. She didn't want Mouse prattling if Bohdan was extra violent with her for some reason. Mouse sighed, and tears began to run down her puffy face again. The sight made Lenka relent. 'I'll tell you something, but you have to promise not to say anything to the men.'

'Promise. I promise.' Mouse sounded pathetic.

'I hear them say that the season is nearly over. Soon we will be able to go home.'

Mouse sagged onto her side, her face a mask of hopelessness. 'No home to go to.'

'Where did you come from?'

'From a house in London.'

'What house?'

'Don't know. I do the same there as here. Don't want to go back.'

'Before that?'

'Odessa.'

Mouse's misery stirred a softness in Lenka. *Soon*, she promised herself. *We'll sort this out soon.* She whispered, 'Stay quiet while I find out more. Then we'll see.'

'You'll help me?' Mouse sounded astonished that anyone would bother.

'You keep your promise. Say nothing.' Lenka gripped Mouse's hand. 'Give me some more time. I'm not going back to Serbia either.'

It was a nice evening. All the gang, even Pavel and Bohdan, were lazing around the firepit. The broken chairs and table had been patched up with electrical tape and Matus had brought out a couple of cushions from the caravan to sit on. Lenka made a pot of tea and handed the mugs round to the seated men. She sat on the kitchen step and watched them, hoping to hear something useful. There was little conversation beyond where they were to be working tomorrow. Even so, home must have been on their minds.

'Can you make *palačinke*?' one of the men suddenly asked her.

'Of course.' Potato pancakes, every Serbian could make them.

'I miss that. Could you do it for tomorrow?'

Lenka nodded.

'That would be wonderful,' Pavel said. 'With *ćevapi* sausages.'

'You can find them here?' she asked.

'Yes, they have them at the supermarket,' said Matus. 'They have a special section now. It's all tins and packets, so I didn't bring anything.'

'Shall I fetch some tomorrow?' asked Pavel. 'I have a vehicle not broken down yet. I could drive over in the morning.'

The Ukrainian men were catching the Serb's enthusiasm, even if it had to be explained in broken English.

'There's *reforma torta* too,' Matus said. It was a special kind of sponge cake they all loved.

'A proper feast.' Pavel was pleased. 'A taste of home.'

With the prospect of this special meal tomorrow evening, one by one the men drifted off to their beds, yawning. Lenka washed up the last of the pots, watching the only man still outside. Bohdan. She wiped the mugs and stacked them ready for breakfast. When she turned back to the kitchen window, he'd gone. She peered out of the door. He was walking briskly along the path that Pavel took every day.

What on earth is he up to? Lenka wondered. *If Kirill finds out, he'll kill him.*

She went to her room, locked her door and got ready for bed. She shut the curtains before bringing out the latest magazine Matus had smuggled to her with that week's shopping. Restlessly turning the pages, she couldn't make her mind fix on the words. Her thoughts kept returning to the old lady who had visited in the afternoon. What had she called herself? Agnes?

Lenka's behaviour that afternoon must have looked very suspicious. But she could hardly have acted otherwise. Supposing she had locked herself in the caravan and refused to come out. That would have looked even worse. After all, why shouldn't the gang have a housekeeper? So, preparing what she would say, she'd watched the two visitors walk up the cart track. It hadn't worked, the old lady was too nosey.

Now Lenka wondered if she dared take Agnes at her word. Could Agnes be an ally? Had the old lady meant it? Could she trust her? There was so much to think about and no one to talk to.

CHAPTER 16

By the time Sara and Edwards had finished talking to Mrs Barker, the SOCOs were hard at work in Crane's cottage. Knowing there was little they could do, the team finished for the day, agreeing to return early Wednesday morning. Frustrated at not being able to get inside the place, Sara sat next to Edwards in silence as they drove back to HQ.

'What did Crane do after he left the force?' Edwards asked.

'Volunteering for the most part. Mrs Barker said something about him doing security reports for a firm in Norwich.'

'We should follow that up, see if we can find out who he worked for.'

'And this fight at the pub,' she added.

'Indeed. Busy day tomorrow.'

As they made for their own cars back at base, Edwards favoured Sara with a smile.

'Well done for today. You didn't rise to the bait.'

'Thank you, sir.'

'There'll be worse than that, I'm afraid.'

'Being a police officer isn't a popular option in London either.'

'I guess not. Are you busy tonight? Or still settling in?'

'As a matter of fact, I have a date.'

Edwards laughed. It was a pleasant, encouraging laugh, which made Sara smile in return.

'Didn't take you long to find your feet, did it? Well, Billy No-Mates here is off to the chippy. See you tomorrow.'

Perhaps she was a bit premature in calling tonight a date, but it had served to break the ice with the DI. Her new neighbour, Chris, had offered to take her on a tour of Norwich. She'd found his company agreeable on Saturday when they'd shared a pizza and watched some inane talent show on the television. He had turned out to be chatty without being too inquisitive, and unfazed when she'd told him what she did for a living. He'd left after a couple of hours, saying she must need an early night and that he was working in the coffee bar on Sunday.

'I'll be free on Tuesday evening if you'd like me to show you around?'

'That would be nice,' she'd said.

'Wear sensible shoes,' Chris had warned her. 'This is a city for walkers.'

As Sara parked behind the flats, she realised that she was looking forward to going out. It was a chance to explore her new home and have a conversation that wasn't about either police work or her secret father.

Her last boyfriend had departed more than two years ago, unable to cope with her job or the strange hours it entailed. Focused on doing well at work, she realised now that she'd become isolated in London. If the SCU was as quiet as the team said, perhaps she might get some semblance of a social life in Norwich.

There was time to shower and change before Chris knocked at her door. Outside it was a pleasant, warm evening, which was tempting people to sit outside the restaurants and bars. The atmosphere was easy-going and convivial. Somewhere, bell ringers were practising in a church, the peals echoing over the city.

Norwich was an ancient place, medieval and Tudor in layout, Chris proudly explained, as they set off across a small green between a row of shops and a pub. Much of the centre was pedestrianised, the ancient streets supporting a hive of independent shops and restaurants. There seemed to be a church on every street corner, most of them no longer active as places of worship and repurposed into everything from antiques centres to a circus training club. Sara's practised eye acknowledged the beauty, but also saw the hidden nooks and crannies that would be a haven for drug dealers. Turning down a small alley beside one of the churches, they reached an incongruous modern-looking white building.

'This is the Maddermarket Theatre,' said Chris. 'I act here sometimes. In fact, I have an audition later in the week.'

'What for?'

'*Romeo and Juliet*.' He blushed. 'Although I suspect I am too old for Romeo.'

'I wouldn't know.'

'They're supposed to be teenagers.'

'Are you an actor, then?'

'Not professionally. We're lucky with the Madders, it's for amateur performers but with a professional staff.' Chris's enthusiasm for the place was clear, though it sounded complicated to Sara. 'If I get a part, will you come and see me?'

'Why not? I've never seen a play.'

'You've never been to a theatre?' Chris sounded shocked.

'Regularly. My mum loves musicals, so that's what we always went to see. I could recite the entire script of *Phantom*.'

With a laugh, Chris led her across the road near a modern multistorey car park. They rejoined the old city by crossing onto a cobbled street called Elm Hill. A large elm tree stood at the top, and Tudor houses leaned towards each other, the top storey wider than the ground floor. There was snow in the gutter.

'They've been filming here again recently.' Chris laughed, digging his hands into the pile of paper. 'Happens a lot on this street. Must be a Christmas one.'

They walked through the Cathedral Close, stopped to eat at a place on Tombland and ended their tour sitting outside a trendy theatre bar by the river, where fashionable types sat in the evening sun to drink craft beer or good-quality wine, even though the theatre itself was shut.

'I'm confused. This isn't the same place you showed me before, is it?' Sara asked. She chose a seat overlooking the river. 'How many theatres are there in Norwich?'

'Six. Three music venues. Two universities.' Chris grinned. 'We're a very cultured lot.'

Sara wondered how the locals found time to commit any crimes. She sipped her wine and began to relax for the first time in weeks. Before they could reach the awkward stage of not knowing what to say next, a couple hailed Chris from the door and joined them at the table.

'We act together sometimes.' Chris made the introductions. 'This is my new neighbour.'

After that, the evening stretched out wonderfully, with a bottle of prosecco, jokes and tall tales of the goings-on in the city. There were endless myths, or at least highly embroidered, half-remembered historical tales featuring a Morris dancer, a giant black dog and a peasants' rebellion. As they drank more wine, oak trees merged into bishops and saints, ghosts morphed with giants, and their stories always managed to come back to Boudicca.

'She's our local hero,' Chris explained. 'Whooped the Romans.'

'Don't forget Nelson,' the husband said. 'We have lots of local heroes.'

When the bar staff called last orders, Chris took Sara's hand to pull her up from the table. He kept her hand in his as they wandered erratically home. He let her lead up the stairs to the flats. She stopped outside his door, unsure how to end the evening, grateful when he turned out to be a gentleman.

'I'll see you again soon, I hope,' he said and gave her a friendly kiss on the cheek. 'You can let me know how the new job is going.'

'It's busy. We've had a big new case just come in.'

It was on the tip of her tongue to tell him what a shitty awful start it had been until discretion stopped her. With a parting smile, she carried on to her flat. Their doors closed at almost the same moment. It had been a pleasant evening, but Sara hadn't had enough wine to confide in someone who was still a stranger, no matter how nice he was.

CHAPTER 17

The SCU team were all outside the cottage at eight in the morning, suited up and anxious to get inside, especially Sara. As soon as they were given clearance, Edwards led them into the cottage. The layout was the same as Mrs Barker's home at the other end of the row, but there the similarity ended.

Crane's living room also served as a study. A desk littered with papers stood against one wall. A SOCO was bagging up the laptop which had been sitting on it, the printer unplugged and looking redundant. Dust lay on top of everything. Open drawers showed piles of papers, computer CDs, old tins with a clutter of pens, office stationery and junk in them. Number markers indicated places of potential interest. Contents were being stored in evidence bags, test results tagged.

Sara took her time to get her bearings. The place looked dishevelled. Typical of a man living alone who saw no need to tidy up or clean all the time. Exactly the opposite of herself and her mother.

This front room also had an open fire. Cold embers and burnt paper spilled out onto the tiled hearth in front of the grate. Sara only saw open fires in the occasional retro pub in London. It would make this room cosy on a winter's night, with its small windows and low ceiling. A sagging armchair stood to one side with its back to the front window and facing a television on a stand. There was an open staircase in the corner of the room, stretching diagonally up the wall to the first floor. The kitchen door was open, and the smell of rotting rubbish came from a waste bin with no lid. Bowen was peering into it.

'Anything?' Edwards asked.

'Only standard kitchen rubbish. But it's needed emptying for a while.'

Unlike Mrs Barker's immaculate kitchen, this one had old units, some with their doors broken off. The sink under the window was stacked with dirty pots, and the work surfaces looked as if they needed a good scrub. One SOCO was taking samples from an elderly-looking, filthy cooker. Sara didn't envy them the task. The cooker was too small to fill the alcove space it sat in. Years of grease and dirt mired the sides and walls. The white-suited man concentrated on the water heater, housed above it in the chimney cavity.

'Any luck?' Sara asked.

'Possibly,' the SOCO said. 'There appears to be some blood sprayed on the side of this heater. May not be anything. He could have cut himself. I'll do a swab anyway.'

Edwards and Sara continued out to the garden. It was overgrown and unloved, apart from an area of grass that Crane seemed to have kept mowed, where a plastic outside table and a couple of chairs stood. Beyond that, it was a tangle of weeds, with a narrow path leading to the bottom, where an old shed looked in danger of falling down. It was about thirty yards to the rickety fence that marked the boundary of the cottage garden with a farmer's field. The shed door was open. It contained little except the lawnmower, a few old tins of garden pesticides and piles of rubbish on a bench. A SOCO had followed them out and peered over their shoulders.

'Anything to bag?' she asked.

'I doubt it,' said Edwards. 'Check it anyway, will you?'

The woman nodded and Edwards and Sara returned to the cottage. Bowen and Ellie were upstairs.

Leading off a tiny landing area were two small bedrooms, one of which Crane had occupied. The bed was unmade, clothes littered the floor, cobwebs hung from the ceiling, the windows were gritty. The other was a dumping ground. An old single bed with a crushed mattress was piled high with files, newspapers, magazines and pictures. There were more piles on the floor, some with sheets of paper on the top marked with names like "Bellows Farm," "Houghton Home Farm," "Jack Ellis," "Grain Expo" or "Norfolk Show." The biggest pile held the legend "RuralGuardian."

'I think we're going to need to go through this lot,' said Edwards. Ellie sighed. 'We'll help you, don't worry. Let's get it back to the office.'

They returned to the cars for evidence bags. The SOCO team leader joined them.

'The laptop will be interesting,' he said. 'Lots of personal stuff on it. I'll get it down to the techie team this morning.'

'Anything else that might be of immediate interest?' Edwards asked.

'Some personal papers, bank statements and the like.'

'Who are RuralGuardian?' Sara asked.

'Not a clue. There's so much paper it's hard to know what everything is,' the team leader said.

'My team will go through that. We can backtrack it to the laptop once you guys have looked at it.'

Looking relieved, the team leader went back inside the house. Everyone helped to pack the piles of paper, even Edwards. Ellie took a photo on her mobile of each stack as they bagged it up and carried it downstairs to the car. The process took well over an hour. The files jammed the boot and back seat.

'Mike, you and Ellie get this lot back to the office, log it in and make a start.' Edwards checked his watch. 'Find out who RuralGuardian are and what they do. Sara, you're with me. We'll pay a visit to the pub once I've cleared something with the CSI team.'

'Can I have another look round, sir?' Sara asked.

'Ah, yes. You were with the neighbour yesterday. Feel free.'

The living room was empty when she returned to it. The wine last night may have helped her to sleep, but this morning her nerves were rattling again. The face of the fifty-something Crane on the office wall had troubled her. Now she had a chance to find out if her instinct was right or her fear was making her foolish.

There were shelves on either side of the chimney breast. The set nearest the window was full of books, the other shelves contained all kinds of random items, from cracked teapots to photo frames. There were pictures of Adam Crane in police uniform, with force colleagues, at some agricultural event. None of them indicated a family or partner.

Viewing the photos systematically, Sara recognised the older man from the picture on their incident board. Like a time-capsule, Crane got younger, picture by picture to the very last one. Picking it up, she stared at the photo of him early in his career, wearing a crisp uniform and a broad smile. He was shaking hands with a senior officer while being presented with a certificate. This young man's face was more than familiar. That smile, the eighties sideburns, the posture of pride, were all making her stomach clench. The air around her seemed to close in, her colleagues' voices receded. Delicately, she touched the glass over the young officer's face. The tip of her finger pattered softly on the surface. Her breathing stilled.

Then she heard the SOCO in the kitchen say, 'OK, that's it.'

Edwards replied, and the real world intruded again.

Her every instinct told her to take the photo to compare it to the ones in her blue tin. But what if someone saw her? The protective overall had no pockets. The frame was too big to hide, and there was no time to take the picture out. With rising panic, she propped the frame back on the shelf and pulled out her mobile. She quickly snapped a copy.

Breathing heavily to fight down her nausea, Sara stumbled past Edwards, through the kitchen and out into the garden.

The thought kept running through her head. *It can't be true. It can't be him.*

Two contrasting images flashed in her brain, as she tried to compute the new information. The unkempt garden swam in front of her. She staggered to the end of the path, as far away from the house as she could. The SOCO working in the shed looked out of the door in surprise as Sara wove past.

'You okay?' she called.

'Fine.' Sara could barely get the word out. Reaching the dilapidated fence, she supported herself with trembling hands. Running out of breath, her heart pounding and her head swimming, she leaned over the edge and vomited into the field beyond. She felt a hand placed lightly on her back. Hunching her shoulders, Sara stepped away.

'You don't look very well.' The SOCO had taken off her mask and hood. She looked concerned. 'Need any help?'

Sara shook her head and muttered, 'Too much coffee this morning.'

'Sure you're not pregnant? Some of the chemicals we use can smell awful.' The SOCO patted her distended belly which pushed the white coverall into a shape it hadn't been designed to accommodate. 'I remember when I had my first, it used to make me throw up too. Been luckier this time.'

'Not a chance.'

'Catch your breath,' said the woman. She returned to the shed and gathered up her equipment. 'Your boss was right, nothing of interest in there.'

It was shock, Sara knew, coupled with disbelief. Pulling in deep breaths, the dominant smell wasn't fresh country air, it was cabbage from the field beyond, where tall plants with multiple yellow heads bobbed with the breeze. It wasn't her favourite scent. Slowly her head settled, though her heart was still pounding. At the end of the row, children were playing in another garden. Mrs Barker's grandchildren must have turned up. Birds called and fluttered from garden to garden, visiting the feeders. She leaned against the fence until Edwards called from the kitchen door.

'Hirst, where are you?'

'Coming, sir,' she replied. She tugged off the protective overalls, took a deep breath and with a double check to make sure her blouse was clean, she hurried back down the garden. 'Just wanted to orientate myself.'

'Time to call in at the pub,' said Edwards. He looked at her but made no comment.

Sara deliberately ignored the shelves as she followed Edwards through the living room, though she sensed their presence like a monster just out of her line of sight. Whatever her suspicions, somehow she had to get through the rest of the day. She had the image on her mobile, and she would have to wait to compare it with her own photos when she got home tonight.

But she was already dreading that moment, because if she was right, then her search was at an end. The murder victim was her missing father.

CHAPTER 18

Perhaps it was the promise of a feast of food from home, or maybe it was the bright warm morning, but the picking gang left without any arguments or bad feeling on Wednesday morning. They had an early start. The farm they were working on today was way out on the Fens, a couple of hours' drive away. Lenka packed them extra sandwiches.

Just after nine, Pavel walked off across the fields to the barns, taking a shopping list, carrier bags and some cash. With luck, he would be away from the barns for a couple of hours. As soon as he was out of sight, Lenka went round to Mouse. She'd made her decision in the middle of the night and was ready to act on it. She couldn't waste this opportunity.

'Get up,' she urged. 'Go to the toilet. Then I bring you breakfast.'

'I can't stay with you today?' Mouse's face fell.

'Listen good.' Lenka pulled her up from the bed. 'I keep my promise. You keep yours. Say nothing.'

'About what?'

'Yesterday.' Lenka hustled Mouse out of her room and into the bathroom. She closed the door after her.

'That visitor?' Mouse called.

'Yes. The busybody lady.' Lenka heard Mouse flush the toilet.

'Can't I have shower?' she asked, opening the door. Lenka hastily pushed her back into her room.

'When I get back. I'll bring your food now.'

'Lenka, what are you up to?'

'Perhaps this busybody lady might help. Say nothing.'

She brought Mouse some breakfast, then, extracting a promise to stay put and not shout, she locked the door again. She had to trust Mouse not to try to break out. Lenka knew that this window of opportunity was small. The chances of being caught were enormous, and she didn't dare think about the consequences.

Walk past the barns onto the lane and turn right. Mine's the next house. Lenka remembered Agnes's instruction.

She paused to check that the yard at Dixon's farm was empty, then set off along the path that Pavel took every day. Although she couldn't see beyond the top of the little rise behind the vans, she was confident it led to the barns. It was at least fifteen minutes since Pavel had left, promising to do the shopping first.

The path skirted left around one of Dixon's large, prairie-like fields. It was full of ripe wheat and due to be harvested within a few days. The smell reminded Lenka of home, though the fields there were much smaller. The hedges were long gone, leaving nowhere for her to hide. Reaching the top of the rise, she bent low, jogging a few paces until she could get a view of the fields beyond. The path continued down the other side of the tiny hill between the two fields until it reached a tall, overgrown hedge. Behind that was a field with a herd of grazing cows, beyond which Lenka could see some buildings that she assumed were Pavel's workshop, then a long hedge that ran across the middle horizon. Behind the hedge was a lane.

Seeing no sign of immediate activity, she stood upright and walked quickly down to the hedge. The path was well-trodden. It led over a stile and across the field with the cows. Her grandfather kept cows on his farm where she had grown up, so they held no terror for her. She passed them and climbed onto the track at the rear of the barns.

Lenka pressed her back flat against the outside wall of the first barn, inching her way along. It was old red brick, which held the warmth of the day. It comforted her, as well as shielding her from prying eyes in the barns or the lane. This path continued to the lane, while another track veered off to the left between two windowless sidewalls.

Reaching the end of the first barn, Lenka paused and strained to listen. There were no sounds of activity. Encouraged by the silence, she dashed across the gap to the final hedge and climbed the stile into the narrow lane. Her luck was holding out. No one came past as she jogged along as far as the first house. It was a large, detached place, with unkempt gardens. A gravel drive went round the house to a yard with outbuildings at the back. The front door faced the lane and was easily visible from it. It was too dangerous to use.

Lenka walked along the drive and round to the back of the house. The double doors to one of the outbuildings were open, a ladder was leaning against the house wall and a radio was playing somewhere. With relief, she saw a kitchen door, which was also propped open.

Now she was here, Lenka suddenly realised she didn't know what she was going to say or do. Getting here had been her main objective. Getting back unseen would be her next. But in between? Would this lady be glad to see her? Would Agnes believe Lenka when she explained what was going on? Steeling herself, she went up to the open door. The radio was playing inside the kitchen, so there must be someone around. She knocked politely. There was no response. The tune on the radio was jaunty and loud. She knocked again, more forcefully this time. When there was no reply, Lenka took a cautious step into the room.

'Hello?' she called. A teapot and mugs stood on the table with a half-eaten packet of biscuits. 'Agnes? Is this Agnes's place?'

Still no reply. In spite of her fear, Lenka stepped further inside. Sweat was beginning to drip down her forehead, running into her eyes.

'Agnes?' she called again.

'Agnes isn't here,' said a man's voice behind her.

With a small shriek of terror, Lenka spun round. The man was standing in the kitchen doorway, blocking her exit. It was the man from yesterday. He was tall and well built, far too big for her to get past.

'What be you wanting?'

'Sorry, sorry,' she shrilled, backing away until her bottom crashed into the kitchen table, halting her retreat. She raised her hands to protect her face. As the man came inside the kitchen, Lenka braced herself for the blow. Instead, he turned to the sink to wash his oil-stained hands.

'Gone to the doctors for her tablets. Hour ago. Back before long,' he said. 'If you want to wait?'

Before he could turn on the tap, Lenka shot back out of the door. Running full tilt around the corner of the house, she skidded back down the drive to the lane. She could hear a vehicle approaching. Terrified that it was Pavel returning, she lengthened her stride, lack of exercise leaving her fighting for breath. Lungs exploding, she reached the first stile. Scrambling over it, scratching her hands on the wood, she fell sideways into the cover of the grass behind the hedge. Rolling onto her front, sobbing into upraised arms, she hid her face and waited for the vehicle to drive past into the barns.

CHAPTER 19

'Just up there on the right.' A uniformed officer pointed along the road. Sara felt the DI glance at her trying to fire up her mobile for a map, her frustrated fingers gripping the casing.

'There won't be much signal up here,' said Edwards. They climbed into the car. 'Or you might not get any at all. Depends what network you're on. It's a "not-spot". Get on to IT. They should have sorted you out with a staff mobile by now.'

The Hall House pub was within walking distance of the cottage. The drive took moments, giving Sara no time to recover from her swirling emotions. She turned the useless mobile off, tossing it onto the front shelf of the car.

They parked on the gravel at the front and went inside. Sara walked behind Edwards, shoving her shaking hands into her trouser pockets to keep them still. She knew she had to remain professional, pay attention to the conversation or Edwards would have an excuse to fault her. On the right was a small restaurant, getting ready for lunchtime service. On the left was the taproom with a long wooden bar, a proud row of hand pumps serving local real ales. It was already busy with customers ferrying drinks out to the large beer garden behind the pub, where families were enjoying the nice weather. Edwards approached the harassed barman and asked for the landlord.

'He's outside. You can't miss him,' the young man said as he pulled streams of amber coloured ale into pint glasses. 'Big chap. Beard. Wearing a pub polo shirt. Pint in his hand. Tim.'

Out in the sunny garden, Sara agreed that it would indeed have been difficult to miss Tim. He was laughing loudly at a customer's joke, his pint glass nearly empty, even though it was still before midday. By the size of his belly, it was clear he enjoyed his products. Tim's smile vanished when Edwards introduced himself and Sara.

'Let's go into my office,' he said, leading them into a long, low building attached to the side of the pub. Inside, three tall, gleaming steel vats hissed, releasing an odour that reminded Sara of baking bread. At another time she would have found this pleasant, but now it made the bile rise in her throat. She paused to calm her stomach, surveying the line of vessels, the set of beer barrels carefully stacked against the far wall and the pristine metal workbench. In some ways, it didn't look dissimilar to the mortuary they had been in yesterday. At least there didn't appear to be a body here. A body that might be her father. She shuddered.

'Never been in a brewery before?' Tim asked her.

'No, I haven't, sir. Smells very pleasant,' Sara lied.

'I always thought so too. It's the yeast fermenting. We're a micro-brewery. Just enough real ale for the pub and to sell the occasional barrel to local restaurants. My office is this way.'

The office was as tidy as the tiny brewery. Tim indicated a couple of visitors' chairs, and sat behind his desk. He took the last mouthful of beer from the glass in his hand. 'So, what can I do for you?' he asked. 'Noise complaint, is it?'

'No, it's not about noise,' began Edwards. If he wanted to lead this one, that was fine by Sara. It gave her a few more moments to try and regain control of herself. 'It's about a man called Ray Fraser.'

'Ah.' The landlord didn't appear surprised. 'Haven't seen him for a few weeks.'

'He was involved in a fight here, I believe.'

'That's right. I barred him after that. To be honest, I expected him back after a couple of days. He's not one for listening to other people if he doesn't want to.'

'Can you tell me what happened?' Edwards asked.

'It should all be on file. Why don't you look it up?'

'Was Desmond Dixon involved in the fight as well?'

'Now, how would you know that? Unless you'd looked it up already.' Tim smirked.

'I didn't know if it was the same incident,' the DI replied. 'Thank you for confirming that it was.'

'We are a family-friendly pub and restaurant. Fights are not a feature in this establishment, not even when we have our beer festival.'

'Can you give us your view of what happened?' asked Sara in what she hoped was a placatory tone.

'He's trouble is Ray Fraser.' Tim sighed. 'Knew it the first time I saw him. You get an instinct working in this trade. He often comes for a drink in the evenings, when he's around.'

'He isn't always around?' Edwards took over again.

'Nah.' Tim looked at his empty beer glass as though he wished it was still full.

'Is he popular with your other regulars?'

'He can get a bit vocal after he's had a couple of beers. Pro-Brexit, anti-immigrant and all that. Being pro-Brexit isn't unusual around here, most people voted leave. Trouble is, we have a lot of customers who might not agree.'

'Your summer visitors?'

'Not just them. We get quite a few migrant workers here, and they like a drink too. What they don't like is Ray Fraser telling them to go home because they're not welcome, that they're stealing people's jobs.'

'What do you do about that?' Edwards asked.

'It doesn't pay for a landlord to have political views, not these days.' Tim shifted in his chair, as though it made him uncomfortable. 'Times are hard enough financially, we need the visitors — all of them. I've dropped a few hints, but the bugger ignores them.'

'What happened on the night of the fight?' the DI prompted.

'Well, it was Adam Crane who was most upset by Fraser's noise that night. He hated that stuff about immigrants. It was as if he took it personally.' Sara stiffened. 'Adam's a good customer, even helps me out at the beer festival.'

'You like Adam Crane?'

'He's a nice bloke.' Tim paused.

'And then?'

'Fraser started banging on about it being all the seasonal workers' fault, stealing everything, from jobs to livelihoods. Then Dixon got in on the act.'

'This is Desmond Dixon from Ridlington Manor Farm?'

'Yeah, he's a regular here too. He has a crop picking gang living out at his place, and he didn't like Fraser drawing attention to them. That's when it all kicked off. Fraser swung at them both 'cos he's not all that bright when it comes to numbers.'

'What did you do?' Edwards said.

'Hit the panic button,' said Tim. 'I'm not dealing with stuff like that myself, and I certainly didn't expect my bar staff to intervene. Anyway, it's never like on the TV. When people get knocked onto tables in a real pub, the tables tend to win, not get smashed. It's more of a rugby scrum than a fight. Crane knocked Fraser out cold.'

Sara exchanged a glance with her boss. Almost any ex-copper would be able to hold his own in a tight situation.

'It takes fifteen minutes for a police car to get here from North Walsham, so by the time your lot turned up, it was all over. That's when I barred Fraser.'

'What about Mr Crane?'

'He came back once, a few days after the fight. I haven't seen him since.'

'Do you have any idea why?'

'He got extremely drunk, which was unusual for him.' Tim frowned at the memory. Sara's heart began to race. 'Said something about having dynamite evidence. I thought it was the drink talking.'

'Did he say what it might be?' asked Edwards.

'No, but whatever it was, he seemed serious.'

CHAPTER 20

Dearest Tegan,

Has something happened? I know the weekend didn't go as planned, but we still had a nice time, didn't we? When I called on Wednesday, your dad said you didn't want to speak to me. Have I done something wrong? Or forgotten something?

I know Norfolk might not be ideal, but I have to stick it out for a couple of years. Even then, I can't come back to London. Perhaps we could move to a bigger city after that? Up north, maybe?

Why don't you and baby come up for a few days? I could take some leave, and we could look around the place, see what you think. I'm sure we could manage for a couple of nights. Please say you'll think about it.

I love you.

The car journey took fifty minutes. Edwards barely spoke, which gave Sara time to take control of herself, to silence her racing thoughts before they drowned out everything else. Should Crane turn out to be her father, then she ought to report the connection to Edwards and take herself off the investigation. If she held back that fact, then she could be damaging the case. It was a no-win situation, which could have disastrous consequences for her career. She had never experienced such conflict in her life and was dreading the moment when she came to compare the two images.

The office looked like a paper bomb had gone off. The DI went upstairs to talk to ACC Miller. The stacks of paper from Crane's spare bedroom littered the unoccupied desks. Someone had dumped the files, maps and other items from the search about the agricultural theft on the chair behind Sara's desk. Ellie and Bowen were logging the Crane material, group by group.

Lifting the theft files onto the window ledge, with a sinking feeling, Sara opened her mobile to check the picture. The photo on the screen was blurred.

Fuck. She silently cursed herself and threw her phone onto the desk with a noisy clatter. Now what should she do?

Glancing up to make sure she hadn't drawn attention to herself, she sat down and logged into her computer, trying to appear normal. The stress was bringing her close to weeping. Blinking through the tears, she tracked down Ray Fraser on their database. Work would help to distract her.

She wasn't surprised to find that he was well known to the police. He had a record for offences ranging from public disorder to assault. Apart from the pub fight, he had also been involved in a pro-Brexit rally in London, when he had assaulted a police officer, and a couple of years earlier had been arrested for using language likely to incite violence at a Nationalist rally. He was drunk on each occasion. Drink and Ray Fraser obviously didn't mix well.

Was there bad blood between this man and Crane, beyond the fight at the pub? Could Fraser be connected to her father's death? She shook her head. *Now who's making assumptions?*

She pushed back her chair and went to the coffee station. The pot was cold. She took her time putting on a fresh one, hiding in the ladies for a few minutes to blow her nose and get back in control of herself.

'Bowen, didn't you pull out the report on the fight at Hall House pub?' she asked, as she watched the coffee pot fill.

'Just the header sheet.' Bowen looked up in surprise. He moved over to one of the paper-littered desks and rummaged until he found a piece of paper, which he brought over to her. 'You still interested in Dixon, then?'

'Not sure. I think there might be more to that pub fight than we first thought.' The coffee was shared out, and Sara filled in the other two on the interview with the landlord, as well as Fraser's record.

'Ray Fraser?' Bowen screwed up his face in disgust. 'I've had the dubious pleasure of interviewing him before.'

'It would appear he instigated the fight.'

Sara returned to her computer and typed in the report number. There were several witness statements taken that evening, including the landlord, Dixon and a couple of other locals. Adam Crane had been followed up for a statement the next day. Bruises to his hand had been noted. They had let off Dixon and Crane with warnings and no further action.

'Perhaps Fraser is more involved than we thought.' Bowen sucked his teeth in frustration. 'I'm not sure this helps us. Apart from his previous and the fight, how do we know he had any other connection to Crane?'

'He might be worth a visit,' said Sara. 'To have a look round his house. He lives in Happisburgh, just like our victim.'

'You'd need to be careful,' Ellie warned. 'He's just the type to call it police harassment.'

When Edwards returned, he agreed with Ellie. 'Let's get this lot sorted.' He pointed to the heaps of files. 'Did we find out about RuralGuardian?'

Ellie briefly outlined that the company sold security equipment to farms and rural businesses like riding stables.

'Good,' said Edwards. 'Then tomorrow we'll start by visiting them.'

It took the three of them the rest of the afternoon to log all the evidence and pile it into boxes stacked in order of interest. Dealing with the paperwork calmed Sara and gave her time to think. When they finished for the evening, she made sure she was the last one to leave.

'No need to work late,' Edwards said as he followed the other two out. 'It won't make that much difference before tomorrow morning.'

'Just shutting down my computer.'

But she wasn't. She waited until she could no longer hear them chatting as they went downstairs and double-checked the corridor. It was empty, the other rooms all seemed quiet too. It was now or never.

Standing in the middle of the office, Sara pulled out her mobile and checked the photo from the house one more time. Magnifying the image made it even more blurry. It was of no help. She pushed the phone into her bag.

Fully aware of the enormity of what she was about to do, Sara pulled on her jacket and picked up her bag to leave. Her whole body was shaking as if she had a fever. She gazed at her trembling hands.

In a way, perhaps she was infected, she thought. Her life and training were all about finding hard evidence, of being sure beyond any reasonable doubt. This time it was personal and bizarre, and she needed to know for sure. It was as bad as an addiction.

Pausing by the spare desk where several evidence bags were lying, she listened for voices again. None came. The bags should have been locked safely away, of course. Things here were so much more lax than she was used to, but tonight, that was to her advantage. By tomorrow, everything would be stored in the secured evidence room.

It was only a second's work to pick up the bag containing Crane's spare front door key, which she had deliberately failed to seal, and stash it at the bottom of her handbag.

CHAPTER 21

Lenka lay prostrate in the long grass for what felt like an age, until her breathing settled and the tears stopped. The car whose sound had made her panic had driven on up the lane. There had been nothing since. Sitting up, she blew her nose with her fingers, then cleaned her hand on the dry grass. She couldn't tell how much time had passed, so she decided to get back to the caravans as quickly as she could.

She sniffed. *I'm just so unlucky. Nothing I do ever comes right.*

After pausing to check that there were still no signs of life at the barn, she walked back up the track. She tackled the washing up, then brought Mouse round to join her.

'No good,' Mouse stated. It wasn't a question. Lenka's body language said more than enough. She busied herself with chores, changing beds, putting washing in the machine, hanging out the clean sheets. Mouse used the shower, then helped a little. Neither woman spoke much. They were sitting outside enjoying the sunshine when Pavel drove up in a vehicle Lenka didn't recognise.

They unloaded the shopping. 'Don't let anyone see you,' he said. Pavel drove off again as they went through the bags.

'He's a nice man. The only one,' Mouse said.

'Apart from Matus. But he's the youngest. No one would listen to him. Pavel doesn't seem to be worried by the others.'

'You think Pavel will help us?' Mouse's face brightened.

'I think he has a gun, doesn't need to care about anything else,' Lenka replied.

'He cared before?'

'Yes, he did. Something bad is happening, I think. They talk of home, but it's not the end of picking season yet.'

'How do you know?' Mouse asked.

'We should work here until the end of September.' Lenka shrugged. They returned to sit on the step of the caravan in the sun. 'That's what they said when I came. It's only early August now, I saw the date on the news.'

'If your busybody lady is no help, then we have to help ourselves.' Mouse kicked at a burnt spot on the grass. Lenka watched her, thinking that a flicker of the old Mouse, the one who fought her fate, was returning.

They didn't know exactly when the pickers would return, so the two women prepared for the Serbian feast in the kitchen, leaving the potato pancake mix in the fridge so Lenka could cook them fresh when the gang returned. Mouse took a slice of cake back to her room.

'I'm sorry,' Lenka murmured. She locked the door again.

'I know,' Mouse said. 'Soon.'

The evening news had finished when the minibus came back. Lenka started the pancakes as soon as she saw it turn in from the road. Pavel had returned earlier and was asleep on his bunk when she knocked on his door to say the food was ready. The food from home cheered the gang up, and for once the atmosphere was bordering on friendly.

'Good pancakes.' Bohdan laughed, slapping Lenka on her backside. She squealed, and Matus looked up. Bohdan grinned at the young man, then at Lenka. 'May have to visit the girly tonight.'

'Not this one.' Pavel frowned, pointing to Lenka. Gratefully, she handed round the cake. Pavel's support was becoming more open by the day.

The men took their cake outside to eat, enjoying the evening warmth. She made a second pot of tea, put it on the table for the gang to help themselves, added cold tins of beer to the selection and left them to it. A tired bonhomie settled on the group. Cigarettes and cards were shared out, the fire-pit set going. Lenka cooked two fresh pancakes for Mouse and herself and carried them round to the other caravan. The women settled side by side on the bed to eat.

'Bohdan might visit you later,' Lenka warned. 'Please don't fight with him.'

'Not if you don't want me to.'

They finished their food and Lenka stacked the tray with the dirty dishes. Mouse pulled Lenka back down onto the bed beside her.

'So, what do we do next?' Mouse whispered. 'You have a plan?'

'I don't know. We'll find some way.'

'Good. I'm not going back to that whorehouse in London.'

The two women faced each other, their hands gripped together. Mouse looked excited, Lenka fierce. In a single breath, Lenka made her decision.

'Promise me,' she urged. 'Don't try to run away. If you go, they will take it out on me.'

'Same for me, isn't it? Together?'

Lenka nodded. 'Yes. When we go, we go together.'

'Together. We shall help each other.'

There was a moment's hesitation and then Mouse flung her arms around Lenka. Her body felt frail and bony. Lenka had placed her safety in Mouse's hands. She had to trust her.

CHAPTER 22

It was after eight by the time Sara drove into Happisburgh. The daylight was fading and above her streams of cloud bunched like fish scales, with a delicate salmon-pink under-glow. The effect was breathtaking, though Sara didn't notice it. She jutted out her chin. She needed to know the answer. The consequences would have to be dealt with afterwards.

The other cottages in the row all had their lights on, the owners or holidaymakers returned from their day. At the far end of the row, a mum was loading children into a car. Mrs Barker was saying goodbye to her daytime charges. She looked up curiously at the new car's arrival.

'Bye, Granny,' called the little girl. 'See you tomorrow.'

'We'll go to the beach again,' Mrs Barker promised. She waved as the car set off.

Sara had checked that the SOCO team were finished at the cottage before setting out, wanting to arrive and search unobserved. Now it would look far more conspicuous just sitting in the car and waiting. Willing herself to move, she took the key from her handbag and got out.

'You back again?' Mrs Barker called.

'Evening,' Sara said. Mrs Barker nodded and headed back inside her cottage.

She had been seen. No doubt the time of her arrival would be remembered too. Anyone could speak to Mrs Barker about an unexpected visitor, and the truth would be out. If Edwards heard about it, he would doubtless be angry, and her job would be on the line. Even if she didn't go inside, they would need to know why she had gone up there. In which case, she may as well get on with her search. It was too late to change her mind.

Walking up the path to the cottage's front door, anticipation and fear clouding her brain, Sara was close to hyperventilation. Slipping a pair of protective gloves on her quivering hands, she pushed the key into the lock. It turned without fuss. She stepped over the threshold and flicked on the living room light.

The room looked even more dishevelled than earlier in the day. A couple of the desk drawers were open but empty and there were dust marks where the laptop and various files had been removed. She wavered by the door, marshalling her courage.

'Who are you, Adam Crane? Why did you leave us?' Sara asked the empty room.

She began with the bookshelves. The contents reflected the two parts of his career. Crime books — fiction and true accounts — sat incongruously beside piles of information sheets on crops, and brochures for the purchase of farm vehicles. Nestled against the chimney wall, a copy of Andrea Levy's *Small Island*. Sara took it down and, flicking through the pages, saw that some passages were underlined in pencil. Sliding the book back into its place, she wondered what it was that Crane had been trying to understand from the story.

At the second set of shelves, she took each framed photo down one at a time, pausing to check the likeness in each one before moving on to the next. The photo of the young Crane at his presentation was still there. Without hesitation, she put it into an evidence bag, then into her jacket pocket. The key to the garden was still on the kitchen hook. Sara let herself out by the back door.

Walking slowly down the path, all she could hear was distant laughter and the occasional bird. Even the wildlife was settling down for the night. The smell of cabbages told her she was nearly at the boundary fence.

This time it wasn't her stomach that was churning, it was her mind. Turning to look back at the cottage, she grasped the photo frame in her pocket with a hand that burned. When her heart slowed to a more normal rate, Sara pulled out the frame to examine the photo in the evening light.

The man's face was achingly familiar. Holding the frame higher, she squinted at it. If she were wrong, she could simply put it back on the shelf and go home. No matter how hard she studied the face, she couldn't be sure. The natural light was too poor, and there were no street lights here. The only way to be certain was to take it home and compare it directly to the photos in the tin. Taking another photo wasn't an option, there wasn't enough light, and the flash would reflect in the glass.

A sense of inevitability swept over her. The journey she'd set herself on months ago must be followed to the end, whatever the cost. With a sigh, she tucked the picture back in her pocket and set off down the garden. She was a police officer in possession of two lots of stolen evidence, the photo and the door key. But Sara, the daughter, was no nearer knowing what sort of man Crane had been.

As she passed, she saw that the shed door was still open. Exclusion tape had been strung over the gap. Closer inspection showed that the door was off its hinges, one end dug into the grass floor, making it difficult to shift without breaking the wood. It was the one place she hadn't been in. She couldn't leave without checking everything. She stepped inside.

It was dark, despite a row of Perspex windows along one wall. Flicking on the torch app on her mobile, she saw more piles of rubbish. The mess only confirmed that Crane was no better at gardening than at housework.

Turning the junk over on the bench with a reluctant finger, she gazed at the old jam jars filled with dead screws, mouldy seed packets and tins of decaying garden pesticides, until something caught her attention. Stuffed under a shelf and covered in debris was a tin with a familiar pattern on it. Laying her mobile on the bench, with the light shining up to the roof, she carefully pulled the tin out.

How on earth had the SOCO woman missed this? Guiltily, she recalled how the woman had come out to comfort her when she had vomited. She had disturbed her. It was Sara's fault.

The tin was a faded burgundy red. Around the edges were some generic oriental patterns. On the lid, a scene of two long-legged birds in gold, battered almost beyond recognition. But Sara did recognise it. With some difficulty, she took off the lid and shone the light on the contents. There were a few faded letters, stuffed back into their envelopes, and a handful of decaying photos, mildew eating into the faces and places they showed. What looked like printed estate agent details for houses or flats were folded in a bunch.

And a ring box.

Dearest Tegan,

It's been three weeks now, and I have called every day that I can. Why won't you talk to me? On this shift rotation, I have a long weekend coming up, and I want to see you and the baby so much. I'll get the train down on Friday morning. I don't have to come back until Monday evening. Can you get someone to babysit on Saturday night so that we can go out for a talk? Please?

I don't know what's wrong, but I do still love you. I want us to be together. I have a surprise for you too. I hope you'll like it.

A

CHAPTER 23

Sara drove back to Norwich in the growing dark. The evenings were getting shorter already, even though it was still warm enough to be out in summer clothes at ten o'clock at night. The faded burgundy box sat on the passenger seat, along with the photo in its frame. She crept up the stairs to her flat, hoping to avoid running into Chris.

Opening the windows to let out some of the heat that had accumulated during the day, she placed the burgundy tin on her coffee table. She brought the blue tin from its hiding place behind the television and placed it beside the new one. Then, throwing her coat over the end of the sofa, she slumped down on the floor in front of the boxes. Greedily she snatched the lid from the new tin and pulled out the contents.

There were several letters from London, and she recognised the handwriting as being that of her mother. There were half a dozen faded photos of Tegan with a baby or toddler. The folded batch of house details showed a selection of terraced or semi-detached houses and flats in Norwich with absurdly low prices.

She took the photos from the new tin and laid them out on the table. Then she opened the blue tin and did the same.

Finally, she placed the photo in the frame between the two sets of pictures. There could be no doubt. Some of the pictures were duplicates of one another. The man in the framed picture was the same as the one in photos from both tins.

Adam Crane had been her father. And he was dead. She was too late.

A long, low keening sound rose from the pit of her stomach, like a trapped animal. It reached her mouth, escaping into the room of its own volition. Her arm swept across the table, scattering photos, letters and tins. Her clenched fists slammed hard down onto the carpet, beating a tattoo of despair that accompanied her 'No, no, no,' until she keeled over onto her side and curled into a ball, sobs racking her body.

It had all been for nothing. Falling out with her mother, risking her career, moving to a new city. Worthless.

Time passed. Her sobbing subsided.

She lay on the carpet until she heard the pub down the road shut for the night, which meant it was at least midnight. Releasing her locked muscles, she went to the bathroom, washed her face and returned to the living room.

With patience and care, she collected the contents of the tins and put them back into their respective homes. She stood the framed photo of Crane on top of her television. He was her father. She would own the photo and the mistake of taking it. Arguments were already forming as to why she should be allowed to keep it. The SOCOs hadn't removed it from the house, so it couldn't be that important. They already knew who he was.

She opened the ring box. Inside was a single small diamond solitaire in a rose gold setting. It wasn't large, but she felt sure it would have cost Crane a substantial amount of money.

Had Crane intended this for Tegan? Why hadn't they got married, then?

Settling onto the sofa, she began to open the letters from her mother that Crane had preserved. The answer must lie here somewhere.

At first, Tegan had answered Adam's letters promptly. Sara could easily match his letters to her mother's replies. Although for some reason, she had delayed a visit to Norwich, there was no indication that they had fallen out. Until she reached one that mentioned a name she'd not heard before.

Dear Adam,

Father has asked that you come back to help us with Clifton again. The police sussed him two days ago, and he was carrying. He is so stupid. I can't begin to say how angry we all are. It's only a bit of weed, but you know they will make a big issue of it. Please call me and tell me you can come help.

Sara and me are looking forward to you coming down anyway. My love always.

Tegan xxxxx

Clifton? Who the hell was Clifton? Why did Adam have to 'help again?' What had happened before? There was only one letter left. It was very short. There was no date or envelope.

Adam,

I feel I should thank you for proposing to me at the weekend. But I can't. You have left Clifton to rot in jail. Whatever you say, surely you must be able to do something. If you won't help him, you can't care for me or my family. How can I love someone like you now? How can I trust you? Please leave me alone.

Tegan.

The harshness of the words stunned Sara. She stared at the ring again. So, Crane had gone to London to propose to Tegan. Had her mother accepted or said she'd think about it? Then what? Why was Clifton 'rotting in jail?' Had this last vicious letter been sent when she returned the engagement ring?

There were more questions than answers. Leaning back on the sofa, Sara tried to comprehend what would make her mother write such an awful letter. Clifton. It all hinged on him, whoever he was. She searched through the photos until she found the only one with a family grouping. There she was, Sara, as a toddler in her mother's arms. Next to her, with the broad smile, was Adam Crane, her father. Standing by Adam was her grandmother, next to Tegan stood her grandfather. Behind them was the block of council flats in Brixton where they'd lived at the time.

So, who had taken the photo?

'You fool!' It had never occurred to Sara to wonder about this before, and she berated herself now for this simple mistake. 'Was it you holding the camera, Clifton?'

CHAPTER 24

Even though Sara had fallen asleep on the sofa in the living room, the alarm in the bedroom still woke her up. She took a hasty shower and left the flat as soon as she could. Crane's house key was burning a hole in her handbag, it must be returned before it was missed. Her knuckles white, she steered the car through the early morning city traffic. Parking at the police HQ was a hit and miss affair but being early helped. She backed the car rapidly into a small space. She rushed up the stairs and along the corridor, passing desk sergeant Trevor Jones who bid her a cheerful good morning. Reaching the office, she dropped the key in its unsealed evidence bag, staggered over to her desk and sat down with a thump. Her legs had turned to jelly. It was just before seven thirty.

God help her if anyone found out.

From the moment she'd woken, Sara knew she wasn't going to admit to any connection with the victim. She mustn't be removed from the case. The only thing she could do for her father now was to help catch his killer. When her breathing slowed to something approaching normality, Sara switched on her computer as if she'd been working. Then she took herself off to the canteen to fetch the morning run of bacon rolls.

'Been here all night?' asked DI Edwards.

Sara smiled, shook her head and plastered her bacon with ketchup. Needing to look casual she bit into the greasy roll with every sign of enjoyment while her stomach churned.

Morning orders were soon completed. Sara was tasked with going through the reports for RuralGuardian. Forensics were working on the laptop, so she began with the manual copies they had brought back from Crane's cottage.

They were stapled into groups of varying thickness, together with a standardised form topped by the RuralGuardian logo. The reports contained details of site visits to various farms in the region to advise on security or carry out an inspection after the installation of new equipment. Crane worked over a huge area, from Norfolk and Suffolk to the Lincolnshire Fenland, Cambridgeshire to Essex, and even Bedfordshire.

Sara checked out their website. RuralGuardian seemed to be a combination of region-wide self-help group and security firm. A page of news items listed recent thefts, ranging from heating fuel, via a variety of equipment thefts to, most expensively, the GPS systems from the cabs of high-end tractors and harvesters. The contact name was the same in each case, the RuralGuardian Office Manager, Donald Cole. Sara checked out the offices on Google Maps. The place looked like a private house on an estate in a small village called Little Litcham, not far from Swaffham, wherever that was. It didn't look like a big business.

By mid-morning Bowen and Ellie had finished logging in the evidence and had carted anything they'd deemed irrelevant to the secure store. Head down over the site reports, Sara kept a covert eye on them. To her relief, no one seemed to notice that the key had been touched. Her stomach and her heart rate began to settle.

'So, what have we found so far?' Edwards called them to order round the evidence board. 'Ellie?'

'Lots of junk, sir. It's going to take a while to get through it all. There's a couple of memory sticks which may be backups from his laptop. Those will be useful.'

'Mike?'

'I've been looking through the other papers. There are several letters from a solicitor and some bank statements. Crane was also working part-time for NFU Mutual.'

'Sara?'

'He did quite a lot of work for RuralGuardian. Mostly site visits to advise on security. They go back years. The office manager is Mr Donald Cole.'

'I think we should visit Mr Cole this morning. Ellie, have a look through those memory sticks and see what might be of interest. Mike, contact those solicitors, there might be a will.'

It took over an hour to drive to Little Litcham. Sara was beginning to understand just how far each place was from everywhere else in this county. It wasn't just that it covered a large geographical area, the main roads were poor — endless A roads, where the average motorist trailed along at forty-five miles per hour. The occasional bit of dual carriageway allowed faster traffic a few miles to get past caravans and tractors.

The RuralGuardian office was an old garage built to the side of a semi-detached house in a 1970s housing estate. Converted into an office years ago, it looked run-down and shabby. Three desks with elderly-looking computers perched on them occupied the space. On the walls were several shelves full of reference books and leaflets that reminded Sara of Crane's cottage. Outside in the drive stood a solitary workman's van, with the RuralGuardian name and logo on the sides.

'Mostly, we sell security systems,' said Cole. He offered them tea.

'Just to the farming community?' Edwards asked. Cole disappeared through a door into what was evidently the kitchen. They could hear him clattering around, putting on the kettle.

'Farmers, smallholders, riding stables. All that sort of thing. It can be a bit specialised, you see.'

'How so?'

'It's not quite like a domestic system or even a factory building. For one thing, they are often remote from any other occupied buildings, and power can be an issue. Besides, this community likes to deal with people who understand what they do, and often more generalised security firms don't.'

Cole placed a mug of tea in front of Sara. 'Why did you become so specialised?' she asked.

'Ah, that would be Tony Martin.'

Edwards grunted, but Sara was surprised. She had, of course, heard of the Tony Martin case — who hadn't? Notorious at the time, it had received endless publicity, not to mention demonstrations outside the courtrooms. Some protestors had supported the victims caught in the act of burgling Martin's house, while others had been vocal in defence of the farmer. In his isolated home in the heart of the Fens in the middle of the night, he had shot two of the burglars, killing one and injuring the other.

'The one thing the farmers took away from all that was how vulnerable they were. How lonely a job it can be. You been out on the Fens yet, Miss?'

Sara said she hadn't.

'It can be very remote. The same is true all over the region. Up to then, farmers had been much more cavalier about leaving equipment in lock-ups or fuel tanks in the yard with the pump left on.'

'And afterwards?' she asked.

'After Martin's trial, one of the coppers who investigated it retired — Robbie Chapman. He decided that something like RuralGuardian was the answer. I was the first employee, and I put in the systems. When Robbie had had enough, I bought him out and I've been running it from home ever since.'

He gestured round the office.

'How many employees do you have now?' asked Edwards.

'Strictly speaking, none at all. The work isn't that regular, so I use sub-contractors. I have an office lady who comes in a couple of days a week, a couple of fitters, several advisors. I do most of the selling myself. I always stick to the same people if I can. It makes my life easier.'

'Where does Crane fit into this?' Edwards asked.

Sara felt her stomach lurch at this mention of her father. She picked up the mug of tea and sipped it, to hide her confusion.

'He's one of my regulars.' Cole went to one of the filing cabinets and brought back a thick file. 'As Robbie had been ex-police, he was always keen to hire others. Adam came to us not long after he retired from Norfolk police. He does farm visits to advise on security. They're chargeable to the farmer, and Adam gets a fee for each visit.'

Opening the file, Cole lifted out a sample invoice from Crane and put it on the desk in front of them.

'I keep a copy of the report and follow up any potential leads. If it leads to a sale, then Adam will get a further commission. Like this.'

Cole put another invoice down. Crane's signature was at the bottom of each item, the first time Sara had seen it in full. Leaning forward in her chair to look at it more closely, she traced the signature with her index finger. The 'A' flourished in the same way it did in his letters.

'He took a real interest right from the start. Became quite knowledgeable about farming, which, given his city upbringing is unusual,' Cole continued. 'The farmers have come to trust his opinion.'

'We believe he also works for the NFU. Do you know what he does for them?' Edwards asked.

'You'd be better asking them, but I think it's also security reports. Look, can you tell me why you're so interested in him? Because I've been wondering where Adam is. I haven't heard from him in a while, and he turned down the last three or four jobs I offered him.'

Sara looked at the DI, then back at Cole. Her back set like a steel bar and she placed her mug back on the desk with great care. *Control yourself*, she silently commanded her tear ducts.

'I'm sorry to inform you that Adam Crane was found deceased earlier this week,' Edwards said.

'Bloody hell.' Cole nearly dropped his mug in surprise. 'I suppose that was his heart, then. He had a weak heart, you know. Took pills for it.'

'I'm afraid not, Mr Cole. It appears that Crane may have been murdered.'

Cole sucked in a sharp breath. 'I warned him. I told him to leave it alone.'

'Sir?' Edwards leaned forward. 'Leave what alone?'

'It's them foreigners.' Cole glanced at Sara. 'Bloody immigrants. I hate them. They always bring trouble.'

CHAPTER 25

Cole's hatred for the migrant workers, or 'foreigners' as he called them, was both extensive and specific. He had trouble hiding his anger.

'It's those gangmasters. They come here every summer with their Eastern Europeans, taking up all the work on the farms. They're all illegal, and half of them bloody stay when they're supposed to go home.'

'What has this to do with Crane?' Edwards asked. 'Was he a gangmaster?'

'Bloody hell, of course not. He said he thought they were up to something and he was going to investigate it, just like the old days. You've no idea what it's like out there in the countryside. The police aren't interested, nor Immigration neither.'

'Interested in what?' asked Sara. 'Why should we be involved?'

'Illegals.' Cole stared hard at her. 'Coming here and claiming benefits. Thieving bastards, the lot of them.'

'Good for business though,' said Edwards. 'All those farmers ordering security systems.'

Cole turned on Sara. 'Used to be just your lot in the cities, sponging off everyone. Gangs and drugs and violence.

Now they're everywhere, and you can't even tell by their colour.'

Sara stared at Cole in disbelief. Mrs Barker's comments yesterday were mild in comparison to this. She felt herself grow hot with anger, and Edwards placed a restraining hand on her arm.

'Mr Cole, it is unacceptable for you to speak to one of my officers in that manner. If you do it again, I will have to charge you,' he said.

'What with?' Cole demanded.

'I'll think of something. My officer's skin colour has nothing to do with her capabilities. Now, what did Crane claim he was investigating?'

With much spluttering, Cole admitted that he didn't know anything more specific, so they left him to fume.

Sara could barely control her anger when they left the building, and trembled with the effort of suppressing it. For once she wished that she smoked or practised mindfulness — anything that would help her to calm down. Edwards drove them all the way to the A47 before he spoke.

'Are you feeling better now?'

'It's prehistoric,' she snapped. 'How can anyone talk like that these days?'

'It's what they've thought all along, to be honest. Up to a few years ago, no one would have used terms like that openly. But Brexit has emboldened people, ordinary working people. When they hear the top brass in Westminster saying things like that, they no longer see anything wrong in doing the same.'

'It's going to make my life a whole lot harder.'

'Yes, it is.' Edwards kept his eyes on the road. 'He was panicked about Crane's death, don't you think?'

'I mean, I expect it from those far-right buggers,' she muttered. 'Just not from ordinary people, small business owners like him.'

'It's going to happen here. You will have to get used to it. What spooked Cole, do you think?'

Tightening her lips to prevent another rant, Sara tried to consider the other things Cole had said.

'I'm showing my ignorance here,' Sara finally admitted as the car reached the dual carriageway and hurtled past some lorries. 'What the hell is a gangmaster? It sounds Victorian to me.'

'It's not really. Have you ever been on a farm?'

'Nope. Monday was my first time ever.'

'Round here it's mostly arable, especially out on the Fens. Quite a lot of the crops need to be picked by hand. The people who do that are mostly foreign nationals who come here for the summer.'

'Seasonal workers?'

'They work in gangs, run by a master, who has to have a licence. There's a special government department that looks after it. That's why we don't get involved.'

'Are they illegal?'

'Sometimes, I suppose they might be, though it's easy enough to get a licence and papers for the pickers. With people like Cole, it's prejudice. Most of the locals don't want to do the work anyway.'

'And do they stay?'

'Some will if they can find longer-term jobs. Food processing factories mostly. Then they might bring their families over. That's what causes a lot of the friction.'

'So, what did Crane think he'd found?'

'The laptop might tell us that.'

It was mid-afternoon before they got back to the office. Bowen was in Norwich speaking to Crane's solicitors, Ellie told them, intent on her screen.

'These memory sticks are backups. One is more interesting than the other. This one looks like day to day stuff.' Ellie pointed to one set of documents. 'Like the RuralGuardian reports you have on your desk or the NFU stuff.'

'What about the other one?' asked the DI. 'You said it was more interesting.'

'I was just getting to that.'

'Keep going, then,' Edwards said. 'Find out what's on there and make a list. It could be the key we've been looking for.'

Sara took the coffee pot to the ladies for water. Somehow the task had transferred to her from Ellie. Doubtless too much caffeine was contributing to the rawness of her emotions, but she did it anyway. As she came back into the office, Ellie looked up and cocked her head towards Edwards's office. Through the glass windows, Sara could see ACC Miller haranguing the DI.

'What's up?' she mouthed to Ellie, who grinned.

'Think the local press have got wind of our little incident.'

The door to the inner office swung open, Miller standing in the doorway to finish his tirade.

'Now I'm going to have to give them a statement.'

'Can't the press office deal with it?'

'Of course, but it's me that's going to have to deliver it. You need to give me much more regular updates.'

'Yes, sir.'

'And stop buggering around. Get a move on with it.'

Miller steamed out of the room without so much as a glance at the two women. Edwards came round his desk to close his door. Sara turned to the NFU reports and began to look through them.

They were all for the insurance side of the group. Crane had done reports for all the branch offices in the county over the years. Copies of each report had been sent to Julie Jones, the manager in the regional head office in Norwich. When Sara rang to speak to Ms Jones, her assistant told her that she was out for the day doing site visits. Sara made an appointment for first thing the following morning.

No one is ever in, thought Sara testily. *This whole county is too laid back for its own good.*

Ellie snarled at her computer screen. 'Goddammit! Open up, you bastard.'

'Problem?' Sara asked. Ellie pushed back hard on her chair in frustration.

'These files are all protected. I can't get into them.'

'Did he protect the ones on the others?'

'No, none of them.'

'Then they must be important if he bothered to lock them.'

'I'll check with forensics.' Ellie stood up, taking the memory stick out of her computer. 'They took the laptop from the house, might have already done it. Back in a bit.'

Sara poured a coffee and returned to her NFU reports. Coffee cooling rapidly, she read through them until a new voice made her look up.

'DI Edwards?' A young uniformed PC hovered in the doorway with a buff folder in his hand.

'In the office.' She glanced over her shoulder. The door was shut, Edwards was on the phone. 'Looks busy. Can I help?'

'Probably.' He held up the folder. 'Are you guys still looking into the agricultural machinery thefts? Trevor on the front desk said he thought that it was your department's area.'

'I guess we still are, though this murder probably takes precedence.'

'Sorry. It's just that we've been out to quite a nasty break-in. Thieves took a bunch of gardening equipment, ride-on mowers, a quad bike, that sort of thing. Then they beat up the man whose business it was and left him on the kitchen floor.'

'You think it might be part of this ongoing investigation we've been doing?'

He nodded. 'I thought it might be connected. I brought you a copy. CSI are going over the place but we don't expect to find much. It's the attack that's worrying.'

'How so?'

'Reckon he must have disturbed them. They gave him a real beating. Broken nose, broken forearm, fractured skull, stitches all over his face.'

'Where is he? The victim?'

'In the NNUH. Going to be there quite a while, I should think. His name's Graham Dack. Anyway, I'll leave this copy with you. If we find out anything else, would you like me to update you?'

'Yes, that could be useful. I'm DS Hirst, by the way.'

'Evans, Constable Evans.'

Sara flipped open the file and skimmed through the top statement. Then she put it on the pile of theft files balanced on the window ledge behind her desk.

Bowen and Ellie arrived back at the same time. Edwards saw them and came out of his office. 'Let's get updates. Mike?'

'Been to the solicitors. Crane was a regular client. Used them when he bought his cottage and had them make a will about eighteen months ago. It's in the archive store, they've ordered a copy for us. Should be here on Monday.'

'Sara?'

'I've put the NFU files in date order, and I booked an appointment with the office manager tomorrow morning. I assumed you would want to do that?'

'Yes, what time?'

'Ten. Oh, and an officer brought in a copy of a report from a robbery he thought might be connected to our other investigation. I put it with the others.'

'We don't have time to worry about that at the moment,' said Edwards. 'It will have to wait. Ellie?'

'Forensics have Crane's laptop, we had the backup memory sticks. I thought they would both be the same, but they're not.'

'In what way?'

'I could read the everyday files on the first stick. There's no passwords on them. They match the ones on the laptop downstairs. I couldn't open the stuff on the second stick.'

'Can forensics?'

'Working on it now, but they are going to have to call in a specialist.'

'That will hold us up,' Edwards said with a resigned shrug.

'That's not all. None of the stuff on the second memory stick is on the laptop we currently have. Not even in a backdoor area.'

'So? You think there must be a second computer somewhere?'

'Makes sense, sir. Forensics say it could be a laptop, a tablet or even a really good mobile phone. They're adamant there was nothing else in the cottage. So, whatever it is, we don't have it. It's gone missing. The stuff on the memory stick is all the evidence we have.'

CHAPTER 26

The picking gang had been working locally on Thursday. Less tired than on the previous day, they became boisterous when they went outside after their meal, joking and play-fighting while they set up the table for cards. As Lenka stacked the dirty pots, the local news came on and a grey-haired man began a report outside a large police station.

'Tonight's main story,' the man said. 'A man's body has been found on a farm in North Norfolk. Police say his death is unexplained. More on this in a moment.'

Kirill ceased eating and stared at the screen. Lenka watched him for a moment, then made a show of noisily stacking the pans. She could see the TV from where she was. The screen moved back from the studio to the reporter standing outside.

'Police have today admitted that a man's body has been found in a farm ditch in North Norfolk. Investigations are underway, and the police are treating the death as suspicious. Local sources have named the man as Adam Crane.'

Lenka approached the table with a slab of cake on a little plate. Kirill didn't seem to notice, his eyes were fastened on the screen.

'Late this afternoon, Assistant Chief Constable Miller of the Norfolk Police gave this statement.'

The screen cut to another older man, this one in police uniform, holding a piece of paper.

'The body of a man was discovered on Monday of this week,' he read. 'He had been left in a drainage ditch on a farm near to the village of Happisburgh and had been deceased for some days. A full investigation is ongoing.'

'Is it murder?' Lenka heard a reporter call out.

'Far too early to say. We are appealing for witnesses who might have used some of the minor lanes in this area over the weekend of Saturday the twenty-ninth or Sunday the thirtieth of July. We are also searching for the victim's car, a dark green Land Rover Freelander, which is missing. It may have some bearing on the case. If anyone has seen this vehicle recently or has been asked to deal with it in any way, I would ask you to contact us urgently.'

The man then read out the car's registration number and a contact telephone number, which remained on the bottom of the screen as the camera switched back to the reporter outside the police building.

Swearing loudly, Kirill stood up and smashed his fist into the front of the TV, shoving it back on its shelf. It flickered and died. Lenka snatched away his empty dinner plate and made for the kitchen to get out of his way. Cursing again, he jumped out of the caravan door and yelled at Pavel.

Lenka watched the men sitting outside look up in astonishment at Kirill, cakes and cigarettes suspended in mid-air.

'What do you want now?' asked Pavel.

'Our little problem just got bigger.' Kirill grabbed Pavel by the arm and dragged him out of earshot.

Washing the dirty dishes, Lenka watched the two men walk off down the track towards the farmhouse. Kirill was doing most of the talking, gesticulating wildly. At the firepit, she saw Bohdan fire up his mobile. Whoever he was ringing didn't answer, and he punched angrily at the screen. Fetching his coat from the other caravan, he set off across the field path towards the barns. Matus and the rest of the gang made no move to stop him.

Lenka made her customary large pot of tea and carried the tray of mugs out to the table outside. She poured drinks for the remaining men, then one for herself and one for Mouse. It was enough to break the silence.

'Shall I light the fire?' Matus asked the others, who agreed he should.

Mouse was waiting behind the door when Lenka opened it. She grabbed the mug of tea and pulled Lenka into her room.

'What happened?' she demanded in a whisper. Lenka told her about the news report. 'You think this is something Kirill has done? He's a mad bastard.'

'So is Bohdan,' said Lenka. 'He's gone out again, doesn't even care if Kirill sees him anymore.'

'What about the others? What about Pavel?'

'I think Pavel does up cars. They call him the grease monkey behind his back.'

'Pavel's no monkey,' Mouse insisted. 'He's the one with a gun.'

Lenka sank onto the rumpled bed. Mouse flopped down beside her, touching her arm tentatively.

'Together?'

'Yes, oh, yes,' said Lenka.

'What do you think is going on?'

'Kirill has been frightened ever since Monday morning. You remember?'

Mouse nodded.

'I think Dixon has something to do with this too. Matus? I don't want to believe that.'

'Matus?'

'I think he likes me very much, he's kind to me.'

'He can help us then?' Mouse grabbed Lenka's arm and shook it.

'I dare not ask him.'

'Then make him want to. You offer him something, anything. Sex. Blow job. But don't deliver until he helps us.'

'What?'

'Men, all they worry about is this act. It's our best weapon.'

'And food,' said Lenka. 'I hoped the feast from home might help. Now it's all spoiled.'

'Not yet. Go back out and be nice to Matus. I'll see if I can talk to the other men if they visit me.'

'Pillow talk?' Lenka almost laughed.

'Why not?'

Why not indeed? Lenka locked Mouse's door again. If something was going badly for Kirill, they were going to need some allies.

Matus had set the fire going. The rest of the men sat around it, smoking and playing cards, subdued. Only Matus looked up when Lenka reappeared. She flashed him a smile, gathered up the mugs and retreated to the kitchen. He followed her. They finished the clearing up, then squeezed behind the table to finish the last of the cake. Matus laid his warm hand over Lenka's cold and tired one.

'What set him off this time?' he asked.

Lenka told him about the news report. Pausing to weigh up the options, she looked Matus straight in the eye.

'You like me?'

'You know I do.'

'If we met some other time, some other place, would we be dating? Girlfriend, boyfriend?'

Matus nodded. 'Like normal people.'

'I've not been off this place since we arrived.'

'You want to go somewhere?'

'Anywhere. To be like normal people for once. Before we leave.'

Matus smiled. 'We're not leaving yet. There's still several weeks left in the season. I know just the thing, though. We'll go on a date. I'll fix it.'

Then he drew her into his arms and kissed her. The others didn't seem to notice.

CHAPTER 27

There had been a couple of newspaper reporters, a single photographer and two local TV news teams outside HQ's front doors when Sara left for the evening. According to Ellie, this constituted a 'scrum,' but it was nothing compared to the turnouts they sometimes got in the Met. Finding Crane's body was good fodder for the local news but it wouldn't reach the nationals unless it was a slow news day.

Chris must have been waiting for her to come home. He opened his flat door as she climbed the stairs.

'Working late?' he asked.

'Yeah, we're really busy.'

'Too busy for a drink? The Vagabonds are on at the pub tonight. They're really good.'

'I'm a bit tired.' Sara yawned for effect. 'At the weekend maybe. Though we might have to work.'

'OK. Well, nice to see you.' Chris, looking disappointed, returned to his flat with a casual, 'Catch you soon.'

She wasn't hungry, though her stomach was bubbling again and she knew she ought to eat something. Unable to face cooking, she boiled the kettle and made up a packet of mushroom soup. It looked like the sort of paste they used in infants' school for crafting, and it tasted the same. Sara left it on the coffee table to congeal as she turned on the television to watch both local news bulletins. The ITV one showed before the BBC but the BBC had the upper hand. The scoop, such as it was, featured Crane's neighbour talking to the reporter. At least Sara knew now how the newsrooms had got hold of the story.

'He's lived here for nearly twenty years,' Mrs Barker was saying. 'Nice man, retired police officer.'

It felt bizarre, watching this woman she had first met two days ago talking about her father. Sara almost felt cheated that Mrs Barker had known him for twenty years when she had only just found him.

'You knew him well?' asked the interviewer.

'Oh yes. He was a good, solid member of our community.'

'If it is indeed Mr Crane, is there any reason he should be targeted?'

'He did investigations for local farmers, after thefts. And he didn't always see eye to eye with one or two locals. Beyond that, I couldn't say,' she said.

The reporter turned to the camera, to sum up. Inevitably, their team didn't come out of it too well. The press usually set up the police as the bogeymen in these things. They always wanted the story and the answer to it on the same damn day. Though the comment about helping farmers after thefts was a bit close to the mark, which was unfortunate.

Sara threw the soup away and poured a glass of wine before settling down on her little balcony with the burgundy box she had rescued from her father's shed.

Taking her mother's letters from the tin, she read them again, this time more slowly. Now she wasn't in the first shock of discovery, they began to make more sense. The disagreement between her parents had been over Clifton, and Adam's treatment of him. But who was Clifton and what had Adam failed to do for him? She put the letters back, picked up her glass of wine and leaned against the balustrade sipping it, gazing without focus into the street below.

There was the usual chattering crowd of smokers on the pavement outside the pub at the far end. A party of well-dressed diners went into the posh Italian restaurant. She was surrounded by the cheerful sounds of the adult part of the city at play. Laughter, teasing, 'Let me get the door for you,' girls in high heels clacking into the distance. Perhaps half an hour passed while Sara stood indecisive and deep in thought. Eventually, she summoned up the courage and went to find her mobile.

Javed answered her mother's landline. 'Good evening. How can I help you?'

'Hi, Javed.'

'Sara? That you?'

'Yes. How are you doing?'

'I'm good. How are you settling in?'

'Not bad so far,' she lied.

'Flat okay? Work good?'

'The flat's lovely. Work is busy. We had a big case come in on the first morning. Lots to do.' She hesitated. 'Is Mum there?'

'Yes.' Javed sounded uncertain. 'I'm not sure she'll speak to you, though.'

'Can you try for me? There is something important I need to ask her.'

'Well . . . OK.' He went off to find Tegan. Sara could hear him in the background, attempting to persuade her mother to come to the phone.

He picked up the receiver again. 'She says you have nothing to talk about.'

'I see. Will you do one more thing for me?'

'Depends if I can.'

'Just ask her one question. Ask her now, while I wait.'

'What question?'

'Just ask her, "Who is Clifton?"'

'That's all?' Javed obviously had no idea what this meant. He couldn't have known of Clifton. Sara's mouth went dry as he put his hand over the mouthpiece and called, 'Tegan, it's only one question. Sara is asking, "Who is Clifton?"'

Her mother's scream was so loud that it came straight into her ears. She heard Tegan scolding Javed, while he tried to defend himself.

'Where did you get that?' Her mother snatched the handset from him. 'That name, who told you?'

'Nobody told me.' Sara wanted to explain, but without admitting to appropriating the box of love letters, or finding her father and the other box, there was no way to begin. 'Someone mentioned it to me. Who is he?'

'Is this what you are a detective for? To spy on your own family?'

'Of course not.'

'Just leave it alone.' Tegan burst into tears. For a moment, Sara heard Javed trying to comfort her before the receiver was slammed down. She stared at the screen of her mobile, panic rising and tightening her throat.

When she had come to Norwich against her mother's wishes, she had assumed that they would make up their differences in time, that it wouldn't take too long for the opportunity to arise when they could talk. Now it was worse than ever.

What have I done? What have I found? She emptied her wine glass in a single gulp.

The bottle in the fridge had an inch of liquid in the bottom. Sara sloshed it into her glass and downed it without thinking. It was all too much — all this grief, the arguments, having no one to talk to. She needed a drink. There were no more bottles in the cupboards she realised. She slammed the doors in frustration. She was going to have to go out and buy some. Usually, she only drank socially, as she had the other night with Chris. Now she longed for the release, if only temporary.

It wasn't until she got to the stairs that it came to her. There was no need to drink alone. If she wanted to set aside her crap week for a couple of hours, the offer had already been made to her. Chris wanted to take her to see this local band. She may not have to spend the night alone with her demons after all.

When he answered her knock, she said, 'I've changed my mind, if you still fancy that drink. Is that band any good?'

CHAPTER 28

Lenka wasn't sure if she felt like a fraud or whether kissing Matus had been a natural thing to do. Surely if they'd met some other time and place, then they would still have been attracted to each other. Here and now it was a means to an end, no matter how pleasurable it was. They weren't left alone long enough to repeat it. A few minutes later Kirill and Pavel returned with Des Dixon in his monstrous Range Rover. Des was outside on his mobile, speaking furiously at whoever was on the other end.

Kirill pointed at Matus. 'You, outside,' he said. 'You, make drinks and get in your room.'

Lenka hurriedly made fresh tea and coffee, loaded tins of beer onto the kitchen counter from the fridge, escaped to her bedroom and locked the door behind her.

'Just get here,' she heard Dixon snap.

These old caravans had Perspex windows in every room. In Lenka's, there was a tiny frame at the top which could be opened for ventilation, as it was now. Looking out, she could see that Matus had gone back to the men sitting around the firepit. He was safe for now at least. If anyone had seen them kiss, then it was unimportant against whatever this other thing was.

Lenka pulled the curtains and turned off her light as if she was going to bed. She waited.

'Well?' asked Kirill.

'Ray is on his way,' Dixon replied. 'You got a drink? I need one.'

'Inside.'

The three men settled down in the living area. There was the sound of mugs clinking, and tins being opened, their voices an insistent murmur. Lenka sat silently on her bed until she heard another vehicle bumping down the cart track from the farmhouse. It pulled up and the door slammed with a tinny echo. She peered around the edge of the curtain.

'Evening,' said the driver to the men outside, then he climbed into the caravan.

The facing light and acute angle made it difficult to tell if she recognised the man, but she thought it must be someone called Ray Fraser. She knew that sometimes Pavel asked for him to be sent to the barns to collect things and dispose of them, the 'rubbish run,' he called it. Kirill also sometimes spoke of him, though only to criticise Fraser's attitude. Lenka had never seen him come to the caravans before.

'About bloody time,' she heard Dixon say as the newcomer helped himself to a drink.

'Shove up,' said Ray. His tin clonked on the table. 'What's set your tail on fire, then?'

Lenka stepped to her door and put her ear to the gap between the frames. It was getting dark outside. She prayed they wouldn't see her shadow.

'Didn't you see the news tonight?'

'Nope, can't be arsed. Why? What happened?'

'You did, stupid fucker.' The edge in Kirill's tone warned that he was close to losing control.

'Me? How come?'

'I told you.' Dixon again. 'I fucking told you. Leave the man alone. He had no proof.'

'What are you on about?' Ray sounded less cocky now.

'It's all over the television,' said Pavel, his voice low. 'The police are asking for witnesses, looking for his car.'

There was a pause. 'So what?' asked Ray. 'We moved him. The Landie must have gone by now.'

Lenka stuffed her hand in her mouth to stifle the gasp. So this man was dead because of them, and Pavel knew all about it.

'Not gone,' Pavel spoke so quietly Lenka could barely hear him. 'Been using it.'

'For fuck's sake,' snapped Dixon. 'You'll have to torch it, then.'

'I can break it down, two days, no more. Ready to go. No trace.'

'After that, there's nothing to connect him to us,' said Ray. 'I'll arrange the lorry for Saturday.'

'There shouldn't be,' Dixon snapped. 'Except for you.'

'What do you mean? What have I done?'

'Don't be an idiot,' Dixon blazed on. 'They won't have to dig very far, will they? The police have already been sniffing around that bloody fight. You were the one who wanted the man charged.'

'Shouldn't have hit me, should he?' Ray threw back at Dixon. 'You were the one that got a fucking caution.'

'Should have left him alone,' Pavel insisted.

'If you hadn't stopped me, I would have got him,' Kirill yelled. There was a scuffling sound, a muted yell from Pavel and a crash of crockery and tins.

'For fuck's sake.' Dixon must have gone across the table to grab one of them. 'There's no time for this. We need to make plans to cover our tracks.'

The scuffling continued for a few seconds until someone broke them up. 'Sit down and shut up, the goddam pair of you.'

'We still have to do Saturday's job,' Ray whined as they settled down again.

'I know,' agreed Dixon. 'It will have to be our last. You tell your end of the line, no more after this. Pavel, you get

159

that last Landie down to parts by Saturday morning, I don't care how many hours you have to bloody do. How many others are there?'

'Two,' Pavel replied. 'They're ready. Finished today. Plus a quad bike, that can go straight in.'

'That will have to be enough,' Dixon snapped. 'Fraser, you get the container up there as soon as you can. The men will pack them up. And don't load my quad bike, I'll move it back to my sheds.'

There was a muttering of general agreement.

'Saturday night's stuff will be another full container. Fraser, you get another driver lined up.'

'Not sure if I can,' said Fraser. 'We've only ever used the same bloke. He doesn't care, so long as it's cash.'

'With all your contacts?' Dixon sneered. 'I thought you were Mr Fix-it.'

'Told you, he's no good.' Kirill sounded triumphant.

'And we need to find that car before the police do. God knows what's in it. We all need to drive around the lanes until we find it.'

Kirill started to object. Dixon cut him off.

'It can't be far. He must have parked near where you guys were that night. I'll start in the morning and so will you, Fraser.'

'Here.' It was Ray's voice. 'Who the hell is that in your yard?'

'What?'

'Look. They're coming over here.'

Lenka shrank back from the door, wondering what on earth was happening now. There was the sound of scrambling from the kitchen. Pavel stamped past Lenka's door and into his room. Two of the men went out of the door, one stayed in the van. Another vehicle pulled up with a squeak of brakes, a door opened and slammed.

'Good evening. Well, isn't this cosy?'

Lenka recognised the cheerful female voice. Moving back to the window, she twitched her curtain open just enough to see out. Beyond the men sitting around the firepit stood the busybody lady, Agnes. A man stood behind her. It was the man from the kitchen at Agnes's farm, the one who had come before.

'Hello, Des.' Agnes moved to the edge of the group, glanced around the faces. 'Is that you, Ray Fraser?'

'Evening, Agnes.' Ray nodded, lighting up a cigarette.

'Fancy seeing you here.'

'I'd say the same to you, Agnes.' Dixon sounded as if he had to work hard to keep his voice calm. 'What are you doing?'

'I was taking Frank home.' Agnes pointed to the man who stood behind her. 'Thought I'd pop by to arrange that salad picking. I think it's ready now.'

'Why did you come over here?'

'I saw the lights and hoped you were with your boys planning for next week. Figured if I could catch you it might kill two birds with one stone, so to speak.'

'Give me half a chance.' Lenka heard Ray's muttered comment as he drifted under her window. She prayed silently for the old lady's safety.

'Why don't we go back to the farmhouse and rota it in?' Dixon offered.

'That would be lovely,' Agnes nodded. 'Nice set up you've got.'

'The guys seem to like it.' Dixon headed across to move her away.

'Could you do with a housekeeper or cook?' she asked. Her eyes searched the curtained windows. 'I could recommend someone.'

'They're happy as they are.'

Agnes let her gaze settle on Fraser, who was standing next to Lenka's window. Briefly, her eyes flickered to the drawn curtains, and she smiled.

'I guess so. It would be too lonely, I suppose. Well, goodnight, then.'

She lifted her hand in a general farewell gesture, which it seemed to Lenka was aimed at her window. Then Agnes turned around and walked back to the parked vehicles with Dixon. The man called Frank followed her.

'How about Monday morning for the salad? Would that be suitable?' was the last thing Lenka heard Agnes say.

Was this for her? Lenka wondered. Had the man at the farm recognised her yesterday morning? Whatever the reason, either the old lady was being stupid, or playing a far more dangerous game than she realised. *Please let it be for me,* Lenka prayed. *Let it be a sign.*

Kirill waited until both vehicles reached the farmyard before going outside. He strode over to where Fraser was still standing, finishing his smoke. Suddenly, he grabbed Fraser by the throat and slammed him against the wall of the caravan. Behind the curtains, the terrified Lenka shot awkwardly backwards onto her bed.

'You're the fucking problem.' Kirill snarled into the other man's face.

'Kirill. Mate,' Fraser spluttered. 'Thought we were buddies. All in this together.'

'I'll kill you if you make one more mistake.'

There was a choking sound and a gurgle from Fraser in reply.

'You sort out those containers. Don't come here to the caravans again.'

To emphasise the point, Lenka heard the sound of a fist landing repeatedly into flesh and the whoosh of air from Fraser's mouth. Kirill dropped the man and returned to the van.

She heard Fraser mutter, 'Bastard. I'll show him,' before he scrambled to his feet and trudged away.

CHAPTER 29

Sara woke to the chimes from the City Hall clock. When had she left the window open? She never left the window open at night. Had she counted the chimes accurately? What time was it? She rolled over to look at her alarm clock and found Chris instead.

Her eyes opened wide as she felt the warmth from his body next to her. His breathing was relaxed, his eyes closed. He looked peaceful. She looked around the room, didn't recognise it. They must have ended the evening in his flat and not hers. With a pounding head, she turned away from him, and, trying not to wake him, she put each leg slowly over the edge of the bed until she was sitting upright. Memories of the previous night came crawling back. The best hope she could find was that she didn't appear to have talked about anything too important. They had danced to the band, who were rather good. They'd drunk too much, of course. Liberated from her sensible self, she had encouraged Chris to kiss her passionately, which had led to this morning. Chris mumbled as Sara collected up her clothes, pulling on the minimum amount that would get her upstairs to her flat.

'Got to go to work,' she whispered. She left him with a kiss on the cheek.

Her alarm clock said ten past five when she reached her bedroom. Breakfast consisted of painkillers, water, coffee and remorse. Showering didn't help much.

To add to her already turbulent emotions, she had embarrassed herself with a neighbour that she would be living next to for the foreseeable future. Or for as long as her boss allowed her to stay in Norwich if he found about her father. At the very least, she needed to find a way to apologise to Chris without hurting him. He was a kind soul, and she felt as if she'd used him.

Bleary-eyed, she arrived at work in time for more coffee, but her hangover stomach couldn't face the bacon buttie. Bowen ate hers as well as his own. Without comment, Edwards had gathered her up to go to their appointment at the NFU Mutual. By then her head had cleared sufficiently for her to recall why she knew the term NFU Mutual. It was the company with the TV ads showing an assessor wading through a waterlogged home. Edwards parked carefully in the multistorey.

'There's nothing the traffic wardens like better than to be able to give us a ticket for bad parking,' he said. They made their way across the city to the office on Prince of Wales Road.

The morning was hot and sunny and the good weather was forecast to last until the end of August. It made the city humid and dusty, busy with tourists and locals alike. Cafés spilled tables out into the pedestrianised areas along London Street. The smell of fresh ground coffee and newly baked scones drifted around them. Even the charity shops charged high prices on this street.

To Sara's relief, the NFU offices were air-conditioned. It was cooler and calmer than the city outside. Julie Jones, the office manager, didn't keep them waiting long.

Sara had expected her to be some horsey or farming type. Or some middle-aged management harridan who had fought her way to the top of her little pond. Julie Jones was stunning. In her mid-thirties, petite, with strikingly ginger hair falling halfway down her back, she was dressed in a dark blue figure-hugging sleeveless dress. Sara felt fat and frumpy in comparison.

'Call me Julie,' the woman insisted as she led them into her office, ordering drinks from her young male PA as she passed his desk. 'Now, what can I do for you?'

'We've come about Adam Crane,' said Edwards.

'Certainly. What would you like to know?'

'You may have seen the news last night.'

'The man they found in the ditch?' Julie Jones looked shocked. 'Yes, I saw that. Do you mean it's Adam Crane?'

'We believe so, though that is still confidential information at the moment.'

'Yes, of course.' The woman held up a finger as the PA came in with refreshments on a tray. 'Callum, bring me Adam Crane's PR file, will you, please?'

The young man retreated, and Julie Jones nodded to Edwards to continue.

'From certain papers we found at his cottage, we understand that Crane worked for you.'

'Yes, he'd been with us for about four years. Freelancer.'

'What did Mr Crane do for you?'

'Security reports mostly.'

Callum returned with the PR file and placed it on his manager's desk. She smiled and dismissed him. Turning the file towards Sara and Edwards, she opened the front cover. It bore a recent photo of Adam.

'Same man?' she asked.

'Definitely,' said the DI.

Sara looked closely at her father, staring back at her from the cover of the cardboard file. Here was a chance to find out more about him, to fill in some of those gaps.

'What did his work for you entail?' she asked.

'Sometimes we commission a security report when we take on a new client,' Julie explained. 'It helps us to do a proper quote for the cover. Other times it can be after a break-in or a theft.'

'To assess the cost of the lost items?'

'No. We have loss adjusters for that. After any theft, the police are informed. Unfortunately, they tend only to come out and look around if the items are of high value or someone has been injured.'

'Injured?' Sara asked.

'Beaten up or injured by something broken during the theft.' Julie grimaced. 'That doesn't happen too often but it's not unheard of. It's the value of the items that normally causes the police to visit. With any claim, we will send in the loss adjuster and someone like Adam to visit the site as part of the insurance claim. He was ex-police, you know that?'

'Yes, of course,' said Edwards. 'So, what were his duties?'

'He would inspect the scene and let us know what he thought had happened. Afterwards, we might make certain stipulations as to further security measures that we would require in the future in order for the cover to continue.'

'So, Crane had a good idea of how many incidents were happening in the area?' Edwards said.

'Pretty much. We only have three of these advisors in the region. Adam is our main man in Norfolk and Suffolk.' Julie sighed. '*Was* our main man. We're the principal insurers for most of the agricultural businesses around here, and theft has been a growing issue for several years now.'

Sara thought of the pile of files on the windowsill behind her desk. The cases that the team had thought too boring to bother with, which they'd abandoned as soon as something more interesting and urgent had come along.

'Have you come to any conclusion about it?' asked Edwards.

'To be fair, it was Adam who said he saw a pattern, and I agreed with some of what he said.'

'Such as?'

'Well, there is a clear increase in the thefts reported between March and September. You'd think that the long dark nights in winter would be a more obvious time to break into these barns and yards.'

'So?'

'Some of that is probably down to the fact that certain pieces of equipment are only brought out at given times of the year. They could have been stolen earlier, but not necessarily missed until they were due to be serviced and used. There was a marked increase in the last two years of smaller, more portable equipment like quad bikes or ride-on mowers and Land Rovers.'

'Land Rovers?' Edwards sounded surprised. 'Why those?'

'Defenders,' Julie specified. 'Probably the most useful farm vehicle ever built. They can be used in the toughest terrains, are easy to maintain and extremely popular everywhere.'

'Everywhere?' Sara asked. 'Can you be more specific?'

'Nope, I mean everywhere. Europe, Eastern Europe, Russia, Africa, the Americas. And for some reason no one can quite fathom, Land Rover stopped building them a few years back. After that, they become the single most stolen vehicle on farms. They are valuable on the black market and easily transported. There's a new model coming out now, and it's even more expensive than the old one.'

'Surely moving large numbers of stolen vehicles would be conspicuous?'

'Not in this case.' Julie chuckled. 'You see, the original Defenders were designed to be easily maintained in difficult circumstances. Consequently, they are built not unlike giant Meccano kits. If you have the right equipment, they can be stripped and crated up in a matter of hours. That way you can get several of them stacked into a container with false papers and it's highly unlikely that Customs would bother to inspect it. At least, that was the theory Adam was working on.'

'You mentioned a pattern?' Edwards asked.

'Adam said he saw a pattern in the geography and timing of the thefts. They rise dramatically at the time the seasonal workers are in the region. The majority of the claims were made between May and September and within a four-hour drive of Norwich.'

'So, this isn't a national problem?' Sara asked.

'Yes, it is,' Julie replied. 'But we have a much higher incidence of activity in this region.'

'Could you let us have specific figures?' asked Sara.

'I can email them to you.'

'What did Crane make of all this?' Edwards picked up the file.

'Adam thought that it was an immigrant gang posing as seasonal workers. He also became convinced that it was organised crime. A single group, or perhaps a couple of related groups, working in this region who were systematically stealing to order and shipping out as I've described.'

'Did he have any particular suspects in mind?'

'He mentioned a group of men in North Norfolk. Said he was going to follow them. That was several weeks ago, and I haven't heard any more from him. I had become rather worried about him, but I didn't know who to speak to about it. You see, he hadn't answered his phones or emails since I last saw him at the Norfolk Show at the end of June.'

CHAPTER 30

'Crane vanished off the radar at both NFU Mutual and RuralGuardian by early July,' DI Edwards mused as they walked back across the city to the car park. 'And no one did anything about it. Poor sod.'

'If he was following something or someone,' said Sara, 'I suppose he would keep his mobile off. But why not answer emails or return ordinary calls at home? All he had to do was decline the work.'

'Crane was methodical in spite of appearances. His instinct was first rate, his suspicions always well founded. Why did he settle on someone close to him? What was the connection?'

'Or who, sir,' Sara suggested. 'It might be a particular person he thought was involved. Those other files might tell us.'

They stopped at a coffee shop for takeaways. Sara joined the queue, while Edwards sat at one of the outside tables making phone calls. Watching through the window, she saw him gesture for her to join him. She hurriedly paid for the drinks and went back outside.

'That was forensics. That blood at the cottage — guess who it belongs to?'

Sara shook her head.

'Fraser. Ray bloody Fraser.' Edwards began to march back to the car park. 'Now, how did that get there? Time to give our man Fraser a visit, wouldn't you say?'

'Definitely, sir.'

'Oh, and Dr Taylor said he needs you to go back to the lab.'

The request came as a bolt from the blue. Her voice wavering, Sara asked, 'What for?'

'Something went wrong with your DNA test. He needs to take another swab. Said to call in later today.'

She didn't believe that for a minute.

They headed straight back to Happisburgh. Fraser lived at the opposite end of the village to Crane. Blacksmith's Lane was narrow, with several 1980s bungalows on each side. Fraser's home was at the far end, as it turned the corner into another narrow country lane, surrounded by neatly trimmed, high, dense hedges, which blocked the house from view. They turned into a small gap in the hedge. The bungalow was ahead of them.

It was a small detached place. What garden they could see was mostly grass. Once trimmed like the hedges, now it was scorched yellow by the hot summer weather. It was packed full of sheds and outbuildings. While Edwards knocked on the front door, Sara walked across to the outbuildings, rattled a couple of shed doors and peered in the windows. The outbuildings were all locked.

'Mr Fraser,' she heard Edwards shout through the letterbox. 'Mr Fraser, it's the police. We need a word.'

'I wonder what he uses all this lot for,' said Sara. 'There's a powerful amount of storage space.'

'Could be anything. Stolen goods, maybe?' Edwards shrugged. 'He could be anywhere. We're going to need to keep an eye on the place until he gets back.'

They sat in the car for a while, until Edwards became frustrated at the wait and drove them back to HQ.

Sara's hangover had cleared by the time they regrouped in the office around the incident board, but worry about the pathologist's request had taken its place. She wasn't sure how much more of this pressure she could withstand.

'The hotline number has received several calls about the missing car,' said Ellie. 'But the only thing of interest was the garage who rang to say they did the MOT and servicing for Crane. Only a couple of people have come forward as being in the area, and neither of those had been there after dark.'

'That's not much help,' said Edwards. 'What else?'

'There's the fact that Fraser has been inside Crane's place,' Bowen said. 'And he left traces of blood.'

'Whatever happened, Crane can't have noticed the spots, or I think he would have cleaned them up,' Edwards said. 'We need to make some progress here. Jones said he talked about a picking group in North Norfolk. Can we trace all the picking gangs in the area? There must be a register.'

'Yes, sir,' said Ellie. 'But they might not be registered.'

'Maybe not, but we should still try. Ellie, take a look. What about those NFU reports?'

'Sir, I think it would be really useful if we compared our reports with theirs.' Sara indicated the pile of files on the window ledge. 'Maybe we can spot the same evidence he did.'

'Good idea, give it a go. Mike, I want you to go and keep an eye on Fraser's place, take a uniform for backup. If he turns up, call it in.'

It took Sara most of the afternoon to compare the files. It soon became clear that, with a couple of exceptions, their files corresponded to an NFU claim. Some of the police reports were little more than logs of the theft, fewer than half had received a visit.

Julie Jones had been right, the largest number of thefts was of Land Rover Defenders, followed by smaller items like quad bikes and mowers. Some larger pieces of equipment did get stolen, though being hard to transport or hide, they got targeted less often. The price of a new tractor or combine harvester made Sara wince. Items stolen from other vehicles included GPS equipment and specialist onboard computers. On one occasion, a boatyard in Wroxham had been turned over and thirty outboard motors stolen from the day boats. These had had trackers on them. Frustratingly, the theft had remained undiscovered for days, and the trackers were out of range.

'Gone abroad,' said Ellie. 'I reckon all this stuff is likely to be going abroad. Though, God knows, it's easy enough to sell the smaller stuff on eBay or Gumtree if you have a solid-looking front man.'

'Jeez.' Sara sighed. 'Look at this.'

Julie Jones had sent over a spreadsheet of claims, which Sara had compared to the other sets of files.

'I think this is what Crane saw.' She printed out the figures and laid them on the desk. 'He's been working for the NFU for more than four years. The claims rose steadily but quietly for the first two years. Then look what happened.'

Ellie studied the figures and whistled. In the last two years, their region had accounted for nearly half the value of equipment thefts, running to nearly thirty-five million each year. The number of claims had risen by 220%.

'These dates indicate that around three-quarters of this is happening during the picking season,' said Sara. 'No wonder he thought it might have a connection.'

'What made him think it was a group based around here?' asked Ellie. 'These gangs live all over the area, especially on the Fens.'

'How many have you found?'

'I've put in an official request to the registration authority.'

'What else happened to make him so suspicious? Was it Ray Fraser? How did his blood end up inside the cottage?'

As the afternoon wore on, the frustration ground them all down. Forensics still hadn't managed to break into the files on the memory stick. Edwards gave them a roasting over the phone for that. Ellie spent over an hour on the phone trying to get someone to send her a copy of the gang register, without finding anyone who would do it without a higher authority signing it off. Bowen sat outside Fraser's house without success — the man hadn't returned by 5 p.m.

Finally, Edwards told them all to go home and the team disbanded for the evening. It had been a dispiriting day.

Sara suspected that her evening wasn't going to be any better. She couldn't avoid going to the path lab on her way home, since Taylor had requested her to do so. All she could hope was that he had already left.

He hadn't. Sara called his office from the car park, and he came to reception to meet her.

'It's a bit of a maze until you get used to it,' he said, leading the way to the far end of the hospital building. 'Let's go into my office. We won't be disturbed there.'

'You wanted to see me, sir?'

'Have a seat, DS Hirst.' Taylor indicated for her to sit in the chair on the other side of his desk. 'On your own?'

'Just on my way home.' Sara sat tense and upright, primed for flight. 'DI Edwards said you wanted to do another DNA test?'

'Well, I could do another one.' Taylor looked at her intently, before opening a drawer in his desk and pulling out a folder. 'But I don't suppose it would bring up a different result. Can you read DNA reports?'

'I'm not an expert, sir, no.'

'You know what they show?'

'Yes, of course.' Sara's voice drained away.

'Well, this was the DNA result from Adam Crane.' Taylor pulled out a paper with graphs and figures on it, laying it on the table for Sara to read. Her heart began to hammer, her skin became clammy. So, this was it. Now she would know for sure.

'And this is the one we took from you for elimination purposes.' He placed another report next to it. 'Can you explain why you appear to be closely related to the victim?'

'How closely?' she almost whispered.

'Extremely close familial relationship. I would say that Crane was your father.'

'You're sure?' Sara was shaking.

Taylor nodded. 'Are you surprised?'

'Not really. I came to the same conclusion yesterday from certain family items I have.'

'You didn't know who your father was?'

'It's a long story.' Sara began to cry. She was so, so tired. Taylor pushed a box of tissues across the desk. *He probably always keeps some there for distraught family members*, she thought, her scrambled brain fixing on the most inconsequential thing it could find.

It had all happened far too quickly for her to take in. The speed with which she had found her father, her mother's reaction to the mention of Clifton, waking in Chris's bed that morning. None of the things that she would normally have done after a bad week at work would help her now. No soak in the bath, no visit to the pub with her colleagues, no home-cooked Jamaican food and a lovely long chat with her mother. Her father had been murdered and was lying in a locked refrigerator in the hospital morgue, on the other side of the wall from where she now sat. Too late to meet him or ask him anything.

'Well, you don't have to tell me about it. However, as Adam Crane is your father, I will have to tell DI Edwards about the results.'

'Yes, sir.'

Taylor's voice became kinder. 'I don't need to know what is going on here, but you should discuss this with your boss. You are aware that you will have to leave the investigation?'

'I've only been here a week,' she muttered, her head drooping in defeat. 'They might use it as an excuse to get rid of me.'

Taylor paused to consider this. 'I know Edwards can be a difficult character sometimes. Can't we all? But I don't think he would be unfair about it.' Sara looked up at the pathologist, who smiled at her. He put the file back in his drawer. 'I'm going home,' he said. 'I have the weekend off. Not back in until Monday morning.'

It was the best he could do for her, she realised, and tried to smile in return. In spite of the fact that he barely knew her, Dr Taylor was giving her the weekend to come clean with her boss. Sara knew that if she kept this hidden from Edwards, even for a day, it could ruin her career.

CHAPTER 31

Friday passed without incident at the caravans. The men went off to wherever they were crop picking, Pavel to the barns across the fields. Lenka was pleased to find that the television had recovered from its beating by Kirill. She brought Mouse round to share the day with her. They sat for a long time outside the caravan, enjoying the sunshine and planning their next move.

'You get Matus on side,' Mouse urged Lenka. They sat on two of the rickety chairs, drinking tea and holding hands. 'Go out with him, fuck him if he wants. Do it and come back for me.'

'Whatever it takes,' Lenka agreed. 'You'll wait for me if he takes me out?'

Mouse squeezed Lenka's hand. *Yes, she would.*

'No one will believe us unless we go together, then people will have to listen,' said Lenka.

Lenka knew that the gang would return early, the job that day being a short one, so the evening meal was ready by 3 p.m. Afterwards, they set up their card game and launched into the beers. The subdued atmosphere had returned. Bohdan let himself into Mouse's room. Since the beginning of this extraordinary week, he had been the only one interested in visiting her. Matus and Kirill sat at the table drinking tea while Lenka cleared up after the meal.

'Someone should stay tomorrow night,' she heard Matus suggest. 'With the women.'

'What for?' Kirill wasn't interested, he was watching horse-racing on the TV.

'If we all go, they could get away.'

'They're always here alone,' Kirill pointed out, then began to shout at a horse. Matus waited until the race ended. The horse Kirill had backed came in fourth. He screwed up the betting slip angrily and threw it on the floor.

'We always come back in the evening though,' said Matus. 'If it's dark, they could get up to anything. They need guarding.'

Kirill looked at Matus. He sat for a moment, weighing up the options, then sneered, 'You want to stay?'

Matus nodded. 'Someone should. I can do it.'

'Why do you want to stay? You want the women to yourself?' Kirill laughed, reaching forward to slap Matus none too gently on the cheek. 'Are you a shy boy? Virgin?'

Matus blushed and shook his head.

'Don't believe you.' The joke seemed to grow on Kirill. 'I think you're queer.'

Allowing his head to droop towards the table, Matus muttered, 'Not gay, just young.'

'Baby boy.' Kirill thumped on the table in delight. 'Ok, you stay and have a fuck with no one listening. Fuck 'em both if you want. Just not in same room, or they'll tie you up. Gayboy.'

Matus stood up to leave. Still chuckling, the other man pulled a newspaper towards him and began to examine his handful of betting slips. As he went outside, Matus looked at Lenka and winked.

Lenka locked herself away as early as she could, not wanting to hear the sounds of Bohdan with Mouse or watch the other men's indifference. She curled up on her bed with the crumpled magazine, reading aloud softly to practise her

English. The horse-racing ended and the television switched to the evening news. She listened for more reports about the body in the ditch, but there were no updates. As it ended, she heard a vehicle coming along the track. Not knowing what might be wanted, she returned to the kitchen and put on the kettle. Kirill was standing outside the main door. Filling the coffee machine, she stole a look out of the window, unsurprised to see Dixon's Range Rover pulling up.

Ray Fraser got out of the passenger side.

'What's that bastard doing here?' asked Kirill.

Pavel flicked his cigarette butt into the firepit and stood up. 'I asked for him.'

Lenka left the teapot, coffee jug, mugs and all the rest of the paraphernalia on the kitchen counter and went back to her room. As she locked the door, the four men moved into the kitchen. She drew her curtains and stood behind the door to listen.

'Did you find it?' began Dixon.

'Find what?' asked Fraser.

'Crane's fucking car,' Dixon snapped. 'You were supposed to be looking for it.'

'Went to Peterborough.' Fraser's tone was surly.

'Why?' asked Kirill.

'None of your business. I had another job booked. It had to be done first. Did you go looking?'

'I took the men to their job.'

'Dixon?'

'I went to an auction.'

There was a silence.

'Nobody looked for the car?' asked Pavel. None of the others replied. 'For fuck's sake,' he snarled. 'Don't you realise how important it is? We need to find it before the police do.'

'I don't see why,' said Fraser. 'None of us have touched it, why should it matter?'

'It's bound to be near the job we were doing that night.' His fist banged on the table. 'Too close for comfort.'

'All right, keep your hair on. I'll do it in the morning.'

'Are we ready for tomorrow night?' Dixon said.

'The containers will be there first thing. I managed to get another driver.'

'Let's concentrate on the job.' Lenka heard the crackle of someone unfolding a paper map. 'The field is here.'

'Only a few miles away?' Pavel didn't sound pleased. 'It's too close. Even the police will think it's us.'

'Why?' demanded Dixon. 'Nothing to lead them here.'

'Apart from that twat,' said Kirill. 'They suspect him, I bet.'

'How do you know that no one will see us?' asked Pavel.

'They'll all be busy.' Fraser sniggered. 'It's "North Walsham Rocks." Big free gig, beer tent, dancing, food. Everyone goes. Once we are off the road and in the field, the lot of them will be on the other side of the town.'

'Fraser will go with you,' said Dixon. 'When they put up the array, they built a bank between the field and the road to keep it private. More fool them. No one bothered to put alarms on the panels. All you need to do is cut the chains and take them off the frames. I've hired a second van. Load both of them as full as you can. Take it in turns to bring them back to the barns to offload.'

'I've measured up.' Pavel said. 'We can get about two hundred in the container.'

'Then two hundred it is,' said Dixon. 'You should easily be able to do that many before dawn.'

'Where will you be?' asked Kirill.

'In the pub. Setting up my alibi. When will the containers be picked up?'

'Sunday morning. Both of them,' Fraser promised.

'Then we'll be rid of everything.' Dixon sighed. 'And you lot can go home. I'll be glad to see the back of you all.'

Lenka curled up on her bed with a tiny whimper. She needed a plan more than ever, and she needed the courage to carry it out. If the men were leaving on Sunday morning, what did they intend to do with her and Mouse?

CHAPTER 32

Sometimes, Agnes thought as she parked in the field entrance, *it would be nice to have a dog again. It would be some company and protection. Mark could advise me if only he'd answer his phone.*

She always rose early on Saturday mornings to listen to *Farming Today* on BBC Radio Four. It was something she and Tom had done together for decades. Now it was a habit she didn't want to break, not so much for the information that she might pick up, more for the link to her deceased husband.

Locking the Defender, Agnes undid the padlock to the field of grazing marsh beyond and let herself in. Jack Ellis was fattening some young bullocks down here and, although the animals were his problem, Agnes needed to make sure the fences were secure. It was another bright and warm morning, so it was a pleasure to wander along the perimeters. These fields lay beyond the ones that Frank ploughed and planted, along the road towards Sea Palling. Most of them could only be accessed from footpaths or through the field gates in tractors or four-by-fours. Small drainage dykes separated them. Feathery reeds, marsh flowers and long grasses waved along their margins, damsel and dragonflies darted undisturbed by the distant road. Agnes made a leisurely circuit of three fields, finding just one place, a walker's stile, where some repairs would be needed.

'Bloody ramblers,' she muttered. She watched the cattle for a few minutes without seeing any that might need attention and decided to pop round and let Jack know about the fence. She could have rung him of course, but Jack's wife, Elsie, would no doubt have the kettle on, and she would appreciate a bit of company.

When she'd returned from shopping on Wednesday, Frank had told her about the young woman's attempt to visit.

'You'd have thought I was goin' to attack her,' he said. 'Terrified, she were.'

Agnes had thought about this for the rest of the day and most of Thursday until she'd decided to try and contact the girl again. She couldn't shake the feeling that this girl Lenka was in serious trouble and needed a friend. Frank hadn't approved of her decision to go up to the caravans the following evening, but he wouldn't let her go alone.

The tension between the men had been palpable, Dixon's desire to get her away from the caravans obvious. There had been no sign of Lenka, unless that had been her peeping out from behind the curtains in the van window. Hopefully it was, and she'd have realised that Agnes had been trying to reassure her. On Friday she'd waited at the farmhouse all day in case Lenka had tried again. There had been no visitors.

The only activity had been at the barns when a lorry had turned up to offload a container. It wasn't the first time this had happened, so Agnes didn't pay it much attention. What did seem odd was that the lorry returned this morning and dropped off another one. There had never been two there before, and the lorry didn't take the original one away.

Jack's farmhouse was on a minor road out of Sea Palling. Agnes turned into it across the stream of holidaymakers' cars. Saturday mornings were busy with people going home. This afternoon the next set would arrive at the cottages and caravans that dotted the coast. The locals called it 'changeover day.'

The lane had high hedges, rather like the ones on her boundaries. She and Jack both believed in leaving the margins for the wildlife. It was something her son Mark had been passionate about when he was younger. With his help, not to mention set-aside money, they'd returned the hedges and field boundaries into mini havens for everything from mice to butterflies. It was something she was proud of.

She was only a couple of miles from Jack's farmhouse when a white van suddenly shot out of a gap in the hedge, just metres in front of her. Agnes flung the steering wheel sideways and stamped on her brakes, and the Defender bumped heavily over the verge and into the drainage ditch, tossing her around like a crash-test dummy. Her head banged against the door window as she struggled to control the vehicle, praying that it wouldn't roll over. The brakes were screaming, dust showering up around her like a fog. She could hear stones banging like machine gun fire against the metal floor. As she ground to a halt, Agnes realised that she too was screaming. Her heart was racing so fast, she thought she might pass out. Instead, adrenaline allowed her to fling open the driver's door and scramble with jelly-like legs out onto the verge.

The van was already departing at speed. She could just make it out through the dust, though it was too far away for her to see the number plate.

Her precious Defender was groaning metallically, the engine stalled, nose dug into the ditch wall, the bumper and one wheel arch both badly dented. The back wheels were off the ground. It would need towing out. As the dust settled, Agnes decided that it looked stable enough and reached inside to rescue her mobile phone and bag. With shaking fingers, she dialled Jack Ellis's number. After her brief explanation, she heard Jack swear roundly.

'Fuckin' tourists. You ok?'

'Rather shaken,' she admitted. 'But not stirred!'

Jack laughed at this. 'Stay put,' he said. 'I'll bring the tractor to get you out. Be with you in a few minutes. Elsie, get the kettle on.'

Her legs began to give out under her, and she staggered a little. Her head was throbbing heavily. Her hands on her knees, she rested for a few minutes. The sound of the tractor approaching brought her head up again.

'Agnes, you ok?' Jack demanded, as he parked the tractor on the verge to survey the damage. 'Poor Landie. Never mind, soon have that out of there.'

'Thanks, Jack.' Her voice was still shaky.

'Where did he come from, then?' Agnes pointed to the gap in the hedge. 'Bugger was on my land? Wonder why?'

'And why was he leaving in such a hurry? All he had to do was look.'

They pushed past the tractor and into the gap. Behind the hedge was an area of unused scrubland. A large concrete pad ran behind the hedge for about fifty yards. The surface was broken up, full of weeds and rotting leaf debris.

'Used to have barns here,' Jack explained. 'When they fell to pieces, I rented it out to the council for their gritting materials for a couple of winters. Ruined it for anything else.'

It was clear that the van had driven down the concrete to the far end, snapping off the tall weeds and grass as it went. They followed the trail and came to a halt where a larger patch of grass had been flattened. Parked against the hedge, carefully tucked away from view, was a dark green Land Rover Freelander. It must have been there since the last rains. It was covered in dust and the windows were smeared where the rain had failed to clean them. Grass was beginning to grow up around the tyres. Someone had smashed the rear passenger window. The door stood open. The registration number was familiar.

'I think we'd better call the police,' said Jack. Agnes dialled from her mobile.

It only took them a few minutes to hitch up her Landie and pull it back onto the lane. Agnes tried to start it and, reliable as always, it fired at the first turn of the key. It proved drivable so she followed Jack back to his farmhouse.

The two police officers who turned up in Jack's kitchen were a serious disappointment to Agnes. She had been expecting someone from the CID but these two were just spotty youths, out for a pleasant ride in the countryside.

'Isn't this the car your boss was talking about on the TV the other night?' she asked one of them.

The young officer shrugged. 'We'd better take a look at it before jumping to conclusions.'

Agnes was now swimming in cups of tea and rapidly running out of patience with the young man's patronising tone. It was time to go home.

'Best you deal with it, Jack, it's on your land.' She nodded to her friend. Gathering up her things, she turned to the young officer. 'If you don't need anything else, you have my contact details. I'm going home.'

'We'll be in touch.' He was far more interested in the tea that Elsie was busy making than in anything Agnes had to say. She drove carefully home, knowing she would have to get the Landie down to the garage soon and have it checked out. She went immediately into her study. If she were any judge, those youngsters wouldn't get around to reporting their find for hours. It took a few minutes searching among the piles of paper on her desk to turn up the torn-off scrap that the new CID sergeant had given her on Monday.

'Sorry I don't have a card yet,' the sergeant had apologised. 'If you or Frank think of anything else, call me.'

There were both landline and mobile numbers on the piece of paper, the name DS Sara Hirst written in a neat, curly hand underneath. Agnes wondered if they would have the weekend off too, though as they were investigating a murder case, they might be working. She tried the mobile first. It rang out, and Agnes left a tentative message asking the DS to call. The landline also rang out. She had reached an impasse. 'Damn it,' she muttered. 'Now what?'

She pinned the paper on the corkboard in the kitchen. Without any expectation of success, she tried her son's numbers again. Nothing. How long had it been now? It must be at least eight weeks since she had managed to speak to him.

She had barely finished leaving another message when the mobile shrilled in her hand.

'Mrs Richardson?'

'Yes, it is.' Agnes perked up. The sergeant had called her back after all.

'How can I help you?'

'Are you working today? Could you come round?'

'Yes, we are working. You need a visit?'

'There's something I think you should know, and I don't trust those two clowns to pass it on to you.'

'Two clowns?'

'Two young constables from Wroxham.' Agnes knew she wasn't making much sense. 'We found the car, the one your boss mentioned on the TV. At least, I think it was.'

'Hold on a minute.' She heard the woman speaking to someone. Then she came back. 'Where was this, Mrs Richardson?'

Agnes explained about her near miss. 'I thought the other officers would be more interested, to be honest. I think it's the same registration number.'

There was more discussion. 'As luck would have it, Mrs Richardson, we are over at Happisburgh at the moment. I think we'll call in at Mr Ellis's farm first, then pop round to you afterwards, if that's OK?'

Agnes couldn't help but wonder what they were doing just a few miles up the road, but it suited her fine. She turned on the TV and settled down in her chair to wait. Her heart was beginning to race, erratically and painfully.

'Just the shock,' she muttered, putting a hand to her chest and rubbing at the tightness. She could feel herself slipping into unconsciousness. 'Bugger. That hurts.'

CHAPTER 33

It might have been Saturday, but Sara, along with Mike Bowen, was out early in the staff car. Their instructions were simple — find and bring in Ray Fraser for questioning. They headed out towards the coast in silence.

Last night she had returned to her flat, locked herself in and sat for hours in the dark and silence, desperately trying to decide what to do. In the middle of the evening, Chris had come to the door and knocked gently. She had pretended to be out because she hadn't managed to think of a way to apologise to him. Finally, she had made herself the simplest of meals and forced herself to eat it. The blue and burgundy tins had stood unopened on the coffee table. She'd snatched some sleep on the sofa again.

'Look,' said Bowen. His voice abruptly cut across her thoughts. 'About the ditch thing.'

Sara blinked. She turned to look at him.

'Did it damage your shoes?'

'Ruined them.'

'Oh.'

They wound their way around the bypass south of the city without further comment. Too preoccupied, Sara didn't realise that Bowen had taken her silence the wrong way until they were approaching Wroxham.

'All right, Goddammit. I'll buy you a new pair.'

'What?'

'Shoes,' said Bowen. 'I'll bloody well buy you a new pair. OK?'

'What are you on about?' Sara was genuinely puzzled until she realised that this was as close as Bowen could come to apologising. She shrugged. 'I see. I don't think that's necessary. A coffee wouldn't go amiss, though.'

He swung into a car park by the river and dashed across the road to a café. Sara waited, watching the tourists having breakfast on the cruisers that, according to Ellie, packed the waterways during the summer holidays. A flotilla of wild birds paddled between the boats, waiting for the crusts of toast and other breakfast remnants that got thrown overboard to them.

She wondered if her father had ever done that, and shivered. There were so many things she would never know. Bowen returned with bags of cakes and a couple of coffees.

'You choose,' he said, propping his cup in the drinks holder. 'Bakewell, Victoria sponge, flapjack or apple slice.'

She selected the slice of Bakewell tart. 'Do you think I need fattening up or something?' she asked.

'You been eating properly?'

'This isn't eating properly.' She handed the other bags back to Bowen. 'But apology accepted.'

They reached Fraser's bungalow at nine. The place was once again empty. Parking in a field gate where they could watch the entrance, they demolished the drinks and all the cakes. Sara's appetite seemed to return when faced with comfort food.

Before long, each of them needed to climb over the gate into the field for a pee. The car became hot under the morning sun, so they wound the windows down. A stilted conversation about 'great stake-outs I've known' helped pass a little time before Bowen began to play games on his mobile.

Sara's mind returned to the mortuary, her inner eye ranging over the body of her father lying on the table. She felt tears forming and climbed out of the car so that Bowen wouldn't see. He might misinterpret what he saw or ask difficult questions. There was no way she was going to confide in Mike Bowen. With a stretch and yawn, she tried to divert her thoughts by planning the conversation she needed to have with DI Edwards before Monday morning.

'Your phone rang,' Bowen said, getting out of the driver's side.

Sara didn't recognise the number but picked up the message and returned the call.

'It's Agnes Richardson,' she said to Bowen, listening to what Agnes had to tell her. She started upright, her spine rigid with excitement.

'Are you sure we should go?' he asked when Sara had told her Agnes's story. But Sara could see he was as keen as she was to check the vehicle out.

'Let DI Edwards know,' she said. 'Shame about the poor signal.'

Bowen grinned at her and left the DI a message. It was nearly midday when they set off towards Jack Ellis's farm. They soon spotted the police car parked in the entrance to a field.

Agnes had been right. The two buggers needed a rocket up their arses. They were poking about in the tall weeds around the vehicle in a desultory fashion. Their surprise at the arrival of the two detectives was obvious.

One of them squared his shoulders when Sara asked what he thought he was doing. 'I was just going to call in,' he said.

'Get a lot of dumped or hidden cars up here, do you?' For once, Bowen's sarcasm was well-placed.

'Some,' the youngster replied. 'Joyriders, mostly.'

'Surely you know about our investigation?' Sara was livid. 'How can you not? Why didn't you call it in straight away?'

'Yeah, sorry.' He was fidgeting with the stick in his hand, his face bright red.

'Bowen, get on to forensics. We need this lifted and taken in as soon as possible. You two can seal off the area. I take it you have some tape with you? Then wait at the gate to stop anyone else coming in.'

The young constable nodded and beckoned to his partner. The two of them stumbled back down the scrubland as quickly as they dared.

'Jesus,' Sara muttered. 'What are they on?'

'Don't ask me.' Bowen was shaking his head. 'Maybe they thought finding something would turn them into the heroes of the day.'

'Totally against procedure. They'll be lucky not to be disciplined.'

'You going to complain, then?'

'Not a chance. Now, what about our lady farmer? I think we ought to go round and see her.'

'I'll wait here with the lads if you like,' Bowen offered.

It would take a while for the SOCO team to arrive, so she might as well use the time to go and thank Agnes. She fired up the car's satnav. The lanes here twisted and turned until a newcomer like her had no sense of direction left. Mercifully, the house was only a few minutes' drive away. Sara tried the front door first. There was no reply, so she walked round to the rear of the house. There was no reply to her knock at the back door either, but she could hear voices. She tried the door and found it unlocked.

'Mrs Richardson?' she called through the open door. 'It's DS Hirst. Are you in?'

The voices were coming from another room. Sara crossed the kitchen, pausing to orientate herself. It was a television, some quiz show.

'Mrs Richardson? It's Sara, from the police.'

Still there was no reply. Following the sound, Sara crossed the hallway and knocked at the door. Pushing it open, she called again.

189

Agnes was there all right, stretched out on the rug in front of the fire. One arm was clutching her chest, the other twisted under her head, her legs drawn up as if to guard herself against the pain. As she rushed over to the prone figure, Sara hauled out her mobile and dialled 999. Thank God she had a signal. Grabbing for the wrist, Sara managed to find a pulse. Agnes was only unconscious. Talking rapidly to the call controller, she gave details of how to find the place. Then she turned Agnes into the recovery position, checked her airways, tried to make her more comfortable. The farmer's skin was ashen, her breathing uneven. When she had done all she could, Sara grabbed the remote and turned the TV off. Perching on the edge of the armchair, she called Bowen, rapidly explaining the situation.

'Have you got your notes with you?' she asked. 'Do you have the number for that farm worker? Frank, wasn't he called?'

'Yes, somewhere on me. You want me to call him?'

'See if he'll come over. They were close, and I don't know of any relatives.'

For a few more minutes she sat there, ears anxiously straining for the ambulance until Agnes let out a huge sigh. As Sara knelt to check, the old lady's eyes began to flicker.

'It's all right, Mrs Richardson,' Sara said. 'Don't worry. Help is on its way.'

Slowly turning her head, Agnes looked up into Sara's face.

'I'm Sara, from the police. You called me.'

'Oh, yes.' Agnes sighed again. 'The police.'

'I think you might have had a fall or something.' Sara knew the latter was more likely — a heart attack or stroke. 'The ambulance is coming. Lie still, and they'll help you.'

'It hurts.' Agnes pressed a hand against her chest. 'The police? Yes, tell the police.'

'Don't try to talk. They'll be here soon.'

'You should be doing something about them.' Agnes's hand left her chest and reached out towards Sara. 'Those girls.'

'What? Which girls? I came about the car you found.'

'Car?'

'You were right. It was the one we were looking for.'

'No. You need to help those girls.' Agnes's eyelids were fluttering again.

'Mrs Richardson, stay with me,' Sara pressed her hand, shook it gently. 'Try to stay awake.'

In the distance she could hear the approaching sirens. She gave another gentle shake but receiving no response, she scrambled up and dashed out through the kitchen. The ambulance was powering down the lane. Waving wildly, Sara guided it into the yard.

'This way,' she shouted, running ahead of the paramedics and into the sitting room. 'She's here.'

'What's her name?' asked one, as they pushed past towards the prone figure, hunkering down to begin their urgent examination.

From where she stood, Sara couldn't see any sign of movement at all. 'Agnes. Mrs Richardson.'

'Come on then, Agnes,' said the female paramedic. 'Let's see how you're doing, eh?'

While the paramedics worked on Agnes, Sara called DI Edwards to tell him about finding the car and then Agnes. Wondering whether she could cope with many more shocks this week, she asked him for instructions.

'Go with her,' he said. 'See if you can raise some friends or family.'

The ambulance drove, lights and sirens blazing, to the main hospital in Norwich. But it still took over half an hour. Agnes was hooked up to several different machines, the paramedic regularly checking each one.

They hurtled round a junction.

'That's surprising,' she said.

'What is?'

'I don't think she's had a heart attack.' The paramedic pointed to a small printout. 'No sign of damage here. They'll do a full test when we get in, of course.'

They got priority treatment when they arrived at A&E, the trolley taken immediately into a curtained-off cubicle. Hovering in the nearest seating area, Sara rang Bowen.

'I got hold of that chap,' he assured her. 'Told him it was best to go straight to the hospital. He should be with you soon.'

'How about that vehicle?'

'SOCOs are here. They'll be lifting it to take it back to the lab any minute. Where's the pool car?'

'Shit.' She spoke in little more than a breath, but an elderly lady sitting opposite her frowned at the language. 'It's in the farmyard. I came in the ambulance with her.'

'No problem. I'll cadge a lift with someone to pick it up. You couldn't let the poor old sod go on her own.'

'Right.' Raised voices at the reception desk caught her attention. 'Got to go. That farm chap has just got here.'

Sara went over to speak to Frank. She flipped her warrant card, placated the receptionist and took Frank to the waiting area.

'They're still working on her. We can't go in yet.'

'Thank God you were there.' Frank slumped down onto a chair. 'I worry about her being on her own so much. Ring her regular in the evenings.'

'I'm sure she's glad to have you.' Sara sat next to him. 'Doesn't she have any other family?'

'Tom, her husband, died three years ago. Heart attack.'

'No children?'

'Oh, yes. A son. Mark.'

'So where is he?'

'Dun't know,' Frank shook his head. 'He's a vet in Cambridge, don't visit too often. Last time was her birthday in April.'

'Do you have any contact numbers for him?'

Frank brought his mobile phone from his pocket and fiddled with the screen. After a couple of attempts that made him grimace in frustration, Frank managed to bring up a number. He handed the phone across. 'That one, I think.'

Sara dialled the number on her mobile. It rang out, so she left a message. ,

'Mr Richardson.' She realised she was using her best official police voice. 'I'm Detective Sergeant Hirst. Can you please call me back urgently, it's about your mother.'

He rang back almost immediately, just as the doctors came out of the cubicle. Sara motioned Frank to go in while she used her best 'breaking bad news' voice, explaining the situation. At first, he didn't respond, except to say, 'Yes,' or, 'Of course.' Just as Sara was putting him down as uncaring, he burst into tears.

'I'm on my way,' he sobbed. 'Tell her I'm coming.'

CHAPTER 34

'I don't believe your mother to be in a critical state,' Sara assured Mark over the phone. She glanced round the curtain at the stalwart Frank settling into an armchair, and was relieved to see him smile at her. 'I'll get an update and call you back. Please drive carefully.'

The doctor sounded quite relaxed over Agnes's condition. Although she was still drifting in and out of consciousness, they seemed to think she was stable enough.

'No sign of a heart attack or stroke,' he said. 'She does have an injury to her head. That could have caused her to pass out, or it could have been as a result of the fall. Either way, I want to keep her in. We'll get her transferred to a ward to keep an eye on her.'

Having ensured that Frank knew Mark was on his way, Sara excused herself and went out into the large square at the top of the hospital to check in with her boss again. It was already mid-afternoon.

'The car is on its way to forensics,' said Edwards. 'Mike's on his way back here.'

'We didn't manage to find Fraser, sir,' Sara said. 'Do you want us to go back and try again?'

'No, let's leave that until tomorrow. There's something else I want you to do, since you're at the hospital anyway.' Edwards explained that he had spent the day going through the theft reports with Ellie. 'It's this new one that interests me.'

'The one from a couple of days ago? I put it on the top.'

'Yes, a gardener called Graham Dack. I think it might be part of this. See if he's still in the hospital and have a quiet chat if he is. Let me know what you find out.'

'Yes, sir.' Sara closed her mobile and looked round the square at the various bus stops. No doubt one of them would go back into the city. It would be good to keep busy because it kept her mind off her other problems. While she still had a job.

The woman at the enquiry desk was determined to be unhelpful until Sara opened her warrant card. Graham Dack was in Dilham Ward, waiting for surgery, the woman said, slapping a map of the hospital down on the counter and turning back to her computer screen before Sara could ask anything else. The ward matron was more helpful.

'They broke his arm in three places, his collarbone, and ruined his nose,' she explained to Sara. 'He's waiting for corrective surgery on his face and pins in his arms. Tomorrow morning, hopefully, if there's theatre space.'

Dack was trying to read a newspaper that lay open on the patient table. His right arm was wrapped in bandages and suspended in a sling, fingers protruding uselessly. He struggled to turn the pages with his left hand. His face was covered in cuts held together with micro-tape, bruises ringed both his eyes and large plasters were strapped across his nose in an attempt to support it.

'Police? Really?' he asked after Sara introduced herself. 'Told you all I can.'

'I'm sorry to trouble you again.' Sara sat on the visitor's chair. 'We've read your statement, and I believe your attackers may be part of a wider operation. I wondered if there was anything else you might have remembered since our colleagues first spoke to you.'

Dack leaned back, seeming to consider this.

'I surprised them. It was night.'

'Yes, sir. Dark, too?'

'I put on the office light as I went in.'

'What did you see?'

'Two men, definitely men. One was tall, big. You know, well built.'

'What did they look like?'

Dack shuddered. 'Can't remember much. The one that came at me had a stubbly beard. And a crowbar.'

'Did you hear them say anything? Would you recognise their voices again?'

Dack once again took his time. 'I heard them talking to each other. One was English and the other was foreign. Did I say that before?'

'I don't think so.' Sara tried to remember. She had only skimmed the statement. 'What do you mean by that? Can you be more specific?'

'Yes, them migrant buggers. Polish or Ukrainian or something. White, but foreign. Thieving bastards. Should all be sent home. That's what we voted for.'

She suspected that under normal circumstances, Graham Dack wouldn't be speaking like this. But this attack wasn't normal. She associated injuries like these with gang violence in the inner city, not the theft of garden machinery, no matter how valuable. He must be in a lot of pain. She saw him try to turn the page of his newspaper, but failed to reach out and help him.

'Did you see a van at all?'

'No time. All I saw was the boot heading towards my face.'

'Well, thank you, sir.' She rose to leave. 'You've been very helpful.'

'Sure.' He gestured with his left hand at his right. 'Catch 'em for me, will you?'

'We'll do our best.'

She had almost got to the end of the ward when Dack called her back.

'There was a van,' he said. 'Not that night. A couple of evenings before.'

'Can you describe it?'

'It was parked on the verge opposite the house.' Grunting with the effort, Dack leaned forward. 'I only noticed 'cos that makes it harder for me to turn in with the trailer. There was two men in it. Like they was watching our place.'

'In the evening?'

'Yeah. It was white. One of those second-hand Vivaros. It upset Sandra. She said it had been there for more than an hour.'

'Sandra?'

'The wife. It worried her so much that I think she took a picture of it on her phone.'

CHAPTER 35

She had a vague recollection of two people leaning over her, speaking to her, urging her to do something. She couldn't work out what they wanted. Briefly, her eyes focused on the ceiling. There was a buzzing noise as she drifted back to sleep.

Next, she was lying on something, being rattled around. It was too bright to keep her eyes open for long, it hurt. The buzzing was now a beeping.

'Come on, Agnes,' said a man's voice. 'Try to stay with us this time.'

She couldn't.

Then she was lying in a room. The walls were blue, or at least the curtains around her bed were. The ceiling was white, less bright than before. A machine beeped with a steady sinus rhythm.

Her head ached, there was something attached to one side of it. She tried to lift her hand to feel at whatever it was, but it was too much effort. Someone had propped her up on a pile of pillows. Looking down, she saw a needle and tube attached to the back of her hand.

Agnes groaned.

'You awake?' asked a familiar voice. As he sat forward, Agnes could make out the figure of Frank. 'You gave us quite a shock.'

'Did I?'

'Can't deny it. Thought the worst for a while.'

'What's going on?'

'You've been lucky.' He tried to smile. 'That nice lady police detective found you.'

'Where?'

'On the carpet in the sitting room. You were out cold. She rang for the ambulance.'

Agnes looked around her. 'So, I'm in hospital?'

'Yes. Everyone thought you had a heart attack. You're too tough for that though.'

'What was it?'

'Doctors aren't sure. How did you bang your head?'

Agnes thought for a while. The morning seemed so far away.

'A van,' she said. 'There was a white van. It drove me off the road. I banged my head on the bloody window. Had to get Jack to tow me out of the ditch.'

Suddenly it began to come back to her. The van, the hidden car, the girl. She was worried about some girl, perhaps two girls. She tried to sit up, struggled to swing her legs off the bed.

'Is that policewoman still here? I need to speak to her.'

'She went home ages ago,' Frank said. 'Here, don't get up.'

Dizziness rose within her, along with the contents of her stomach. Bile belched up into her mouth.

'Nurse, nurse,' shouted Frank. Through the haze, Agnes saw someone in a uniform come briskly to her bedside. A paper tray appeared miraculously under her chin as the vomit shot up her throat and into her mouth. She spat gratefully, her legs and arms shaking. The nurse cleaned her up and gave her a sip of water.

'At least it will clean your mouth out,' said the young woman in a kind tone. 'No more trying to get up until we say. All right?'

Agnes agreed, settling limply against her pillows. Frank followed the nurse beyond the curtains and she heard them talk in low voices.

'Gone to find a doctor to have a look,' he said when he came back. 'She reckons you got concussion. Explains the head stuff. You nodding off again?'

'No, I don't think so.'

'Good. You should have another visitor soon. Feel up to it?'

'The police lady? Sara? I need to speak to her. It's important.'

'No, not her.' Frank shuffled in his chair. 'Mark is on his way. DS Hirst called him, told him to get here as soon as he could.'

Well, thought Agnes, *it comes to something when it takes me having an accident and a police officer calling him before my son comes to visit. I think it's time I had the truth from him.*

A man in a white coat who looked young enough to be her grandson arrived to examine her.

'I want to keep you in overnight,' the doctor said when he'd finished. 'Pop you down for a scan in the morning to be sure. Concussion is the most likely answer.'

'My accident was hours ago.'

'Can take days for it to come out. We've checked your heart. I'm pleased to say that the reading was clear. Is this your son?'

'No, I'm not,' Frank replied. 'Friend of the family.'

'Mrs Richardson was fortunate. It might have been much worse.' He turned back to Agnes. 'You could have been there for hours. I want you to rest and eat something if you feel up to it.'

'A cup of tea would be wonderful.'

'There's a café downstairs. Your friend could bring you a decent one from there. I'll pop back later to see how you're getting on.'

He handed the notes to the nurse, who was waiting at the foot of the bed. She smiled at Agnes. 'Fancy some more company?' she asked. Pulling the blue curtains back, the nurse beckoned to a figure who stood waiting at the end of the ward.

Mark approached the bed. 'I'll fetch that drink,' said Frank. He gestured to the chair he'd been using. 'Nice to see you, Mark. You can sit here. Fancy a cuppa?'

'Yes, please. Milk, no sugar.'

'I remember.' Frank left them to it.

'Bloody hell, Mum, what have you been up to?' The young man sat down. He crossed one long leg gracefully over the other and reached for Agnes's hand. 'What a fright you gave us all.'

'I had a bit of an accident, that's all. Nothing serious. I should have got checked out, I suppose.'

She inspected him while he looked around at the equipment she was attached to. He had a tan as if he'd been on holiday abroad, but underneath he looked pale. His hair was a lighter blond than she remembered it being in the spring, as if that too had caught the sun. He was biting his lip as he scanned her tubes, going over it all with a professional eye.

'Look at me,' she said. Mark brought his gaze up to meet hers. 'Where have you been? Why haven't you been answering my calls?'

'You should stay calm,' he insisted. He dropped his eyes to the bed. 'I don't want you to get upset. The doctor says—'

'Bugger the doctor,' said Agnes. 'This isn't about what you want or what you feel. What's been going on with you? I want a straight answer.'

'Truly?'

'Absolutely. I'm fed up with all this nonsense.'

'All right.' Mark sucked in a huge breath. 'I've met someone.'

'And what's his name?' asked Agnes. Mark's head shot up. She returned his gaze. 'Is that what all this was about? You think I don't know you're gay?'

'R-Richie,' he stammered. 'His name is Richie. I thought you'd be shocked. Angry.'

'No, darling.' She smiled a little. 'That would have been your dad. He never realised, and I didn't enlighten him.'

'He's a vet, like me.' Mark's words fell out in a hurried jumble. 'Joined our practice a few months ago. It's been a whirlwind romance. You asked for a straight answer. How could I ever give you one of those? I'm not straight.'

'What did you think I'd say?'

'I thought you would cut me off,' he admitted. 'Who can you pass the farm on to if I don't have kids? Why did we never talk about this?'

'I assumed you would tell me in your own time. Besides, it was obvious to me from when you were a teenager.'

'How? What do you mean?'

'You only ever brought one girl home — Sally from Young Farmers. Do you remember?'

'Yes.'

'It didn't last long, and you never showed any interest in girls after that.'

'I was concentrating on my studies.'

'I know you worked hard. But you never really told us much about university, or your social life. What you did do was talk a lot about a friend called Jamie. When we came to your graduation, Jamie was there. Dressed as a woman.'

'Came out as trans, just before the ceremony.'

'Your dad was so proud of you that he had no time for anyone else and didn't make the connection. I did. I know we should have talked years ago, but I never knew how to start the conversation. When you wouldn't take my calls, I thought I'd done something wrong, don't you see that? You haven't spoken to me for weeks.'

'I wasn't here.' Mark squeezed Agnes's hand.

'Where were you?'

'Aruba. It's in the Caribbean.'

'Nice, but you could have told me that.'

'We were getting married.'

Agnes dropped her grip on Mark's hand. 'How dare you?' she said. 'How dare you get married without your mother there?'

'Bloody hell, Agnes.' Frank was standing at the end of the bed with three takeaway cups. 'I'm gone five minutes and you two are fighting already.'

'Little bugger got married without me being there.' Agnes held out her hand for the cup. 'Typical!'

'Oh, Mum!' Mark burst into tears. Then he began to laugh. 'That isn't the reason I thought you'd be upset about it.'

'Congratulations.' Frank held out his hand to the young man. 'Who's the lucky fella? When do we get to meet him?'

'You both knew? For fuck's sake. You didn't say anything either.'

'None of my business,' said Frank. 'Your mum mentioned it. Doesn't stop you being a good vet.'

'Or being my son. You daft thing. Now, tell me all about it.'

Frank brought another chair for himself as, with a smile, Mark began to tell them about his new husband and the wedding.

CHAPTER 36

Sara caught a bus in the hospital square, which took her back into the city centre. It was after seven by the time she got there. Threading her way through the empty streets, past the windows of the independent shops near her flat, she nursed the feeling that she was already being sidelined by her boss. DI Edwards had decided to speak with Mrs Dack himself and had sent Sara home for the evening. It was as if he already suspected her.

She opened the doors onto the tiny balcony to let in some fresh air. She knew she ought to try to eat something, the cakes Bowen had bought this morning had been her last meal. She didn't want to listen to music, or watch the happy people in the street below, or turn on the TV. It felt as if her skin was crawling with indecision. In her mind, the vision of Agnes in the ambulance and her father on the slab in the morgue were beginning to merge. Tears were pouring down her cheeks. The knock at the door was so unexpected that she almost shrieked.

Chris, she thought, *Please don't be Chris. I can't cope with that as well.*

'I've been waiting hours for you,' said a tall figure. It took her several attempts to focus through her tears. It was her step-father, Javed. 'Sat in my car downstairs. You been at work?'

All Sara saw was someone she cared about, and who cared about her. Blindly, she reached out towards him. Javed stepped inside and pulled her into his arms.

'Hey now,' he murmured. 'What's causing this? You not pleased to see me?'

Javed steered them both inside, closing the door with his foot and helping Sara to sit on the sofa. He cuddled her with one arm, digging in his pocket with the other hand to bring out a hankie. Her stepfather was the only person Sara knew who still used cotton hankies rather than tissues. As he pressed the folded white material into her hands, it gave her a sense of security that she hadn't realised was lost.

'I'm a fool,' she sobbed.

'No, you've never been that,' Javed assured her. 'You homesick? Or just a bad day?'

'Too many things, happening way too fast. I've made a big mistake, and I can't get out of it.'

'I believe nothing is ever so bad that it can't be changed,' said Javed. 'Why don't you tell me all about it?'

'It's a bit of a long story.'

'Best I put the kettle on, eh?'

By the time he returned with their drinks, Sara had recovered herself enough to talk coherently. 'Do you remember, back in February, we went to that eighties night?'

'At the social club?' Javed nodded. 'Good evening, that was. Soul and reggae sounds, all those old-fashioned clothes. You got drunk.'

'That was the start of it all.' She sipped her tea for courage, and then launched into her story. Finding the tin, searching online, deciding to move to Norwich, being unable to talk to Tegan about it all. How events had run out of control since she had started her new job on Monday. Javed listened patiently.

He raised a finger like a child in a classroom. 'So this man?' he asked. 'You think he's your long-lost biological father?'

'I don't think it, I know.'

'How come?'

'The photos, for a start.' Sara lifted the blue tin from the coffee table and put it on the sofa between them. 'This is the tin I found in Mum's wardrobe. You can read it all in a minute.'

'You sure you want me to? It's nothing to do with me. I don't want to be nosey.'

'I need to share it with someone.' She offered him a couple of pictures. 'Look, this is the man. Here's Mum and Granddad and me.'

'So this is why you came here?'

'Ultimately, yes.'

'Why do you think this dead man is the same one?'

'I wasn't sure at first. I began to wonder when the boss put up the picture from Crane's personnel file at work. The face seemed familiar, but I didn't have a recent photo to compare with these in the tin. Then we identified him and searched the house. There was this photo.' Sara brought the framed picture she had taken from Crane's house. 'Looks the same, doesn't it?'

'Possibly.' Javed wasn't yet convinced.

Sara picked up the second tin and put it on Javed's lap. 'This blue one,' — she patted it — 'contains Adam Crane's letters to Mum. This other one I found in Crane's shed. It has Mum's replies to Crane and the same photos. Look.'

Her stepfather took the lid from the second tin. 'This convinced you?' he asked. 'You sound sure.'

'I'm sure. Because when we found the body, it was badly damaged and rotting in a ditch.'

'You get all the best jobs.'

'Right. I was hazed, fell into the water next to it and threw up.'

'Not like you.'

'I might have contaminated the scene, so they had to do a DNA test.'

Javed compared a photo from each box, shaking his head as if he couldn't take it in.

'The DNA was a match,' said Sara. She leaned wearily back into the sofa. 'The body is definitely Adam Crane, and Crane is my father. I found him as soon as I got here. But he was already dead.'

They sat in silence, Javed reading his way through the letters one by one. He made no comment when she got off the sofa to go to the kitchen.

'You eaten?' she asked. Javed shook his head.

Sara busied herself making a basic meal, chucking handfuls of rice in water, adding chilli, peas, chopped red pepper and finally coconut milk. It was her grandmother's version of that Jamaican staple, rice and peas, passed from her grandmother to her mother and eventually to Sara. As a teenager, she would proudly prepare it for the family on those evenings when Tegan worked late at the hairdressing salon. Serving it out for Javed and herself, she felt hungry for the first time in days.

Javed had spread the letters and photos on the coffee table in much the same way she'd arranged them earlier in the week. It made a visual sense of the exchanges that reading alone didn't offer.

'What will you do?' he asked, forking up rice as if he too had been starving.

'I have to tell them at work.' Sara was eating more daintily. 'They might sack me. Or, if I'm lucky, they might just take me off the case.'

'Is that how you found out about Clifton?' Javed asked. 'Here in this letter?'

'Exactly. Who the hell is he?'

'Another man, another secret. This time it cost us both.'

'What do you mean?' Sara looked at Javed. He looked at the floor. 'Why are you here, anyway?'

'After your call, Tegan went mad. We had a big row. Biggest ever.'

'For God's sake, it wasn't your fault.'

'She said I helped you, so it is my fault.' Javed rubbed his face. 'I walked out. Slept on Charlie's sofa for a couple of nights.'

'Have you spoken since?'

'Nah. I tried to call, but she won't answer. I thought you might be able to help me. So I came up here to ask.'

'I'm so sorry.' Sara stared at him. She began to cry again.

Javed took her hand and pressed it. He looked resigned. 'Not your problem.'

'I'll help if I can.'

But she didn't know what she could do. Why had she been so determined to uncover secrets that had been best left hidden? Had this need to know about her father been worth the cost they were all paying? Now her mum was alone again, and Javed was devastated. Her career was on the line. Everything she cared about was being damaged, and everyone she loved was being hurt. It was all her fault.

CHAPTER 37

On Saturday morning, the gang had all been taken to the barns. They went unwillingly, grumbling and smoking — it should have been a rest day. As soon as they returned, most of them headed to their bunks for a nap. Once they had finished their evening meal, they loaded the minibus with bags of tools that Pavel had spent the afternoon sorting out. Dusk was falling when, just before eight, Ray Fraser's van bumped its way down the track to the field, followed by Dixon in a tatty white van with a hire company logo on the side.

As she tidied up outside, Lenka strained to listen to their conversation. Kirill, Pavel and Fraser gathered round as Dixon gave final instructions.

'It's too early,' Pavel objected.

'It'll be dark by the time we get there. Everyone will be down the park anyway.'

The gang finished loading the minibus, and then the little cavalcade set off along the track to Dixon's farmyard. Fraser led the way in his van, Kirill followed in the minibus, Pavel brought up the rear in the hire van. Fraser paused to drop Dixon off in the yard, then led them out into the lane.

Lenka took herself back inside the caravan. Matus joined her and watched until Dixon got into his vehicle and headed off in the opposite direction.

'You want to go to "North Walsham Rocks?"' Matus asked.

'Go out? How?'

With a triumphant grin, he pulled a set of keys from his pocket and jangled them at Lenka. 'Pavel has a quad bike over at the barn. I stole the keys this morning.'

'What if we get caught?' Lenka's determination wavered. Perhaps she could take Matus to bed right now, that would be enough.

'No chance.' Matus grabbed her hand and began to tug her out of the door. 'They'll be busy all night. You want a dance? You fancy a drink? I'm taking you on a date, just like I promised.'

Laughing, breathless, stumbling, they hurried over the hill to the barns.

'It's OK,' said Matus. 'I have a motorbike at home. I know how to do this.'

He unlocked the door and went inside, using his mobile for light. Lenka stood on guard, shaking with a mixture of excitement and fear. With an electronic whine, the quad bike engine started and Matus rode it out.

'Come on, then,' he shouted. 'On the back.'

They jammed their bodies as close as they could on the single seat, Lenka wrapping her arms tightly around Matus's waist. He twisted the throttle and they lurched out of the yard towards North Walsham. Lenka screamed with delight.

It wasn't a long drive into the town. Lenka enjoyed every second — the wind billowing her hair, rippling the folds of her shirt, the sensation of speed. Most of all, freedom. She was off the farm at last. It made her giddy and giggly.

Matus turned into a housing estate at the edge of the town and parked the quad bike in a small cul-de-sac. They could see coloured lights flashing, could feel the beat from the music drubbing up through the pavement. Following the noise, they got into the park through a side gate. A security guard nodded at them, stamped the back of their hands with an identifying mark, added two more to his list, and beckoned them through.

'You want a drink?' Matus asked. He pulled out his wallet. It was full of twenty-pound notes.

'Where did you get all that from?'

'I saved it up. From when they make me do the shopping for you.'

'How did you manage that?' Lenka asked.

'Easy. I tell Kirill it's more than I need. He gives me what I ask for. He's not interested what we do so long as the meals are all right. I hide the difference.'

As Matus brought them beer from the bar tent, the idea of getting one over on Kirill made Lenka laugh, a genuine belly laugh. The park was crowded, people were dancing in front of the stage to a local band belting out classic soft rock. Lenka recognised some of the tunes from the TV. Sitting behind the dancers were smaller groups of people on blankets or folding chairs. Everyone seemed to have a drink in their hands. Stalls, booths and tents stood around the perimeter of the arena selling everything from food to silly hats and over-colourful clothing.

The band finished their encore. A man came out to announce a break to allow the next band to set up. Music blared from the speakers to keep people entertained while the stage was rearranged. The crowd began to ebb and flow around the stalls, the young pair walking along with them.

The first stall that caught Lenka's eye displayed a strange assortment of hats and hair decorations. She picked up a green circular headband. It had tiny flowers twisted around it, held in place by pink ribbons which cascaded out of the back. She tried it on, admiring herself in the mirror that was hanging from one of the stall poles. Before she could decide, Matus had already paid for it.

'You look like a princess,' he murmured. One by one, Matus loaded her with gifts from the stalls. A purse shaped like a flower that folded open to reveal pockets underneath the petals — Matus stuffed twenty-pound notes into it. A giant bag of children's sweets, a pretty, diaphanous cream blouse, a canvas shoulder bag to put everything in, with a handsome horse's head printed on it. He bought them some more beer and a giant bag of doughnuts, warm from the fryer, the sugar sticking their fingers to the sides of the plastic beer glasses.

There was a cheer as the last band of the night arrived on stage — a group of local lads who specialised in playing songs from the movie *The Blues Brothers*.

'Oh! I saw this movie on the television,' Lenka shouted with delight. 'I know this song.' Wiping her sugary fingers on her T-shirt, she headed towards the dancers and joined in. Matus willingly followed her, his eyes shining. Between two songs, he wrapped his arms possessively around Lenka. She smiled up at him.

'Happy?' he asked.

'This is the best night of my life,' she promised him and knew that it was true. They kissed amid the catcalls of the crowd around them. The band played until nearly midnight. When the last song ended, the announcer came out to say goodnight to the crowd, urging them to be good neighbours as they left. People packed up their belongings and left the park by the main gate in a steady stream. Caught up in the crush, they headed towards the exit with everyone else.

Lenka guessed she must be drunk, something she hadn't experienced before. It made her euphoric. Never before had the world felt this good to her. Matus held her hand tightly. Her whole body tingled in response. Sleeping with Matus wasn't going to be difficult at all. It was going to be a pleasure. Then, suddenly struck by another thought, she stopped. The crowd log-jammed behind her.

I'm in love with him.

'Come on.' Matus tugged her forward and the crowd surged past with a good-natured grumble. 'I can find the bike from here.'

Beyond the park gates, the crowd began to break into different streams. Some milled about on the road, not sober enough to sense any danger. There were police on duty, stopping the traffic and keeping people moving. Turning left with one group of revellers, they headed away from the park and along the pavement to the estate where they'd left the bike. The crowd around them thinned as they came to a playing field serving as the car park. A queue of vehicles was trying to pull out onto the road. One pushy driver was revving his engine at the people walking past, forcing Lenka and Matus to stagger out into the road.

A moment was all it took. There was a rubbery squeal as a vehicle on the main road swerved to avoid them. The noise was shocking after the music, the friendliness of the crowd. A woman screamed as the frightened pair tumbled back onto the pavement. Matus turned to swear at the driver.

The vehicle stopped. It was a white van. Blinking in the headlights, it took Lenka a moment to focus on the faces of the people inside. The driver was Ray Fraser. The passenger was Bohdan. He was already opening the passenger door.

Matus dragged at her arm. 'Run!' he shouted.

CHAPTER 38

The van door slammed behind them. Matus and Lenka ran through the dwindling crowd, dodging adults, children, baby buggies and festival carts. They could hear Bohdan, his heavy feet hitting the pavement, the curses of the people he shoved aside.

Fear drove the couple. Anger drove the man. He was gaining.

They reached the side road ahead of him, racing round the corner just as the white van turned in behind them. Fraser accelerated past, driving onto the pavement to cut them off. Matus dragged Lenka into the road to avoid it. She staggered as she fell off the kerb edge, Matus tried to get her upright again. It was too late.

Lenka felt a heavy blow to the back of her head and let out a scream. The force sent her staggering forwards, her knees smacked down onto the rough tarmac, her outstretched hands unable to save her. She pitched towards the road with her face foremost, turning onto her shoulder at the last possible moment. A heavy boot kicked her in the stomach as she landed. Her head exploded with pain, the breath rushed from her lungs and she couldn't replace it. Streaks of lightning blinded her vision. She raised her arms just in time, as a heavy boot crashed into them. It was aimed at her face.

Lenka knew it was Bohdan — he loved to hurt women, and now he had his excuse.

With a guttural cry, Matus leaped at the heavy-set man who was twice his size. Lenka rolled to her knees, trying to catch her breath. Vomit was rising from her battered stomach and she retched.

'Help us,' she sobbed. 'Somebody, please help us.'

She raised her pounding head to see Matus clinging to Bohdan's back with his legs wrapped around the bigger man's waist. He had one hand covering his attacker's face, battering him on the top of his head with the other fist. Bohdan swung around like a crazed animal, catching at Matus's legs, trying to pull him off. It looked like some hideous children's game. Matus was landing blow after blow on Bohdan's head, ribs, neck, anything he could reach.

In an instant, the battle was lost. Ignoring the beating, Bohdan reached up to the hand over his face to bend one finger back until Lenka heard it snap. Matus screamed and let go, dropping to the ground. Bohdan was back in control. He spun to face Matus, crashing his huge fist into his opponent's head. Fraser jumped out of the van and ran towards Lenka.

'Help us,' she yelled before Fraser could catch at her arms. 'Help! Police!'

Matus was rolling around, Bohdan kicking and stomping at him. Fraser dragged her along the road. Lenka pulled back against him, struggling and howling loudly. A light went on in a bedroom across the street.

'Help me!' she screamed. 'Stop him! Matus!'

Bohdan raised one foot high and brought it down as hard as he could on Matus's head. Lenka wailed like a banshee as Matus lay still.

The bedroom window opened and a man shouted, 'What the hell is going on? Shut up, can't you?'

'Help us,' Lenka shouted up at the man.

Fraser pushed her against the wall of the van. He clamped a dirty hand over Lenka's mouth. 'Bohdan, come on, man,' he urged. 'Leave the bugger. Get her in the fucking van.'

'I'm calling the police,' the man shouted down. 'I'm fed up with you lot causing trouble.'

Bohdan pushed Lenka round to the back doors. Fraser flung them open. Inside the back were dozens of solar panels, black and angular and sharp, stacked almost to the ceiling. The two men half forced, half lifted Lenka onto the top of the pile. She fell, adding vicious cuts to her already bleeding hands and knees. It went dark as the doors slammed shut. She struggled to find a purchase among the heavy panels shifting underneath her. The engine accelerated, the van shot forward. She clung desperately to the panels, wedging herself between them and the roof. Over the noise of the engine, she could hear sirens. The sensation of speed, the lurch around every corner made Lenka vomit again. It ran, stinking, down the panels onto the van floor. Her wounds opened, bloody handprints peppered the roof as she braced herself. Her clothes were shredded, her beautiful green princess crown tangled in her blood-matted hair.

The van slowed and began to bump up and down. She guessed they were back at the caravans but couldn't see in the darkness. The doors wrenched open again. Four hands reached up to her, she was too exhausted to resist. The men pulled her out onto the grass.

'Lock her up,' Fraser said before Bohdan could start to beat her again. 'We need to offload these fucking panels.'

'Where?' Bohdan held Lenka's arm high up her back. 'With the other whore?'

'Yes. Good idea.'

Fraser went into the caravan and unlocked the door to Mouse's room. Bohdan dragged Lenka along, twisting her matted hair in his other hand until she screamed, then he forced her into the room. In the half-light, Lenka saw Mouse shrunk into the far corner, cowering on the floor like the tiny rodent she was named after. Her mouth was open. She might have been screaming, Lenka couldn't hear for the noise in her head, the overwhelming pain in her whole body. Bohdan snarled something she couldn't make out, and shoved her into the room. As she stumbled forwards, he landed a heavy kick in the small of her back. She sank onto the bed and the world receded.

It was still dark when Lenka struggled up from the noisy void. Everything was in shadow, indistinct. She hurt everywhere. Her scalp felt raw, her stomach bloated with bruises, her hands throbbed. As awareness grew, she realised that she was lying on the bed, her head on the pillow, the duvet pulled over her. Mouse lay next to her. At the first flickering of her eyelids, the other woman's face came into close focus.

'Lie still,' she murmured. 'Everything will hurt. They beat you bad.'

'I know,' Lenka croaked. Her mouth felt dry, stale with old vomit.

Moving round to the side of the bed and easing her up a little, Mouse placed the rim of a plastic water bottle to Lenka's broken lips. She sipped gratefully, the water running across her gums, dribbling down her bloodied chin. Enough of it went down her throat to alleviate the immediate dryness. With a gentleness Lenka would never have guessed at, Mouse took her towel and wiped Lenka's face.

'I'll try to clean you up,' she said. 'I'll have to break that thing in your hair. I won't undress you. They will come back.'

'How long have they been gone?'

'Not sure. Two, maybe three hours. Try to rest.'

'Did they bring Matus?'

'Not here.' Mouse shook her head. 'They beat him too?'

'Yes.' Lenka leaned back on the pillow again. 'Much worse. Bohdan stamped on his head.'

'Fucking bastard. They catch you?'

'Coming out of the park.'

Lenka stared up at the dirty caravan ceiling, tears running down her cheeks onto the pillow. Mouse went back to her place on the bed and gently lifted Lenka, cradling the weeping woman in her arms, rocking her like a distraught child.

'I think I love him,' Lenka moaned. She began to slip out of consciousness again. 'I think he is dead.'

CHAPTER 39

It was after dawn when the gang returned. Lenka woke at the touch of Mouse gently shaking her shoulder. They both lay still, taking in the slamming of doors, the grumbling male voices. Some headed to the other caravan, expecting Lenka to be in the kitchen with food and tea. One set of feet headed towards them.

'Up, you bitches,' snarled Bohdan. He unlocked the door and flung it open.

'Where's that damn woman?' shouted Kirill outside. 'I want some breakfast.'

With an evil grin, Bohdan put a finger to his lips. He slammed the door behind him and walked round to Lenka, unzipping his flies as he went. He was going to rape her, he was erect and eager for action. Mouse tumbled out of bed, heading for the door as fast as she could.

'Help us!' Mouse screamed as she raced out of the bedroom. 'Bohdan, he's hurting Lenka.'

'What are you going on about?' demanded Kirill. Lenka could distantly hear raised voices.

Bohdan pinned Lenka to the mattress, one burly hand round her throat. She tried to pull at his arm. It was futile. He released himself from his jeans, kneeling between her legs and reaching up to yank down her knickers, leaning his whole weight on her neck. She began to choke. He increased the pressure on her throat. Lenka began to pass out, her head swimming, her breath choked, her lungs bursting.

Suddenly she was free. A huge dragging breath filled her grateful lungs, she began to cough up bile, rolled onto her side and curled into a foetal ball. Dimly, she was aware that Bohdan was being dragged outside by at least two other men. As they went out, Mouse came back in, running to help Lenka.

'Can you come?' she asked the stricken woman, pulling her arm urgently.

'Don't know,' mumbled Lenka. Mouse tried to rearrange her clothes, and lift her from the bed. 'Wait, wait.'

'They need to see what Bohdan did to you. Come. I help.'

Mouse took her weight and raised her off the bed. They adjusted her clothes for decency then, leaning on Mouse, Lenka moved stiffly out of the caravan. Outside, they could hear a loud argument begin.

'What's been going on?' Kirill yelled.

'Teaching her a lesson,' Bohdan snarled in reply. 'They left the caravan.'

Each step was painful, her bruised stomach forcing her to bend almost in half. She cried out as Mouse took her down the steps to the area by the firepit. The whole gang was gathered outside, warily watching the row. Ray Fraser was hovering, having a quick smoke. He looked up as Lenka appeared. Cigarette suspended halfway to his mouth, his jaw dropped open. 'Fucking hell,' he said. No one else spoke.

Pavel was the only man who moved. The rest were mesmerised by the sight of the two women. He caught Lenka as she stumbled towards them, taking the weight from Mouse and ordering, 'Bring a chair.' There was complete silence as he lowered the stricken woman into the plastic seat. Mouse stood by her, holding her hand.

'He did this.' Mouse pointed at Bohdan. 'Last night. Now he tried to rape her.'

Pavel gripped Lenka's chin, turning her face this way and that to inspect the wounds. She coughed up bile which dribbled over Pavel's hand. Releasing her chin, he rubbed away the yellow liquid on his trouser leg.

'Bastard women,' said Bohdan. 'Only good for fucking. Why are they here anyway?'

He lunged at Lenka. Kirill grabbed him by the arm, and another of the gang moved quickly to grasp the other one as Bohdan raised it to gesture. He was standing arrogant and tall, prepared to brazen it out.

'I brought them,' said Kirill. His quiet tone was considerably more frightening than his rage. 'The whore for your man-needs, the housekeeper to feed you. You've fucked it all up.'

'Not me.' Bohdan laughed and pointed at Lenka. 'Ask her. Ask why she got the beating she deserves. Ask her how she got into the town.'

Kirill's eyes moved from the smirking man to Lenka. Mouse pressed her hand.

'Well?'

'Yes, we went into the town.' Lenka knew there was no turning back now. 'To hear the music.'

'How?'

'Matus took me. On a four-wheel bike.'

'Were you coming back?'

'Yes.' She whimpered as she tried to stand. 'After the music finished. Why not? We just wanted to be normal for one night.'

'So why this?' Kirill turned back to Bohdan. 'Why do this?'

'We saw them in the town. We thought they were escaping maybe.'

'We?'

'Fraser and me.' It was obvious that Bohdan felt he was on the winning side of the argument. Fraser glanced from side to side, hunting for an escape route.

'They chased us,' said Lenka, holding out her arms for inspection. 'He beat us. Kicked me in the stomach, my face.'

'Fraser?' asked Kirill.

'No, him.' Lenka jabbed her finger at Bohdan.

'How many times do I have to tell you?' Kirill prodded at Bohdan, making the big man turn around again. 'Leave the fucking housekeeper alone. No touching.'

'Why? She's just a fucking whore.'

'Not the point.' Kirill's face was reddening. 'You do exactly what I say.'

He shouldn't have laughed, Lenka thought, as Kirill landed the first heavy punch on the side of Bohdan's face.

The bigger man was ready for the second blow. He parried and swung in return, catching Kirill with a glancing blow. Within seconds, the two men were slogging at each other with their fists and feet, neither managing to gain the upper hand. As they rolled onto the grass, shouting and gouging, Pavel stood up. 'Stop them,' he ordered the other men who were looking on.

For a second, Lenka thought they wouldn't obey him, until one picked up the heaviest of the broken chairs and smashed it across Bohdan's back. The shock made Bohdan roll free and galvanised the others. They grabbed at the big man's arms and legs, pinning him to the ground while he struggled and cursed. It took four of them to hold him down. Kirill rolled away, spitting blood and swearing. He rose and planted a boot in Bohdan's ribs before Pavel spoke again. 'Enough, Kirill.'

'Up,' Pavel said. The four men wrenched Bohdan to his knees. The big man snorted like a trapped animal, coughing as he tried to catch his breath.

'Who do you think is in charge here?' asked Pavel. Standing over Bohdan, he gripped the other man's jaw with both hands, wrenching the neck up until Bohdan met his gaze.

'Kirill,' choked out Bohdan.

'Wrong.' Pavel brought his face closer. 'It's me.'

Lenka's eyes opened wide in surprise. Mouse gasped.

'Kirill does what I say.' Pavel glanced at Kirill, who was spitting blood into the grass. 'My gang, my operation, my contacts.'

Bohdan's eyes swivelled to Kirill.

The other man grinned bloodily back and nodded. 'Everyone needs a hard man,' Kirill sneered. 'You're not it. Not as hard as you think.'

'Where is Matus?' asked Pavel. Bohdan snorted defiantly, locking his lips tightly.

'Last time,' Pavel warned. 'He took Lenka to the music in town. That's okay with me. Now, she's here, no Matus. Where is he?'

'What do you care?' Bohdan said. 'He took her away from the caravans. He stole the quad bike. He disobeyed you both.'

'You killed him!' Lenka screamed. She staggered towards Bohdan and tried to hammer him with her fists. 'I saw you do it.'

'What you mean?' Pavel grabbed her flailing hands.

'He hit me on the head,' she sobbed. 'Matus tried to help me, jumped on Bohdan.' She lunged at Bohdan again. 'You broke his finger, beat him on the floor. Then you stamped on his head. Bastard! Wanker! You killed him.'

'Where is Matus?' Pavel asked Lenka.

'Don't know. When we drove off, Matus was lying in the middle of the road.'

'You stamped on his head?' Pavel turned back to Bohdan.

'We're not allowed in town.' Bohdan's defiance was turning to a whine. 'We all get caught if he grasses on us.'

'Why would he do that?'

'It's good if he's dead. Why do you care?'

'Because he is my nephew,' said Pavel. 'My sister's son. My only living relative.'

Bohdan didn't waste words or breath. With an almighty effort, he heaved at the men holding him down, scattering them in all directions. He was on his feet and running before they staggered to their feet.

Pavel reached into his inside pocket, brought out his gun and shot the running man.

CHAPTER 40

It took a moment to sink in. The deliberate aim, the single gunshot. Bohdan pitching forward with a deep grunt, blood spattering in front of him as the bullet passed through the shoulder blade and out of the front of his chest. He collapsed onto the grass with a sigh, then lay still. The silence was total. No one breathing, no bird singing, no traffic noise, not even wind in the grass. Nothing. Then Mouse screamed. Long, loud, high-pitched, it was a scream of utter terror.

As one, the men drew a breath.

'Be quiet, stupid whore.' Pavel turned to Mouse and slapped her face. It did the trick. Her mouth snapped shut, her hand flew up to her reddening cheek. 'He got what he deserved.'

Lenka pulled Mouse to her side, placing her aching arm around the smaller woman's shoulder. The men groaned.

'What have you done now?' Ray Fraser said, his voice shaking. 'What are we going to do with that? It's not going in my van.'

Fraser's whinging seemed to wake Kirill from a trance. He pushed the other men aside, dragged Fraser forward and shook him. 'You shut up,' he growled. 'Help us move him.'

'Not a fucking chance.' Fraser's fear was making him brave for once. 'I'm not touching him.'

A weak groan came from Bohdan. Mouse cried out again, Lenka pulled her tighter into her arms. The men returned their attention to the man on the grass.

'Not dead, then,' said Fraser. 'Not your best shot, eh?'

'If I want him dead, I'll make him dead. Now shut up and carry him to his bed. You, housekeeper.' Pavel turned to Lenka. 'Make breakfast. Do it quick. You, whore. You clean him up.'

'I'm not touching him,' said Fraser. 'I don't want anything else to do with this lot.'

Kirill grabbed Fraser's arm and dragged him to where Bohdan was lying. Kirill rolled the big man over, forced Fraser to take him by the shoulders. Bohdan was heavy. It took three of them to carry him into the caravan.

Lenka brought the first aid bag from the kitchen. 'Do your best,' she said. She shoved the bag into Mouse's hand. 'Get water from bathroom. Clean him up.'

Then she limped into the kitchen, pulling cereal packets, milk, bowls and mugs out onto the counter. She put the kettle on, threw tea bags into the large communal teapot ready for it to boil.

At the back of the work surface was a plastic box with basic medicines in it. Lenka helped herself to a strip of painkillers, gulping the whole lot down to ease her aches and pains. She took the box to the bathroom, washed her face, then looked at the damage. Cuts, bruises. The skin under both eyes had turned purple. There was a lump protruding from the top of her skull. Rubbing antiseptic cream on everything that she could bear to touch, Lenka grabbed a jumper and pulled it on over the ripped and shredded remnants of her clothes.

Led by Pavel, one by one the gang filed through the kitchen, choosing cereal, slopping on the milk and sugar. They found seats and ate in silence, as Lenka put bread in the toaster, laid out plates, tubs of margarine and jars of jam.

225

Hot water in the teapot made the lid rattle. The sound of her activity was the only real noise in the caravan. With a shaking arm, she began to pour out the tea, taking the first and weakest one for herself. She looked at Pavel, who was intent on shovelling cornflakes into his mouth. It all seemed so prosaic.

How can he do that? she thought. *Doesn't he care if Matus is dead? He just shot a man in cold blood and he's eating as if nothing happened.*

Lenka glanced out of the window. They must have dumped Bohdan because she could see Fraser gesticulating and backing away from Kirill. Fraser's shirt was covered in blood, his reedy voice beginning to rise in pitch and volume. As Kirill stepped towards him, Fraser turned and fled, running as fast as he could, past his van and down the track. Kirill shrugged and came into the kitchen.

'He'll be back.' He sneered, loading up his bowl with cereal. 'Needs his van.'

Placing toast on a big plate on the counter, feeding more bread slices into the machine, putting the kettle on again, Lenka kept busy. Still, the men didn't say anything. She looked out of the other window at the track. Fraser had slowed down but was still running. She sipped her tea and watched. Fraser reached the farmyard. For a moment, he stopped, bending over, hands on his knees. Then he strode up to the farmhouse door and began to hammer on it.

The pile of toast grew, the teapot was refilled. Lenka poured out another mug, tucked a packet of biscuits under her arm and went to the door.

'I'll see how they're getting on,' she said. Pavel looked up and nodded. Lenka limped out.

Bohdan lay on his side, his clothes soaked in blood. Mouse was trying to clean him up. Her hand was pushed under the shirt. Blood was seeping down her arm to the elbow, dripping onto the bed.

Lenka put the drinks and biscuits down. The room stank of warm blood. Rummaging in the first aid kit, she found a pair of scissors and slowly cut away the ruined shirt.

Mouse let go of the wound and helped manoeuvre Bohdan's arm until they had removed all the fabric. Fetching a bowl of water, Lenka cleaned the entry wound on his back. The man groaned and as she wiped, she could feel sections of the fractured shoulder blade moving under her fingers. She wiped the area with an antiseptic cloth, then moved on to the exit wound on his chest.

It was an impossible task. The flesh where the bullet had exited was ripped and shredded. Blood and muscle were caked into his chest hair, fragments of the shirt were embedded in the wound. Lenka surveyed the mess, realising that if she tried to cut away the hair or fabric, it would open the wound further. Left untouched, it would probably never heal.

'I don't know what we can do,' she said. 'We're not nurses. If we try to clean it, he might wake up.'

'If we leave him, then what?' Mouse surveyed the bleeding body of Bohdan and shrugged.

'Don't know, he's bleeding very much.'

'We could make him bleed some more,' said Mouse with a slow, evil, half-smile. She made a snipping motion with her fingers. 'Cut it off while he's knocked out. No more raping, no more sex.'

'You mean cut off his dick?' Lenka looked at Mouse in astonishment.

'Why not? He hurt me many times. He tried to rape you. Serve him right.'

'The other men would kill us,' said Lenka with conviction, although the idea did have its justice. She took a thick pad of cotton wool and fixed it over the gaping mess with some sticking plasters. They looked at their blood-caked hands and arms. 'There, that's all we can do.'

The sound of a car engine drew the two women to the window. Dixon was climbing out of the Range Rover, his clothes flapping open where he had rushed to get dressed. Seated in the passenger side, Ray Fraser made no effort to get out. Dixon slammed the door and stormed into the kitchen.

'You go and get clean.' Lenka nudged Mouse. The blood on their hands was congealing into a sticky mess.

'I'll miss the sport,' grumbled Mouse. She went to the bathroom anyway. Lenka retrieved her mug. Leaving bloody fingerprints on the handle, she sipped at the half-cold brew. She could hear Kirill and Dixon in the other caravan shouting at each other. There was a clatter of crockery as one of them thumped on the table. A quieter voice intervened, and the two men fell silent.

Pavel stepped outside to stand between the two caravans. Dixon and Kirill followed.

'Here is what will happen,' said Pavel in a level tone. He looked at Fraser in the Range Rover, who slithered down in his seat, trying to escape the gaze. 'You,' — Pavel pointed at the angry and out-of-breath Dixon — 'will find out where Matus is.'

Dixon began to bluster.

'Find him, even if he's dead. You,' — this to Kirill — 'round up the others, drive over to barns. We load the other container this morning.'

With a curt nod, Kirill went back inside the kitchen and began to issue orders. *So that's why he is getting them fed*, Lenka thought. *Their work isn't finished.*

Pavel walked to where Fraser sat in Dixon's vehicle. He opened the door and grabbed Fraser by the shirt, then dragged him out onto the grass.

'You,' said Pavel. He twisted Fraser's shirt into a knot under the quaking man's chin. 'Find your driver friend, make sure he is coming to pick up the containers. Then go to the barns and help clear things out.'

'What about him?' Dixon pointed at the caravan where Bohdan lay. 'Do I take him to the hospital?'

'No.' Pavel glanced at Lenka, standing at the window. 'The girls keep him here. He's not awake anyway.'

'Then what?' Dixon was scrolling on his mobile looking for information. 'You have to clear out. The police could be here any time.'

'After we clear the barns, Kirill will take the men to the ferry in the minibus.' Pavel had it all worked out.

'And the women?'

'I'll sort them out. Bohdan too.'

Horrified, Lenka stepped back from the window. Did he mean to abandon them there with the wounded man? Or send them in the minibus with the men? Or was he going to shoot them, too? After all, they were witnesses and Pavel was capable of anything.

CHAPTER 41

There were no days off in a murder investigation, at least not in Norfolk. Sara rose early, showered and dressed and went into the kitchen. Sharing her secret had been cathartic, and for the first time since her move, she'd managed to get some sleep. Even so, she was still exhausted and unable to decide what to do for the best. She wanted to help bring her father's killer to justice but not if her involvement jeopardised a conviction. She also needed to keep her job and patch things up with her mother, not least for Javed's sake. So many secrets, so many lies. She couldn't see a path through them that didn't lead to one disaster or another.

Javed was snoring on the sofa in his sleeping bag. Sara had some cereal and made them both a cup of tea. She left his drink on the coffee table, where it would almost certainly go cold.

The team gathered in the office. Crane's car was in the lab. The theft reports were in some kind of order. Graham Dack's mention of Eastern European accents might be of help. Best of all, Dack's wife had taken a photo of the van that had loitered outside their house.

'You'll never guess who it belongs to,' said Edwards. 'Our old friend, Ray Fraser. Doesn't prove it was part of the robbery. It does mean we need to find and interview him urgently.'

'There are dozens of these gangs in the region,' said Bowen.

'Did you get anywhere with the register?' Edwards asked Ellie.

'Sorry, no. They won't give out the full list without authorisation, and there's no one in until tomorrow morning.'

'Helpful civil servants, as usual. Something made Crane think they were local,' said Edwards. 'Could the connection be Ray Fraser? The neighbour says he strongly disliked him. They had a fight at the pub and Fraser's blood is in Crane's cottage. How did that get there? We have a lot of questions for Mr Fraser.'

'What about the information on the other memory stick?' asked Ellie.

'Should be with us this morning,' replied Edwards. 'That may well be the key. The car might give us something too. Any other suggestions?'

'Should I have another word with Mrs Richardson?' Sara asked. 'She's very clued up about the people in the area, and Crane was found on her land. And I think she was trying to tell me something else yesterday.'

'Will she be well enough?'

'We can go and find out.'

'Take Ellie with you,' said Edwards. 'It might seem more friendly with you two. Mike and I will go back to Happisburgh, see if we can find Fraser at home. Let me know how you get on.'

'Two women going to interview another woman,' said Sara to Ellie, as they went out to the car park. 'The gentle touch?'

'You were the one to find her, and probably saved her life. Besides, she's your witness, really.'

Agnes was sitting up in bed eating bacon and eggs when they found her. She looked well, apart from the drips and tubes around the bed.

'I'm so glad to see you,' Agnes said. She was eating her breakfast with enthusiasm. 'Do sit down.'

'How are you this morning?' asked Sara.

'I'm feeling well, thanks. Thought the noise would keep me awake. Not at all, and I woke up hungry as anything.'

'What does the doctor say?'

'Not a heart attack, thank God. Probably concussion from when I got driven off the road by that van. I intend to go home this morning.'

'If they'll let you.' Sara smiled, though she suspected that if Agnes meant to go home, there wasn't much the medical staff would be able to do to dissuade her. 'Do you feel up to a chat?'

'If you hadn't come, I was going to ring you anyway.' Agnes put down her breakfast things and pushed her table aside.

'Agnes, did you know a man called Adam Crane?' It felt odd to Sara to be talking about her father so objectively.

'Adam Crane? Yes, I met him a couple of times at farming events. Worked for the NFU Mutual, didn't he?'

'Yes, that's right. Did Crane ever speak to you about thefts in the area?'

'No, he didn't.' Agnes became impatient. 'I don't see what Mr Crane has to do with any of this. I want to know what we are going to do about these girls.'

'What girls? You said the same thing yesterday, but I thought it was because you were ill.'

'This is all to do with that bloody Des Dixon.' Agnes frowned. 'Trying to bully me out of my land, foisting those men on me at the barn. Well, Mark is here now, so there'll be no more of that nonsense.'

'Your son?'

'Yes. I have you to thank for that, don't I? He got here late yesterday. It's all cleared up. He thought I didn't know he was gay.'

'Slow down, Mrs Richardson,' said Sara. 'I'm getting confused. What has your son's sexuality got to do with Des Dixon?'

'Never mind about Mark. He's here now, and he'll stop Dixon from bullying me, that's all. It's the other stuff.'

'One thing at a time. Let's start with Dixon and his bullying.'

The story poured from Agnes in much the same way Sara's had to Javed the night before. How Dixon was trying to buy her land, the late evening visits, the suggestions about her being all alone. 'Ha! Well, I said Mark would come back, and he has.' Agnes smiled. 'It is difficult on your own, I couldn't have managed without Frank. Then there is this gang.'

'What gang?' Ellie asked.

'Crop pickers. They live in some old caravans on Dixon's place. Do up old cars in their spare time. In my barns, no less.'

'Old cars?'

'That's how Dixon described it to me. Said they wanted to make a bit extra on the side and could they use my barn for the summer. Like a fool, I said yes. That's not what I saw when I went up there on Monday. Crates everywhere, quad bikes, Defenders, engines, you name it. That Polish man shooed me out. It's the girl I'm worried about.'

'What girl?' asked Sara.

'Might be two of them. Found her at the caravans — she appeared to be cooking and cleaning. She was terrified. Didn't want to be caught talking to me. And I'm sure I heard another one. Poor thing was shouting to be let out. I got hustled away after that.'

'These caravans, are they down a dirt track behind Dixon's farmhouse?'

'Yes, they're the ones.'

Sara sat still for a moment, trying to recall the first day of her new job, the visit she made with DI Edwards to talk to Dixon about the pub fight. It had to be the same caravans, and she felt sure she'd seen a young woman at the time.

'Can you tell me about the van that drove you off the road?'

'It came out of the gate that leads to Jack's bit of scrub-land, where we found the missing car. Came out like a bloody rocket, that's why I banged my head.'

'I don't suppose you got the registration number?'

'Sorry.' Agnes drained her mug of tea. 'I was too busy trying to control my Landie.'

'Do you remember anything about it?' asked Ellie.

'It was white,' said Agnes. 'One of those second-hand Vivaros probably. There's a lot of them around here.'

'Why's that?'

'Fleet vehicle for the local water company. They replace them every few years. There's a chap out at Potter does them up. Good workhorses, lots of local small businesses have them.'

Sara looked at Ellie, who nodded in agreement. Ray Fraser's van was a white Vivaro. 'Thank you for all your help, Mrs Richardson.' Sara stood up to leave.

'You know how to find me.'

They headed back to the car. 'I swear that woman is more on the ball than we are,' said Sara. She tried to sort the evidence in her mind, but her tired brain was refusing to cooperate. It made her grind her teeth in frustration.

'It certainly looks to revolve around those two farms,' Ellie said. 'Ray Fraser must be involved somehow.'

'Dixon too, I bet. Have we stumbled on the answer to both crimes? Is this why Dad thought the gang was in this area?'

'Dad?' asked Ellie. 'What's your dad got to do with this? Who is he?'

CHAPTER 42

After she had cleaned herself of Bohdan's blood, Lenka returned to the kitchen and began to clear up. The men gathered outside, smoking and grumbling about the extra work. Dixon drove back to the farm. Fraser stood by his van using his mobile. She had only got as far as stacking the dirty pots on the kitchen counter when Pavel appeared from his room.

'You.' He pointed at Lenka. 'Leave that. Get over to the other caravan.'

'I'll get some food,' she said. She rapidly loaded cold toast, margarine and jam pots onto a tray.

'Hurry.' Pavel pushed Lenka out of the door in front of him. 'Everyone must hurry.'

She rushed to the other caravan, Pavel close on her heels. Mouse was sitting on her bed. Lenka carried the tray into the bedroom.

Bohdan's room was directly opposite. Pavel opened the door and went in to check on the injured man. Lenka could see that Bohdan had rolled onto his front. If he had been conscious, it would have been unbearably painful. The sheet underneath him was soaked in blood. Pavel made no attempt to touch the other man. Instead, he grunted in satisfaction and backed out of the room. Before Lenka could stop him, he slammed the door to Mouse's room and locked it. Now they were both trapped.

'I'm sorry,' he said. 'I've got to go. I need time.'

Mouse stared at Lenka. Her face was blank, her breathing shallow as if all the life and resilience had drained out of her.

'Anya?' Lenka asked. The use of Mouse's real name brought no response. Lenka sat on the bed beside her. 'Look, I brought food.'

She heard the minibus start up outside, then the vehicle rattling away down the cart track to the farmhouse. Ray Fraser's van followed it.

'Listen to me.' Lenka shook Mouse. 'We don't have much time. Pavel is making them load up and ship all the stuff they stole. They will only be gone a couple of hours. I don't want to be here when they get back.'

'He will shoot us,' came the trembling reply. 'We're no more use. We've seen things.'

'I think that too.' Lenka went to the tray and loaded some cold toast, handing the jammy slice to Mouse. 'Eat. We may not get a chance later. Then we go.'

'How?' Mouse took the proffered slice and nibbled at the edge. Lenka loaded a slice for herself and lifted up her prize. Hidden under the breakfast debris was a large kitchen knife.

'I brought it for insurance. We can use it to break off the lock. Eat up, get some clothes on.'

They gobbled their food while Mouse pulled on trousers and trainers. Mouse threw the rest of her clothes, a meagre selection, onto the bed for Lenka to choose from. They didn't fit, the jeans were too short, the tops too tight, the shoes pinched her feet. She pulled them on anyway. Time was too precious.

Lenka picked up the knife. The lock was firmly wrapped around the key barrel. For a desperate minute, she hacked away at the Formica around the lock, puncturing tiny holes in the fabric of the door. They were making a lot of noise but little progress.

'You got anything heavy?' Lenka asked, doubting that the reply would be helpful. Mouse burrowed under the bed and emerged triumphantly with a log that must originally have been intended for the firepit.

'I took it a couple of days ago. You didn't see.'

'Why?'

'When we leave, I was going to hit Bohdan with it. Pavel saved me the bother.'

Lenka jammed the kitchen knife between the door and the lock. Using the log as a hammer, she swung at it with all her might. It took three huge blows before the door cracked, and the lock began to give way. Two more blows separated the key barrel from the door panel, a final couple of thumps smashed the lock onto the floor. Lenka pushed open the door, Mouse crowding behind her.

Blocking out the light from the opposite room, the unsteady figure of Bohdan leaned against the doorframe to his room. The noise must have woken him. Blood from his heaving chest dripped onto his feet. Moving had opened his wound — it was bleeding freely again. His face contorted in pain. His eyes radiated pure evil. His right arm hung uselessly, but he stretched his left hand out towards the petrified Lenka.

'Got you at last.' He closed the bloodied hand around her throat.

A scream of rage came from behind her. Mouse slammed her whole body into Lenka's back. The force sent Lenka crashing forward into Bohdan. With a howl of pain, the injured man fell backwards onto the floor of his room and released his grip. Lenka struggled to rise, rolling to her knees. Mouse flashed past her, the kitchen knife raised above her head.

'Bastard! Bastard! Bastard!' She matched each cry with a stab.

As she raised the knife for the fourth time, Lenka caught her arm. 'Stop,' she begged. 'Just stop.'

Mouse dropped the blade. The pair climbed up to survey the damage. Bohdan was on his back, blood bubbling from his mouth. The bullet wound was in the shoulder. The new stab wounds were in his chest. They spurted blood rhythmically — perhaps Mouse had severed an artery. His breathing sounded tortured. As they watched, the breathing slowed, then stopped with a sigh. More blood ran down his face. Bohdan's eyes became as still as glass.

'He's dead, isn't he?' asked Mouse.

'I fucking well hope so,' replied Lenka. She looked at her clothes, then at Mouse. 'Come on. We need to clean up and get out of here.'

Abandoning everything else, they ran round to Lenka's room and washed as quickly as they could, putting on the first practical clothes they found. Within a couple of minutes, they were standing on the grass between the caravans.

Lenka surveyed their ill-fitting outfits. 'Good,' she said. 'Nothing too colourful.'

'Now what?' Mouse pointed at Dixon's farmhouse. 'We can't go that way. He might come back.'

'We'll go to the busybody lady,' said Lenka. 'She knows we are here. I think that's why she came here the other night. But we have to go past those barns.'

'Where the men are working? Fucking hell, I don't want to do that.'

'That's the only place I think we can get help,' Lenka insisted. 'Better than walking on the road.'

She tugged the reluctant Mouse onto the field path, and they set off up the hill. The wheat in the field was now fully ripe, its harvest overdue. When they neared the top, Lenka made Mouse wait, while she crouched behind the tall wheat to look down at the barns.

There were two containers. One had its doors open. The men were loading the solar panels into it and someone, probably Pavel, was directing them to stack it. Fraser's white van stood in the entrance to the yard. He was loading equipment from the barn into the back of it.

Lenka waved to Mouse. 'Come on, try to stay low.' It took longer that way, but the wheat kept them hidden from view until they got to the hedge lining the field of cows. Crossing the stile, they worked their way around the edge. The cows looked up, uninterested.

Heart pounding, Lenka climbed over the second stile at the rear of the barns. The grass at the side of the path was unkempt and long, dry and brittle. She ran the few steps to the first barn, pinning her back against the warm bricks. In the yard, she could hear the men working, raised voices calling for instructions, the clanging of the panels being stacked in the metal container. She turned and signalled to Mouse.

The tiny woman ran to join Lenka and settled against the wall. Her breathing was heavy, and she spread her hands as if to say, 'Now what?' Lenka indicated with her head, and the pair inched along the barn wall until they reached the gap between the barns. She could only hope that the gang would be too busy to notice them. She peered around the edge of the barn, and was relieved to see that one of the containers was blocking the path from view. She took a deep breath and dashed across the gap to the far barn, threw herself against the second wall, and looked back.

Mouse appeared to be pinned to the wall of the first barn. Her face turned up to the sky, she was muttering. If it was a prayer, the answer came immediately. Down the lane thundered Dixon's Range Rover. They saw the shape of it through the hedge they were aiming towards. It pulled up at the entrance to the yard. The engine shut off and the farmer climbed out.

'Fraser, you should have gone by now,' yelled Dixon. The men stopped working. 'Bugger off home, Ray. Pavel, I want a word with you.'

Pavel shouted at the men, who resumed their packing. Lenka looked at Mouse again. The other woman nodded, peered around the wall to check it was clear, then stumbled across the gap as quickly as she could. They began to edge along the second wall, heading for the lane. Lenka pointed at the long grass behind the hedge, where she had hidden before. The doors of Fraser's van slammed shut. They heard the engine start, and the van turned into the lane away from them.

Lenka made it to the end of the barn, ran the few steps across the path and squirmed under the cover. Lying on her side, she parted a few strands of the dry grass to keep on an eye on the other woman.

Mouse waited for her to settle, but she waited too long. They both heard the voices at the same time. Pavel and Dixon were deep in conversation, their words echoing off the brick walls as they came down the gap. With a loud gasp, Mouse threw herself down in the grass at the end of the barn.

'He's in the hospital,' Dixon was saying as they came out at the path. He looked up and down, then turning to the far barn wall, he unzipped his flies and began to urinate against the bricks. Lenka prayed that Mouse was far enough away, well enough hidden and would lie still.

'You find out how he is?' asked Pavel.

'Not good.' Dixon was looking down, concentrating on not splashing his boots. 'He has head injuries, a broken finger, broken ribs, broken nose.'

'He's not dead?'

Lenka sucked in a ragged breath. They must be talking about Matus.

'Not yet. Unconscious, but stable, they said. He's in intensive care. Best place. Bohdan did a thorough job on him.'

'Bastard. I should have killed him, not winged him.'

'Either way, he's a bloody big problem now.'

'Leave him, he'll bleed out,' Pavel said. 'No more problem.'

'Except what to do with the fucking body.'

'Ooh, ladies, look away.' A male voice sounded from the direction of the cow's field. Dixon looked up, shook his member and zipped up his flies. Lenka shifted her gaze back to the field stile.

A short queue of middle-aged men and women had formed by the stile, all in walking boots, some carrying rucksacks. The leading walker had a map in some sort of plastic carrier on a string round his neck. It was his voice they'd heard. Laughing and chatting, the group climbed over one by one, then milled around waiting for one another.

Dixon turned his back on the ramblers. Pushing Pavel back up the gap between the barns, the pair went back to where the men were still loading. The group of walkers passed Lenka, chatting cheerfully about their proposed lunch stop. With offers of assistance to the ladies, they climbed noisily into the lane. The leader checked his map, called out, 'This way,' and the party set off up the lane in the direction of Agnes's farmhouse.

Lenka checked the barns again, then, using all her courage, stood up from her shelter. She trotted over to Mouse, pulled her out of the grass and pointed at the walkers.

'Quick,' she mouthed. The two scrambled into the lane, moving swiftly to catch up with the group. An elderly couple turned to look at them and the man smiled as they approached.

'Morning,' he said. 'Nice day for a walk. You want to join us?'

'Just going home.' Lenka nodded. 'Up there.'

She pointed up the lane, slotting herself and Mouse in front of the couple, who were walking side by side. The group were more amblers than ramblers and progress was frustratingly slow.

'Is everything all right?' asked the woman, eyeing Lenka's cuts and bruises.

'Bit of an accident,' Lenka replied. 'Yesterday. I'm okay.'

'Lovely area to live. You're very lucky,' said the woman. 'We're going to the Roses for lunch. Is it nice?'

'Oh yes, very good,' said Lenka, although she had no idea what the woman was talking about. As they came to the farmhouse, a lorry drove along the lane towards the barns. The group paused to let it go past, Lenka and Mouse huddled in the middle. The walkers began to move on and Lenka whispered to Mouse to head up the drive.

'Thank you,' she said to the couple. 'We're home now.'

The couple set off to catch up with the rest of the group. Scurrying down the drive, Lenka heard them talking.

'What was that all about?' asked the woman.

'Who knows,' the man replied. 'I hope that girl's going to get some help.'

Lenka urged Mouse around the back of the house. Agnes's battered Defender stood in the yard. The house looked empty. There was no reply to her knock at the kitchen door. She rattled the handle, but it was locked. Mouse sank onto the doorstep in exhaustion.

'We can't sit out here,' said Lenka. 'Help me.'

They checked each of the outbuildings' doors without success, until they reached the largest one. Set into the main door was a smaller one. She twisted the handle. It opened.

The two women stumbled inside and pulled the door shut behind them. In the gloom they could make out a tractor. Its bonnet was up. Someone had evidently been working on the engine. As their eyes adjusted to the gloom, they made out junk stacked around the sides of the space. A pile of machinery parts lay on a long workbench that had a large space underneath. Behind the tractor was another, smaller vehicle covered in a tarpaulin. Lenka lifted it to reveal a quad bike underneath.

She wasn't interested in the bike. They wouldn't be able to get it past the tractor in any case. They would have to wait.

'Any sacks?' she whispered. Hunting in the rubbish, Mouse found some sacks and offcuts of foam, while Lenka removed the bike's cover. Piling the soft stuff onto the floor, the two climbed under the workbench. Pulling the stinky tarpaulin over themselves, they sank back, wrapped in each other's arms. Lenka could feel sleep sweeping over her. Mouse quietly began to cry.

CHAPTER 43

'Adam Crane's your father?' Ellie asked. Sara's fingers couldn't manage the seat belt buckle.

'I've only just found out,' she said.

'When are you going to tell the DI?'

'Soon.' Sara tried to take Ellie's hand, but she snatched it away. 'Please, let me do it. Don't tell him yourself.'

'Why on earth should I keep this quiet? You stole my job.'

'That was hardly my intention. How was I to know what politics were going on up here? The job was advertised, I applied. That's all there was to it.'

'Take yourself off the case.' Ellie powered the car up the bypass slip road. 'You're jeopardising the whole thing. Get your seat belt on, for God's sake.'

'I was going to tell the DI in the morning. It was just such a shock when I realised. Dr Taylor told me about the DNA results on Friday. I just needed a bit of time to sort my head out.'

Ellie concentrated on the road until they turned off the dual carriageway. Sara sat in silence, chewing her lip. They joined the slow-moving queue to cross the bridge in Wroxham. Hundreds of cars jammed with families were heading to the coast in front of them.

'You realise that if we make arrests, the prosecution could have a field day?' Ellie asked. 'Why not just go home?'

'I need to find his killer myself.'

'You don't trust us to do our jobs?'

'I do trust you,' said Sara. Her anger rose, her emotions burst through all restraints, and her voice rattled out of control. 'But could you blame me if I didn't? All I've had since I arrived is racism, sexism and jealousy, not to mention Bowen hazing me. I've seen more mistakes in a week than I would expect to happen in a year. Items missed at the cottage, computer information that hasn't been unlocked, those clowns from the local nick who hadn't bothered to report finding Crane's car. I've been looking for my father for years. When I find him, he's dead. Murdered. You can't begin to imagine how I feel.'

Sara began to sob. She scrabbled in her pocket and pulled out a packet of tissues. As her tears subsided, she spoke again. 'The locals treat me like some circus freak. I gave up my career in London to join a team who don't want me. That includes the boss, by the way. He wanted you to have the bloody job. I'm a stranger to this place and not one of my colleagues has welcomed me. I've fallen out with my family to move here, though you wouldn't know that. All to find a man I never knew, because he abandoned my mum and me when I was two years old. When Taylor told me, I was stunned. I didn't know what to do, or how to do it because I can't afford to lose this job or I'll have nothing left.' Sara's voice trailed away. She slumped back in her seat.

Ellie crawled along with the rest of the queue. She seemed deep in thought. They had drifted past homes, the local library and then the boatyard by the bridge before she spoke again. 'You're right. I can't begin to know how you feel. Edwards really wanted me to have the job?'

'Yes.'

'ACC Miller made the decision, then?'

'I assume so.'

'He was probably trying to protect you. It won't be easy for you, all this casual racism stuff that has resurfaced here.'

'I'd noticed. I think Edwards was trying to keep his team together.'

'That too.'

'All this personal stuff.' Ellie hesitated. They drove over the bridge to stop yet again at some pedestrian lights on the other side. 'That's really tough.'

'Incredibly.'

'It's not that we don't want you. It was a shock. We don't know you as a person.'

'You haven't tried.'

'I suppose that's true.' The lights changed, and they headed out of Wroxham. Ellie glanced at Sara and smiled. 'Okay.'

'Okay to what?'

'I won't say anything to Edwards, so long as you promise to tell him tomorrow.'

'I promise. Whatever happens today.'

They found Edwards and Bowen parked at the same field gate that Bowen and Sara had used the day before. There was still no sign of Fraser. Edwards, seething with impatience, desperate for action, listened as Ellie told them what Agnes had said. Sara leaned exhaustedly on the field gate.

It dawned on her that the countryside was anything but quiet. Birds with their myriad different chirps and squawks, lawnmowers cutting lawns before the day became too hot, the sound of a distant vehicle, children's voices calling eagerly for holiday treats . . . and wasn't that the sea?

'We'll need a search warrant, sir,' Bowen was saying. 'Can't see Dixon letting us in there without one.'

'No, of course he won't,' Edwards said. 'I'm not sure we have enough evidence to get one signed off. What about Mrs Richardson? Do you think she'd let us into her barns without one?'

'I think she would, sir. She's still at the hospital, won't be home until later.'

'Right.' Edwards turned away in frustration as his mobile rang.

'DI Edwards.' Putting the call on speaker, he motioned for the team to gather round. 'What have you got for me?'

'We've got into the memory stick. I've sent you all the contents,' said the caller. 'Some of it is useless. The video stuff is especially poor quality. There's an interesting spreadsheet, comparing what appears to be bookings for a crop picking gang with agricultural thefts. Starts two years ago with the activity increasing each season. There's quite a few written reports too. I hope all that helps.'

'I can't wait to start going through it.' Edwards smiled at Ellie and Sara as he ended the call. 'Guess where you're going. Find enough of a link to get us a warrant for Dixon's place.'

'Sir,' they said in unison. They didn't reach the car.

The vehicle Sara had thought she'd heard suddenly drew nearer and a white van turned into the entrance to Ray Fraser's bungalow. Bowen was in the drive seconds behind Fraser, so close that at first, the driver didn't notice them. Ellie parked the other car across the entrance, ensuring that the van couldn't leave again. Fraser had climbed out of the driver's door before realising he had company.

'Mr Fraser,' DI Edwards shouted as he scrambled out of his car. 'A word, if you please.'

At the sound of Edwards's voice, Fraser looked up in horror. His face was grey with fatigue, his hands were black with grease and oil, the front of his shirt covered in blood. He dropped his van keys, reached behind him to grab a large spanner from the pocket in the van door, brandished it, then changed his mind and set off in a ragged run across the lawn. Bowen was still climbing out of the driver's seat, Ellie marooned in the lane. It was down to Edwards and Sara. Edwards was quick to run, Sara quicker, adrenaline charging over her exhaustion. Fraser ran at an angle across the grass, heading for a small gate in the hedge on the far side of the garden.

Running at full stretch, she cut across Fraser's route, closing the gap between them. Beyond the hedge, she could hear Ellie pounding along the road in the same direction. Fraser almost got to the gate but baulked when he saw Ellie arrive at the roadside. A large shed shut off escape on the other side. Sara closed off the garden behind him, Edwards only a few strides behind her.

'Keep away,' Fraser shouted, spinning on the spot, brandishing the heavy spanner. 'Leave me alone. I haven't done anything.'

'We only want a talk, Mr Fraser,' said Sara. She held up her hands. 'Why don't you put the weapon down.'

'Weapon? I know you lot, you buggers might do anything.'

Then he threw the spanner straight at Sara. She hit the grass and it whistled over her head as Edwards streaked past her to rugby tackle Fraser to the ground. Wrestling her way through the gate, Ellie cuffed the writhing Fraser. Puffing unhealthily, Bowen reached Sara, skidding down beside her on the lawn.

'My God. You all right?' he asked. Sara levered herself up onto her elbow and surveyed the panting DC.

'In better shape than you, apparently,' she said, and added a smile. 'He missed me by a mile. I'm fine. Now let's see why Mr Fraser is covered in blood.'

Edwards and Ellie had Fraser on his feet. Dead grass clung to his shirt front and hair. He looked defeated and sullen. Bowen took great delight in escorting their prisoner back to the car.

'Think we'll have those few words in an interview room, Mr Fraser,' he said, putting the regulation hand on top of Fraser's head to get him into the back seat. Edwards brushed the dry grass and dust from his clothes before he got into the front seat next to Bowen.

'Look over the van carefully,' he said. 'I'll call for a SOCO team. We are keeping them busy, aren't we?'

As they drove away, Ellie brought the other car into the drive. It might be a long wait. The two of them donned gloves, Sara picked up the keys and opened the back of the van. It was covered in grease and dirt, with what looked like giant rubber skid marks on the side panels. Looking up, Sara saw a pattern of bloody handprints on the underside of the roof.

'You better look at this,' she heard Ellie call from the driver's cab. 'What's the betting these belong to Crane?'

Stuffed into the map pocket of the passenger door were a rather battered laptop and a mobile phone with a broken screen.

CHAPTER 44

The CSI team assembled yet another crime scene. The exclusion tape was up, their vans blocking the view to the road, the protective suits in place. The photographer got to work first.

Sara showed the laptop and mobile to the SOCO in charge. 'Can I take these two with me?' resting on them. A cup of stale tea stood untouched at his elbow. From where they stood behind the viewing mirror, neither Sara nor Ellie could tell if he was asleep. A uniform officer stood near the door, his eyes glazed with boredom. They had been waiting for the duty solicitor for over an hour.

'I'm going to have a look at those computer files,' said Ellie. 'You coming?'

The laptop was out on one of the spare desks in the office. A computer specialist from forensics had come to start it up. The password was different from the one on the locked memory stick. The contents proved to be the same. The printer began to rattle off the spreadsheet and some of the reports. The forensics man moved on to the mobile phone.

'It's got a number access code,' he said. 'Got any suggestions? It's usually significant birthdays or anniversaries.'

Sara retrieved Crane's personnel file from Edwards's office and pulled up a chair next to the specialist. Starting at the front, they tried everything they could find — Crane's birthday, his parents' birthdays, his start dates at the Met and Norfolk, his retirement date. Nothing worked. Sara wrote six numbers on a Post-it note and handed it over. The phone unlocked. Crane had used her birthday.

'Great guess.' The forensics man looked quizzically at Sara. When she didn't enlighten him, he placed the note in the evidence bag. 'Let's see who he'd been in contact with.'

Everyone had been occupied with something, too busy to notice. Sara carried the personnel file back to her desk.

Crane had been in the force for over twenty-five years. The time he had been absent from her life began to fill. Photographs charted his ageing, reports listed annual reviews and health checks. It was a good, solid career until his heart attack, though no partners or girlfriends were ever listed. The 'next of kin' and 'in case of emergency' boxes remained resolutely empty. Was Crane so hurt by her mother that he'd never allowed another woman into his life? If so, she felt sorry for him. Her mother had moved on eventually. Until now. She thought of Javed asleep on her sofa and sighed. She became so absorbed that a hand reaching across to shut the file made her rattle back in her chair. Ellie laid some printed spreadsheets on top of the file, nodding her head briefly at Edwards, who was coming out of his office.

'Hirst, you're with me. Duty solicitor has arrived at last. Fetch them to the interview room.'

The solicitor was a woman in a businesslike grey skirt suit, her hair scraped back untidily into a ponytail. Looking flustered, she scrabbled through her briefcase for a notepad and pen as Sara escorted her upstairs. When the three of them entered the room, Fraser still had his head on his arms. He looked up with a yawn.

'Keeping you up, are we?' asked Edwards. 'Late night?'

Fraser said nothing. The duty solicitor sat down next to him and introduced herself as Mrs Chapman, while Edwards turned on the recorder and pronounced the formal introductions.

'So, Mr Fraser.' Edwards settled into his chair. 'Let's get started. Can you explain to me why your clothes are covered in blood?'

'No comment.'

'Why are you so tired? Where were you last night?'

'No comment.'

'What made you run when we tried to speak with you at your house?'

'No comment.'

'What's your association with Desmond Dixon of Ridlington Manor Farm?'

'No comment.'

'This is going to get very tedious, Ray.'

'No—' Fraser began. Edwards slammed both his palms on the table and pushed himself upright. For a moment, Sara wasn't sure what he intended. Fraser leaned back in his chair, equally unsure. Mrs Chapman looked up in surprise.

'Well, if you don't want to help us with our enquiries,' Edwards said, 'then I'll have to see what charges can be brought. Let's try one more. Did you know Adam Crane?'

'You know I do.'

'We know about the fight at the Hall House pub. You know this is a murder investigation?'

'Saw it on the telly.'

'So, tell me, Fraser, why are there traces of your blood in Adam Crane's cottage?'

Fraser turned white. He looked at the solicitor, who shook her head.

'No comment.'

'We are applying for a warrant to search your premises,' said Edwards. He turned to leave the room. 'While we await the outcome of the search, you'll be taken down to the holding cells. Sorry to disturb your Sunday, Mrs Chapman, but it looks like we won't be needing your services today after all.'

'Ok, ok,' Fraser said. 'Can I have a cup of tea first?'

At a nod from Edwards, the uniform officer left to find the drink. Edwards sat down again and Sara settled back to listen. Mrs Chapman furiously scribbled notes as Fraser began to speak.

'I went to the concert last night,' Fraser began.

'Which one?'

'"North Walsham Rocks,"' said Fraser. 'I was up late, that's why I'm tired. Drank quite a bit, so I parked up in a lay-by to sleep it off. I'm not sure why I've got blood down my shirt — it might be mine.'

'Were you in a fight?'

'Don't remember. I was a bit out of it. That's why I parked up. When I woke up, it was morning, so I went home. You lot were bloody waiting for me. Of course I ran.'

'We only wanted a quiet word.'

'No such thing with coppers. You know me, I've got form.' He smiled as if this were something to be proud of. Mrs Chapman leaned over and spoke to him in a low voice.

'I can enlighten you, Mrs Chapman,' Edwards said. The uniform officer came back with a cup of tea, which he placed in front of Fraser before returning to his station by the door. 'Our friend here has a bit of a record. Not least, assaulting a police officer.'

'Got to keep our country safe from people like you.' Fraser turned to Sara, not bothering to conceal his anger.

'People from London, you mean?' asked Sara.

'No,' replied Fraser. 'Immigrants.'

Mrs Chapman whispered urgently to Fraser, who shuffled in his chair. He uttered a grudging, 'Sorry.'

'What's your connection to Des Dixon?' Edwards asked.

'I do a few jobs for him, run stuff around. Man with a van and all that.'

'What I don't understand, Ray, is why you would work with Dixon when you feel the way you do. After all, he has migrant workers living on his farm. Surely you object to that?'

'I need the work,' Fraser muttered.

There was a knock at the door. Bowen stuck his head inside.

252

'A word, guv.' Edwards suspended the interview, and he and Sara went into the corridor. Bowen was shifting uneasily from foot to foot. 'I've been checking for connections. An incident came up last night after the gig in North Walsham. Only just been logged.'

'Well?'

'There was a big fight, in one of the side roads near the park where the concert took place. Occupant of one of the houses called us. Said it was vicious. The nearest to respond were a couple of the traffic guys. They'd been clearing the car park, doing crowd control stuff. The witness said that it looked like a young couple were being attacked by a big guy and his mate. There was a white van. Said the big fella beat up the young man, while the other one dragged the young woman off and forced her into the back of the van.'

'Did he get the van plates?'

'No, but traffic did. They came round the corner, all sirens blazing.' Bowen pulled a sour face to show he thought that traffic were overfond of running on sirens. 'They saw the van drive off. The victim was lying unconscious in the road — they had to help him first. Ellie's ringing the hospital now.'

'And the number plate?'

'Ray Fraser.'

CHAPTER 45

DI Edwards gave Bowen some instructions, nodded to Sara, and the two of them went back into the interview room. He started up the recorder.

'Mr Fraser,' he began. His tone had suddenly become formal. 'I want you to tell me again about the concert last night. Don't leave out any details.'

Fraser shifted uneasily, aware of new tension in the room. He looked at the duty solicitor, who turned her gaze to the notepad on her lap. Fraser began uncertainly to repeat his former story. Edwards's gaze was unflinching. After a few words, Fraser's voice petered out.

'The trouble is, Mr Fraser,' said Edwards, 'that we have a witness who places your vehicle in the street by the park in North Walsham at about twelve thirty last night.'

'How do you know it was my van? Lots of white vans around here.'

'A police officer took note of the number plate.' Edwards leaned forward, looking intently at Fraser. 'It's your registration.'

'I already said I was at the gig.'

'Indeed. Our witness also saw you with another man. Who was that?'

'Must be mistaken.'

'What about the young couple?'

Fraser jolted upright in his chair. His mouth opened and closed a couple of times before he said, 'No comment.'

'Who was the woman? What did you do with her?'

'Don't know what you're on about.'

'We're bringing your van into the forensic garage. Whose blood is in the van, Mr Fraser? What is it doing there?'

'No comment.' Fraser folded his arms. 'I'm not saying anything else.'

Edwards rose to leave. 'DS Hirst, take Mr Fraser down to the holding cells while we complete the van and house search and take further statements. Mrs Chapman, you can expect formal charges tomorrow morning.'

Sara left Fraser in the cell, still dressed in his white paper suit. Shivering with cold, he picked up the blue blanket, wrapped himself up in it, lay on the plastic mattress and yawned. Leaving instruction for a meal to be brought, she went back up to the office.

'I've sent Ellie to wait at the hospital with this victim,' said Edwards. 'Mike's gone to get the search warrant for Fraser's place signed off. SOCOs are waiting at the property to get started inside the bungalow and outbuildings. I bet it will be an absolute Aladdin's cave. I want you to download a photo of Fraser, there should be one on file. Then I think we'll pay a visit to our witness in North Walsham and see what he can tell us.'

'Anything else, sir?' Sara fired up her computer to find the photo. Waiting for the picture of Fraser to emerge from the printer, she went over her conversation with Agnes in the hospital that morning. Sara turned to the DI. 'Sir, I think we should speak to Agnes Richardson again. This stuff she keeps going on about — a young woman, possibly two women. She thinks Des Dixon is keeping them in those caravans on his farm. With that crop picking team. If Fraser works for Dixon, surely that might be the connection we are looking for? Crane told the NFU manager he thought it was a gang in North Norfolk. It all fits.'

'You might well be right,' said Edwards. 'Come on. Let's see what she can tell us. Hopefully, it will give us enough to get a search warrant.'

Grabbing the still-damp picture and her mobile, Sara hurried downstairs after her boss. The main road wasn't busy, and they were soon turning off the lane into the drive-way of Agnes Richardson's farm. A classy green Volvo SUV was parked in the yard next to the Defender that Sara recog-nised as belonging to Agnes. Frank must have seen them pull up. He opened the door to let them in.

A family party, or what Sara at first assumed it to be, were assembled in the kitchen around the table. Agnes was fussing around making tea, and a handsome, tall man of about Sara's age was preparing sandwiches. Two bedraggled young women sat at the table. Both were covered in dirt and dressed in torn, ill-fitting clothes. There were scratches on their arms, tear stains streaked their faces. One had longish dark hair which was tangled into knots by twigs. The other had matted, lank blonde strands, dark with oily patches and brown stains. Both looked exhausted. They looked up fear-fully when Edwards and Sara walked in.

'DS Hirst,' said Agnes. 'Just the person.' She pointed to the dark-haired woman. 'Look who was waiting for us when we got home. This is Lenka, and this is Mouse.'

The smaller blonde woman screamed and leaped out of her seat, looking around wildly as if for some means of escape. The second woman caught her and pulled her, sob-bing, into her arms. Lenka turned an exhausted stare at the officers.

'Don't let them take us back,' the blonde woman moaned. Her body was shaking with sobs.

'I won't,' Lenka assured her. Holding Sara's gaze, she added, 'If you take us back, they will kill us. Just like Bohdan.'

It took some time to calm the sobbing woman. Edwards and Sara took them into the front room, away from the oth-ers. Agnes bustled in and out with tea and food, until Sara thanked her for allowing them to use the room and gently persuaded her to leave. She watched the lane out of the big sash windows while she waited for her boss to ring for backup. Two lorries with containers on their backs wound their way past the house.

Unusual to bring those down a lane like this, she thought. *It must be tight for space.*

'They'll be here as soon as they can,' said Edwards. 'I think we can guess what's going on here, so I asked for the human trafficking specialist to come with them.'

The young women were huddled on the sofa, still clinging together. Edwards settled on a chair opposite. Lenka was covered in bruises and held herself stiffly as if she were in pain. They were going to need a doctor as well. Edwards opened the voice recorder on his phone, which he placed on the table between them and the two women.

'I know it's dodgy on the legal front but it saves having to remember everything. I don't want to wait for the specialist to arrive before we get the preliminaries. Let's see what this is all about.'

'Would you like a drink or something to eat?' Sara settled in another chair, preparing herself for what might come. She tried to sound reassuring. 'Help is on the way. We'll get you somewhere safe as soon as we can.'

'Can you tell me about yourselves?' asked Edwards. 'Where is home?'

Lenka released herself gently from Mouse's arms. She passed Mouse a cup of tea and took one for herself. Then she said, 'Serbia. I think Mouse comes from Ukraine.'

'Do you have papers? Work permits?' asked Edwards.

Both women shook their heads. 'No, nothing,' said Lenka.

'How did you manage to get into the UK?'

Mouse put down her mug, pulled herself back on the sofa, tucked up her legs and wrapped her arms around her knees, defensively. Lenka looked at him, then spoke to Sara. 'This man came to our village,' she explained. 'There is no work there, it is very poor. He said if we paid, they would bring us to France or the UK. My grandfather, he is a farmer. So, he sold a cow to raise the money. First, we travelled in a minibus, then they took our clothes and passports. Eight of us, all women.'

'How did you cross the borders?' asked Edwards. Sara wished he would stop interrupting. She threw him a glance and raised a hand. Edwards blew out a frustrated breath, then gave her a nod.

'Carry on, Lenka,' said Sara. 'You're doing well. Anything you can tell us will help.'

'We crossed the borders late at night.' Lenka resumed her story. 'The papers were false, but money made them real. We travelled for days, only stopped for toilet and food. Until we got to the sea.'

'At Calais?'

'No. Quiet place, by the side of the road. They got us all out, made us climb into the back of a lorry. I don't know how long we hid in there, but we crossed the sea. I felt it.'

'And when you got to England?'

'Same happened again. We got out of the lorry, were put in another minibus. This man called Kirill Klimenko took us to London. To a house. It's a brothel.'

'Not what they promised you?'

'I think maybe dancing, in a nightclub or something.'

'So, you became a sex worker?'

Lenka smiled. 'Not me. I am no good at it. Lie too still. Men don't like it.'

'Kirill Klimenko was running this house?'

'Yes, and I think he has other houses too.'

'Could you find it again?'

'No.' Lenka shook her head. 'We were not allowed out.'

'How did you end up in Norfolk?' asked Sara. She knew that if women like this didn't perform, they might be disposed of in the Thames, like the flotsam they were to their traffickers.

'Sometimes other men came to stay in the house. Not for sex, waiting for something. Pavel, he came in the spring.

He told me to cook if I can't fuck. So I did, and he liked it. When they came up here to farm, they brought me too, to cook for them, look after them.'

'Pavel?'

'Pavel Babich.'

'What about you, Mouse? What was your journey?' The young woman's eyes darted from one officer to the other, until Lenka whispered encouragement.

'Same way,' Mouse whispered. 'I got here in May. I was good at fucking, so they kept me at the house.'

'At the farm, the men started to complain,' said Lenka. 'They work very hard all day, sometimes all night. They are not allowed to go out if not for work. Not allowed to go out for a drink or to find company. So, Kirill brought Mouse to the caravan for the men to use.'

'Why didn't you run away?' Edwards asked. Sara flinched.

'Where could I go? Who would believe me? I do not know where I am, there's no one to talk to. I have no friends, apart from Matus.'

'Who's Matus?'

'One of the crop pickers, Pavel's nephew. My boy-friend,' said Lenka with a shiver. 'He took me out to the concert, but Bohdan beat him up. I don't know for sure what happened to him.'

'Was this last night? In a place called North Walsham?'

Lenka nodded, twisting a tissue in her grubby hands.

'I think he might be in hospital.' Sara leaned forward. 'There's a young man there, we don't know his name. He's injured, Lenka, but they say he will recover.'

'Were you there at the time?' interrupted Edwards. Lenka nodded. 'What happened to you?'

'Ray grabbed me, forced me into the van, and they took me back to the caravan.'

'Ray? Ray Fraser?' Sara produced the photo and offered it to Lenka. 'This him?'

'Yes, that's the man. You know about this?'

'Some of it.' Sara said. 'What you're telling us is helping to make sense of some things we didn't understand before. Thank you. Where are these caravans? How have you ended up here with Mrs Richardson?'

'We live on the farm over there.' Lenka pointed behind the two detectives. 'It all started to go wrong on Monday when it was raining.'

'How did it start to go wrong?'

'Don't know, but Kirill and the farmer got very upset. Agnes, she came to see the farmer on Tuesday. He wasn't there. She came to the caravans, spoke to me, said I could visit her. There was lots of arguing and meetings. Last night, everyone went out except Matus, who took me to the park. When they got back, what Bohdan did to Matus, it caused a big fight, and Bohdan was hurt bad. They locked us in the caravan.'

'This farmer,' said Edwards. 'Do you know what his name is?'

'He is called Des Dixon.'

'Got him.' Edwards was triumphant.

'What made you come here today?' asked Sara.

'We were too frightened before, and today is our last chance.'

'Why?'

'The men are leaving.'

'Bastard,' Mouse suddenly spat out. 'Bohdan, he is a bastard. Hurt me, beat Matus, tried to rape my friend.' She indicated Lenka. 'He got what he deserved.'

'How did you manage to get away?'

'They all went to the barn to load up the lorries. We broke out, came across the fields and hid here until Agnes came home.'

'What barns? What lorries?' asked Edwards.

Lorries. Sara shot out of her chair. Two bloody container lorries, in the wrong place, on an unusual day. She'd seen them not twenty minutes ago.

CHAPTER 46

Sara was almost incoherent as she pulled Edwards out into the hall.

'Lorries, sir,' she said. 'I saw two lorries, just a few minutes ago. Why would there be container lorries down a lane like this on a Sunday afternoon? Mrs Richardson told me that Des Dixon had bullied her into allowing the crop pickers to use her barns. It must be the same people. They must be our thieves.'

DI Edwards walked to the kitchen, where Agnes, Mark and Frank were still sitting round the table.

'Mrs Richardson, DS Hirst tells me that Des Dixon leaned on you to allow his crop picking friends to use a barn. Where is it?'

'I was dreadfully upset about that,' Agnes began. She turned to Mark. 'I want you to go and tell them to clear out. When I tried, the man pretended he didn't speak English.'

'This barn,' said Edwards. 'Where is it?'

'Down the lane. Why?'

'I can show you,' said Mark. 'What man, Mum?'

Edwards cut across his question. 'These men are dangerous. I don't want you getting hurt. You take your car and show us the way, then drive on. Do you understand?'

Mark nodded, reaching for his keys.

'Mrs Richardson,' said Sara, 'we have to go out for a while. Backup is on its way to help with Lenka and Mouse. Can you keep them comfortable until one or other of us gets back? Don't let them leave, keep them safe.'

'You can rely on me,' promised Agnes.

Sara ran out of the door, just managing to reach Edwards's car before he set off. Both cars shot out of the drive and down the lane towards Happisburgh. Mark indicated left as they passed the entrance to the yard, then carried on down the road as agreed. Edwards swung into the yard, braking sharply and splattering gravel.

There were several buildings around the yard. The door to the main barn was swinging open. Edwards headed straight for it, and Sara followed. There was plenty of light inside. Regular narrow vertical windows pierced the top of the walls, the light flooded through making the place seem like a church or cathedral. The wide open doors let in the summer sun.

The place had obviously been used as a workshop. Tools, a hoist in a red frame, crates, car parts, cans of oil littered the floor. There was a workbench in one corner, in another some old furniture. Lying on the floor in the centre was a rectangular frame of welded metal. Edwards was inspecting it closely.

'What is it, sir?'

'Doesn't look much, does it?' he asked. 'I'm no mechanic, but I think we'll find it's a chassis. For a Land Rover Defender.' He stood up and grimaced. 'We missed the bastards. The girls were right. They've cleared out and left Dixon and Fraser to take the fallout. Let's get up to the farm.'

He marched back out of the barn. As Sara strode after him, the sound of a distant explosion filled the air. They turned to look. Above the line of hedges at the end of the barns, a writhing mass of white and black clouds rolled up into the sky. A second explosion shattered the peaceful summer afternoon. She knew that sound, she'd heard it on riot duty. Edwards turned back and raced for the car.

'Come on,' he yelled. 'It's a fire.'

Edwards drove as fast as he could on the narrow country lanes, following the billowing clouds of smoke. 'It's Dixon's farm. Call for the fire crews.'

They were not the first to arrive in the farmyard. Dixon was beside his gleaming Range Rover, dancing from foot to foot in agitation. The fire was across the field. Bright orange flames engulfed the caravans where the crop pickers lived. Black smoke belched up into the sky.

'Dear God,' said Edwards. 'Please tell me there is no one in there.'

'No, they've all gone out. They were down at the barns.' Dixon waved in the direction of Agnes's buildings over the brow of the hill.

'And the women?' asked Sara. She knew this was cruel, they had just left them at Agnes's.

'No.' Dixon turned a ghostly white. 'There was no sign of them.'

'When did you last see them?' asked Edwards.

'How do you know about them?' Dixon asked.

'We know,' Edwards assured him. 'We know about the girls, about Matus, about the barns. We have Ray Fraser in custody.'

Sara could hear the fire engines in the distance. They needed to be here fast. The fire was spreading along the margins of dry grass and into the wheat field.

'My fucking crop,' wailed Dixon. He was wringing his hands, watching the fire intently.

'Never mind that.' Edwards sounded incensed. 'What about the *people*?'

'They're just bloody immigrants,' snarled Dixon. Sara and Edwards stared open-mouthed at the farmer as another vehicle raced into the yard. Mark and Frank leaped out.

'It's spreading.' Frank pointed at the fire. 'If that field goes up, the whole area could be ablaze in minutes. Where's your irrigation kit?'

This practical question galvanised Dixon more than Edwards's words had. 'It's in the end barn.'

'We should run the hose from the ditch, or the firemen won't have enough water,' said Frank. 'I've never seen a fire spread so fast. It's been that dry this year.'

The pair shot off across the yard. The fire brigade were close now. Edwards headed back to the road to flag them down and directed them into the yard. As two huge fire trucks began to bounce down the cart track, a tractor manoeuvred out of one barn and reversed up to another. Frank jumped down and ran to the back, where Dixon was hitching up a trailer. When it pulled forward, Sara could see that it was a giant reel with a hose like a python wound around it. It looked like something you could buy for your garden, except this one had been on steroids.

As soon as the trailer was attached, Frank climbed back up into the tractor and headed down the cart track in pursuit of the fire trucks. He got about halfway to the caravans, then veered off through the scrubby area under the trees and into the wheat field. The tractor forged a path directly through the crop until it came to a drainage ditch. The firemen were already beginning to aim water onto the burning caravans. The fire was intense, their tanks would soon be exhausted. One firefighter was already scouting around, looking for a water source. Spotting Frank, he waved furiously. Frank waved back as he fed one end of the giant hose into the ditch. He unhitched the reel and locked its wheels steady. He attached the other end of the hose, climbed back into the tractor cab and drove slowly across the field towards the fire. The hose lengthened out behind him. In the distance, the onlookers in the yard could hear more sirens. This time they sounded to be coming from two different directions. Another smaller explosion ripped out of the side of one of the caravans.

'Gas bottles,' said Dixon. 'They had them for cooking. I forgot about the gas.'

Frank had reached the fire crew with the other end of the hose. There was a short discussion, and for a moment Sara wondered if the two hoses weren't compatible and Frank's efforts had been for nothing. Two more fire crew came over to help, and before long, they were pumping water.

The fire was spreading with a fierce dry crackle deep into the wheat, leaping from the dry grass margins to the crop and back again. Heated ash carried on the breeze gave rise to pockets of flames that sprouted further out into the wheat.

Another fire engine roared through the yard and turned off the track to follow the route Frank had taken in the tractor. As it bounced across the field, two more fire brigade vehicles turned into the yard. One was a large van, the second was another fire engine. They headed towards the blazing caravans. Frank pulled the tractor out of their way. Two uniformed fire officers climbed out of the van, consulted rapidly with the head of each engine crew, then sent the extra tender across the field to help tackle the crop fire.

Sara stood watching as the crews doused the caravans and the field. Agnes's son stood beside her, anxiously scanning the scene.

'It could reach our fields in no time,' he said. 'How did the damn fire start?'

Sara's mind was racing, her hands twisting in impotent frustration. How had the fire managed to spread so quickly between the two caravans?

Two patrol cars arrived, sirens blazing. Edwards strode off and identified himself, sending the officers to get rid of the spectators whose cars were already gathering on the verges along the lane. The fire officer drove back to the yard in the van.

'Anyone know about this place?' he asked.

Sara pointed out the dumbfounded Dixon.

'Sir,' the fire officer asked urgently. 'Is there anyone in those caravans?'

'I don't think so,' replied Dixon.

'Are you sure?' demanded the fireman. 'I don't want to risk my men's lives unnecessarily.'

'The girls. There were two girls.' Dixon shuddered. 'I didn't see them.'

'It's all right,' said Edwards. 'We know where the girls are, and it's not in there.'

'Why didn't you tell me?' Dixon's face was ashen.

'We wanted to know if you knew where they were.'

'Sir,' Sara said to Dixon. 'What did you mean when you said you didn't see them?'

'When I came back here,' Dixon blustered, 'I saw the fire, I didn't see any people.'

'How would you know unless you were close to the vans?' asked Sara. 'And what did you mean by "forgot about the gas bottles?"'

'Just what I said.' Dixon turned away.

'Mr Dixon, how did the fire start?' asked Edwards. 'Where were you this afternoon?'

'Out.'

'Fine.' Edwards looked around the yard, then moved towards an open workshop door.

'You can't go in there without a warrant,' called Dixon.

'Well, what have we here?' said Edwards as he halted at the door. 'Looks like some fuel cans to me. Lids are off. They look wet, too. Recently used, wouldn't you say, DS Hirst?'

Sara joined him and peered inside the workshop. The containers were industrial-sized, made of heavy-duty white plastic. Four of them lay scattered on the floor, dripping the remains of their contents from open necks. She smelled the familiar stink of diesel.

'Dribbles all over the floor, sir.' She pointed in the dust. 'I wonder why that is?'

'Can you explain all this, Mr Dixon?' asked Edwards.

'No comment,' said Dixon. His voice trembled like that of a small boy in front of the headmaster. Edwards sighed in exasperation.

'Desmond Dixon, I am arresting you on suspicion of arson,' the DI said. Sara had the handcuffs on the farmer before he could protest.

'Bastard,' said the fire officer. 'It'll be an insurance job. It usually is with these buggers.'

Borrowing one of the uniforms to accompany him, Edwards took the sulking Dixon off in his car. Sara volunteered to go and wait with the escaped girls, and Mark agreed to take her back.

They watched for a while. The fire crews were getting the caravan fire under control, the various other engines were containing the crop fire. Steam rose from the blackened wheat and the grassy margins. The fire had stopped spreading. Frank stood talking to one of the firemen as they dampened down the caravans.

'I think we can safely leave now,' Sara said to Mark, who seemed more than willing to get away from the scene.

There were two other cars in the yard when they returned. Agnes was brewing yet more tea for a grateful female police officer. The two girls were still in the sitting room, this time talking to the human trafficking officer. Lenka looked pleased to see Sara and raised a little smile.

'What was the noise?' Lenka asked.

'Your caravans.' Sara felt they deserved the truth. 'They've been burned down. So there is no question of anyone being able to go back there.'

'The men have gone then?'

'We think so. We don't know where or how.'

'Bastards,' Mouse sighed. 'They get away with everything. We'll get the blame. You wait and see.'

'You can give us descriptions of them,' Sara said. 'We might find them that way.'

'You should find the minibus,' said Lenka. 'Pavel told them all to go to the ferry in the minibus.'

'Can you give me a description of it?'

'Yes.' Lenka smiled. 'I can do better than that. I can give you the registration number.'

CHAPTER 47

Sara called Edwards and gave him the minibus registration. He immediately put out an all ports warning and traffic call. She travelled back to police HQ in the car with the two women and the human trafficking officer. As soon as they arrived, the HTO headed to her office to organise the safe house.

'We only need to get a brief statement from you,' Sara assured Lenka and Mouse. She led them to the witness suite. A female officer was waiting to greet them. 'You won't be here long.'

The officer smiled at the women, handing them cups of water and offering food or drink. Lenka settled her friend onto the sofa, and Sara left them with a promise to return very soon. To her relief, the whole team were in the office.

'Where's Dixon?' she asked.

'We're letting him sweat in the interview room for a while,' said Edwards. 'He's sent for his solicitor. Good work on the minibus number.'

'We've picked it up on a traffic camera,' Bowen said, pointing to his computer. 'Going south towards Ipswich. Likely to be heading to Felixstowe for the Rotterdam Ferry. It's the nearest.'

'Norfolk and Suffolk Traffic are putting cars out to stop them as soon as we can find them,' said Edwards. 'Let's hope they can get to them soon. Otherwise, we'll be relying on Immigration at the ports.'

'I don't get it,' said Ellie. 'Why aren't they going to Dover? Hiding in the crowds?'

'They may still do that, but the cameras picked them up going off the bypass on the A140 about an hour ago,' said Bowen. 'Our cars will be much faster. We should be able to get to them before they get that far.'

'CSI team are on their way to the barns,' said Edwards. 'Let's see what they come up with there. How are your ladies doing?'

'Mouse, the smaller one, is very shocked,' said Sara. 'Lenka is more helpful. It will take time to get full statements from them.'

'Don't push them too hard for now. Mike, you and I will deal with Dixon. Sara, Ellie, you get a basic statement and make sure they are taken to the safe house as soon as possible.'

Sara couldn't resist taking a peek at Dixon as she passed. She watched through the two-way window as the farmer sat with his arms folded, listening to his solicitor advise him to admit to nothing. When Edwards and Bowen entered the room, he gave the two detectives an arrogant smirk.

He thinks he's got away with it, she thought, watching Dixon. *He reckons he is only facing the accusation of an insurance scam.*

With Ellie's gentle assistance, they took a simple statement from Lenka and Mouse. How they had arrived in the country, where they had been kept and, in the briefest of terms, what their lives had been like at the caravans.

'Can you say if the farm owner knew about all of this?' asked Sara.

'Yes, of course,' Lenka said. 'He often came to the van for meetings and making plans.'

'Anyone else from round there?'

'Ray Fraser. He helps them a lot when the men go out at night. But he never came to the caravans until this week.'

'Fraser saw you both there?'

'Yes.'

'You mentioned a man called Bohdan. Can you tell us what happened with him?'

'He beat up Matus.' The energy that had been keeping Lenka upright suddenly seemed to leave her. Her arms were lying across her knees, now her body shrank and folded until her chest was resting on her arms. Her head dropped, her gaze settled on the floor. She began to cry.

'I'll tell them.' Mouse placed a gentle hand on Lenka's shoulder. Sara pushed a box of tissues towards Lenka, nodding encouragingly to the other woman.

'There was a big fight, like we said before. Pavel shot Bohdan.'

'Shot him?' asked Ellie.

'Yes, then they put him in the van and went off. Made us look after him.'

'He wasn't dead, then?'

'No, but not awake. The men locked us in, then went off to clear up and run away for the ferry.'

'Was there anyone else there when Bohdan got shot?'

'Yes,' said Mouse. 'We all saw. All the men. Me and Lenka. Fraser and Dixon.'

'Yes,' sobbed Lenka. 'Fraser helped carry him inside. He deserved it. Bohdan's a bastard to everyone.'

What a life they've been leading, thought Sara as they handed the two women over to the HTO who had arrived to escort them to the safe house.

They watched the car depart.

'I've never heard anything like it,' Ellie said.

'Do you realise what this means for Dixon?' asked Sara. Ellie shook her head. 'If he set alight to those caravans deliberately, and didn't go inside to check first, then he burned that man alive. He knew Bohdan was there and still set fire to the vans. If he didn't check inside, and he didn't know where those two women were, then he intended to burn them all alive. We'd better tell the boss.'

Sara and Ellie went up to the interview room. Edwards was as shocked by this revelation as they were.

'Jesus.' He wiped his hand over his face to clear the sweat. 'I would never have thought of him as being that cruel. I need to know for sure if he checked inside before he set light to the things. At the moment, he's just refusing to admit to anything. Bring Fraser up to interview room two. I have some questions for him as well.'

Fraser had been asleep in his cell all day, the custody officer told Sara. She escorted the still-yawning man up to the second interview room. The duty solicitor had been called again. They didn't have long to wait. Edwards came into the room with Mrs Chapman at his heels. Sara perched on the edge of her chair. As soon as the formalities had been dealt with, Edwards launched into Fraser. 'Mr Fraser, were you at the caravans on Mr Dixon's farm this morning?'

'No comment.'

'Did you witness a fight there?'

Fraser shrugged.

'Did you witness a shooting there?'

'What shooting? I didn't see anything.'

'Well, that is most peculiar because we now have two witnesses who place you at the caravans on Des Dixon's farm first thing this morning. When a man, known to us as Bohdan, was shot by another man, Pavel.'

'No comment.'

'Oh, come on Fraser, you can do better than that. Our witnesses also state that the man was injured but not dead. What did you do after that?'

'No comment.' Fraser looked away, his reply far from confident.

'When we arrested you this morning, your shirt was covered in blood. Forensics are testing it right now. Whose blood will it turn out to be?'

Fraser said nothing. Edwards let the silence hang, giving Fraser time to weigh up his options.

'Did you shoot this Bohdan?' he asked.

'No,' Fraser almost yelled. 'No, it was Pavel. Just like Dixon said.'

Edwards raised an eyebrow, but let the incorrect assumption go. 'What happened?'

'Pavel,' said Fraser. 'Pavel shot him. I didn't even know he had a gun. We were all outside. Everyone saw who it was.'

'And then?'

'He wasn't dead. Pavel made us carry him to his room. I had the head end, he was bleeding loads, so I got covered. We put him in bed and left the girls to clean him up.'

'What girls?'

'They keep two girls at the caravans.'

'What did you do next?'

'We went off to clear out the barns, left them all behind.'

'Would it shock you to know that those caravans have been destroyed by fire? That someone set fire to those caravans on purpose?'

'Not me,' rattled Fraser. 'You can't pin that one on me.'

'No, Mr Fraser,' Edwards agreed. 'You were in the cell by then.'

'Did they get out?'

'Who, Mr Fraser?'

'The girls. Pavel locked them in the van.'

'And Bohdan?'

'Passed out on his bed.'

Edwards returned to the other interview room, leaving Fraser to worry. From his thunderous expression, he intended to give Dixon a hard time.

'Bring me that photo of Fraser, will you?' he asked Sara. 'And prepare yourself. It might be a long session.'

She returned to the office, pulled the picture out of her bag and examined Fraser's face. He didn't look evil, though the picture was hardly flattering.

Over the years she had seen lots of difficult stuff in the line of duty, especially among the gangs involved in the London drug scene — young women and young men trapped into prostitution, addicts acting as mules to ferry packages of product in all directions, knife crime, gun crime. Informers maimed and terrorised. This situation was a first, and particularly unexpected. The thought that three people had been locked in a caravan and the place deliberately set on fire was deeply unsettling. It made her think of witches or heretics being burned alive at the stake. The image was so striking it made her feel sick, and it took her a moment to register that the desk phone was ringing.

'Is DI Edwards there?' asked the man on the other end.

'No, sir, he's interviewing at the moment.'

'Can you get a message to him? I'm Group Manager Miles, Norfolk Fire. We're out at the fire on Ridlington Manor Farm.'

'I think we may have met earlier. What can I tell him?'

'You were the young woman who helped arrest the farmer?'

'Yes, sir.'

'Good for you,' said Miles. 'You've still got him there, I take it? Tell DI Edwards that Dixon lied to me. There was someone in the caravans. We've found a body in one of the bedrooms. We'll send it on to the mortuary asap. The poor bugger must have suffered.'

'How so?'

'He was behind the door. From the position the body was in, it looks like he was trying to get out when he was overcome by smoke. Let Edwards know, will you?'

'Right away, sir,' said Sara, and replaced the phone.

So, Bohdan had still been alive when the fire had started. It seemed that Dixon had deliberately burned the man to death.

CHAPTER 48

Events moved at considerable speed after Sara had spoken to the fire brigade manager. After she conveyed the message to her boss, Edwards had promptly arrested Des Dixon on suspicion of murder. The shocked and whimpering farmer had been led away to the cells. In interview room two, Edwards had charged Fraser with conspiracy because he had helped move the body, along with a variety of other charges relating to the savage beating of the young man in North Walsham. Finally, the call they'd been waiting for arrived. Suffolk traffic police had pulled over the minibus on the A14, three miles short of the ferry port of Felixstowe.

Edwards insisted on driving, his siren and lights clearing the road to Ipswich. Sara leaned forward in her seat, almost urging him to drive faster as they passed vehicles and tore down the outside lane on the A45. Squad cars jammed the car park at Ipswich police station as, one by one, officers led the handcuffed men into the building. Edwards and Sara followed. The desk sergeant was having trouble processing so many people all at once.

'Not been a football match has there?' he asked, allocating the men to cells until they could be formally processed. 'Not that our lot make any trouble. Where are these all from?'

'Eastern Europe,' Edwards answered.

'Going to need an interpreter, then. Can you be any more specific?'

Sara stood, statue-like, the calm centre of the vortex. Officers, arrested gang members, the DI, some of the Suffolk CID team, Ellie and Bowen who had been following them, swirled around her. Amid all the noise, the slamming of doors, the repeated, 'No speak English,' she listened for one name. It didn't come. Another one did.

'Kirill Klimenko? asked the desk sergeant. 'How are you spelling that?'

'Sir.' Sara grasped Edwards's arm. 'That's the man who brought the girls to the brothel in London. We should interview him immediately.'

Edwards looked pointedly at her hand. She let go her grip.

'We'll get him brought up in the morning. Too late to do anything now.'

'With all due respect, sir—' she began.

'Think carefully before you say anything else,' said Edwards.

He turned away to speak to his counterpart in the local CID. Klimenko stood at the booking-in desk window. He looked around, meeting Sara's eye, and maintained his stare. A sneer spread across his face and he mouthed, 'No comment.'

Sara knew she couldn't cope with anything more. Her emotions stretched beyond endurance, the ground rushed up to meet her. She had the vague sensation of being lifted and carried. Fresh air helped her breathe, and she heard Ellie's voice. As the swirling settled, she realised that she was sitting in the passenger seat of a car, head lowered. Ellie was holding her by the shoulder.

'I should have told Edwards you weren't fit to stay on this case,' said Ellie. She rubbed Sara's back. It was a brisk but comforting sensation. 'Now I'll be in trouble, as well as you. If you don't speak up first thing tomorrow, you'll be too late.'

A door slammed, and Sara watched as Edwards reluctantly approached them.

'You all right?'

'Sorry, sir. I'll be fine, just needed some air.'

'Why are you so concerned with that man?'

'It's the girls, sir. What a bastard. How could he do that?'

'Surely you've seen cases like this before?'

'Yes, sometimes,' said Sara. 'But it's not what I expected to meet in a Serious Crimes Unit that has no serious crime to investigate.'

'You're a DS, and you deal with whatever comes your way. No questions. Are you pregnant? Is that it?'

Sara snorted. 'Why are all the men here so awful?' She stood up, ignoring her churning guts. 'You know you can't ask me that. Nor can you discriminate against me if I am.'

'I wouldn't be much of a detective if I didn't suspect that a young woman who has been vomiting and fainting all week might have a reason to account for it.' Edwards folded his arms. 'Nor can you accuse me of discrimination when you make a statement like that about "all men."'

'Since Monday morning, all I've heard is men moaning. You didn't want me to have the job. Bowen making his feelings clear by pushing me into that ditch. That farmer not caring if he burns three people alive. Fraser and all the rest spewing their anti-immigrant rhetoric and tabloid sound bites.'

'Which, quite frankly, in this instance, would appear to be well founded. This lot are all immigrants.' Edwards paused. 'Bowen pushed you, did he?'

Sara felt her legs wobble. Reaching behind her to grab the car door frame, she collapsed back into the passenger seat. 'All of you judging me by the colour of my skin.'

'For God's sake, Ellie, get her away from here. Take her home. Bowen and I will see that this lot get charged.'

'Yes, sir.'

'I knew I was right. I knew we should have given the job to someone local. You're a bloody embarrassment, Hirst. If you can't cope, you shouldn't have taken the job.'

He turned his back on them and headed back inside.

'You idiot,' said Ellie. 'Why did you say that? We caught them, didn't we? We've got the evidence. What's wrong with you?'

'That man killed my father.'

'We don't know that, not yet.'

'One of those bastards did it. One of them will pay.'

'Shut the fuck up,' said Ellie. 'You've done enough damage for one day.'

It was after ten when Sara finally got back to her flat. She could hear the TV as she let herself in, which meant that her stepfather was still there. She dropped her coat on the floor. Javed greeted her with a hug. It was enough to make her want to cry, but her body was too weary even for that. She slumped onto the sofa. In seconds, Javed appeared with a large helping of Jamaican pot roast — he must have been shopping and cooking. Sara ate the food gratefully, though she couldn't taste it. She stared at the TV where some adult cartoon was showing and took none of it in.

'Long day?'

'Insane. You wouldn't believe everything that happened.'

'Can you talk about it?'

'No. How about you? Did you try Mum again?'

'Yes, but she won't answer. Don't you worry about that. I'll sort it myself. We just need a few days' break, if that's okay with you?'

'Sure, stay as long as you like.'

Her clothes held the acrid smell of the fire they had witnessed, Sara realised as she stripped to get into bed. For a moment, she wondered if the prospect of facing her boss and the team again tomorrow would keep her awake. It didn't.

CHAPTER 49

Her call was for ten o'clock. Knowing that the morning could see her suspended from the investigation or from the force itself, Sara dropped her Police Federation card into her purse. The phone number for the legal support department was on the back. Despite the bone-deep tiredness starting from the moment she'd woken up, Sara decided that she wasn't going to lose her career without a fight. She was also determined to see the case through if they would let her. For her father, her mother, for Javed, and finally for herself. She'd beg if necessary, she owed them all that much. Had it only been a week ago that first day nerves had robbed her of her appetite? It seemed little had changed — the smell of her early morning coffee made her want to throw up.

The office was buzzing with activity. Sara had no idea where all the additional staff had appeared from. The evidence was being listed, recorded and assessed. The forensic results were mounting. Bowen and Edwards were coordinating a timeline that would piece it all together. As she came in, Ellie glanced up and scowled. Sara went over to Edwards and said quietly, 'I'd like a private word, sir.'

'Let's go to my office, shall we?'

He closed the door and allowed her to settle before he asked, 'What's this all about, then?'

'First of all, I'd like to apologise for my behaviour last night,' she began.

'Well, it was decidedly unprofessional,' he said. 'Not to mention embarrassing for myself and the team. I don't discriminate against members of my team, whatever their gender or heritage.'

'No, sir.'

'Nor do I appreciate being shouted at by a junior officer, especially when I'm on a neighbouring force's premises.'

'No, sir.'

'While I appreciate you may have experienced some difficulties this past week,' — Edwards paused and glanced outside to where Bowen was working at his computer — 'nonetheless, I expect you to be up to the job, whatever it might be.'

'Yes, sir.' Sara knew she sounded like Ray Fraser repeating, 'No comment.'

'I wanted a local because they are used to the kind of comments that you seem to have taken exception to. You can either work with this sort of situation or you can't. Which is it?'

'I believe that I can, sir.'

'That's a start, I suppose.' Edwards sighed and turned the pages in Sara's HR file. 'I had changed my mind about you, thought you were going to be a real asset. Now I'm not so sure.'

'I've allowed myself to get too involved with this case. Not something I would normally do. But this one is different.'

'Go on.'

'I have a personal connection with the murder victim, Adam Crane,' she said.

There, she thought. *Now it's out.* Relief flooded through her.

'Such as?'

'I have reason to believe he's my father.'

Edwards held her gaze for a moment. He seemed to be waiting for her to add something more, but she didn't know where to start. The DI pulled a manila folder from a pile of paperwork on his desk.

'That would explain this, then.' He opened the file and handed Sara a legal document. 'It's Crane's will. Did you used to live in Brixton?'

'Yes, sir.' Sara stared at the paper. 'When I was little. We moved to Tower Hamlets after my grandmother died. I'd have been about ten.'

'Was that your old address?' Edwards pointed to a paragraph in the will. Sara nodded. 'Seems like you are about to become a woman of property. Crane has left you his cottage. I thought the name might be a coincidence when I first read it, until I spoke to Dr Taylor this morning.'

Sara scanned the will, hardly able to take in the contents. Edwards let her finish reading before he spoke again.

'Taylor told me about the DNA results. He is obliged to, you know that?'

'Yes, of course, sir.'

'He also told me of your conversation on Friday.'

'I never knew him.' Sara blurted out. 'He moved away when I was tiny. Abandoned Mum and me. All I have are these old photos of when I was a baby. Then I found these letters from him, posted in Norwich back in the eighties.'

'Is that why you wanted to move here?'

'Partly.' It felt like such a flimsy excuse now. 'But it wasn't the only reason.'

'What was the other reason?'

'I wanted to be part of a smaller team so that I could make a real difference. The Met can be really impersonal. This post was the first opportunity that came up and it seemed ideal.'

Edwards grunted. 'When did you realise our victim was your father?'

'When we searched the cottage.' Sara knew her voice was trembling, but she couldn't control it. 'I recognised him in

280

the photos on the shelves. When Dr Taylor confirmed it, I didn't know what to do about it.'

'You should have told me immediately.'

'Yes, sir. I couldn't get my head around the coincidence. Now it makes sense because he was almost acting like a private detective. One that got out of his depth.'

'Have you discussed this connection with anyone else?'

'One member of my family.' Sara shuffled. She didn't want to get Ellie into trouble.

'Your presence on the team could jeopardise the case.'

'Possibly, sir. It hadn't altered my actions, except for last night when I got upset.'

'Do you often "get upset", as you put it?'

'No, sir. Extreme circumstances.'

'I don't often lose my temper either,' said Edwards. He closed the HR file. 'Perhaps we could call yesterday a one-all draw.'

'I want to finish the case, sir.' Sara was pleading now. 'Those girls, they trust me, and I can be of use, I'm sure.'

'Given your behaviour last night, I have every right to remove you from the case.'

'Yes, sir.'

'ACC Miller will expect you to receive a formal reprimand, and your relationship to the victim does put things in a difficult light.'

Sara nodded. It was what she had expected. The energy and determination that she had felt driving into work drained away. Edwards drummed his fingers on the table.

'I knew your dad. He was a good copper, and I liked him. Helped me a lot when I first moved into this department. In time, he might have expected to become the DI. I got the job instead.' Edwards frowned and paused. The will in Sara's hand trembled. She folded it in half, then in half again, until it was too tight to fold again.

'It's a shame you never knew him,' he said. 'I suspect you'd have found you had a lot in common. Pity.'

'I am beginning to think so too, sir.'

'For his sake, I'll let you finish the case,' he decided. 'You can't speak to any of the suspects. You can help with other things — looking after those young women for a start. There'll have to be a formal review. I know it's been a tough start, but you remind me of your father. I think you're a good copper too.'

'Thank you, sir,' breathed Sara. *How long had I been holding my breath?* she wondered.

'I want you to get down to forensics to pick up some evidence. They've come up trumps at Mrs Richardson's barns.'

'Sir.'

'Bring the bacon rolls with you when you come back.' Edwards glanced out of the window. 'Twenty should do it.'

The evidence was a broken camera and a bloodstained shirt. The technician waggled a memory card.

'Got this out of it,' he said. 'Not sure it will be readable.'

'Why is it important?'

'We found it wrapped in the shirt and stuffed down a corner of that knackered sofa. Our victim was ex-police, wasn't he?'

'A detective sergeant.'

'He'd put his initials and postcode inside here.' The technician opened a tiny flap and held a UV light pen over it. 'Where the card fits. Look. In case it got stolen, I would imagine.'

How had the camera ended up at the barns? she wondered, turning the Canon over in her hands. She headed back to the office with a tray of rolls and the camera.

Ellie helped herself to one of the rolls. 'Did you shop me?' she hissed.

'Of course not. Where's Edwards gone?

'Suffolk's transport has arrived. He's interviewing the picking gang, starting with Kirill Klimenko.'

CHAPTER 50

Using the camera as her excuse, Sara went into the interview room. It was crowded. Klimenko sat on one side of the desk. Next to him were the duty solicitor and another man, who she assumed to be an interpreter. Bowen was sitting next to Edwards.

'Was this what you were looking for, sir?' she asked. Klimenko looked at her and grinned. She left and, checking the corridor was clear, went into the observation room.

Klimenko was in room two. Ray Fraser sat nervously in the adjacent room one, the duty solicitor tapping her pencil rhythmically on her notepad. The CSI team at Fraser's house had rung in a preliminary report. The outhouses were full of everything from stolen goods to packets of weed and endless amounts of rubbish. The second team at the barns on Agnes's farm were collecting ample evidence to show that the place had been used for stripping down vehicles and machinery, then packing them up for shipment.

Edwards held up Crane's camera in its evidence bag. 'Do you recognise this?' Klimenko shook his head.

'Can you explain what it was doing at Mrs Richardson's barns?'

Klimenko shrugged. 'Nothing to do with me.'

'What was the barn used for?' There was no reply. 'Can you explain why we should find traces of the victim's blood at the barns?'

'Not me,' he snarled in English.

'Do you know the whereabouts of Pavel Babich?' Edwards continued.

'No.'

'Where were you on the night of the twenty-seventh of July?'

'At the caravans.' Klimenko asserted through the interpreter. 'Everyone will say so.'

'We have a witness who can place you at the farm of Jack Ellis around midnight that night.'

'They're lying.'

'I'll ask them for confirmation,' said Edwards standing up. Sara kept silent as he and Bowen moved past the back of the observation room to speak to Ray Fraser.

'We have found several items at your bungalow which appear to have been stolen. Can you explain why you have a ride-on mower and trailer belonging to Graham Dack in your possession?'

'It was Bohdan,' said Fraser. 'You've got them all now, right? The whole thing was his idea. The money from the thefts wasn't enough, he wanted more.'

'How were you involved?'

'He spotted Dack's place when they were picking. Said it looked an easy target. I didn't think . . .' Fraser's voice trailed off.

'Didn't think what?'

'That anyone was there. I told him to stop. He wouldn't. It was out of order what he did to that old guy.'

'Where were you on the night of July twenty-seventh?'

Fraser touched his face nervously but didn't answer. In the observation room, Sara clenched her fists.

'Where were you?' Edwards insisted. 'What were you doing? Who were you with?'

'I was out.'

'Who with?'

'I just went along to keep a lookout. Pavel was there to start the engine, Klimenko for muscle. Dixon dropped us off.'

'And then?'

'We saw a camera light flashing.' Fraser's voice lowered to a whisper. 'Dixon told me it would be easy money. Just pinching a few second-hand cars. Said he was doing it for the cash himself.'

'Why would he need money?'

'His wife cleaned him out.' Fraser sneered. 'He smacked her about, so she took him to the cleaners when she divorced him. He's desperate.'

'Slimy little bastard,' Bowen said when they were back in the corridor. Sara listened as the two men returned to the first interview room. She moved forward to the two-way window as if it would make it easier to hear.

Edwards seated himself opposite Klimenko. 'I can confirm that our witness places you at Jack Ellis's barns on the night of the twenty-seventh of July,' he said through the interpreter. Klimenko laughed.

'Our witness says that you hotwired a Land Rover Defender and drove off in it.'

'I was not there, I couldn't say.'

'Did you see someone else there that night?'

'Not there. You don't have any witnesses,' Klimenko said.

'We have another witness, someone who overheard you at a later time talking about that night.'

'Fucking women,' Klimenko snarled. 'You got them too?'

'I didn't say they were women. If you don't help us, we will charge you with murder on the evidence we currently have. Do you understand?'

The interpreter had barely finished before Klimenko turned bright red. He spluttered with anger. 'Not me,' he said. He stood up and leaned across the desk. 'Pavel Babich. He's the one. You ask him when you find him.'

'Calm down now.' Bowen rose from his seat and pushed Klimenko back into his chair.

Klimenko grabbed Bowen by the wrist. 'Don't you set me up. Babich was driving.'

Both the duty solicitor and the interpreter were on their feet now, backing out of the way.

'It wasn't the car that killed him.' Edwards rose to face the gangmaster.

Klimenko let go of Bowen's wrist and slammed his fists down on the table. 'Not me. I wasn't there. You can't prove it.'

'The pathologist's report shows the victim was strangled. Who did it?'

The gangmaster's face was red, furious. He spat out a string of Ukrainian, spittle flying from his mouth. His arm pulled back and he aimed a punch at the DI. Bowen pushed in front of Edwards and grabbed the swinging fist. In seconds, the uniform officer and the DC had Klimenko on the floor, his arms handcuffed behind his back, His head reared up, his back arching and feet drubbing on the floor, he hurled a stream of abuse at the officers.

'I don't expect I want that translated, do I?' asked Edwards.

The interpreter shook his head. 'Wouldn't recommend it.'

'Take him to the cells.'

In the observation room, Sara let out a frustrated grunt. Her head was swimming, only her balled fists resting on the glass were holding her up. They still didn't know who had killed Adam Crane.

CHAPTER 51

The Kent police had stopped two lorries containing stolen solar panels at the Dover Customs checkpoint. Pavel Babich was one of the men arrested. It took twenty-four hours to transport him back to Norwich. On Tuesday morning, Sara hovered in the office, helping Ellie with the paperwork, her presence being tentatively welcomed. Bowen furnished the bacon rolls.

He offered Sara some ketchup. 'Crane was your dad, then?'

She nodded, accepting the sachet and ripping it with her teeth.

'I'm sorry.' He sounded sincere, and Sara took it at face value. 'The last one's here,' Bowen continued. 'Edwards says you can watch from the observation room if you take Ellie with you.'

Pavel Babich was a short, thick-set man with several days of stubble shading his chin. A new interpreter sat on one side of him, the same duty solicitor as yesterday on the other. Edwards started the recorder and began the interview. The interpreter interrupted.

'Mr Babich would like to ask a question,' he said. Edwards agreed that he could. 'Do you know how Matus Petrović is?'

Bowen leaned over to the DI and whispered, then answered, 'We think he is in the local hospital, in the ICU. They say he came round this morning and is doing quite well.'

The interpreter conferred with Babich. 'Do you know where Lenka Jevtić is?'

'One question at a time, Mr Babich,' Edwards said. 'One each, is that fair? Why do you want to know about these two?'

The interpreter conferred again. 'Matus is Mr Babich's nephew. He says that he promised his sister, Matus's mother, that he would keep an eye on him just before she died earlier in the year. That's why he brought him to England. Lenka is Matus's girlfriend.'

'We are keeping Lenka in a safe place,' said Edwards. 'Where were you on the night of July twenty-seventh?'

'Out with two other men,' the interpreter confirmed. 'They all went to a local farm.'

'Are you aware that we have all the other members of the crop picking gang in custody?'

Babich nodded. He looked relieved. He spoke to the interpreter again. 'Mr Babich would like to confirm that Matus and Lenka had nothing to do with the robberies.'

'I can accept that,' said Edwards. 'Who did you go out with and why?'

With the interpreter working hard to keep up, Babich began to speak. 'I went with Klimenko and a local man, Ray Fraser. We went to take a vehicle.'

'Klimenko says he wasn't there.'

'He was,' the interpreter confirmed. 'There was someone else, someone taking pictures. We saw the camera flash, but the man escaped across the fields.'

In the observation room, Sara stood rigid, unable to move. Ellie stood beside her in silence.

'So, we left,' the interpreter said for Babich. 'Hid behind a hedge and waited. We wanted the camera. When the man emerged, we chased him in the car.'

'And then?'

There was a brief flurry of Serbian, after which, the interpreter said, 'If Mr Babich gives you a full statement, do you agree to leave the young man, Matus, and his girlfriend free of all charges?'

'I can't guarantee that,' Edwards said, 'but so far, there doesn't seem to be any evidence that would cause them to be prosecuted.'

There was a silence after the interpreter relayed this reply. With a sigh, Babich came to a decision. He began to speak, the interpreter's words galloping after him. 'I promised my sister, so now I'll take care of Matus as best I can,' he said. 'When the man came down the road, Klimenko was driving. We only needed the camera, but Klimenko drove straight at him. I grabbed the steering wheel and tried to turn it so we didn't hit him full on. The man got knocked across the road.'

Ellie put a comforting hand on Sara's arm as a single tear ran slowly down her frozen face. Here was the truth at last.

'We got out, I grabbed the camera. Ray was talking loudly about calling for an ambulance. Klimenko got angry. Have you seen him angry?'

'We have,' said Edwards.

'He hit Fraser, nearly knocked him out. Then the man on the ground started groaning. He was covered in blood and Klimenko dragged him up onto the verge. I didn't know what to do. Then I saw Klimenko grab the man by the throat. I tried to pull him off, but he shoved me aside and carried on. By the time I got up, Klimenko had throttled the man.' Babich paused, looking into the distance, evidently replaying the scene in his mind.

'We were still near the barns where we took the car. The man was dead. So, we put him in the back of the vehicle, pushed Fraser in the rear with him. He was squealing like a baby. Klimenko threatened him again and he stopped. I drove round the lanes until we came to one with big ditches and high hedges. Klimenko made Fraser help get the body out, and they rolled it into the ditch.'

'What happened next?'

'We went back to the barns, where I broke down the things we'd stolen to ship back to Odessa. Fraser drove off in his van. I made Klimenko take off his shirt. It was covered in the dead man's blood. I gave him my jumper. Then we went back to the caravans.'

'We found the camera and the shirt at the barns,' said Edwards. 'Why did you keep them?'

'Klimenko was getting out of control.' Babich looked at Edwards. 'The stealing, that was my idea. I've been working with Dixon for three years now. This year I brought new people, recommended to me in Odessa. They were a mistake. I bought a gun in London.'

'Where is that now?'

'I threw it away somewhere on the road to the ferry. Can't remember where.'

'Why did you need a gun?'

'I thought it would help.' Babich shrugged. 'I know how to use one. But it didn't frighten him as much as I'd hoped. After he killed this man, I needed something else to control him. So, I kept the camera and the shirt as insurance.'

The air around Sara grew thin. Her body began to buzz all over. If she didn't get out of the observation room soon, she might collapse. Her locked leg muscles painful, she went to the door.

'Did you shoot a man called Bohdan at the caravans, Mr Babich?' Edwards asked.

'Yes.'

'Did you kill him?'

'No, I winged him. He's another bad choice I made in Odessa. He beat up my nephew and hurt Lenka.'

'Then you put him in the caravan?'

'Yes.'

'What about the two women? We know about Mouse.'

Sara turned back to the window. Babich looked ashamed. 'I locked them in while we packed up the barns.'

'Did you go back to the caravans, Mr Babich?'

'No, we left from the barns. Dixon said he would go back and let the women out. You have them safe, yes? Dixon told me he would take Bohdan to the hospital.'

'The caravans have been burned down.'

Sara heard Babich suck in a heavy breath.

'The firemen found Bohdan's body. He was burned to death.'

CHAPTER 52

Sara made her way unsteadily back to the office. Ellie followed closely behind.

'Christ,' said Ellie. 'You look so grey.'

'That bastard Klimenko strangled my dad.' Sara sat on her chair, folded her arms and rested her head on them. Ellie patted her shoulder uncertainly, then headed to the water cooler.

Edwards and Bowen returned to the office, congratulating themselves, as Ellie put a drink on the desk. 'This is too much for you. I think you should go home for the day.'

'Everything all right?' asked Edwards coming over to her desk. Sara raised her head. 'You know?'

'Yes, sir. I was listening in the observation room.'

'Was Ellie with you?'

'Yes, sir, I was,' said Ellie.

'Good.' He turned to the rest of the room. 'Great work, team, we have our man.' There was a rustle of approval, a spattering of applause. 'Let's make sure our evidence is locked up tight.' He turned back to Sara. 'Do you want to go home?'

'Rather not, sir,' she said. Having begged to stay on the case, she didn't want to leave now.

'Then take a uniform and go over to see how those two women are getting on. Lenka's boyfriend has come round.

You can take her to see him and find out what you can from the man.'

Sara drove to the safe house. It was in the middle of an unassuming newbuild housing estate not far from the airport. The two women were in the kitchen, an HTO with them. New clothes had been provided, and a doctor had visited to patch up Lenka's injuries.

Mouse declined the offer to go to the hospital with them, saying she wanted to rest. 'I feel clean,' she said. 'I haven't felt like this for a long time.'

The ward was quite small. There were six beds, all with their curtains drawn. The blinds were half open to mitigate the harsh hospital light and give the place a restful feel. Matus was at the far end of the room. He seemed to be sleeping as they stepped quietly round the curtain to his bedside. With an effort, he partly opened his eyes. The sight of Lenka made him sit up, and he held out a bandaged hand to her. She took it gently, stroked the bandage lightly, then placed it on the bedcovers. Sara found a couple of chairs and sat Lenka close to Matus, removing herself to the end of the bed at a discreet distance. The young couple spoke in what Sara assumed to be Serbian. She let them have their reunion, too drained to feel jealous of their good fortune.

'Matus?' Sara pulled her chair closer. 'I would like to ask you a few questions. How is your English? Do you need an interpreter?'

Matus frowned at Lenka, who answered for him. 'My English is better,' she said. 'I will translate for him.'

'If you don't mind helping for now, can you start by telling me a little about what went on at the caravans?'

Lenka asked the question, listened to the reply, then said, 'Matus did not take part in the stealing.'

'So, what did you do, Matus?'

'He worked picking crops with the others,' Lenka said. 'Sometimes he went to help pack the lorry. He brought the shopping for me so I could cook.'

'What was he doing in England?'

'Pavel is his uncle,' explained Lenka. 'Matus wanted to come to England, to get away from Serbia. There is better work here.'

Why on earth did they think that doing back-breaking work like crop picking was better than staying at home? 'Who was at the caravans?' Sara said.

Matus named the members of the gang. He became agitated at the mention of Bohdan.

'Was he the man who saw you in North Walsham?' asked Sara.

Matus nodded. 'He tried to kill us both.' He held up his bandaged hand. Lenka began to soothe him, lapsing into Serbian again. Sara could see that there was no doubt about their affection for each other.

'I think I'll go for coffee. The other police officer is outside if you need anything. I'll come back in a few minutes.' Leaving them to talk in private, Sara called the mortuary and asked Dr Taylor to allow her to go along for a visit.

'Give us fifteen minutes,' Dr Taylor said.

He dealt with grieving families all the time, Sara realised, when she reached his office. He understood why she needed this moment. Her father had been placed in the viewing room, neatly arranged, a sheet pulled up to his neck to hide the worst of the wounds and scars. Dr Taylor took her in and stood quietly next to her while she looked down at the man who had abandoned her so long ago. He'd never forgotten her, he'd remembered her in his will. He had left her his home.

'I'm sorry I was too late, Dad,' she murmured. 'You'll get justice, I promise.'

Sara leaned down and placed a kiss on the cold cheek, which the pathologist had sewn up with care. She didn't cry. There were no tears left in her.

'You'll need to make arrangements soon,' Dr Taylor explained when they returned to the corridor. 'We will keep him here until the investigation gets wound up.'

'Thank you,' she said. She shook Dr Taylor's hand.

'Did you speak to Edwards?'

'Yes. I was grateful for the time you gave me.'

'He's not such a difficult man, is he?'

'He's treating me fairly,' Sara agreed. 'I need to get back to work. Did they bring the body in from the caravan?'

'Yes, I'm working on him now. Want a quick précis?'

Dr Taylor led Sara into the lab. All the tables had been cleared, apart from one. He drew back the sheet from the charred corpse. The air stank of stale smoke, baked flesh and cleaning fluids. The body was open. A variety of bowls with grotesque contents stood on a wheeled trolley next to the table, where Sara's request had interrupted Taylor from his examination.

'Male, late thirties, gunshot wound to the shoulder.'

'Did he die in the fire?'

'No.' Taylor pointed to one of the bowls. 'There's no smoke in his lungs. I think our friend here was already dead when the fire started.'

'The fire officer thought he'd been trying to get to the door to escape,' she said.

'I doubt it.' Taylor bent over the cadaver. He pointed at the ribs around the heart. 'If you look here, these are stab wounds.'

'Stabbed?' Sara was stunned. 'He was shot outside, then carried into his room and cleaned up. That's the story we have so far.'

'That could all be true. Perhaps someone attacked him in the caravan after that. Besides, he was lying on his back on the floor when the fire broke out. I can tell by the pattern of the burning.'

Sara spoke to the DI on her way out of the mortuary and went to the coffee bar. She needed caffeine.

'See if either of those two women know any more about what happened to this Bohdan after he was shot,' said Edwards. 'Perhaps it was Dixon who stabbed him.'

She collected Lenka. The journey back to the safe house was quiet.

'Lenka,' Sara asked tentatively, as the other woman gazed silently at the passing city suburbs. 'When you escaped from the caravan, was Bohdan still in his room?' Lenka turned to look at Sara but didn't reply. Sara tried again. 'Do you know if he was still alive when you left?' She shrugged.

When they reached the house, the HTO was sitting on the sofa listening to something on her mobile. Earbuds in place, she failed to notice them letting themselves in until Sara stopped in the doorway to the living room.

'Oh, you're back,' she said, looking startled.

'What the hell are you doing?' asked Sara.

'Mouse said she wanted a nap,' the woman explained. 'She went upstairs half an hour ago. I didn't want to disturb her, so I used my earphones.'

'I'll check on her,' said Lenka climbing the stairs. 'Sara, come here,' she yelled.

The bedroom was empty, the bed undisturbed, the new clothes had vanished, the hold-all was missing. Sara checked the bathroom — the new toiletries had also been taken. She ran downstairs to the kitchen. The patio doors were wide open. Knowing it was too late, Sara ran to the back gate and checked up and down the street outside. Mouse was gone. When she got back into the house, Lenka was sitting at the kitchen table, crying.

'She left me,' Lenka sobbed. 'She promised she would wait, now she's gone without me.'

Dismissing the HTO with a flick of her wrist and telling her to call in the runaway, Sara waited. Eventually, Lenka looked up, pulled a tissue from the box Sara had placed next to her and blew her nose.

'Why has Mouse gone, do you know?' Sara asked.

Lenka wiped her face with more tissues, and stared out of the window. 'She is afraid.'

'Why? Afraid of who? We can protect her here, much better than if she's on the streets or on the run.'

'Not from that.' Lenka kept her gaze outside.

'From what?'

'They're putting out street teams, to see if they can find her,' the HTO interrupted from the doorway.

'We promised to stay together,' said Lenka. She stood up abruptly and hurried upstairs to the bedroom. Sara followed her. Lenka lifted the mattress and ran her hand along beneath it, feeling for something.

'It's gone,' she said. 'The only thing I brought with me. My petal purse, the one that Matus bought me. It has money in it. English money. Plenty of it.'

Clean and rested, Mouse had a head start, new clothes and a purse full of cash.

Good luck to her, Sara thought.

CHAPTER 53

The weather was still hot, though the summer holidays were fast coming to an end. A couple more weeks and the families would head home, to be replaced by the retirees who came to enjoy the quieter days of September. The CSI team at the barns took three days to complete their investigations. Mark was staying with his mother at the farm, his husband due to join them for the weekend, so he could meet his mother-in-law. Agnes stood with her son in the open area between the barns, surveying the buildings.

'I'd forgotten how much space there was here,' he said. 'What will you do with them?'

'That partly depends on you,' said Agnes. 'If all of this has taught me anything, then I think it's the need for honesty.'

'From me?'

Agnes shook her head. 'Just in general. All these secrets, all those lies, all that violence. So unnecessary. But I do need you to be honest with me about one thing.'

'What's that?'

She tried to keep her voice steady. 'Do you intend to come back here to farm?'

Mark looked around the buildings, at the field beyond where the cows were grazing. Finally, he turned to his mother.

'Not to farm, no.' She turned to walk away, but he grabbed her hand. 'I'm no farmer. You know I love being a vet. I also miss home. I miss this place, and you.'

Agnes looked at him, unable to hide her disappointment.

'This is just an idea,' he rushed on. 'We can talk more about it when Richie comes to visit. The other thing I miss is working with big animals, the cattle and the horses. We could open up a new practice, right here in the barns.'

Agnes smiled. It was a long time since she'd seen her son this enthusiastic about anything. Mark gestured around.

'We would need to do this lot up, perhaps even make a flat in one of them. We'd need to use three or four of the grazing fields for exercise paddocks and outdoor rest areas. I think it could work.'

'You could live in the farmhouse until you refurbished it,' she said. 'There's cash in the bank, we could use that to get started.'

He squeezed her hand. 'I'd love that. We'd have to see how Richie feels about it, though.'

'Of course.' Agnes stood deep in thought for a while. Over the fields they could hear the last of the skylarks calling their familiar song. 'Actually, Des Dixon was right about one thing.'

'Surely not?'

'I'm getting on a bit.' They began to walk back down the lane towards the farmhouse. 'I refused to accept how vulnerable I am here on my own.'

'We could get you a housekeeper. Perhaps we should do that, whatever else happens.'

'I have someone in mind.' She smiled. 'Two people, actually.'

'Frank? Would he want to bring his family here?'

'No, I mean that young woman, Lenka, and her boy-friend,' said Agnes. 'You remember DS Hirst called yesterday?'

Mark nodded.

'She told me that one of those youngsters had run off, they can't find any trace of her. Lenka has to stay here for a while. She's an important witness at the trial. Her boyfriend got beaten up — he's a witness as well.'

'Is this wise?' Mark looked unsure.

'I don't know. What I do know is that they'll be kicking their heels, waiting for months before this lot comes to trial. She was a housekeeper before, perhaps she'd be willing to help me. He can come here to recover, help Frank and you once he's a bit better. There's plenty of rooms in the house.'

'Will they allow it? With the current antipathy to migrants, they may want to send them to a detention centre.'

'I'm not sure who "they" are, but we can ask. I'd pay them, of course. A proper job, with proper wages.'

'I hate to say this, Mum,' said Mark, 'but they're illegal immigrants. Once they've served their purpose in the case, they'll want to send them back to Serbia.'

'We can cross that bridge when we get to it,' said Agnes. 'Besides, there would be time to sort out their papers so that they can stay. If they want to, that is.'

They reached the farmhouse. Frank was in the yard, tinkering with the tractor again. Agnes called to him that she was putting the kettle on.

'There's one more person I need to take care of,' she said. 'I want to make provision for Frank, and I want you to know about it so there are no arguments later on. I've been worrying about this for a long time.'

Mark settled himself to listen. Opposite him, Agnes reached out to take his hand. She felt that he was paying attention to her for the first time in years.

'I love your idea about the veterinary practice. If your Richie is up for it, I'd like to split up the farm. You can have the good grazing fields and the barns. I want Frank to have the rest. You say you're not interested in farming and that's fine, I can accept that. Frank is a natural farmer. He loves the place and the work. He would get the buildings here and the land, including the grazing marshes. That would be enough to run a small business on.'

'What if he doesn't want it?'

Agnes smiled. 'That won't be a problem. Do you agree with the idea, or are you going to get all possessive about it now?'

'No.' Mark returned her smile. 'It sounds fine to me. I think Richie will love it out here. He misses his horses.'

Frank walked into the kitchen. 'Is that tea ready?'

Agnes poured them all a drink, then sat Frank down and explained her plan to him. At first, he looked delighted, then his expression clouded. 'People will say I bin taking advantage of you,' he muttered.

'I don't care what people say. Do you?' asked Agnes.

'And I don't know how to do all that paperwork,' he said.

'I can do it for you,' Agnes assured him. 'I wasn't planning on retiring yet. I can teach it to you over time. My only stipulation is that I will be allowed to remain here in the farmhouse for as long as I'm able. It's my home until I can't use it anymore. Then it will pass to you.'

For a moment, she wondered if Frank was going to refuse. He twisted the mug of tea round and round on the table as if that would somehow aid his thinking. Then he looked up at her. 'That would be wonderful. Best thing that ever could happen.'

'For me as well,' said Agnes. She took Frank's hand in one of hers and Mark's in the other. 'I will have my family around me again. The farm will survive for another generation, and perhaps we will even do some good for that young couple. I can't think of a better way to put an end to all this unpleasantness.' She raised her drink in a toast. 'To the future,' she said.

They clinked their mugs of tea.

CHAPTER 54

The team worked hard, pulling together the threads of the case, interviewing all the gang members and matching forensic evidence to witness statements. They compared all this to Crane's spreadsheets and reports. The pattern he had discerned was now clear to see. Perhaps because it was on his patch, or perhaps because he was uniquely placed, he'd understood what was going on long before anyone in the Norfolk force had taken an interest.

Fraser admitted to his part in the thefts. His involvement dated from the previous season. He also admitted to visiting Crane at his cottage following the fight at the pub. Still drunk when he arrived, Fraser had shoved past Crane into the kitchen, where Crane had punched him again, and thrown him out. Terrified of a longer sentence, he gave full statements regarding Bohdan's beatings of Graham Dack and Matus and took great care to ensure that Kirill got all the blame for Adam Crane's murder. But he could throw no light on the death of Bohdan, insisting that the man had still been alive when they left for the barns on Sunday morning.

Dixon had been involved with the thefts all along. Pavel Babich had approached him at his most vulnerable moment. After years of abuse and neglect, his wife had finally walked out on him and the subsequent divorce settlement had crippled him with debt. Talking about it now, three years after the event, still made him spit with fury. He had taken a cut of the proceeds from the thefts and used the gang's crop picking services for free. On advice from his lawyer, Dixon admitted to starting the fire but denied that he had gone inside either of the caravans or touched Bohdan.

The team could not fathom what might have happened to Bohdan. A kitchen knife had been found in the debris of the burnt-out caravan, too damaged to show fingerprints but a match to the wounds in the man's lungs. Edwards interviewed Lenka about it, but she denied all knowledge, saying that the man had been lying on his bed when they'd escaped the caravan. Dixon admitted he had only looked through Bohdan's bedroom window before setting alight to the caravans. He'd seen the injured man lying on the floor but hadn't gone in to check. The other bedroom door had been open, leading him to assume that the two women had run away. His fear when they had found him watching the fire had stemmed from the thought that his assumption had been wrong, and they might still have been inside. The fact that he hadn't properly checked to see if either of the girls or Bohdan were still alive sickened the whole team. Edwards started a long discussion with the CPS to see if there was some charge that could be brought against him for this, but so far, they hadn't come up with anything.

There had been no sign of Mouse. Sara was glad about that, though she kept her opinion to herself. She also wondered if Lenka knew more about the death of Bohdan than she was admitting. She kept that thought private as well.

Sara's formal review turned out to be a rather one-sided affair. She was called to the personnel office with Edwards. The HR manager and ACC Miller were waiting for them. Sara began by apologising again for her outburst in Ipswich.

'I know it was extremely unprofessional,' she admitted.

'It didn't do us any good in the eyes of our neighbouring force,' Miller grumbled. 'We have to work with them regularly. However, as DI Edwards does not wish to pursue it, there will be no further action taken on the matter, except for an official reprimand in your file.'

'Yes, sir.'

'Now, let's hear why you became so personally involved.'

Sara took them back to the beginning — Crane's disappearance, her youth without a father, the discovery of the letters and her subsequent decision to move to Norwich.

'You took evidence from the victim's cottage?' the HR manager said.

'Yes, sir.' Sara produced the framed photo. 'It was when I saw these early photos of the victim that I recognised him.' She produced the two tins and opened them. 'The blue one is mine, the red one was in the shed at the house. It had to be the same man.'

'You thought you had found your father?' asked Edwards. 'And Dr Taylor's DNA results confirmed it?'

'Yes, sir. I was too late. Now I'll never know his side of the story, or why he left us.'

Sara sat exhaustedly outside the office, her evidence gripped tightly in her lap, while the three men deliberated on her fate. There was one other person she still needed to contact. After all this, she felt justified in asking her mother to fill in the gaps between those letters.

'We feel that your actions were not consistent with your previous unblemished record,' ACC Miller said when she was brought back in. 'Apart from recommending some grief counselling, we do not intend to take this matter any further. I hope that this won't affect your decision to stay with us in Norfolk, as DI Edwards feels that you are already a valued member of his team.'

And that was the end of it.

On Thursday evening, Edwards declared a long weekend. 'I don't want to see any of you again before Monday. We can finish the paperwork next week.'

Friday morning was hot and still. Sara dressed for comfort, took the two tins, along with the photo she had removed from Crane's cottage, and drove to London. Javed led the way in his car, and she tried to follow. She lost him somewhere on the M11, but it wasn't as if she didn't know where she was going. He was waiting for her in the allocated parking spaces outside the block of maisonettes. It was Tegan's day off from the salon, and they had calculated that this would be the best time to find her at home. Javed led the way into the house, calling for Tegan as he went.

'Where have you been?' Sara heard her mother's voice from the living room. 'I've been worried sick.'

'You should answer your phone,' said Javed. 'Been trying to call you every day.'

Sara hovered in the doorway until Javed had finished greeting her mum. Tegan let Javed go when she saw her daughter waiting. 'What are you doing here? I'm not ready to talk to you yet.'

'Please, Mum, there are things I need to tell you.' Sara stepped into the kitchen. 'I found him. I found Adam Crane.'

'Why?'

'I needed to know. I thought you might like to know what I found out.'

'Not me. I gave up on him years ago.'

'He didn't give up on us.' Sara tried to explain. 'Mum, please hear me out.'

Tegan nodded curtly.

'He made a new life in Norfolk, did well in the force. He never found anyone else. Lived alone until he died.'

'He's dead?'

'He was murdered, Mum.' Sara reached out towards Tegan, but her mum folded her arms. 'He's the man that we've been investigating ever since I started. And he didn't forget me either. He left me his house in his will.'

'Good for you.' Tegan didn't sound like she was changing her mind about Crane.

It incensed Sara. 'This is pointless if you're not prepared to listen. I came all this way to show you what I found at his house, to tell you about his life, and you don't care. I still don't know why he moved there. Only you know that, and you don't care enough about either of us to tell me.'

She retreated from the kitchen, slamming the door behind her. The drive back to Norwich was long enough for Sara to calm down. Sitting on her balcony as the evening gathered, she watched Chris in the street below locking up his coffee shop for the night. They hadn't spoken since the night they had slept together. *God knows what he must think of me*, she thought. She went down the stairs to meet him. He smiled when he saw her.

'Good evening, lovely lady,' he said. 'I take it you've been busy at work.'

'Insane.' She held onto the banister to ground herself. 'We had a murder case, but it's over now.'

'So, you have the weekend off?'

'I do.'

'I have to work tomorrow. I'm off on Sunday, though. We could go to the coast if you like. The forecast is good.'

'That would be nice.'

'I got a part, by the way. The audition I went for.'

'You're going to be Romeo?'

'I'm definitely too old for that.' He laughed. 'I'm going to be Tybalt, so I get a good sword fight. Will you come and see it?'

'Of course.'

'I've got a bottle of wine in the fridge,' he said. Sara nodded and followed him into his flat.

CHAPTER 55

On Saturday evening an email arrived in Sara's inbox. It was from her mother.

Dear Sara,

I am still very hurt by your actions and do not understand why you feel you have to find this man who hurt our family in the past. Javed tells me you have the letters that I hid in the wardrobe. That you found more at this man's house, that you will not stop until you know what happened.

It's not something I feel easy talking about, so I have decided to write this to you.

You cannot know what it was like back then, in Brixton in the 1980s. Our skin colour ruled our every waking moment. The police could stop and search anyone they liked, it was called 'sus.' Black boys were always being stopped on 'sus,' white boys not so much, even though we were all poor together. It wasn't possible to lead an ordinary life. We were a law-abiding family, all had jobs. Well, all but one. Still we got caught up in it. There had been fighting before. The police came down heavy on anyone they thought was 'sus,' until the kids couldn't stand it anymore and a big riot broke out. You must have heard of this.

For me, it was like this.

At that time, I'm training to be a hairdresser, loving my work. The first evening, I am walking home, and the fighting starts all around me. I am terrified. Don't know what to do.

Police come down the street in a long line, riot shield by riot shield. Boys at the other end of the road, throwing stuff. People getting hurt. They say a young black boy has been beaten to death by the police. It wasn't true, but everyone thought it was. The police line comes towards me, and I am trapped, gangs throwing things on one side, riot shields on the other. The only place I can go is into a pub doorway, even though the door is locked. As the line gets nearer, the boys throw more and more bricks and things. One hits me on the head, I go down like a silly girl fainting. My head hurts, blood runs down my face. I lie here, police ignore me, the line goes past. Still missiles are falling, one hits my leg. Now I cannot even walk. I cry so much, my nose starts bleeding.

The policemen push the boys back down the street and now I am behind their line. There are many more policemen there, waiting behind the ones with the riot shields. One comes over to me, looks at my wounds and says, 'Will you let me help you?' I agree. He picks me up, like a bride on a wedding night, carries me up the street to where ambulances are waiting. Stays with me while they dress my wounds. I'm still too frightened to move, so this man's boss tells him to fetch me home. He carries me some, I limp some and we get to our flat. That policeman, he's my knight in shining armour. He's Adam Crane.

We start to go out. Fall in love. We love each other so much. But it's very hard. No one likes it that we are going out, that we sleep together. At the hairdressers, they say to me, 'Why you sleeping with a honky?' You can guess what they say to Adam at work. I can't bring myself to write it. Granddad makes it difficult. Clifton makes it impossible. Clifton is my brother. Granddad let Adam and me be together in the end after your grandma spoke out on our side. Adam moved into the flat with us. But Cliff is always picking arguments with Adam. Besides, Clifton thinks he is not treated fairly, thinks the world owes him a living. Says we are stupid for working hard for so little money when there are easier ways to make a fortune.

Adam and me are very happy. You arrive, and it seems we can ask for no more. They promise us a council flat. It's paradise. Until Clifton gets arrested. Stopped on 'sus', pockets full of dope. He goes straight to prison. So Granddad asks Adam for a favour. He does what Granddad asks him, won't tell me what it is. Granddad told me after he left. Adam stole the evidence against Clifton and burned it. Cliff is released, no evidence. But Adam's boss knows it must be Adam's doing, tells him he won't ever get a promotion.

What else can he do but move? Adam goes to Norfolk, to start again. He gets a small place, starts his new job. When I go to visit, I hate the place. I'm the only black face I see. People stare at me in the street. I want him to come back to London. He says he can't.

Adam is gone a few months, then Clifton gets into trouble again. Granddad asks Adam to help, but he can't get into the police stations here, he doesn't work for them. Adam comes to see me, Granddad and him have a big fight about it. After that, Clifton goes to jail. For ten years.

Adam let us down. He didn't understand us. How could he? We were from different tribes. Without us, there were no more ties to London. His parents had died when he was young.

He keeps trying to contact me, he is always ringing, writing to me. Your granddad gets angry, refuses to let him speak to me. He makes me write to Adam and tell him to leave us alone. I turn down his proposal. I think, how can I marry a man who abandons his family? Then Grandma gets ill. She has cancer. They don't know why, but I think it's all the stress. I have to help nurse her, look after you, keep working. No time for myself. Adam writes no more.

Clifton does his time. When he comes back, he's like a different man — taking drugs all the time, being violent. I don't like him around you. He's only out a few months, then he's arrested again. This time he is terrified. Somehow gets a passport and the next thing we know, he's gone. Back to Jamaica.

I am sorry I haven't told you this before. It hurts me too much. Do you understand? All these years, I feel so guilty about not doing anything about finding him again later on. Why would he have wanted anything to do with me, anyway?

Good luck with your new life. Perhaps one day, Javed and I will be able to visit you.

Sara closed her laptop. She thought of that final letter, stored in the red biscuit tin along with the engagement ring and the details for houses. He must have been devastated. Crane had wanted to be her father. It all came back to her uncle Clifton. No wonder her mum and granddad hadn't wanted to talk about it.

The weather was breaking up, rain clouds were gathering above the city skyline. As the first drops of rain pattered on the dry and dusty decking, she opened the window to the balcony. Watching the rain suddenly gather in intensity, she could hear people laughing and running for shelter in the street below. *Perhaps I'll get some pot plants for the balcony*, she thought. *Then again, I might have a cottage garden to deal with soon.*

She took the two tins and hid them in her suitcase on top of her wardrobe and placed the ring box safely with her jewellery. Sara thought of Chris. If they couldn't go to the coast tomorrow, there would be other things to do together.

What had happened to Clifton? Had he stayed in Jamaica? *No*, she scolded herself. *Enough of the family history. No more private investigations.* Then again . . . she'd never been to Jamaica.

The scent of the city, freshly washed, came in through the open windows.

THE END

ACKNOWLEDGMENTS

This novel is the product of the MA in Creative Writing (Crime Fiction) at the University of East Anglia. I want to thank course director Henry Sutton for taking a chance on me. As well as my tutors Tom Benn, Laura Joyce, Nathan Ashman, William Ryan and Julia Crouch for their encouragement and wonderful teaching. My cohort became my good friends, and we are carrying on together as a writer's group and beta-readers for each other's work: Laura Ashton; Antony Dunford; Jayne Farnworth; Natasha Hutcheson; Louise Mangos; Elizabeth Saccente; Matthew Smith; Karen Taylor; Wendy Turbin; Bridget Walsh. I couldn't have managed without you guys! I also received invaluable assistance from Charlotte Salter of the UEA Medical School for medical details and Mark Wilkinson of the NNUH for forensic advice.

My eternal gratitude goes out to Jasper Joffe for welcoming me to Joffe Books, and to Emma Grundy Haigh, Anne Derges, Matthew Grundy Haigh and Cat Phipps for helping me improve the novel with very helpful edits and generous comments.

Last but not least, my husband, Rhett. Always there for me whatever happens and an invaluable source of farming knowledge. Thank you.

FREE KINDLE BOOKS

Please join our mailing list for free Kindle books
and new releases, including crime thrillers, mysteries,
romance and more!

www.joffebooks.com

Follow us on Facebook, Twitter and Instagram
@joffebooks

DO YOU LOVE FREE AND BARGAIN BOOKS?

Thank you for reading this book. If you enjoyed it
please leave feedback on Amazon, and if there is anything
we missed or you have a question about then please get in
touch. The author and publishing team appreciate your
feedback and time reading this book.

www.joffebooks.com/contact

We hate typos too but sometimes they slip through.
Please send any errors you find to
corrections@joffebooks.com.
We'll get them fixed ASAP. We're very grateful to
eagle-eyed readers who take the time to contact us.

Printed in Poland
by Amazon Fulfillment
Poland Sp. z o.o., Wrocław

62436894R00188